mas

D0561279

Willow springs

JAN WATSON

Willow
SPRINGS

Tyndale House Publishers, Inc., Carol Stream, Illinois

TYNDALE and Tyndale's quill logo are registered trademarks of Tyndale House Publishers, Inc.

Willow Springs

Copyright © 2007 by Jan Watson. All rights reserved.

Cover photograph of models copyright © 2006 by Brian MacDonald. All rights reserved.

Cover photograph of country house copyright © 2006 by Franz Aberham/Getty Images. All rights reserved.

Author photo copyright © 2005 by Brenda Metzler/ Hart Studios. All rights reserved.

Designed by Jessie McGrath

Edited by Lorie Popp

Scripture quotations are taken from the *Holy Bible*, King James Version.

ISBN: 978-0-7394-8336-7

Printed in the United States of America

For Charles and Catherine Prather Watson

≈ ACKNOWLEDGMENTS ≈

He spoke the wondrous word, and lo,
Creation rose at His command:
Whirlwinds and seas their limits know,
Bound in the hollow of His hand.
    —FROM THE BAPTIST HYMNAL, 1875

My humble gratitude to:

Jerry B. Jenkins, the Christian Writers Guild, and Tyndale House Publishers for opening the whirlwind of publishing to me.

Lorie Popp, my editor, and Jan Stob of Tyndale for caring so much about the rest of the story.

Mark Sweeney, my agent, for your belief in me.

Terry Taylor, my first reader: you have an editor's eye.

Grass Roots Writers, my wonderful and talented compatriots.

Special friends: You've carried books, arranged signings, chauffeured, repaired my house, provided nourishment for my body as well as my soul, and even walked the dog. You kept me bound in the hollow of His hand.

Ed Maxwell, MD: You steered Drew and me through yet another storm. I could not give myself to writing if I did not know my son was safe.

The staff of Oakwood Residential Facility in Somerset, Kentucky—my heroes and Drew's friends at his home away from home.

My children–Charles, Catherine, Andrew, and Stephen: you are my richest blessing.

Maggie, who keeps everything in perspective and reminds me that life's about chasing sunbeams.

My readers: I love and appreciate you.

And to my own angel. Honey, this is all for you. I'll see you on the other side.

CHAPTER I

1883

With each turn of the buggy's wheels, each jaw-jarring rut in the well-traveled road, Copper Brown Corbett felt more alone. She wished she could rewind the clock, take back the day, and return to Troublesome Creek. Why was she here? Who was the stranger beside her? She'd never known a man who wore a piece of silk knotted at his throat like a notice saying who he was, and she wasn't sure she wanted to. Why didn't Simon take off his coat and roll up his sleeves?

This was all a mistake. She never should have married him.

The early summer sun beat down on the rolling carriage. Taking off her hat, a silly concoction of feathers and lace, she fanned herself with its brim. Perspiration soaked her hair at the temples. If she were home, she'd run to the creek, and if Mam wasn't watching, she'd shuck her dress and jump in for a swim. It would be so cool there where the willows wept upon the bank.

The sway of the buggy lulled her. She leaned back and propped her unshod feet on the old dog who snored on the buggy's floor.

Clip-clop. Clip-clop . . . The horse's hooves pounded on the packed-dirt trail. *Click-click-click* . . . A stick announced its presence, trapped in the spoke of a wheel. Sunlight sparkled through a canopy of leaves as the buggy entered a shaded tunnel of towering beeches, oaks, and maples. Copper's hat dropped to her lap. Resting her head against the leather seat, she dreamed of home. . . .

Compared to the other houses up and down the holler, the cabin on Troublesome Creek was spacious with its big front room and two tacked-on bedrooms. Copper Brown's great-grandparents had first homesteaded on the creek. There had still been a few marauding Indian bands about when her grandfather built the sturdy cabin, but most of the uprising was over, settled by Daniel Boone and Simon Kenton and their ilk many years before. They'd had more trouble from bears and wolves than from scalp hunters.

Copper could see her family—Daddy with his bushy white beard; Mam, shoulders squared, her hair pulled back in a bun; and the twins, Daniel and Willy, teasing each other, causing no end of trouble—sitting around the round oak table for supper. They'd all clasp hands, and Daddy would say grace. But there was no plate set for her. She wouldn't have a piece of the crispy-brown fried rabbit. Her chair sat empty and forlorn, pushed back behind the door.

The dream of supper made Copper's stomach growl. She cast
a sideways look at her husband and hoped he hadn't heard the
indelicate sound. Sitting up straight, she gazed ahead; then disbe-
lieving what she saw, she got on her knees to look out the back.
The mountains—*her* mountains—were behind her now. Way in the
background she could see their proud silhouettes, like the humps
of kneeling camels, a shadow land fading from view. The horse
pulled the carriage up puny knobs and across fields as flat as a
skipping rock.

Panic seized her heart in a moment of wild fear. "Stop! Let
me off."

Simon Corbett turned his head at the sound of Laura Grace's
voice. "What is it? I thought you were sleeping." He reined in the
horse, glad for a moment's rest, and reached for the hand of his
seventeen-year-old bride.

Ignoring the offer, she jumped down from the buggy without
his help. He watched as she hitched up her long skirts and ran
back the way they had come.

She didn't run far, and he caught up with her easily enough.
"Laura Grace?"

She flinched at the touch of his hand but more so at the name he
used. Her name was Copper. Copper Brown. Nobody but Mam
ever called her Laura Grace and that too often in reprimand.

She looked toward the mountains. A fool could see their
colors ebbing, the trees bunching up, the rock faces wavering,

running together like a watercolor painting left out in the rain. A spurt of hot tears stung her eyes.

"You never told me this would happen, Simon," she sobbed. "You didn't tell me the mountains would disappear."

Resting his hand on her shoulder, he said, "Oh, sweetheart, I never thought you wouldn't know."

"How was I supposed to know they'd be all ironed out flat like this?" Her voice hitched. "How do you catch your breath when there's nothing to hold things in place?"

He took her arm and turned her toward him. "Close your eyes and take a deep breath."

Stubbornly she tucked her chin.

He raised her head. "Breathe!"

Her breath was ragged and painful when it hit her lungs.

"Deeper," he insisted, his fingertips pressing into her soft flesh. "There, that's better. Now keep your eyes closed and tell me what you smell."

"Trees and grass," she murmured, "and, oh, there's lavender and day's-eye blossoms." Her eyes popped open. "Wet moss and rocks. There's a creek nearby!" Comforted, she leaned her face against his chest.

"The air you breathe is the same everywhere," Simon said. "It's a gift from God that goes wherever you go. All you have to do is close your eyes, and He will send the mountains back to you."

Copper took in the fresh, starched-linen scent of him, relished the strength in his embrace, felt the tickle of his mustache against her cheek, and remembered, with a rush of feeling, why she'd left her dear mountain home, why she'd married this stranger. Oh, the heart was a treacherous thing.

Stretching up, she kissed his cheek, then danced away. "We've got to find that creek."

"I'll unhitch the horse," he replied. "We can use a break."

"Oh, look!" She laughed and pointed at the gray-muzzled hound loping toward them on three legs. Her black high-tops dangled from his mouth.

"Paw-paw, you silly old thing. Thank you." She knelt to retrieve her shoes and patted his head. "Come on, boy. Let's go get a drink."

⤜⑧⑧⑧⤛

"Can't we stay here tonight, Simon?" Laura Grace asked from her perch on the bank of the gently flowing stream.

Simon Corbett looked at his young bride. Her discarded hose lay beside her, and she splashed water with her naked feet. He was mesmerized. Had there ever been an ankle more per- fectly formed? an arch in a foot so exquisite?

"Harrumph." He cleared his throat, then took off his spectacles and cleaned them with the corner of a spotless handkerchief. "I had thought to have our supper at the Wayside Inn, where we will trade out the horse, Laura Grace. I've secured a room there for the night."

"This is ever so much better. Don't you reckon?" The eyes that looked up at him were the same curious silver green as the under- side of the leaves that shaded her there. "We have that picnic Mam packed," she pleaded. "There's sure to be pickled eggs and fried chicken and cake. Makes me hungry just to think on it."

Inwardly Simon groaned as he hooked his wire-rimmed eyeglasses behind his ears. He'd looked forward to this night. He'd arranged for a spacious room with clean linens and a bouquet of fresh flowers picked from the innkeeper's garden for his bride. *Time enough,* he cautioned himself. *Time enough when we get home.*

With a sigh, he gave in. "Of course we shall stay here if that pleases you, my dear. I'll fetch the basket."

The young couple spent their wedding night on a creek bank somewhere between her home in the serene mountains of eastern Kentucky and his in the bustling city of Lexington.

The groom was happy. So happy, even though he had to share his bride with the raggedy hound who slept at her feet, twitching the night through in his old dog way, chasing rabbits in his dreams . . . aggravating Simon's sleep, but he didn't mind, really. He was content to finally hold Laura Grace as she slept, his nose buried in her glorious red hair.

The folded quilt the bride slept upon did nothing to protect her from a maze of disquieting dreams of rushing water and endless hallways leading to countless doors, none of which opened for her.

And much farther up the road, Alice Corbett Upchurch couldn't sleep at all. She threw back her covers and eased out into the hallway. Bending her ear to her husband's bedroom door, she was rewarded by seesawing snores.

"Why can drunkards sleep when I cannot?" she muttered. But all the same, she was glad for his slumber. It gave her a measure of peace. Tugging the sleeve of her dressing gown over the ugly place on her wrist, she tiptoed down the winding staircase and into the kitchen.

All she wanted was a cup of tea; no need to wake Cook. But where was the tea? Where was the tea ball? Why had Cook moved the everyday spoons? She rummaged through drawers and cabinets. At least the stove still gave off heat, and the kettle held hot water.

"Ma'am?" She heard Joseph's soft drawl. "Will you be taking tea in the dining room?"

The butler soon had her seated at one end of a long table, a tea service before her, one cup already poured.

"Will you want anything else?"

A question formed on Alice's lips, but it wouldn't do to have a conversation with a servant. "No, thank you, Joseph." She dismissed him with a flick of her wrist. *Does the man ever sleep?*

She drummed her fingers against the gleaming cherrywood tabletop. Portraits of her husband's ancestors—all round-headed, bald men with ears that stuck out like sprung screen doors—looked down on her from their lofty positions on the dining room walls.

She couldn't believe Simon was doing this to her. He'd thought she would accompany him to his sham of a wedding. Humph, Mrs. Benton Upchurch consorting with backward hill people? She thought not. She had a reputation to uphold; Benton *was* the president of the bank after all. And what of her plans for her brother?

Well, we shall see. All I have to do is show Simon what a monumental mistake he has made. It shouldn't take long.

Taking herself to the library, Alice retrieved a sleeve of onionskin, her favorite tortoiseshell pen, and a small bottle of black ink from the lady's desk. She returned to the dining room, turned up the gaslight, sat down, and began to write. The words flowed as she scripted the menu for a special dinner party. Everything would be just so: flowers, candlelight, several courses of food, and invitations to all the best people in town. Laura Grace Brown–Alice refused to acknowledge the Corbett–wouldn't stand a chance.

CHAPTER 2

Copper snuggled between soft sheets and wondered why Mam was allowing her to laze about, this being a Monday, wash day and all.

"I'd best get stirring before Willy and Daniel come drag me out," she said before she remembered that she was no longer in the cabin on Troublesome Creek. She was alone in someone else's bed, a stranger in a strange place.

She tried to remember how she'd got here the night before, after two and a half arduous days of travel over roads so rough she was quite sure she would never sit again. Exhaustion overtook her several miles from the city, and she had fallen asleep, her head resting on Simon's shoulder. Vaguely she recollected being carried up the stairs and Simon's murmuring reassurance.

She recalled a melodious feminine voice and gentle hands pulling a nightgown over her head, then darkness and blessed rest.

The scent of woodsmoke and the wisp of a hymn sung sweet and low drifted in through an open window and piqued her curiosity. Padding barefoot across the carpeted floor, she peered down into the backyard. A tall, thin woman, with skin as silky brown as earth turned over with a spade, stirred a pile of whites into bubbling wash water. She must be the housekeeper Simon had told her about. Sheets and pillowcases, already hung to dry, flapped in the early morning breeze.

"Why did nobody wake me?" Copper called to the empty room, unsure whether to make her bed or rush out to help with the wash before she wasted any more time. Her cheeks stung with embarrassment as she frantically searched about.

"Oh, land sakes. Where's the necessary?" She peeked under the four-poster, then looked about the room. An ornate dresser with a three-sided mirror sat in front of an armless stool with a needlepoint-cushioned seat. She rose to examine what seemed like half a dozen cut-glass vanity pots on top of the dresser. A note addressed to a Mrs. Corbett—wasn't Simon's mother dead?—leaned against a sterling silver posy holder filled with fragrant pink rosebuds and tiny violets. Slipping the note from the cream-colored envelope, she read:

> *My darling wife, you are so beautiful in sleep. I couldn't bear to wake you. I will see you midday. Searcy will tend to your needs.*
> *I love you, my own.*
> *Yours,*
> *Simon*

Copper laughed at herself. *She* was Mrs. Corbett! She pressed a kiss upon the note before she continued her search. There were three doors in the room. She tried the first and saw a hallway leading to a staircase. The second opened into a dressing room, where she glimpsed her clothing hanging from padded hangers. Her dressing gown was draped across a fainting couch.

Fainting is not what I'm about to do, she thought as she opened the last door and found, of all things, an indoor outhouse! There was a wooden seat that had a box fastened to the wall above it. A long chain with a pull clattered noisily when she brushed against it.

With relief, she looked around. A porcelain tub, big enough for two, stood on claw feet against the wall. A sink with a brass spigot held a man's shaving mug and a straight razor. Below the chair rail the walls were paneled with white beaded board, and above they were papered in the same cabbage-rose print as the bedroom. There was a mirror, framed in the same beaded board, above the sink, and thick white towels hung on a rack beside it.

Curious, she turned the knobby handle on the sink and jumped back in surprise as cold water splashed into the basin. "Well, I never!" She washed her hands and dried them on the merest corner of the sparkling clean towel.

Closing the wooden lid to the pot, she hurried to the dressing room and knelt before her trunk. She ferreted out a favorite feed-sack shift and one of Mam's worn aprons, nestled under the little pile of rocks she'd brought from Troublesome Creek. Selecting the smallest rock—just a pebble really—she held it to her nose before tucking it in the pocket of the apron.

It's a good thing I squirreled some of my work clothes in here before

Mam gave them all away. I guess she thinks people don't do wash in the city. Adjusting her sunbonnet, she decided to forgo shoes. She always worked faster when her feet were free.

Down the stairs and out the back door on the run, she approached the quick-moving woman who stirred the laundry and stuck out her hand. "You must be Searcy. I'm Copper, and I'm so sorry to have overslept on wash day. Why, Mam would have my hide if I did that at home." She let her hand fall, hefted a basket to her hip, and started across the yard to the clothesline.

<hr/>

Searcy nearly dropped a box of bluing into her kettle of rinse water. "Ma'am? Miz Corbett? We can't be having none of this now. Folks be saying Searcy can't take care of her fambly."

Searcy jerked the basket away more roughly than she'd meant to and shooed the new Mrs. Corbett toward the porch. "You all be going back in the house now. Searcy done left you some biscuit on the sideboard. They's honey or blackberry jam—your wish."

The girl halted halfway in the screen door, looking like she didn't know what to do next.

"You be wanting to change before Mr. Doctor comes home. Searcy put your pretties in the closet. Sure do like that green dress; sure would look good with them black boots with all them little buttons. You call you need help with anything."

<hr/>

Copper closed the screen door. The blue-and-white tiled floor was cool to her bare feet. The kitchen was big. A huge cast-iron stove with two ovens and a warmer dominated one corner. Painted shelves held various green and blue enamel pots and pans. Four cast-iron skillets, graduating in size, hung from hooks below the bottom shelf. The walls were white beaded board below the chair rail, like the indoor outhouse, but above they were painted a soft blue the color of a robin's egg. The ceiling was punched tin. Against one wall, a double sink with a funny-handled thingamajig sat under a window.

Leaning against the sink, Copper retrieved a bar of lye soap from a small wire container. She closed her eyes and breathed in the clean scent of it, the only familiar thing in the room. Tears sprang to her eyes as she pictured Mam and the boys doing their Monday wash without her. She pumped the handle with vigor, figuring it would gush like the bathroom sink, and let the water flow to splash away her tears.

A quiet voice and a hand on her shoulder startled away her momentary homesickness.

"Here, now, Miz Corbett," Searcy said. "Let's set you down and get you something to eat. 'Spec everything's right strange to you this morning."

Soon Copper was seated at the kitchen table, her bare feet perched on the chair rung, a plate of biscuits, butter, and jam before her, a cup of hot tea in her hand.

❧

The housekeeper's heart melted. She had been in a stew of apprehension for weeks, not knowing what manner of mistress Mr. Doctor was going to bring into the house. Would she be bossy and haughty like Miz Alice, never satisfied with anything, or whiny and needy like Old Doctor's wife, Miz Lilly, had been? Why, that woman had been so frail that even after Mr. Simon's birth half the time Searcy had to blow her nose for her. But no manner of imaginings could have prepared her for the teary-eyed little creature in the black bonnet and shapeless dress sitting there as puny as a newborn mouse at Mr. Doctor's kitchen table.

"You set and rest a spell," Searcy instructed before she turned toward the hallway, her arms full of sun-drenched bedding, her brown leather house slippers, castoffs of Mr. Doctor's, slapping out her steps.

"Oh my, oh my, Searcy's corns be killing her today," the house-keeper said as she climbed the stairs to the second floor.

Finished with her biscuit, Copper followed.

"Pardon me, Miz Corbett, would you be wanting these sheets ironed? Mr. Doctor likes them right off the line. He likes the smell of fresh air. Onliest time his linens is pressed is when they ain't no sunshine about." With a jerk of her arms, Searcy snapped the top sheet in place.

"Whatever Simon wants," Copper said, reaching out to help. "Mam likes everything ironed to a fault, but in the summer we put the pillowcases to dry over the lavender beds. Oh, they smell so good." She helped tuck the heavy, rose-colored bedspread up over the bolster. "May I ask you something, Searcy? How do you empty that funny chamber pot?"

"Come on in here, Miz Corbett. This be easy. You get hold of this here chain and pull down. Just like that."

Whoosh . . . whirl . . . Copper watched, mouth agape, as the contents of the toilet drained away, replaced by clean water. "But where does it go? Won't the ceiling below be ruined?"

Searcy understood. When the newfangled fixtures were first put in she'd refused to enter the room to clean it. Seemed like voodoo to her. It was only after Mr. Doctor patiently explained the pipes and faucets and showed her how it all connected to the buried tank out back that she had lost her fear of it. Now she did the same for Copper, leading her down the steps and out the back door to the prized septic system.

Working in a house with conveniences elevated Searcy's position among the other housekeepers on the street. Her Mr. Doctor was always the first with anything new, and there had been a flurry of new things since his trip to the mountains last summer. So far, she liked the gaslights and the boiler system with radiators in every room but the kitchen best. They still used the fireplaces but not nearly as often. Sure made her work easier.

"How do, Searcy," Mallie, the Lauderbacks' housekeeper, called over the fence. "That a fine-looking wash you got out today."

"Good day for laundry, Mallie," Searcy replied loudly. "Yours be white as snow."

Searcy stepped between Mallie's prying eyes and her new mistress. She didn't want that nosy Mallie to fetch Miz Lauderback to come out and gawk at Miz Corbett, dressed like she was, barefoot and all. Miz Lauderback would report everything she saw back to Mr. Doctor's sister, Alice. They were as thick as cold molasses.

"I've never seen so many pretty flowers in my life." Copper followed the housekeeper through the flower garden and back into the kitchen. "I brought some seeds from Mam's garden. I can hardly wait to plant them."

"We'll get Reuben to dig you up a spot," Searcy replied. "Reuben, he's good at growing things. We got the best truck garden on the street, and when he ain't planting vegetables he be pinching flower heads and pruning lilacs." She filled the teapot at the sink, then pointed out the window. "That's him digging new potatoes, there under that straw hat."

"Simon told me that Reuben is your husband and that you have been married for a long time. He said he didn't know what he would do without the both of you."

"We been taking care of Mr. Doctor's fambly these many years." Searcy looked thoughtful. "Old Doctor, he bought Reuben when Reuben just a boy, then give him his freedom when he turned eighteen. Reuben, he frame them papers. They on our kitchen wall."

Never still, Searcy punctuated her reminiscence with swipes from a wet dishrag to the stove, the table, the sink. "Searcy come to be Miz Lilly's house girl when she be marrying Old Doctor. 'Course we didn't call him Old Doctor 'til Mr. Simon hung out his shingle. Then he be Mr. Doctor and his daddy be Old Doctor." Pumping the handle, she rinsed the rag and draped it over the sink. "We used to live in that cabin out in the cornfield yonder, but Mr. Doctor, he bought us our own house, said everybody ought to have a place of their own. You be marrying a fine man, Miz Corbett."

Copper followed her up the stairs again.

"Us be fixing your bath now," Searcy said. "Get the road dust offen you. You was too tuckered out last evening." With a quick twist to the top of a flowered tin, Searcy shook sweet-smelling toilet water into the tub. "Things be changing too fast. Seem like a dipping bath in front the fire come Saturday night be plenty good enough."

Copper was swimming in a lilac-scented pool. She soaped and scrubbed and rinsed, then pulled the plug, thankful she knew where the water went, wrapped herself in a clean towel, and stepped into the bedroom to dress her hair. She found her dresser set—her brush and combs on a glass tray with silver handles, a gift from Mam on Copper's sixteenth birthday—on the vanity.

Fingering the raised initials *LGB* on the handle of the hairbrush, her thoughts turned to her stepmother, whom she'd always called Mam. It seemed they had just begun to come to terms with one another, just begun to understand their troubled relationship, when Simon entered the picture and whisked Copper away from her home and her people.

Her lip trembled. "Help me, Lord," she whispered. "I can barely stand this missing my folks. I didn't know it would hurt so bad." Even Mam's temper would be welcome at this moment, and, oh, she might die from the longing to see her little brothers, though she'd been gone from them for only a short time. And Daddy . . . her rock . . . her fortress . . . A shake of her head tumbled him out of her thoughts. Best not to dwell on home.

It was easy to do her hair, sitting there with everything close at hand. Scooping the mass of red curls up and away from her face with a ribbon, she secured the twist with pins.

Searcy thought of everything, she realized as she fastened a lightly boned, button-front corset over her soft knit chemisette and full-cut muslin drawers. Copper pulled one of the petticoats she and Mam had made last winter over her head and smoothed it over her hips. Catching her reflection in the cheval glass, she admired the trim of lace and openwork. "Such a lot of work just to be covered up," she fretted as she slipped into the dress Searcy had laid out on the bed. *I hope Simon doesn't expect this every day, else I'll never get any work done.*

Copper rubbed her thumb against her finger. Where had she left her apron with the pebble in the pocket? She looked out the window, down into the backyard, and spied it on the line beside her wash-day shift. Looked like Searcy was as fond of Monday as Mam. She hoped she wouldn't see Paw-paw there, hung out to dry by one floppy ear.

She was halfway down the stairs when her own bare feet greeted her in the hall mirror. "Fiddlesticks," she said as she hurried back to the bedroom. Hefting her dress and petticoat, her fingers fumbled to secure long, clay-colored cotton stockings to garter straps dangling from the hips of her corset. After she retrieved the buttonhook from her dresser, she leaned over to fasten her shoes.

A funny feeling fluttered in her stomach. She took a deep breath. It didn't go away. She rubbed the little creek rock Searcy had left next to the silver posy holder, then secreted it deep within her dress pocket. *I wish I were home.*

CHAPTER 3

Dr. Simon Corbett strolled from his office to his house at 212 Willow Street. It was his practice to walk back and forth to work on pretty days. With a hearty "Good morning," he tipped his derby to Mrs. Miller, who replied in kind with a twirl of her fancy parasol, then picked up his pace. He couldn't wait to get home.

There she was, the reason for his haste. His heart swelled when he saw Laura Grace waiting for him on the front porch. Her hair was swirled on top of her head, held in place with a ribbon that matched the light green linen dress she wore. She was swinging gently, book in hand, but looked up as he approached.

"Laura Grace, I can hardly believe you're here," he said. "I've been afraid it was all a dream." He prodded the old dog, Paw-paw, from beside her and settled himself in the wicker swing.

She handed him a glass of cold lemonade poured from a cut-glass pitcher. Paw-paw stretched, yawned, then curled his body around a patch of sunlight on the top porch step.

"Simon, I'm all agog." Laura Grace's voice rushed out in a torrent. "I feel like Alice when she fell down the hole and had lunch with the queen. Everything here astounds me. The icebox in the kitchen . . . the outhouse–excuse me, lavatory–with water coming out of pipes in the wall. I'll bet I've flushed the pot ten times just to see the water swirl." Her eyes danced with excitement. "And you can turn the gas lamps on and off, and you don't have to fill them with anything! Oh, how silly. You know all this already. Your house is lovely, just lovely."

"*Our* house," he said, taking her hand. "This house is yours, too. If you want, we could go to the bank and let Benton make it legal."

"Benton is your sister Alice's husband, right?"

"Yes, they've been married for fifteen years. Benton is a lawyer as well as a banker. He aims to acquire more money than a Vanderbilt."

"Speaking of Alice and Benton, when will I meet them? I know I will just love your sister."

"She will love you too. How could she not?" Simon prayed it would be so. "She's having a dinner party for us on Wednesday. I wanted to give you a few days to acclimate before you had to meet everyone."

Laura Grace pushed the swing with one foot. "Tell me about your morning. Did you see many patients?"

After taking a long, welcome drink of lemonade, Simon placed the glass on the tray before replying. "Several. Todd Bowman broke his arm when he fell out of Mrs. Jon's apple tree—a green-stick fracture. Then Harley came by with a painful case of printer's finger. He's a typesetter for the paper. I gave him some laudanum salve. He can't afford to miss any work what with Mary's being in the family way again." He settled an arm around her shoulders. "No more talk of work. I'm sure I'm boring you to tears."

"Oh no." She faced him. "I want to hear everything about your work."

"When it is appropriate, my dear. Come, let me show you the garden before we eat."

"I saw some of it this morning—the lilies and the hollyhocks. Did you know you can make dolls from hollyhock blossoms?" she asked, swinging his hand. "We used to act out plays with our flower puppets. Of course, Willy and Daniel always wanted to have wars. It is hard to make soldiers from hollyhocks."

They strolled around the garden. Simon pointed out his mother's favorite roses and the small fishpond that Alice had commissioned. Then he showed her the vegetable garden and introduced her to Reuben.

Reuben doffed his straw hat and tipped his head. "Pleased, missus, mighty pleased."

Laura Grace reached out to touch the dark brown hand that hung at his side. "As am I, Reuben. Simon tells me you've taken good care of my Molly."

"Yes'm. Molly a fine cow. Gone dry though, after her journey down from the mountains. I got her out in the pasture. She be right-natured again once she fattens up."

JAN WATSON

"Let me know when she's ready, Reuben, and I'll help you with the milking."

"Yes'm," Reuben replied, his eyes seeking Simon's.

⚜

Noon dinner was green beans with new potatoes in their jackets, fried corn, and cabbage slaw, all fresh picked that morning. Searcy served the vegetables with honey-basted ham and yeast rolls, and for dessert there was a three-layer chocolate cake.

Copper pushed back from the table and carried her plate to the kitchen, but Searcy shooed her away when she tried to wash up.

Simon had closed his office for the afternoon. He wanted to take Copper riding to show her Willow Springs, the creek that ran across the back of their property, and so he presented her with a suitable frock. The brown, hip-length, close-fitting jacket made of ladies' cloth fit over a narrow skirt that fell just to the ankle of long leather riding boots. There was even a little hat that was held in place with a hatpin.

Copper felt perfectly silly, being more accustomed to riding in a pair of her daddy's old overalls, cut off at the ankle and cinched at the waist, until she paused to look in the cheval glass. What the mirror revealed was startling. The narrow-hipped woman in the mirror could have been a model in one of Mam's dressmaking magazines. They'd seen a jacket much like this one in *The Standard Designer* and had wished for just a yard of the narrow gilt-and-jet passementerie trim. Twirling to see herself from the back and side, she faced the mirror and placed her hands on her hips. With great relief she appraised herself. *No one can tell that aggravating corset is at the bottom of my trunk.*

Fairly skipping down the stairs to the foyer, she found Simon waiting patiently. "You've thought of everything," she gushed. "I'll bet there's even a real sidesaddle. Daddy jerry-built one for me at home. Mam wouldn't let me ride otherwise. She had some peculiar ways."

"I owe your mother a debt of gratitude for her protection of you," Simon said as he kissed Laura Grace's gloved hand. *And for sending me your measurements to take to the dressmaker,* he thought. Keeping his promise to Grace Brown, he had delivered the envelope to Mme. Pacquin's House of Couture still sealed. He couldn't be more pleased with the riding habit Mme. Pacquin had stitched nor the figure it revealed.

Thoughts of his bride's stern stepmother took him back to the day he'd met the Brown family, to his surprise on finding an educated, refined woman living in an isolated hollow in the hills. And then he was more than surprised when his heart tumbled and never righted as he first caught sight of Laura Grace.

The afternoon was spent on horseback. Pard and Rose made good companions, Rose being a gentle mare purchased especially for Copper. They rode the property behind the house: a few acres of land bordered by a deep, spring-fed creek. They paused at a break in a copse of drooping willows that nearly hid the water.

"This land is so flat, Simon," Copper said, dismissing the gently rolling hills with a wave of her hand. "I'll never get used to it. But at least there is water enough for fishing and swimming." Leaning forward in her sidesaddle, she patted Rose's long neck. What fun to have her own horse. "We'll bring a picnic here soon."

Simon turned his horse and Rose followed. "We'd best head back now before I tire you. I expect Searcy will have left us a light supper."

The young couple stood at the screen door and looked out as the shadows deepened over the well-tended backyard.

"Oh, Simon, let's eat in the garden," Laura Grace begged. "We can spread a quilt and sit there 'til the lightning bugs come out. We can listen for peepers and katydids. It'll be just like home."

It seemed a silly idea to him. They had a perfectly good dining table, and Searcy had left it set for supper. But on this night of all nights, he could deny her nothing. If she asked to dine on the rooftop, he would fetch the ladder.

Supper over, dishes washed, kitchen tidied . . . nothing left but to retire.

"I'll wind the clocks, sweetheart, and join you shortly," Simon said as Laura Grace started up the stairs.

"Don't dawdle. I haven't slept alone since Daniel and Willy were born."

Simon appraised his surroundings while he waited for his bride. The bedroom was beautifully appointed. The deep rose of the bedspread matched the color of the cabbage roses in the paper that adorned the walls. Burgundy damask drapes at each of the two floor-to-ceiling windows were drawn over lace curtains against the darkness of the night. The furniture was solid cherry, burnished to a glow from years of polishing. He'd cut an armful of roses and put the vase on Laura Grace's dresser. Their sweet perfume filled the air. He had not lit the gas lamps in favor of the softer, more romantic glow cast by candles in silver candlesticks strategically placed about the room. This night would be perfect—perfect for his perfect bride.

The bathroom door slowly opened, and he caught his breath.

Laura Grace was dressed for bed in white silk. She stayed at the door and gripped the knob. "Simon," she said softly, "I swan I'm not the least bit sleepy. Couldn't we go down to the kitchen and make some fudge or pop some corn?"

"Laura Grace—" Simon held out his hands to her—"let me look at you."

She came to stand before him. "This is a pretty gown, isn't it? Mam and I sewed all winter. And my underclothes! Why, you wouldn't believe how many pairs of pantalets I have, all lacy and such," she babbled. "I don't know why Mam was in such a dither about my night things." With a shaky hand, she fingered the pink ribbon threaded through eyelet lace that decorated her robe. "She made me redo this a thousand times. Everything had to be just so."

"You are so beautiful. My own sweet wife." His voice caught. "Let me." He unbraided the plait that captured her hair. Loose, it tumbled past her shoulders to the small of her back, fiery red in the candlelight. He sank his hands deep within her tresses. "You must always wear your hair down for bed."

"It gets so wild and tangled. I'll never get it right in the morning." Her voice shook a little.

With one hand he tilted her chin and kissed her trembling lips. "Don't be afraid, my darling," he murmured, caressing her shoulders.

"Simon! Whatever are you doing?" She pushed his hands away as a deep blush covered her cheeks.

He cupped her chin and captured her eyes with his own. "Laura Grace, did your mother talk to you? Did she tell you about husbands and wives and wedding nights?"

"Well, of course," she replied. "Mam said you would want to sleep with me and that I should obey you, and that is perfectly fine with me. I'm sure you will make a better bed partner than Willy and Daniel, what with all their squirming."

She put the palm of her hand to his forehead. "You look a little feverish. Should I make you some tea?" Cinching the belt of her robe tightly, she turned away.

Sighing deeply, reluctantly, Simon followed her down the stairs and to the dark kitchen.

"Help me, Simon. I don't know where anything is. Should we use these cups and saucers? They seem too good for just a cup of tea." She chatted away as she stoked the cookstove, filled the heavy kettle, and arranged china and pieces of cake on a tray.

Simon stood in the doorway and watched her. How had he managed to capture such an enchanting creature?

"This must be hard for you," he said while pulling out a chair for her at the kitchen table. "You must be feeling homesick."

"It just feels really strange," Laura Grace sighed and took her seat. "I keep expecting Willy or Daniel to burst through the door. And I get lost in this house." She looked around. "Why, this kitchen is twice as big as any kitchen needs to be." After blowing on her tea, she took a sip. "There is so much furniture; how will I keep it all dusted?"

"You don't have to learn everything at once." His hand covered hers. "Alice will be glad to help you. She has had the responsibility of this house as well as her own for far too long. She never trusted me to keep everything together." He chuckled. "I'm sure she is relieved to have you take over."

"I'm starting to feel a little sleepy now," Laura Grace said, hiding a yawn behind her hand. "Aren't you going to finish your cake?"

Sitting here in his kitchen, watching his bride lick chocolate icing from her fork, Simon felt complete. He would just have to be patient with Laura Grace. At seventeen, she was still young, and he was an educated, well-traveled man of twenty-seven. Her parents had carefully raised her and had sheltered her from the ways of the world. For this he was grateful. His desire for her was like a living thing, the need nearly overwhelming, but he would never force her. He determined to take his time, moving slowly to awaken the woman in her, waiting until she desired him as he desired her.

They stood together at the kitchen sink, washing their few dishes. She laughed when water gushed over her hands. When they finished, Simon led her up the stairs. They snuggled spoon fashion in the big, comfortable bed he would share with her for all their nights to come.

With a big yawn, Laura Grace wiggled her way even closer to her husband. "Ummm, this feels good. I could get used to sleeping with you, Simon."

"One can only hope, sweetheart," he replied. "One can only hope."

CHAPTER 4

The day of the dinner party with Alice and Benton Upchurch finally arrived. Wednesday afternoon Copper sat at her dressing table in her petticoat, and Searcy dressed her hair. The evening gown she'd brought with her from Troublesome Creek was pressed and laid out on the bed. Copper thought it beautiful, though it had been tedious to sew. The fine-washed China silk puckered and pulled with the slightest provocation and had tested her patience endlessly. She would have thrown it into the front yard on numerous occasions had it not been for Mam's steady hand.

"I hate this," she'd told Mam. "I despise sewing."

Mam had countered, "When you get to the city you can hire a dressmaker, but for now mind your stitches."

Now she was glad Mam had been so particular about finding the latest pattern and the very best material and trim.

Copper undressed to her chemise; then Searcy proceeded to torture her with the whalebone corset Mam had sent to go with her dress.

"Hold your breath, Miz Corbett." Searcy pulled on the laces with all her might.

Copper sailed backward, arms windmilling, nearly knocking Searcy down. "I can't breathe," she gasped. "Searcy, unloose this thing."

"Miz Corbett, you cain't be going to no party at Miz Alice's without a proper corset. Now you stand still."

Copper obeyed and watched in the mirror as her waist nipped in and her lungs collapsed. She didn't complain because she couldn't. She was swooning, seeing stars.

"Do like this," Searcy instructed. She minced about the room on tiptoe, batting her eyes, her old house shoes flapping, for all the world the grandest of ladies.

Copper collapsed on the bed, flat on her back, laughter choking her, tears streaming down her face. "Searcy, have mercy."

Unimpressed, Searcy hauled her up. "You gots to learn, child."

Copper spent the rest of the afternoon learning to breathe. The corset smothered her and made it impossible to bend at the waist. She meandered around the house touching and admiring things.

The parlor was off the entrance hall to the right. It had a pink marble fireplace with a wooden mantel and surround painted glossy white. The fireplace was closed off for the summer with a brass, fan-shaped fire screen. A wrought iron plant stand, holding a lush green fern, sat in front of the screen. A gilt-framed mirror dominated the wall above the mantel and reflected two glass vases filled with blue hydrangeas. A settee and matching chair upholstered in a paisley print of burgundy, pink, and cream sat angled by the windows, and two cream-colored horsehair chairs were positioned just right for conversation.

Copper perched on the edge of one. She felt like she might pop. The mantel clock chimed five. Where was Simon? The party was at seven, and he'd promised to be home early. Anxious, she wandered out to the kitchen. She opened the screen door for a breath of fresh air, even if it wouldn't get past her throat.

Copper was kneeling in the garden, smacking a cat on the head, when she heard someone call her name.

"Miz Corbett? Hey! I'm Andy Tolliver."

Startled, she looked around. "Well, hello, Andy. It's nice to meet you."

"Doc sent me to tell you he was tied up and would be home later. Said for you to go on and dress. Old lady Wilson keeps swooning, and he can't rightly go off and leave her 'til she gets some gumption. Miz Corbett, what're you doing with that there cat?"

"I'm trying to get this old mouser to let go of this chipmunk. He wants to have the poor thing for supper."

The cat set to growling low in his throat and took a mean swipe at Copper's arm. Blood beaded up from two lengthy scratches.

Andy pulled the mangy cat's tail. "Here now, you old tom, let that varmint go."

Old Tom, if that was indeed his name, gave up his prize and let the hapless chipmunk fall, limp and still, to the garden path. He stalked away, stiff tail twitching, meowing his protest.

Andy held the tiny body in one grimy hand and pushed unruly brown hair out of his eyes with the other. "Been better for this feller if Tom'd finished."

Copper looked up at the slender lad, not much older than Willy and Daniel. "You're probably right, but I just couldn't stand to watch him bat it around." She held up her hand, and Andy helped her to her feet. "Thanks. I'd never have gotten up by myself. Let's take him to the kitchen and see how bad he's hurt."

Copper found a small box, lined it with an old rag, and laid the trembling animal inside. Andy slid the box under the pie safe as she directed. The little thing could recover or die in peace.

Standing at the sink, Copper scrubbed her arms. She patted the cat scratches with a clean tea towel while looking over her shoulder at Andy. "You must be hungry from running over here. Wash up and I'll fix you something to eat."

Andy sat at the table in tattered overalls a size too small and wolfed down cookies and slurped his milk. His hands were only a little less dirty than they had been before he washed. He looked at Copper with a direct, honest gaze. "Ever'body's talking about you and wondering what Doc's brung home. I say he done a good job even if he did have to go more'n a hundred miles." Another cookie disappeared. "Are you a hillbilly? I reckon not 'cause you got shoes on, but I'm barefoot myself so's you can't rightly tell by that."

"You may call me a hillbilly if you like," Copper said, hiding a smile.

"I ain't so sure that'd be proper, Miz Corbett, but I'd like to see your corncob pipe next time I come."

"Andy, if I ever decide to smoke a pipe, you will be the first to know. Now you hurry on home. I'm sure your mother will have supper waiting."

"Nah, she don't cook much. I mostly rustle up something for my sisters." Andy stuffed cookies from the platter into his pants pockets. "I'll be stopping by now and then to see if you need any help with Old Tom or anything."

"Would you take a saucer of milk out to the garden for Tom before you go, please? While you're out there, pick whatever you like to take home with you."

"Thanks, Miz Corbett. See you later." The screen door slammed behind him.

Copper chuckled, wondering where she could find a corncob pipe to smoke at Alice's dinner party.

Copper waited in the parlor while Simon changed into evening dress. She studied her reflection in the mirror. The bodice of her deep green gown, with its frill of mint-colored crepe de chine, revealed her shoulders. She turned her back to the mirror and looked over her shoulder. Her five-gored skirt, with its Spanish flounce, hung just right over the wire bustle Searcy had tied to her waist. Under all, besides the pantalets, corset, bustle, and petticoats, she wore fine silk hose and low-cut pumps made of kid, dyed to match her dress.

Leaning forward, she studied her hair, swept into a chignon and held in place by mother-of-pearl combs. She wore the emerald choker that had belonged to her grandmother—a gift from Mam. The cat scratches stung like fire under her opera-length glove.

"Oh, my dear," she sighed as Simon entered the room, freshly shaved, black hair brilliantined, mustache waxed. "You are so handsome." He was dressed in white tie and tails. He'd had his tailor make the new style, shorter frock coat with satin lapels. His cummerbund matched the silk roses in her hair. She touched the V of her gown. "How did you know?"

"Your mother and I were in collusion. She sent me swatches. You can't know how much I want this evening to be just right for you."

He turned her to face the mirror, then circled her waist with his arms and tucked his chin into the curve of her shoulder. Reaching inside his coat pocket, he withdrew a square, satin-covered box. He snapped open the lid and pulled out an emerald bracelet.

"Oh, Simon," Copper said breathlessly as she held out her right arm.

He fastened the bracelet to her wrist, turned her hand, and kissed her gloved palm.

The clock struck seven.

Copper's eyes widened. Her hand flew to her mouth. "We're late! What will your sister think?"

Their carriage turned from the street onto a curved, tree-lined lane that led to a house so big Copper thought it must be a mansion. Light sparkled from every window, and the massive front door was held open by an impeccably dressed, dark-skinned man who took her wrap and Simon's hat.

"Thank you, Joseph," Simon said. "I expect we're a little late—fashionably so, I hope."

The gentle pressure from Simon's hand at the small of her back ushered Copper into the music room. Several couples surrounded a grand piano, where a rather plump, plain-looking young woman dressed in yellow taffeta held court. Her fingers flew effortlessly over the keys, and Copper recognized the strains of Chopin.

A tall, elegantly dressed woman broke away from the laughing group and kissed Simon's cheek. Alice was thin, Copper noticed, and beautiful. She had the same black hair as her brother and arched brows over brown eyes as sharp as twopenny nails. When she leaned toward Copper with pursed lips, her face soured, and the hand that brushed Copper's was cold even through their gloves.

"Late as usual, Simon," she said in a low, aggrieved tone. "Not the best introduction for your bride, but . . . nonetheless. Everyone! Look who has arrived: Simon and the new Mrs. Corbett!"

People swirled around Copper as she was introduced. Mr. This and Mrs. That and everyone so important sounding. How would she ever remember their names?

The last people she met were the pianist and her mother. When the pianist arose from the piano bench, her gown was creased and stood as stiff as cardboard around her. Mam always said taffeta was an unforgiving fabric, and now Copper saw why. The pianist looked like a yellow tent, but her smile was genuine and dimpled her round cheeks.

"I'm Hester Lauderback, and this is my mother, Margaret. So pleased to meet you, Laura Grace," she gushed. "Let me show you Alice and Benton's lovely home before we dine." She took Copper's arm. "You don't mind, do you, Alice?" Her eyes shone with mischief. "Let's go switch place cards," she whispered as she pulled Copper away from Alice and her guests. "Then we can sit together."

Nothing had prepared Copper for the opulence of the place. Each room dripped with rich fabric, glittering chandeliers, huge mirrors, and impressive works of art. Patterned carpets in deep colors of burgundy, gold, and navy graced the floors. The walls were decorously papered—no cabbage roses here—or had murals depicting hunting scenes.

On the upstairs landing, Copper and Hester paused before a magnificent rosewood étagère. It stood at least ten feet high with shelves displaying figurines on either side of its mirrored center, which reflected the two women, Hester with a slight smile, Copper with her mouth agape.

"Parian," Hester said.

"Pardon me?"

"The statuary . . . Parian. Benton has an extensive collection. You'll see it throughout the house."

"Oh." Copper touched one of the smooth white sculptures with the tip of her finger. "How could you keep your mind on your dusting with all these little naked people standing about?"

Hester laughed, her voice a delightful light and airy tinkle. "Laura Grace Corbett, I like you." With a squeeze to Copper's hand, she said, "We'd better get back before Alice comes looking."

They made it just in time to hear Joseph announce, "Dinner is served."

Benton Upchurch gave his arm to Copper and escorted her to the lavish table where she was to sit at his right hand. Hester ensconced herself at Copper's side as the other guests took their assigned seats. Alice, escorted by Simon, brought up the rear.

As she faced the formal dining table, Copper sent a silent thank-you Mam's way for all the nights of table etiquette. Her dinner card, beautifully scripted with her title, Mrs. Simon Alexander Corbett, rested conspicuously on a white folded napkin. She recognized all the dining instruments: the large-bladed cutting knife; the butter knife; the soup and dessert spoons; the dinner, salad, fish, and oyster forks, but what of the little knife and fork placed on an angle across her plate? Her stomach felt queasy. The gloves she wore made a scratchy sound when she rubbed her finger with her thumb. Was everyone watching?

An elbow nudged her arm. Hester drew off her gloves, one finger at a time, laid them across her lap, then sliced a bit of the toast points on her plate with her little knife and fork.

Copper tried a bite and suppressed a shudder.

"Anchovy," Hester said behind her napkin. "Just push it around on your plate if you don't like it."

At the other end of the table, Alice surveyed the room with a critical eye. A large circular arrangement of yellow jonquils, purple and white Catawba grapes, and Japanese honeysuckle commanded attention in the middle of the table. Candles in many-armed candelabra flanked the centerpiece and cast a flattering glow on the faces of her guests. The monogrammed silver was old and heavy, the linen aged to a creamy white. The half dozen serving maids were dressed in stiff black dresses, starched white caps, and frilly white aprons. Every detail of the dinner spoke of old money and privilege.

One course followed another. First an anchovy relish, then raw oysters, followed by a palate-cleansing tomato bisque, before cucumbers, dressed exactly as she had requested—the French way with oil, salt, and pepper in vinegar. The main course was a joint of beef with fresh asparagus, peas, and corn.

Alice was known for her social decorum. She settled her sleeve over her wrist and forked a bit of beef into her crimped mouth. She watched with some surprise as her brother's wife acted as if she'd eaten at the queen's table all her life, watched as Simon's little ninny of a wife fawned over Benton, who sat there, his bald head shining, his bulbous nose reflecting the veins of excess, as he soaked it up. The old fool.

Maybe it wouldn't be too bad; at least someone had taught her a few table manners. She didn't eat everything with a spoon. If they could just get through the meal without any major faux pas, perhaps Alice could relax a little.

❧

Copper was enjoying the meal as much as her constricting clothing would allow. She leaned closer to Benton, who regaled her with tales of big-game hunting in exotic locales like India and Africa.

"My goodness," she replied to his story of the elephant he had shot when it stormed his tent, killing his safari guide. "The wildest thing I ever killed was a bobcat, and that was with a sling. My little brother Willy talked about David and Goliath for weeks afterward." She touched a monogrammed napkin to the corner of her mouth. "Mostly I hunt rabbit and squirrel. Do you like squirrel, Mr. Upchurch? Mam fries up the best you ever ate."

Suddenly every eye was on Alice, who was gasping and clutching her neck. Simon's chair crashed against the floor as he leaped up and pounded her back. One dreadful sound—*arrgh*—escaped her throat before a chunk of beef plopped onto her plate. Tears streamed from her eyes.

"She's all right," Simon said.

Margaret Lauderback escorted Alice from the room.

In a flurry of movement the serving girls cleared the table. With just a nod from Joseph, they placed a finger bowl, floating a single rose petal, in front of each diner.

Copper dipped her fingers and dried them on her napkin. Quick as a flash the finger bowl was replaced by dessert: a fruit ice and fresh strawberries.

Conversation flowed. Hester was engaged in discourse with a handsome young man. Simon listened intently to an elderly woman. Benton described another account of his hunting prowess. A couple to his left laughed at his jokes.

Copper took the opportunity to slip away. Hoping to check on Alice, she followed the sound of voices down the hall to the parlor. The door was ajar, and as she put out her hand to push it open, she heard Alice speak.

"Heavens above, Margaret, how can I bear this? I am just mortified." Copper heard Alice wheeze and the soft sound of Margaret patting her back. "How could Simon do this to me when he had every debutante in Lexington, not to mention your beautiful Hester, at his beck and call? We'll be on every wagging tongue in Lexington."

"Now, now," Margaret soothed. "Here, take a sip of water, and let's tuck your hair back up. She's quite lovely, and Simon seems very happy."

"Margaret—" Alice coughed a few times—"she eats rodents!" She cleared her throat. "You know the story about her family. . . ."

"Oh, Alice, that was such a long time ago. I'm sure people have forgotten or don't connect Simon's wife to those Taylors. She's never lived in Lexington, after all."

"I hope you're right, but those kinds of things taint the blood. Mark my words; no good will come of Simon's bringing her here."

The last thing Copper heard as she eased herself away from the door was Margaret's low voice. "I wonder who her dressmaker is."

After dinner, Benton insisted on showing Copper his collection of mounted heads. He had hunted on nearly every continent, and the darkly paneled walls of the billiards room bore witness to his expertise. Black and brown bears, a lion, an elephant, and an ugly thing that reminded her of the hogs that ran wild on the mountain behind the cabin stared at them with lifelike eyes.

"Wild boar. Those tusks can gut a man." Benton held her elbow captive as he steered her under a whole stuffed tiger and started another story.

Copper's mind wandered back to the unclosed door. She was at a loss to understand why Alice didn't like her. Questions swirled through her mind like tea leaves stirred from the bottom of a cup. And what was that about her family? Had she really stolen Simon away from another? Had Hester been his intended? What would Mam say?

She looked up at the great striped beast. Its huge mouth frozen midsnarl, its polished fangs as sharp as razors. "Don't be so quick to take offense." Mam's voice from the tiger's mouth. "If you hadn't been eavesdropping, you wouldn't have heard words not meant for your ears."

Copper glanced over her shoulder as Benton escorted her from the room, still gripping her elbow. Mam was surely right. Given time, Alice would come to love her. If not, there was room on those polished walls, right between the laughing hyena and the shy antelope, for her sister-in-law to hang a head of her own choosing.

It seemed to Copper that she met more people that evening than she'd known the whole of her life on Troublesome Creek. Finally, after the last guest departed, Alice, Benton, Simon, and Copper stood outside saying good-bye. Simon pecked his sister's cheek, thanked her for the lovely evening, and went to fetch the buggy.

Impulsively, Copper hugged Alice. "Please come to our house for Saturday night supper."

"You don't extend dinner invitations on porch steps," Alice sniffed.

"Nonetheless, we'll be there," Benton interrupted. "Won't we, dear?"

A quiver of pain crossed Alice's face as Copper watched her twist her elbow from his grip. Her sister-in-law's voice was as cold as a mountain stream when she said, "Whatever you wish, Benton."

The carriage arrived, and Copper nearly flew down the steps to Simon. *We'll start over*, she thought as she settled onto the seat. *Alice was just overwhelmed with everything. We'll soon be as close as sisters*. She yawned and snuggled under Simon's arm.

"Did you have a good time?" he asked.

"Mostly. Everything was wonderful, but Benton's quite boring, and I don't like anchovies. I hid mine under a lettuce leaf."

Simon laughed. "At least you didn't put them in the table drawer. That's what I used to do every time Alice insisted I eat peas. It worked until the day she watched Searcy wax the dining room furniture. When she pulled out that drawer, I thought my world would come to an end."

"I don't understand, Simon. Sounds like Alice is your mother."

"Alice and I are very close. . . ." He paused and traced his mustache. "My mother was so frail I hardly knew her except for

supervised visits to her bedside. I owe a great debt to my sister."
A frown furrowed his brow.

"What did you do tonight?" she teased, playful. "Did you put
the peas in your pants pocket? If so, I shall make you eat every one."

"For you, I would eat a boxcarful." He nuzzled her neck. "You
were by far the most beautiful woman at the party."

"Simon! Reuben will see."

He pulled her closer. "There's nothing wrong with a man
kissing his own wife."

"All the same—" Copper pushed him away—"we're in a public
place."

"Later then, sweetheart. Your yawning is contagious; now I
am sleepy too."

CHAPTER 5

Jarring sounds sailed up the staircase and woke Copper from a deep sleep. *Crash*, then *thump, thump, thump*.

"What in the world?" Simon jumped from the bed, grabbed his glasses, and threw on his robe.

Yawning, Copper followed as he dashed down the stairs and into the kitchen, where Searcy was yelling and flailing away with a broom.

"Get out of Searcy's kitchen!" she screamed as she swept a hapless chipmunk toward the propped-open door.

As fast as a greased pig, the fat-cheeked pest slid off the broom and darted behind his box under the pie safe.

"This vermin's set up housekeeping," Searcy huffed, breathing heavily. "He done made hisself a bed."

Simon took the broom and poked under the cupboard.

The chipmunk dodged it, crumbs of corn bread spilling from his mouth.

"For goodness' sake." Copper shook her head and glared at Simon. "You'll scare him to death." She knelt on the floor, plucked up the trembling creature, and carried him outside. They all watched him tunnel through the dew-soaked grass, making a beeline for the garden.

"Watch out for Old Tom," Copper called. "You might not be so lucky next time."

❦

Simon smoothed his hair with the flat of his hand. "Laura Grace, you can't be handling strays. That mangy old cat has already scratched you. I've a good mind to have Reuben shoot it."

"Simon Corbett, I can't believe you would think of such a thing! Tom was only hungry, and the chipmunk was hurt; that's why I brought him in." She dismissed his concern with a toss of her head. "Such a fuss over nothing."

Simon's temper flared. He looked at her standing there in her nightgown, her hands on her hips, sassing him in front of the housekeeper. She hadn't even dressed her hair, and it flared in wild disarray. He had to stop himself from pulling her back into the kitchen, sitting her down, and having a word with her. She wasn't on Troublesome Creek anymore; there was such a thing as decorum.

Instead he took the mug of coffee Searcy handed him. "No breakfast for me," he flung over his shoulder as he headed for the stairs. "I'm late."

Miz Corbett sat at the kitchen table. Tears trickled down her cheeks. "I'm sorry, Searcy. I always seem to do the wrong thing."

Searcy was at a loss. She had never had a white woman share a confidence with her. Oh, she'd heard plenty. Most acted like she was stone deaf unless they wanted something fetched or washed. Now here sat this little girl-woman talking to Searcy like they were the same kind of people. Her heart wanted to hug Miz Corbett, pat her back, tell her everything would be all right, but her brain told her to mind her own business. She settled on offering her a cup of tea and a clean hanky.

Copper mopped her tears. Simon slammed the front door. A punctuation mark for the argument they hadn't even had. She sighed and stood up. "I'll go get dressed; then I can help you."

"Oh no, Miz Corbett, you find something light to do. Maybe some needlework or some reading. When Miz Alice lived here, she had her nose in a book all the time."

"I'll soon cease to be a guest, and you will have to find me some work to do," Copper replied. "I can't bear being idle. Besides, it's not fair to put all the work off on you, Searcy."

"Ain't no hardship. Searcy been taking care of this house most all her life."

Back in her bedroom, Copper chose a muslin day dress with pink satin-ribbon trim and a matching sash. The white dress was covered with tiny pink dots. She studied herself in the mirror. *Looks like I have the German measles. Maybe I should change.*

She picked up her Troublesome Creek pebble and squeezed it so tight that it left a perfect impression on her palm. Finding her trunk, she took out the rest of her treasures: a flat, gritty piece of sandstone; a tumbled-smooth creek rock; a jagged edge of shale; and her prize—a lump of shiny black coal. She arranged them on the windowsill, where a little zephyr blew and puffed out the curtains. Kneeling on the floor with her nose to the sill, she let the warm wind blow the scent of the mountains around her. Her heart ached with longing as she prayed her morning prayers.

Finally comforted, she went downstairs and into the library. Early morning sunlight, filtered through lace curtains, streamed across the table that sat precisely in the middle of the room. Mahogany barrister bookcases with glass fronts filled one wall and held important-looking books bound with burgundy- and camel-colored leather.

Over the fireplace hung oval portraits of Simon's mother and father, Old Doctor and Miss Lilly. Copper saw a strong resemblance between Simon and his father: the same clear, direct gaze; long, straight nose; full bottom lip; and dark, wavy hair. Instead of a mustache, however, Old Doctor sported a clipped Vandyke beard. She saw nothing of her husband or Alice in Miss Lilly. The painting revealed a slip of a woman with a narrow face and wispy gray hair.

"I think I would have liked you," Copper said to the lady on the wall. "Perhaps you would have liked me too."

What am I to do with myself? Wandering about the room, she picked up the morning edition of the Lexington newspaper and settled into an overstuffed chair. She kicked off her black patent leather pumps and rested her feet on the chair's matching ottoman.

I never heard of such mayhem, she mused. The city seemed full of wanton destructiveness. A whole column was devoted to the arrest record of people, mostly men, for robberies, public drunkenness, petty thefts, and such.

Poor Henry Thomas would be in jail all the time if he lived here. She wouldn't mind seeing Henry, her longtime friend, even though he was a chicken thief. She shook her head to remember how people said he'd stolen from Brother Isaac's henhouse to make the money to buy her pie at a pie supper. Then just before Henry had plunked down his quarters, Simon had parted the crowd and claimed her pie. Claimed her, too, truth be told.

Hmm, strange how things turn out. If that copperhead hadn't bitten Daniel, I'd never have met Simon. Funny, his visiting his elderly relative at just the time my little brother decided to play snake handler.

Copper closed her eyes for a moment only to drift off to sleep. A dream carried her home to the dear place she'd never thought to leave. Her bare feet caressed the log porch floor, rubbed smooth from years of wear. Her ears picked up the rush of water over rock; the creek was up. It must have rained. And, oh, there sat Daddy in his rocker. Smoke from his pipe of sweet-smelling tobacco tickled her nose.

Her heart soared. "Daddy," she said in her dream, "I'm back. I never should have left."

But he didn't answer, just tamped his pipe and walked into the cabin as if she were invisible.

Her head drooped to her shoulder and she startled awake, not sure where she was for a moment. Wiping drool from the corner of her mouth, she glanced about, glad to see there was no witness to her laziness. She folded the paper and put it back on the library table. Hands overhead, she stretched backward until she felt the release of tension in her neck and lower back. She drifted around the house, idly filling time before boredom drove her back to the library with its treasure trove of mystery.

❧

The library was where Simon found Laura Grace midday when he returned for dinner. She lay on her belly on the Venetian red carpet, elbows bent, her hands supporting her chin, engrossed in one of his hefty medical tomes. Her legs, clad in white stockings, were revealed to the knee as she swung her crossed ankles slowly back and forth while she read. He could have stood there all day, quietly observing her, taking her in. He cleared his throat and stepped into the room.

Her welcoming smile dazzled him. "Oh, Simon, I'm glad you're home. Are you hungry? My stomach is growling."

He sat down in the chair that faced her. She sat up, holding the heavy book open in her lap. Her sunny greeting surprised him. After their spat, he'd been prepared for days of silence. Leaning forward, he cupped her jaw, stroking her cheek with his thumb. "I'm sorry I was short with you this morning, sweetheart."

"I'm sorry too." She looked up at him. "I didn't mean to make you angry."

He pulled her to his lap. The book fell to the floor; he reached around her and closed it. "You don't need to fill your mind with this, Laura Grace."

"But it has wonderful color plates of the human body!" she exclaimed. "Did you know there is a tube that runs from your throat to your . . . well, never mind. . . . But it has to do with digestion, and it pushes food along with little waves called . . . peri . . . something or other. Makes me think of a slithering snake."

"Peristalsis," he said, pulling on his mustache. "Your analogy was good; peristalsis does somewhat mimic the movement of a snake. I may crib that for my next lecture."

They stood, and Simon put the volume back in its proper place, thankful she was reading about digestion and not procreation, else they might never consummate their union. Not that they were making any progress in that department anyway. She was so much just a girl still—except in looks, of course. Her verdant beauty threatened to be his undoing.

"I'll stop by Hester's and ask her to bring you some appropriate reading material."

Laura Grace took his hand and pulled him along to the dining room. Her good nature filled the space around them, sweet as clover honey, a balm to the ache in his heart, a soreness he hadn't known was there until he met her.

His mind took him back to that humble cabin on Troublesome Creek and to the hardworking family he had met there.

The boy had been his main interest when he'd stepped onto the rough-hewn porch that muggy evening last summer. Daniel lay on his father's lap, nearly comatose from the snake's venom coursing through his young body. Daniel's twin, Willy, showed such concern for his brother. Grace, the mother, puzzled Simon before he learned her story. He'd never expected to find a scholarly, cultured woman in the hollows of eastern Kentucky, but she was there, and because of her Laura Grace was educated, albeit unsophisticated. And because of her father, that bear of a man, she was too self-reliant, much too rash.

It was as if Simon had caught a wood sprite or a whisper of smoke. He'd captured her, but could he hold her?

He resolved to visit his sister after office hours. He needed some advice.

⚜

After a noon meal of fried chicken, potato salad, and strawberries with clotted cream, Simon settled his derby on his head, kissed Copper lightly on the cheek, and strode purposefully down the sidewalk, off to a waiting room full of patients.

Copper leaned against the wooden porch railing, waving him away, absentmindedly touching her face where his mustache had tickled her cheek, glad for his good-bye. She couldn't wait to get back to the library. A whole world of knowledge awaited in those forbidden books. What was the harm? She would just be careful to put them back exactly as she found them.

The library was cool and filled with shadows cast by the huge sugar maple in the side yard. Copper raised the window, thankful for the screen to keep out flies, and propped it open with the stick left there for that purpose. Retrieving the tome titled *Disorders of the Digestive System*, she lost herself in the alimentary canal. Who knew there were thousands of feet of intestines curled up in the human body? How could such a thing be possible? She marveled at God's creation as she smoothed a hand across her own flat belly.

That afternoon she learned that the silver-dollar term for belching was *eructation*, and indigestion, or dyspepsia, was caused by impure air, inattention to diet, and drinking cold water with meals.

Taken aback, she read that pork in the diet was the cause of diphtheria and wondered if she could give up her morning sausage and bacon. She decided she would rather be plump than take the fat-reduction drink made from the juice of pokeberries mixed with a little powdered licorice root, used by G. Million, MD, to reduce a lady's weight from 247 pounds to 198 pounds in fifteen days.

Shuddering to study about water brash and bloody flux, Copper was surprised to hear her own stomach growling in response to the tantalizing smell drifting her way from the kitchen, where Searcy was cooking supper. The afternoon had flown by. Simon would be home soon.

She carefully positioned the borrowed book between its cousins on the polished shelf and pulled the curved front of the bookcase closed, pausing to wipe a smudge from the glass with the tail of her skirt. Before leaving Simon's study, she glanced about, pleased to leave it as she found it . . . save for the open window, where lace curtains fluttered in the late-afternoon breeze.

When Simon made his way home from his visit with his sister, he found his bride in the dining room arranging zinnias in a vase. Even though it was still light out, candles were burning on the dining room table, releasing the fragrant scent of vanilla into the air.

Perhaps Alice was right. He just needed to take a firm hand, show Laura Grace who was in charge instead of spoiling her. Just look what his stand on her reading material had wrought. Obviously she'd spent the afternoon in the flower garden instead of in his library reading about matters much too weighty for the feminine brain. He silently congratulated himself. *It is going to be easier to train a wife than I had imagined. A firm hand and she will learn her proper place, enjoying it all the while.*

They ate their meal in pleasant silence, each lost in thought, Simon dreaming of the acquiescent little wife Laura Grace would soon become.

Returning from a late-evening call on Mrs. Wilson, who lived five miles out in the country and wasn't sick at all, Simon found Laura Grace asleep on top of the bed, a fashion magazine spilling from her hand. He gently eased her beneath the light quilt that would protect her from the night air. He traced the outline of her shoulder before she stirred and brushed his hand away.

"Oh, Simon." She stifled a yawn with the back of her hand. "I meant to wait up for you. Was Mrs. Wilson all right?"

"She was fine, merely lonely, as I would be if not for you."

She burrowed under the covers, already asleep again.

For a moment he sat on the edge of the bed, watching her. Her light breath stirred a lock of hair that had fallen across her face. He tucked it away and then knelt there, as he did each night, and thanked God for the goodness of his day, for Mrs. Wilson's continued health, and for the gift of Laura Grace.

Prayers finished, Bible read, teeth brushed, Simon trod down the stairs to close up the house. While winding the grandfather clock in the front hall, a drift of air gave him pause. He stepped into the library. The curtains gusted. The window was propped in a way that he would not have left it, the propping stick slanted across the opening while he would have positioned it straight up.

Laura Grace came back in here after I asked her not to! Indignant, he pulled a ring of keys from his pocket and turned one in the lock of each bookcase, then took himself up the stairs.

It's my duty to protect her, he thought, puffed up with righteousness, never owning that what he really wanted was to make her over to his specifications, break her will, have her be the wife he thought he wanted, the one his sister told him he needed. Climbing into bed, he tucked her sleeping body into his own and drifted off into the deep and dreamless sleep of the pure in spirit.

⚜

Copper stared at her breakfast. Weighing starvation against diphtheria, she shook pepper on her eggs and took a bite of crisp, thick-sliced bacon. She spied Searcy through the screen door, sluicing water over the stone porch floor, scrubbing mightily with an old mop. "Searcy, come and eat with me. I need company."

"Miz Corbett, this ain't no time for socializing," Searcy huffed. "Mallie done scrubbed all her porches. She be like a fox. No matter how early a body starts, she be finished first. Her floors wet before the sun come up. Sometime Searcy like to ring her head with this here mop."

"If you would let me help, we could finish way before Mallie."

Searcy cast a silencing look Copper's way, then sank to her hands and knees and dipped a scrub brush into the steaming water. "Don't need no help," she mumbled as water splashed about. "They be plenty work left in these old hands."

CHAPTER 6

Simon and Laura Grace were up early Saturday morning, he to attend a symposium at Transylvania University, his alma mater, where he was to deliver the opening address.

"Hold still." Laura Grace pinned a freshly plucked rosebud to his lapel. "I wish I could go with you and listen to your speech."

He pulled her into his arms and nuzzled her neck. "You would be bored silly."

"You'll make me muss your coat," she replied, wiggling out of his arms.

Taking a small comb, he stood before the mirror and groomed his mustache. His eyes met hers in the looking glass. "What will you do with yourself today?"

"Well, since Alice and Benton are coming for supper tonight, as well as Hester and her mother, I'll have plenty to do."

"I don't want you to tax yourself."

"Don't fret; it's just supper. I want to do something nice for Alice. I want so much for her to like me."

"I . . . I'm sure she does." The lie tripped on Simon's tongue and gave him pause. His sister didn't like his wife much at all. His visit with her after finding Laura Grace in the library had made it obvious. . . .

He'd found Alice in the dining room, sitting alone at the end of the long table, composing her week's menus, writing on the finest onionskin as if it were the most important task in the world. The afternoon was unseasonably warm, he'd noticed on his walk from the office, and he mopped perspiration from his brow as he approached his sister.

"Simon," she chided, "why do you insist on walking instead of having Reuben bring your carriage around?" She offered her cheek for her brother's light kiss.

"It gives me a chance to meet people. . . . Oh, thanks, Joseph." He took a long swallow from the glass of chilled water Alice's butler handed him. "Folks are more likely to ask for help if they see me on the street. They won't come to the office because they think they have to pay if they do."

"Why shouldn't they?" She put aside her writing supplies and arched her eyebrows, just like she used to when he was a boy with his hand in the cookie jar.

"Why shouldn't they . . . ?"

"Pay, Simon. Why shouldn't they pay for your services?"

"You miss the point, Alice. If they had funds, they'd come

to the office. Oh, never mind. We've had this conversation before. It's not why I came."

"I don't know why you insist on hobnobbing with every derelict in Lexington instead of claiming your proper place in society. Why did you come?"

He sat down, bouncing his hat on his knee. "I wanted to thank you for the dinner party."

"It was my duty. Now that you are married you will have to think of how your actions affect your wife's social standing. I suspect she will have trouble enough without your adding to it."

A sharp retort formed on his lips, but he held it back. He loved his sister. She was more like a mother to him than his own frail one had ever been. "I'm sorry to disappoint you, but someone must care for the indigent."

Standing, Alice moved behind his chair and put her hand upon his shoulder. "It is not your place to save everyone. Now you've gone too far. Laura Grace will cause you nothing but grief."

"Please don't say that," he replied, angry.

"She'll never be happy here. You know that, don't you?"

"Then I shall take her home."

"That might be best for all concerned. . . . Benton could arrange an annulment." Sadly, he heard the relief in his sister's voice.

"Ah, Alice." He patted the hand that rested so heavily upon his shoulder. "If she goes, then so do I."

CHAPTER 7

Copper took a moment to clean and oil her rifle. Loving the heft and feel of it, with its sleek wood stock, she looked down the sight and then fitted a shell into the chamber. A pang of homesickness, sharp as a whetted blade, caught her off guard as the memory of hunting the mountain hollows with her father crept into her mind.

She'd swiped a pair of Simon's old britches, and now she cinched them tightly about her waist with a length of grosgrain ribbon. They fit much better than the ones of her father's she used to wear. Dipping a piece of cloth in a tin of kerosene kept for the lamps, she swabbed a ring around her ankles. She hated chiggers with their mean bites and didn't care if she smelled like a smoky lamp pot if it prevented that infernal itching. As she pulled on her work boots, she laughed to think of the difference in her attire from Wednesday night when she had been all in splendor.

"What are you laughing at, Miz Corbett?" Andy Tolliver peered through cupped hands held against the screen door.

Copper opened the door, and Andy barreled in. "Well, I suppose you are right funny-looking," he said around the mouthful of biscuit and bacon she set on the table for him. "I ain't never seen a woman wear pants before." He continued to eat like a starved dog, and his eyes grew wide when he noticed her weapon. "What're you doing with that there gun? Doc told me you'd be getting the house ready for company and for me to come help."

"I'm about to get supper. Do you want to come along?"

Copper and Andy climbed the fence to the back pasture and hiked out to the woods they could see in the distance. Paw-paw snuffled and snorted his way alongside them, his excellent nose pressed to the ground.

"This is real exciting, Miz Corbett. I ain't never hunted for anything 'cept something from the cupboard to feed my sisters."

They made their way to a rolling hillside, thick with trees. Here and there Copper spied a few stately hickories and walnut trees too numerous to count. These woods should be thick with squirrels. The air was dense and moist with dew, perfumed by the fertile smell of the earth itself, of buried rock under soil made up of eons of decaying leaves and animal droppings. From somewhere came the sound of water burbling up out of the ground, a spring close by. A quick wind stirred the tops of the trees, and their branches clicked out a tune her ears were hungry to hear.

Copper inhaled deeply, the first full breath she'd had since she left her mountain home.

They pushed on and soon came upon a clearing, where they sat a moment. "We must be very still so the squirrels won't spook," she whispered. "If they see us, they'll stay on the back side of the trees and we'll not get a clear shot."

Killy . . . killy . . . killeeee. A shrill call interrupted Copper's caution. A hawk soared above them; sunlight flashed off its slate blue wings.

"There's a chicken hawk," Andy cried. "I hate them things. Minny Gerhard gave us eggs 'til them chicken thieves killed all her hens."

"That hawk is too small to kill chickens, Andy. It eats field mice, chipmunks, and sometimes even small snakes. Let's lay back and watch the sky. Chances are we'll see a chicken hawk. Their cry sounds like *keeer . . . keeer.*"

Andy mimicked her movements and rested the back of his head on his laced fingers.

"It'll give you the shivers when they scream," she continued as she stared into the blue sky, where little puffs of white clouds romped like sheep in a pasture, "for you know they are about to kill something. Once one carried off my pet rabbit, but I have to admit, they are beautiful to watch."

"Look!" Andy pointed.

High above, three hawks circled the meadow. Ever so slowly, other redtails joined the three. Copper and Andy watched, mesmerized, while dozens of the raptors spiraled together, forming a funnel-shaped mass of dancing birds.

"That's called a kettle when they bunch in the air like that," Copper explained.

"Wow, that was something to see. You sure know a lot of things, Miz Corbett. How'd you get so smart?"

"When I was about your age, my daddy and I lay out on a rock ledge high up on the side of a mountain, and he showed me just what I'm showing you. I love to be outdoors just watching things, don't you?"

"I ain't had much time for watching," Andy said in a voice too grown-up for a boy. "I have to take care of my family. I do jobs for anybody who'll pay me, 'specially Doc Corbett. Why, sometimes he'll slip me a fifty-cent piece when I ain't hardly done nothing. Like today, he'll likely pay me for having fun with you."

"Do you go to school?"

Andy turned onto his belly and began to pull the heads off long stalks of ryegrass and pop them in his mouth. "No'm, but I'm real quick. I learned to read, and I cipher real good, so I don't need no more schooling." A long green stem bobbed in his mouth as he talked. Sitting up, he scratched his bare shin. "Bothersome chiggers, they get me ever time. I hope Ma's friend left some whiskey at the house. That'll stop the itch."

Copper sat up beside him and stared at him, alarmed. "You shouldn't be into whiskey."

Andy looked at her as though he were the adult and she the child. "Don't you go worrying about that. There's never more than a taste in the bottom of his bottle. I keep it in case Dodie gets a earache. I wouldn't ever drink it. It'll make you puke your guts out."

"Is Dodie your sister?"

Andy jumped up. "Dodie's the baby, Marydell's my sister."
He looked away from Copper. "Ma gets lonesome sometimes.
. . ." His voice trailed off. "Hey, ain't we going to shoot that gun?"

"Sure, Andy." Copper picked up the rifle. "See that black walnut tree? See that patch of bumpy-looking bark? That's a gray
squirrel. He's supper." She raised the gun to her shoulder. One
clean shot felled her prey.

Half a dozen squirrels later, Andy had his turn. Copper stood
behind him, helped him sight his target, and held his shoulders
steady.

When the squirrel fell, Andy let out a war whoop to rival any
brave. "Boy, Miz Corbett, I could do this all day. I never knowed
you could have fun getting supper. Can I have this one to take
home? Do you cook it like chicken? How do you get the fur off?"

"That's the next lesson, Andy. But first we need to find a nice
fat rabbit. Alice doesn't like squirrel."

As evening drew near, Copper dressed simply in a brown broad-
cloth dress trimmed with black silk braid. She sat in front of the
mirror and tried to tame the curls that escaped the tortoiseshell
combs catching her hair in a roll at the back of her neck. Frus-
trated, she put the brush aside and opened the top drawer of her
dressing table, searching for another comb.

Her grandmother Taylor's emerald necklace lay nestled on a
bed of lace handkerchiefs. Picking it up, she let it dangle from her
fingers. The jewels cast dazzling green prisms of light across the

cabbage-rose wallpaper and flashed at her from the mirror. Mesmerized, she wondered about the things she'd heard Alice say at the party. What was the secret of her grandmother's past? Why had Mam not told her about her family? Why hadn't she asked?

All Copper knew was that her natural mother and her stepmother were sisters and that Mam had once been a teacher at the Finishing School for Young Ladies right here in Lexington. The fall before Copper married Simon and left Troublesome Creek, Daddy had told her about the tragedy of her mother's demise just two days after Copper's birth. Shuddering, she remembered his words. She could almost feel the rush of dark water that carried her mother to her death.

A solution came to mind. She could write Mam and ask her. Pen and paper would be ever so easy, and Mam wouldn't be able to ignore her or change the subject.

"You look very far away." Simon's voice startled her as he entered the room. She let the necklace fall back into its nest and closed the drawer as he planted little kisses on the back of her neck. "Supper smells good," he continued. "I'm starving."

⁂

Alice sat ramrod straight at the table on the porch. The evening breeze felt fresh and cool, but whoever heard of eating out of doors? And such a menu: squirrel meat with gravy, soup beans, fried potatoes, corn bread—a lowlife's supper. Where was Searcy? She'd have a word with her for neglecting her duties while Laura Grace kept jumping up to pile more food on her guests' plates. So common . . .

Alice picked at her plate. Everyone—even her friend Margaret, who should be miserable out of loyalty—seemed to be having a good time. Church would be an ordeal for Alice in the morning. If gossip were a newspaper, she could see the headline: "Local Doctor from Prominent Family Marries Hillbilly of Questionable Heritage." Tittle-tattle for those who had nothing better to do than sit in judgment.

She waved her hand at a pesky fly and looked across the table at Benton. He was laughing with his mouth full and gesturing with a squirrel leg, making a proper fool of himself. Stiffening her spine, Alice reached down inside her stubborn heart and pulled her pride up around her shoulders like a coat of mail. Some things just had to be endured.

Sunday morning, Copper and Simon walked, her hand in the crook of his arm, to the big redbrick church on the corner. She marveled at its stained glass windows and would have stood on the sidewalk staring, openmouthed, if Simon hadn't nudged her on toward the door.

Right in front of them, two ladies in old-fashioned full skirts tried to enter the vestibule at the same time. Their hoops collided and recoiled wildly, flinging one of the women out onto the lawn. She lay on her back like an overturned turtle, her feet churning the air, her white pantalets exposed to the knees among a froth of petticoats before Simon rushed to help her up.

Copper approached the door with caution. Her church dress was rose-colored washed silk. The overskirt was caught up with ribbon rosettes and pulled back to form a bustle. A moss green, silk shantung mantle covered her shoulders. Her hat was of the same material on a buckram base and boasted satin ribbon and veiling, and she wore moss green spats over her patent leather pumps. Simon was as nattily dressed in a black morning jacket over a gray silk vest and a dark blue tie. His trousers were gray wool, and his high-topped shoes had the newly fashionable boot-cut toe.

The sanctuary was nearly full as they made their way to the pew bearing the Upchurch name. Simon held the low door open, and Copper slid into the seat beside Alice. Giving Copper's gloved hand a squeeze, Simon removed the hymnal from the rack in front of them.

A young boy hurried to the front of the church. Standing on tiptoe, he whispered a message to the minister.

The reverend tented his hands and addressed his flock. "It seems our pianist has suddenly taken ill. Would someone serve in her place?"

Every woman who had ever taken a piano lesson suddenly seemed to become dumb as a stump. Even Alice squirmed in her seat beside Copper.

"Surely, ladies, one of you could grace us with your talent on this fine Lord's Day," the reverend pleaded. "My voice is not harmonious without an instrument. Anyone?"

"Hester?" Copper whispered behind her glove.

"She goes to the Methodist church on High Street," Simon whispered back.

Without thinking Copper said, "Then, perhaps, with your permission, Simon, I should . . ."

As if the congregation truly were one body, every head turned in unison as Dr. Corbett rose from his seat to hand his wife into the aisle. Gasps of surprise escaped pursed lips as he escorted her toward the pulpit. Hats bobbed as mouths whispered behind pasteboard church fans. Every neck crooked so every eye could take in Alice Upchurch and watch the color drain from her face. Then everybody settled in to watch the show.

Copper conferred with the reverend before positioning herself on the piano bench. Her foot hovered over the pedals for a moment as her fingers gently stroked the keys.

After playing one verse of "Upon the Mount," she honored the preacher's request and lifted her voice to the Lord. The words to the sweet hymn stilled the murmuring voices:

> *"My soul is on the mount today, and life's glad bells are*
>   *ringing,*
> *While unseen angels round me stay, their songs of sweetness*
>   *singing.*
> *Sweet and low, sweet and low, are the joy-bells ringing.*
> *While the golden harps resound, and angel hosts are singing."*

With a flutter in her stomach, Copper played on. She had sung nearly every Sunday at the church in the valley of her mountain home, and her stepmother had tutored her in piano from a very young age, but this was different. She didn't know these people. Sneaking a sideways look, she could see the reverend's foot discreetly tapping out the tune, and in the front row smiles creased every face, save one. Alice did not appear so easily swayed.

Following the service, the young couple took a circuitous route home. Simon often stopped to introduce Copper and exchange pleasantries with people they met during their promenade. Every church they passed disgorged beautifully dressed women who raised parasols against the sun and stylish men who tipped their hats in greeting.

Copper had never imagined such wealth. No one was barefoot or shabbily dressed. Even the children wore silk and satin. It made her sad somehow, sad and homesick. Her own dress seemed like a betrayal of the folks on Troublesome Creek. In her church, Brother Isaac would be promising hellfire to every backslider there. So different from the proper, controlled sermon she'd just heard. There'd be no frilly hats, just shapeless sunbonnets, no hoops or bustles but simple cotton or feed-sack shifts as often as not covered by clean, starched aprons to hide a tear or a stain.

She wished to be back there, where the afternoon would be spent reading the Bible and doing chores, but Simon's firm clasp on her elbow claimed her for himself. Copper prayed a silent prayer that she would learn to like the big city she lived in and that she would learn to love the people she was now a part of.

❧

Searcy stood right outside the dining room door, near enough to hear if she was needed but not close enough to be seen, just as Miz Lilly had taught her many years before.

She hoped Miz Alice was pleased with the meal she'd set on the table just minutes before she and Mr. Upchurch swept in for

Sunday dinner with Mr. Doctor and Miz Corbett. She'd made roasted chicken, mashed potatoes, snap peas with pearl onions, cucumbers in sugared vinegar, wilted lettuce with green onions, rhubarb, yeast rolls with fresh-churned butter, and Miz Alice's favorite dessert, banana pudding piled high with meringue.

Miz Corbett's little supper last night had set Searcy back some. She'd insisted on preparing the Saturday evening meal and serving it to her guests without any help from Searcy. She even had a notion that Searcy and Reuben would join them at the table and that she, Miz Corbett, would serve them! My, oh my, that woman child had heaps to learn.

Shifting her weight from one swollen foot to the other, Searcy kept her ears pricked toward the dining room. Her shoes were cutting into her ankles; she'd put her house slippers back on when Miz Alice went home.

Tink . . . tink . . . tink . . .

Oh no. Miz Alice was pinging on her water glass with her fork. Searcy had put the bell by Miz Corbett instead of by Miz Alice. She should have known better.

Searcy approached the table. "Yes, ma'am, Miz Alice?"

Miz Alice never even looked at her. She just said, "The peas are cold."

Searcy was mortified. Had she forgotten to heat the bowl before she filled it?

"Goodness, Searcy." Miz Corbett's chair scraped across the floor. "You don't need to be waiting on us after cooking all morning. I'll heat up the peas."

"Laura Grace, keep your place," Miz Alice said, her voice

frosting Searcy's heart. She had threatened more than once to find a replacement for Searcy if she couldn't keep up her job, and Searcy knew it wasn't an idle threat. Searcy never figured Mr. Doctor would let that happen, but you never could take nothing for granted. Miz Alice had a way about her.

Mr. Upchurch looked up from his plate and asked, "Is there any squirrel left over from last night?"

Searcy beat a retreat to the icebox, where she found two squirrel legs wrapped in waxed paper. After heating them and the peas, she carried the serving pieces back to the dining room. Cold sweat stained the front of her uniform as she served Mr. Upchurch before taking the peas to Miz Alice.

"No, thank you," Miz Alice said. "I couldn't eat another bite."

After their company left, Simon and Laura Grace sat on the porch in companionable silence, reading the Sunday paper. Every once in a while someone would stroll by and stop to chat for a short time, conversation passing from the sidewalk to the porch.

"Shouldn't we ask them to join us?" Laura Grace asked at one point.

"No need, my dear," Simon replied. "It wouldn't be good form to visit unannounced."

"We sure had some strange forms up in the mountains then," she said. "Anyone might come unannounced and stay for supper or a week."

Simon polished his spectacles with his perfectly ironed white handkerchief. "This is much more civilized, you must admit."

"Civilized but surely not very Christian."

Just then Paw-paw stuck his grizzly head around the corner of the porch. Alice had gone to pieces earlier when she saw him sleeping by the front door in a patch of sunlight. She'd summoned Reuben to tie him up out back, but the dog had obviously chewed through the rope and now dragged the tail of it behind him up the steps.

Laura Grace patted a place for him on the swing.

"Laura Grace, I thought we agreed–"

"*You* agreed," she said, an edge to her voice. "I don't understand why Alice was so upset."

"She's right," Simon answered, although Laura Grace made him feel a little pompous. "Dogs don't belong on the front porch."

"And servants don't belong at the table?" Laura Grace took Paw-paw's rope. "Come on, buddy. We mustn't upset the master."

Simon folded his newspaper in precise squares as his wife disappeared around the corner of the house. He knew Alice was not pleased with her behavior. Must every lesson Laura Grace needed to learn be met with such stubborn resistance? He had been much too lenient. After all, he'd let her bring the dog, not to mention the cow, with her from Troublesome Creek. Was it too much to ask to keep Paw-paw off the porch? Who was the master at 212 Willow Street? Laura Grace needed to find out.

◈

Copper stomped across the backyard. Paw-paw's yelps from his exile in the stable followed every step and made her feel like crying. Passing the garden on her way from leaving him, she spied a tomato plant heavy with green fruit. One fit her hand like a ball in a glove, and she could not resist the temptation. A tiny tug and it was hers, then another and another, all lobbed with a vengeance against the side of the barn.

"They be better if they ripe," Searcy said, startling Copper out of her anger. "Then they go *splut* and slide down the wall in a satisfying way when you throws them."

Copper bet her cheeks were as red as a ripe tomato. "I'm sorry, Searcy. That was childish of me. And I ruined one of Reuben's tomato plants."

"We got plenty," Searcy replied. "Reuben, he plants enough for Cox's army. Come on in the house now and let Searcy fix you some sweet tea."

Copper drained the tea and set her glass on the kitchen table. "Searcy? May I ask you something?"

"Yes'm. Ask away."

"When do you go to church? Seems you're always here, and you always cook Sunday dinner for us and our company, so when do you get to worship?"

Such a perplexed look clouded the housekeeper's face that Copper may as well have asked, "When do you feed the alligators?"

"Searcy don't expect that'd be proper, Miz Corbett."

"But don't your friends go?"

"Some do. Now Mallie, Miz Lauderback's girl? She's one to run off to service anytime she's a mind to. But Miz Alice, she liked me close to home." Searcy turned to face the window and wiped the already-spotless sink with her sun-bleached dishrag. "Who would cook if Searcy be singing and shouting on Sunday mornings?"

Paw-paw's yelps faded away, and the kitchen became so quiet that Copper could hear the tick-tock of the grandfather clock from the foyer. She went to stand at the sink beside Searcy. "Do you know the Lord?" Copper said gently.

"Know *of* Him . . . this dream come sometime of my mama singing 'bout Him. 'Swing low,' Mama sang so pretty whilst she stirred the wash. . . . 'Swing low, sweet chariot.'"

"What else do you know of Jesus?"

"Know He be in that big black book in Mr. Doctor's study. Searcy looks in there sometimes when she be dusting." She shook her head. "Can't figure them little squiggly lines nohow."

"Would you like to? Would you like to learn more about Him?"

"How that happen?"

With a gentle touch on Searcy's arm, Copper replied, "I could teach you if you'd like."

One worn hand patted Copper's own. "All right, child, but don't let's tell Miz Alice."

CHAPTER 8

Monday morning saw Simon off to the office as usual. Searcy refused to let Copper help with the wash, so Copper spent the morning dusting the dining room furniture. She carried the dishes and crystal from the china cupboard to the table and then wiped the shelves. When that was done, she put every piece back exactly as she had found it.

Next she dusted the chocolate cabinet, a gift, Simon had told her, from his father to his mother. The glass doors on its front had intricately carved wooden inserts that revealed the serving pieces behind the glass. Ever so carefully opening the door, she removed the ornately painted pitcher, tipped it, poured air into a dainty gold-rimmed cup, and sipped pretend cocoa. She wondered if Miz Lilly had ever served chocolate from the pitcher. It seemed like something to look at rather than to use. *Like every-thing else in Lexington.*

While she worked, Copper thought of the letter to Mam she'd posted this morning. All her questions and Alice's comments were contained in that missive sealed with mucilage, stamped, and sent on its way to Troublesome Creek. What a relief to know she'd soon understand why Alice didn't like her. Then she could mend some fences.

Finished with the dusting, she inspected the hand-crocheted tablecloth for stains; finding none, she stripped it from the table and carried it to the backyard for a shake. The morning was beautiful, so warm and inviting. She'd put the tablecloth back, then spend some time in the garden.

Barefoot, Copper was tamping dirt around the last of Mam's morning-glory seed, her work overseen by the mangy cat, Old Tom, when Alice appeared with a lady Copper remembered from the dinner party, Mrs. Robert Inglepond—or creek or something like that—cochair with Alice on the hospital auxiliary.

"Good morning," Copper said. "What a pleasant surprise."

Alice's black eyebrows arched. "Laura Grace, you remember Mrs. Inglebrook."

After dusting her hand on her apron, Copper held it out. "Of course."

Mrs. Inglebrook touched just the tip of her white-gloved fingers to Copper's. "So lovely to see you again, Mrs. Corbett."

"Come sit on the porch, and I'll fix us some sweet tea," Copper replied. "I made a jug this morning."

"Not today," Alice said, cold as a frozen-toed rooster. "We have a committee meeting. Did you forget?"

Copper's mind raced. Oh no! Alice had said something at Sunday dinner about taking her to a meeting, but between the cold peas and the banishing of her dog, she'd forgotten. How could she be so stupid? Feeling the heat rise from her neck to her face, her fingers sought the little creek rock in her pocket. "I'm sorry, Alice. I guess it slipped my mind."

With perfect timing, Paw-paw lumbered up, snuffled around Mrs. Inglebrook's shoes, then stuck his nose under Old Tom's tail.

Old Tom took offense and dashed under Alice's skirt. The cat sailed out from under the froth of material, propelled on the end of one polished shoe. Landing on his feet, the fur on his body stuck straight out, like a dandelion gone to seed. *"Meeerowh!"* he screamed, then shot up a little plum tree. The skinny branch he chose wavered under his weight, and he bobbed up and down like a dunking apple directly over Alice's head.

Copper could fairly see the chits stacking up against her in Alice's eyes. "I could get dressed . . . ," she offered.

Alice turned on her heel and started off across the yard, her back a stiff reproach. "Another time. We must hurry, Charlotte, or we'll be late."

Copper leaned on her hoe and watched them until they were out of sight. Mollified, Old Tom wound himself around her bare ankles. "Paw-paw!" She shook her finger in the old dog's face, then sank to the ground, pulled off her faded sunbonnet, and laughed until her belly ached and she couldn't catch her breath.

Finally spent, she got up and headed to the house for a glass of tea, a remembered caution from Mam ringing in her ears: "Laugh today and cry tomorrow," she'd say when Copper was too merry.

Stopping at the door, she wiped her feet on the rug Searcy kept there. "Better than not laughing at all, Mam," she said as if her mother could hear her—and, oh, how she wished she could.

Copper and the cat spent the rest of the afternoon in the garden. She would be glad when the morning-glory seeds sprouted. Maybe she'd be less homesick by the time the vines climbed the trellis she'd planted them under.

It was almost time to wash up and change for supper, so she laid her hoe aside and cut some red zinnias and a few sprigs of forsythia leaves, carried them to the house, and arranged them in an old, crackled, white pottery vase she found in the pantry. They'd look pretty on Simon's desk.

The library was cool and dark after the bright sun of the garden. *Tomorrow I will dust his bookcases.* A force she couldn't resist drew her to the books. So much to learn. Giving a happy sigh, she pulled on the knob of one bookcase door; it was stuck. She gave a yank, but it didn't yield so she tried another.

Hmmm, this is odd. They're all stuck. Then it came to her. Simon had locked the doors against her. Her face flushed as tears stung her eyes. She was just a little girl playing hob again. Always in trouble. Mam might as well be here with her wooden spoon.

She carried the vase of flowers to the entrance hall and set it on the table where Searcy kept the mail, which was delivered twice a day. Simon liked to check the post as soon as he came in the house. She reached over the table to straighten the painting that hung there—a pastoral of sheep grazing beside a quiescent, meandering stream.

An anxiety unusual to Copper settled around her heart; she didn't know what to do with the feeling. It was obvious her sister-in-law wasn't pleased with her; nor was Mrs. Inglebrook, and she wasn't so sure about Simon. Yes, he loved her, but was that enough? And did she really love him?

"You've made your bed," Mam would say, and truly she had. But her bed was a peacock's nest and she a small brown wren unable to find a perch.

The painting drew her in. "'He leadeth me beside the still waters,'" she murmured. "'He restoreth my soul. . . . Surely goodness and mercy shall follow me. . . .'" Copper knelt there in the entrance hall with bowed head over folded hands. "Please, Lord," she prayed aloud, "help me find the still water. Help me find my place in this house, and help my husband love the woman I am, not the one he wants me to be."

CHAPTER 9

Simon Corbett was bone weary. He'd never made it home for supper last night but instead had shared some kind of meat-and-potato stew rustled up by Avery Morton while they waited for Avery's wife to deliver her first baby. A long and tedious process. They'd sent for Simon much too early. Mrs. Morton was screaming before she'd dilated even three centimeters, and Avery kept going outside to throw up.

Finally home, Simon kept the lavatory door open so he could observe his wife, still abed. If he stood to one side of the mirror, he could see her while he lathered his face. He liked to watch her wake . . . that sleepy smile, that tangle of red hair.

He could smell coffee brewing and bacon frying. He was ravenous. "Laura Grace?" He sat on the bed beside her and smoothed the hair away from her face, pleased that she'd left it loose as he had requested. If she would only turn to him, only need him, but she swung her legs over the side of the bed, stood, and headed for the bathroom.

"Was the baby born, Simon?" she called over her shoulder. "Is it all right?"

"Hale and hearty. An eight-pound boy. I left him screeching like an out-of-tune fiddle. Takes after his mother."

"Are you going to sleep awhile?"

"I'm too hungry for sleep," he replied.

"Smells like Searcy's got breakfast ready," she said as he watched her bundle up her hair. "Go ahead without me. I'll be there directly."

Simon was standing by the hallway door with a cup of coffee when Laura Grace made it down for breakfast. She looked so pretty and fresh in a lavender day dress with a starched white collar, her hair pulled up with a plain white ribbon. Dropping her shoes beside her chair, she swung her feet, clad in clay-colored hose, back and forth.

"Laura Grace, I need to talk to you."

She tucked into the stack of pancakes Searcy flipped onto her plate, then glanced up. "What is it, Simon?"

He cleared his throat. "It's about shoes, dearest. Alice stopped by the office last afternoon. She said she and Mrs. Ingle-brook visited with you in the garden yesterday."

"Yes, they did." He watched as she poured more maple syrup on her pancakes. "I was sowing flower seed by the trellis, but it wasn't much of a visit." She licked her fork and looked at him. "What does that have to do with shoes? I wasn't planting shoes."

Simon leaned against the doorframe and ran a finger under his collar. Suddenly it seemed very tight. After taking a sip of coffee, he continued. "It was your lack of shoes that upset Alice, sweetheart. She was concerned about what Mrs. Inglebrook would think. You simply can't be going about the city in bare feet."

"I was not going about the city! I was in the yard you said was mine. What's the point of being in the garden if you can't feel the dirt between your toes?" Her eyes flashed. Two bright spots of color bloomed on her cheeks as she pushed back from the table and shot straight up, overturning her chair in the process. "Oh, that sister of yours makes me so mad!" She fairly spat her words across the table. "Miss Alice Upright! If you put that pious old biddy in a stewpot, she wouldn't make a broth."

He looked at the floor. His shoes could stand a polishing. "There's no need to call Alice names, Laura Grace." He modulated his voice to a proper calm-the-patient tone. "She has your best interest at heart."

Out of the blue, something sailed past Simon. Amazingly one high-topped shoe struck the wall beside his ear and thumped to the floor. A whish of air caused him to duck just in time to miss its mate. Hot coffee spilled on his shirtfront and dripped off the end of his new silk tie.

Her hands on her hips, she faced him. "My name is not Laura Grace! It's Copper! Just plain Copper!"

"Shush," he cautioned, one finger to his lips. "The neighbors."

Laura Grace answered by reaching under her dress, jerking off her stockings, and flinging them in his face. "I'm barefoot; do you hear?" She stamped both feet on the tile floor. "Barefoot, and I'm never wearing shoes again!" The screen door slammed once behind her before she turned and slammed it full force again.

Stunned, Simon watched as his wife climbed the backyard fence and tore off across the pasture. He stood rubbing his right ear; one of her stockings trailed from his cup, dripping coffee down his leg. Searcy handed him a clean towel, and he blotted the stains the best he could. He unknotted his tie, loosened his collar, then removed his glasses and pinched the bridge of his nose.

Shoulders slumping, he righted Laura Grace's chair and sat down. "Searcy," he said, the little boy he used to be turning to her for comfort, "what am I to do?"

Searcy stood at the sink running cold water over the charcoal gray tie he had handed her. "You be asking Searcy's opinion, she 'spec she be good enough to give it."

"I am, Searcy. Please, I am."

"That girl child be missing her mama and her folks," Searcy said without stopping her work. "She feel lost, and she don't know why she here, 'cept for you, and that ain't hardly working out."

"I know." He hung his head. "I don't know how to make her happy."

"She gots to be needed, sunshine." Searcy called him the baby name he hadn't heard for years. "Miz Corbett gots to have something to do. She ain't a decoration. She ain't just a play pretty."

Standing, Simon embraced her bony shoulders. Memories

came back to him of boyhood, when he'd run to the kitchen and throw his arms around Searcy whenever he needed a hug, before it became improper.

"Thank you." He rolled up his sleeves. "I'm going to find my wife."

⚜

Copper sat on a jutting rock looking down on Willow Springs. The pasture ended in a steep hill crested by a ridge with a precipitous drop to the creek below and gave the illusion of mountains if you didn't look to the flat field behind. A plethora of weeping willows, their spindly branches drooping, shaded the ridge and, she supposed, gave the creek its name. Simon had told her it was fed by many underground springs. The dark pool below her swinging legs looked cold and deep.

She drew up her legs and rested her head on her knees. Her new lavender dress, one she and Mam had labored over, was dirty where she'd dragged it along the ground, and it had torn loose at the waist—popped some stitches during her tantrum most likely. Her ribbon was long gone, and her hair fell in her face as she sobbed.

What am I to do? I'm seventeen years old, and my life is ruined. Why did I come here? Why?

Her mind drifted back to the past January—that cold, wretched month—to Simon's pleading and Mam's prodding. She'd had her own plans, firm plans, to farm the home place by herself once Mam hauled Daddy and the boys off to Philadelphia. Copper knew Daddy was supposed to have consumption, but she couldn't believe he wouldn't be all right once the summer sun burned the damp coal dust out of his lungs. But Mam had to have her way, had to take him off to be doctored, had to live where she wanted to live instead of taking him to Texas as Simon had recommended. Mam had never liked the mountains, never gotten over being a schoolteacher, never gotten over being born a flatlander.

But Copper had loved her mountain home—loved it more than she loved Simon, truth be told. If Mam and Simon had left her alone, let her take her time instead of rushing her into a marriage her heart told her she wasn't ready for, she'd still be there and she'd be content.

Copper pushed her tousled hair out of her face and tried to tuck it behind her ears. She'd let Simon sway her with his pretty words and his hard kisses, and now here she was, sitting on a rock in a torn dress, way too far from home. No help for it—she'd put the bridle on herself. Standing, she fished the little creek rock from her pocket and put it to her nose. But the scent of the mountains was gone; it was of no comfort. Holding out her hand, she opened her fingers and let the rock drop to the quiet water below.

Startled, she felt Simon's arms circling her from behind.

"I'm so sorry, sweetheart," he whispered in her ear.

"Why did you bring me here?" She twisted out of his embrace. "You should have married some society girl. I can't be what you want."

"I want you."

"No, you don't!" she snapped. "You want someone who's just

like everyone else. Someone to show off, someone to make your sister happy."

He turned her to face him. "You ask why I brought you here; perhaps the better question is, why did you come?"

"Because . . . because I . . . because you and Mam . . . Simon, I don't rightly know anymore."

"Do you love me?"

She collapsed against his chest, wailing, "I don't know. I don't know what love's supposed to feel like."

"Here, sit with me." He eased her down, then put his arm around her shaking shoulders. "Love feels like the morning sun or a cold drink of water on a hot day. It feels like Mrs. Morton looked this morning when I put her baby boy in her arms."

Copper leaned back into the comfort of his strong arms and choked out, "I'm not a very good wife."

"It's just because everything is so new, so different. You'll grow to love me."

"That doesn't sound right." She'd cried so hard that now she hiccuped. "You deserve better."

"Honey, I'll take whatever I can get." He rubbed her cheek with his thumb. "No matter what, I'll never let you go. You could come to work with me in the office. Would that make you feel better?"

"Really, Simon?" she said, pulling away and looking into his eyes. "You mean it?"

"Of course I do. I should have thought of it sooner. What do you think? I could really use your help."

"I'd like that, but you'd have to teach me what to do."

Simon pulled her close again. "Now that could be fun. I might have to keep you after school some days."

"All right, but I'm not standing in the corner." She fanned herself with her hand. "Whew, I'm as hot as a lizard in July on this rock, and I'm real tired of crying."

Standing, Simon took her hand and led her down the rocky bank to the secluded pool below. "We're going swimming." He shucked off his trousers and his coffee-stained shirt and stood on the bank in his long underdrawers.

She didn't protest when he swooped her up, just shivered in the cold water.

"I love you, sweetheart," he said, his voice suddenly gruff.

Copper put her arms around his neck and lifted her face for his kiss. Giving in to strong feelings she'd tried to keep at bay, she kissed him back, finally aware that he was her husband and she loved him.

Afterward, they let the water take them. Holding hands, they floated upon the surface of their marriage bed, their sacred place, and pledged their vows again just as they had done days before in the little church in the valley of the mountains.

Simon led Copper from the water and covered her with his shirt. Somehow, they'd let her shift and pantalets float downstream. Snapping his suspenders over his shoulders, he held her close. "Are you okay?" he whispered tenderly.

"I feel a little woozy. I need to rest a minute."

"Stay here, just rest, and I'll go fetch some clean clothes."

Copper slept after he left, stretched out in the shade of a tree, her ruined dress rolled up like a pillow under her head, until the cawing of a raucous blue jay woke her with a start. In the leafy world above, a pair of robins fussed about their nest, afraid for their babies, afraid of the murderous jay. Sitting up, Copper tossed a small stone at the marauder. All the birds, except the fledglings, burst from the tree, the robins chirping alarm, the jay screaming in protest. She stretched out again. Soon the mother bird was back, a fat fishing worm in her beak. Little heads with wide-open mouths popped up and down in the nest. Father robin landed on a branch above his family, keeping guard.

She pondered what had just happened, her time in the water with Simon. *This is what the Scripture means when it says to leave father and mother and become as one. I am one with my husband. This is what Mam was trying to tell me with all her talk about cleaving and obeying. Mam always did use three words when one would do.*

She was just starting to get up when she heard a horse approach. Simon dismounted and entered her leafy little world with an overflowing basket. First he spread a quilt on the grassy creek bank. Then he helped her dress in clean, dry clothes before they enjoyed the picnic Searcy had prepared. They fed each other bites of cheese, cucumber spears dipped in salt, hard-boiled eggs, and crusty bread slathered with butter, then washed it all down with cold sweet tea.

After their repast, Simon leaned back on his elbows and watched her eat a piece of spice cake.

"Don't you want a bite of this?" she asked.

"No, I'm watching my dessert eat dessert." He smiled a slow, lazy smile at her.

"I must look a mess . . . my hair . . ."

JAN WATSON

"Here—I brought a brush, and I found your ribbon in the pasture." He sat behind her, his knees making a resting place for her arms, and took his sweet time brushing her wild, thick tresses. When he finished, he tangled his hands in her hair, tipped her head back, and kissed her upside down.

"Copper?" His need a whisper in her ear, then his lips upon her own. "I love you."

She turned in his arms and kissed him back. "Let's rest awhile. I want to think on things."

Simon slept with his head in her lap, his legs crossed at the ankles. She stroked his high, clear forehead, traced his rather prominent nose, leaned down to place a little kiss on his lower lip. She knew this man. He had brought her into the inner sanctum of marriage, that mysterious union of God's design. She was now privy to the rights and passages of a married woman. A sense of completeness filled her like a gentle mist.

She fell in love with Simon then, as a wife loves her husband, as a part of herself, with loyalty and a tender passion. His needs would be her needs, his ways hers. Her love would underlay his every endeavor. Because she loved him, he would need no other. Copper lowered herself to his side and slept with him there, married in spirit and in flesh as it was meant to be.

CHAPTER 10

It seemed to Copper as if a wagonload of broken bodies had been dumped on Simon's waiting room benches. It was her task to sort out who needed what, who needed him first, and who was there mostly because they were lonely and wanted an audience. The bleeding and the gasping were the easiest to decide, the whining and the nagging the hardest. It was nearing noon, and she'd marked off almost every name on the registry. There were only a few patients left.

A tiny, sharp-boned woman flitted about the waiting room like a homeless sparrow, her nostrils flaring. A striking red hat, sporting peacock feathers, dried hydrangeas, and enough cherries to make a pie, trembled on her head while a grimy, paisley-patterned carpetbag hung nearly to the floor from the crook of her arm. "Mrs. Archesson," she'd trilled when Copper asked her name and "female trouble" when she'd asked her complaint.

"Would you like a seat?" Copper pointed to a space between two overly nourished ladies, hoping their girth would anchor the annoying bird woman.

"No time to sit. No time to sit." Mrs. Archesson twisted her thin hands into knots. "Doctor always sees me first. Always sees me first."

"I'm afraid you'll have to wait," Copper said politely. "These people were here before you."

One of the rotund ladies snorted a laugh, which set her three chins to jiggling over her ample chest. Copper saw her poke her companion in the ribs. Evidently they'd seen this show before.

"Can't wait. Can't wait," the woman chirped. "I'll come undone!"

Copper pictured Mrs. Archesson flying about the room like a punctured balloon, leaving feathers everywhere as she deflated.

The exam door opened and Simon leaned out. He motioned for Mrs. Archesson to enter as portly Johnny Underwood, a teller at Benton's bank, squeezed his considerable girth through the doorway while gingerly protecting his sore right foot.

"Mrs. Corbett," Simon said, his hand on Mrs. Archesson's shoulder, "prescription number ten for Mr. Underwood and some powdered charcoal, please."

"Certainly, Dr. Corbett." She matched his clipped, professional tone. "Mr. Underwood, please follow me."

The small room Simon used as his apothecary barely left space for Copper to turn around once her patient joined her there. "Let's see . . . hum . . . why, number ten is dried garlic and powdered onion. Does that help your foot very much, Mr. Underwood?" She held her breath as he opened his mouth to answer.

"It's calmed the gout down right smart, but it doesn't seem to help these chalkstones on my fingers. Doc said he'd do some reading and see if he could come up with a remedy for them. That's why I switched to him from Dr. Thornsberry. Doc T.'s good, but he never wants to try anything new." Mr. Underwood held a folded handkerchief over his mouth as he talked; still the apothecary reeked.

Copper felt a wave of sympathy as he continued with his complaints. "He never told me about brushing my teeth with charcoal like Dr. Corbett just did. Why, it's got so bad people don't want to stand in my line at the bank."

Copper handed him an envelope of number ten and one of powdered charcoal.

"Thank you, Mrs. Corbett. Put me down for same time next week."

As soon as Mr. Underwood closed the door to the pantry-sized room, Copper threw open the small window, took deep gulps of fresh air, and fanned the room with the skirt of her apron. Then she put the jar of charcoal back in its rightful place.

Simon's pharmacy had two sets of floor-to-ceiling cabinets made of dark wood. The uppers had glass-paned doors with glass knobs. She recognized Simon's fine hand in the black-ink script of the labels that marked the place of each product on the meticulous shelves. He had given her a key to the locked door that held expensive drugs and powerful narcotics. She opened a door in the lower cabinets and saw carefully arranged jars, pots, pans, mortars, pestles, boxes of dried herbs, and all manner of stuff that she couldn't name.

In a narrow space between the two sets of cabinets hung a full skeleton, its yellow skull grimacing a toothy smile. She felt the bones in her own face. *It's hard to imagine we all look like that underneath.*

As Simon's office assistant, one of Copper's jobs would be to keep this room in order. She was already learning to follow the scripts Simon wrote to prepare medicines for dispensing. She liked counting pills and weighing powders before pouring them into little paper packets and securing them with string.

Through the open door she could hear a commotion in the waiting room. Copper rushed out. What could be causing such a ruckus?

A near-grown boy had banged through the front door, screaming for Dr. Corbett.

Simon rushed from the exam room. "What's wrong, Hiram?"

"It's Father, Dr. Corbett. We were felling trees, and one caught him square across the back. I brought a horse to carry you there."

Grabbing his hat from the hall tree, Simon snatched up his medical bag and followed Hiram out the door.

The doctor wasn't likely to be back soon, so the few remaining patients went home. That left Mrs. Archesson, fretting in Simon's office, and Mrs. Johnson in the treatment room with baby Matilda. Mrs. Johnson had come to see the doctor because the baby refused to nurse. The infant's hungry cries rose into piercing wails of frustration.

Copper stood in the middle of the empty room. "Now what?" she asked, though there was no one left to hear. "What am I to do with the bird and the baby?" She pondered the situation. *Why would a baby stop eating so suddenly? It must be like Molly's calf when Molly got into the wild-cherry leaves and ruined her milk. There must be something about her mother's milk that offends little Matilda.*

She took a teapot-shaped invalid's cup into the treatment room and asked Mrs. Johnson to express some milk. Then, hefting Matilda onto her hip, she carried the baby into Simon's office so she could check on her other patient, the one she'd nicknamed Birdie.

Birdie's beady black eyes fastened on the squalling infant. "Come, come now, baby," Mrs. Archesson cooed, holding out her sticklike arms to Matilda.

The roly-poly baby went to her readily and laid her little head on Birdie's shoulder.

"I'll be right back," Copper said, leaving the door open between the two rooms.

Mrs. Johnson held the white granite cup out to Copper. "Here's the most I could get. My chest's as hard as a rock."

"Tell me what it tastes like," Copper said.

Matilda's mother stuck her index finger in the cup, then popped it into her mouth. "Oh my, just like the green onions I had for supper last night. I fixed some with wilted lettuce and bacon grease. Poor little Matilda."

"I think you will need to dump your milk until the onion taste is all gone. Twenty-four hours does it for cows. I'm sorry, Mrs. Johnson. I didn't mean to imply . . ."

"That's all right, sugar." Mrs. Johnson patted Copper's arm and laughed. "Matilda's my fourth. I been making milk as long as most cows, I reckon, but this never happened before." She rose to take her daughter from Mrs. Archesson, who hovered in the doorway. "I can't take a chance on Matilda weaning herself this soon. I ain't wanting another one yet."

"Put warm compresses on your chest to make your milk flow," Copper instructed. "In the meantime, feed the baby boiled cow's milk from this cup. She can nurse from the little spout."

Mrs. Archesson was quiet as they watched Mrs. Johnson gather her things and leave the office. "I had a baby, had a baby once," she said, her voice wistful. "Long, long ago. When Bob was alive, and I had someone who loved me. Bob loved me." She pushed her face up close to Copper's, plucking at her sleeve with fingers like talons. "Aunt Annie drank my tonic. Drank it all. I didn't drink it. I didn't drink it all."

Copper pried Birdie's fingers off her arm. "Mrs. Archesson, you'll have to come back when the doctor is in."

"*Eeeeee!*" she screeched. "Can't leave. Can't leave without my nostrum."

The eyes that stared at Copper were challenging, like a territorial dog's. "Let me take you home," Copper offered. "The walk will calm you down."

As quick as a hawk on a mouse, Birdie had the ties of Copper's

stiffly starched apron twisted into a noose. She jerked it tight, and
Copper saw stars as her knees buckled.

"Get my tonic," Mrs. Archesson hissed. "Get my tonic now!"

"All right," Copper gasped. "Just let me go." The words
sounded muffled, as if she had her head down a rain barrel.
The knob on the door to the pharmacy slipped from her
sweaty hand. "Wait here," she wheezed, "and I'll get your
medicine."

Copper closed the door behind her and leaned against it. Her
blood pulsed as loud as thunder in her ears. What should she do?
Sticking her head out the little window, she looked into the narrow alley that ran behind the office and saw that there was no
one to help her.

She'd have to make the tonic. Reaching with a trembling
hand toward a row of brown medicine bottles, she set a dozen
or so of them clinking together. One fell over and skittered across
the counter. She grabbed it just before it fell, poured some dis-
tilled water in, added a hefty measure of whiskey from the jug
under the sink, swirled some of the garlic powder in, and topped
it off with Epsom salts. Copper printed *Mrs. Archesson's Nostrum*
on a gummed label and stuck it on the bottle. She plugged the
bottle with a small cork and took it out to Birdie.

"That's better," Mrs. Archesson said. "That's better." She
secreted the bottle deep within her ratty bag, then straightened
her hat. A bunch of cherries, hanging by the slimmest of threads,
spilled over one piercing black eye.

Birdie cocked her head and stretched out her long neck.
Copper thought she looked like a chicken with the gapes. "I'll be

on my way. On my way," her thin lips pecked. "Thank the doctor for me, for me." Finally, thankfully, she fluttered out the door.

Copper watched Mrs. Archesson dart down the brick path that dissected the front yard and led to a gate in the wrought iron fence. Someone had left the gate open, and Birdie paused on the sidewalk to fish in her bag and take a swig from her bottle before she closed it behind her.

Copper retied her apron strings and smoothed the bib against the front of her blue serge office dress. Her hands still shook. *If I weren't a teetotaler, I'd have a swig of that whiskey myself.* She was just turning the key in the lock of the front door when Andy pounded up the porch steps.

"Doc sent me with a list of things he needs out at the Cloughs'. I'm supposed to take the buggy back with me too." He stopped and looked at Copper. "You look like you seen your own ghost, Miz Corbett."

"I just had a run-in with Mrs. Archesson; that's all, Andy."

"Oh, her?" Andy said. "Ever'body knows she's tetched."

"I'm beginning to understand a little of what Dr. Corbett deals with every day," Copper replied. "But how is Mr. Clough?"

"It's right bad. It took five men to lift that old black walnut off him. I thought sure he was dead. There was blood oozing out his ears. Doc had the men carry him on up to his house. He said jostling him about in a wagon might paralyze him. What's that mean anyways?"

"If a person is paralyzed, they can't move. Dr. Corbett's probably afraid Mr. Clough's back is broken. Poor man, we must pray for him."

"Miz Corbett, do you want to pray right now? I'm in a hurry."

"You don't have to be on your knees to pray, Andy. We can pray while we work." She took the list from his hand. "Do you know where this back brace would be?"

"Doc keeps it beside the buggy with the crutches and that rolling chair. I'm going to the house to get Reuben and Pard."

"Ask Searcy to make up a dinner pail to take with you. You'll all need something to eat."

"No need for that. There's ladies coming from every direction with food in their hands. Mr. Clough's surely got good neighbors."

Copper made her way across the backyard to the carriage house, fiddling with the ring of keys secured to a chatelaine at her waist. Simon had given the ornamental clasp to her two weeks ago on the first day she had come to help him with his practice. On it she kept the keys, a small pair of scissors, a vial of reviving ammonia, a locket with Simon's picture, and a clean lace hanky. Awkward in her haste, she dropped the keys twice before she managed to turn the proper one in the large brass lock and free the carriage house door.

She searched through a stack of crutches and splints before she spied a back brace behind the log roller, an aptly named device for moving very heavy people from one bed to another. The leather brace looked like a torture device with all its straps. Copper put it and the roller in the back of the carriage. Simon was smart to keep his doctor's buggy housed where he could load it with supplies. The buggy they used was kept in the stable at home.

In no time Reuben and Andy were back and had Pard

hitched up to the buggy. Tearing off, they left Copper watching, wishing she could go along. She wasn't alone long, however, for before the dust settled a contorted young man made his halting way to her side.

Chapter 11

"You must be Dr. Corbett's bride," the man rasped as he stuck out a trembling hand. "I'm Tommy Turner."

Copper captured his hand between her own. It jumped and bumped in her clasp like a mouse in a trap. "Pleased to meet you, Tommy Turner. I'm Copper."

Tommy tried to tip his hat but smacked his forehead instead. "I'm here to clean the office. If you'll excuse me, I'll get my supplies."

Copper tried not to stare as he jangled a set of keys toward the lock on the carriage house door. She wanted to rush across the small yard and help him, but obviously he'd done this before. Instead she went into the office kitchen and started some tea. Standing beside the window, she peeped out as Tommy fitted a leather glove that appeared to be attached to a broom handle onto his right hand and started sweeping the back walk.

Copper assembled a tray, took it outside, and sat on the edge of the porch, resting her feet in the thin grass of the lawn. "Tommy, would you take tea with me?"

He paused and studied her in his jerking way. "I've got a lot to do, Mrs. Corbett."

Funny, she thought, *his hand didn't jerk as long as he swept with his glove broom.*

"Copper," she insisted. "Please? I don't want to eat alone."

He laid his broom aside and stuck his hand in his pants pocket, then gazed at her seriously through gray-blue eyes. "I might offend you."

"Tommy, I have twin eight-year-old brothers. It would be hard to offend me." She poured tea into two cups like the one she'd given Mrs. Johnson and sipped hers from the little spout.

He leaned against the porch beside her; his legs locked rigidly. Clasping both hands around his cup, he lifted it and poured a stream of tea into his mouth. "This is clever."

"Take that one home," Copper offered, "and I'll mark another for you to use when you're here."

He took a sugar cookie from the tray, managing one bite before the rest of it fell to the ground. "I'm sorry," he whispered, his voice ashamed. "I can't seem to hold on to these treats."

"It's nice out here, what with the breeze and all," Copper said as she broke a piece of cookie and put it to his mouth, then broke a piece for herself. "The walk looks good. It surely needed sweeping."

Tommy had a drink of tea with only a little choking. "Thank you. Dr. Corbett fixed the broom so I could hold on to it." Finishing another bite of cookie, he turned those serious eyes on Copper again. "He means all the world to me. He rescued me, you know."

Copper chanced putting a comforting hand on his arm. "Now I'm afraid of offending you, Tommy, by being nosy, but please tell me what you mean."

"It seems odd to talk about myself. I know people think my brain is as twisted as my body." He sighed and set the cup down, then anchored his hands under his hips as he leaned against the porch. "Dr. Corbett holds a clinic at the state hospital once a month–"

"What is that?" Copper interrupted.

"It's the lunatic asylum. I lived there from the time I was a baby until just a year or so ago. My mother abandoned me." The eyes that gazed at Copper revealed deep pools of pain. "Threw me away as if I were a half-wit, without even bothering to give me a name. An old man who worked at the asylum dubbed me Tommy Turner, and I have been Tommy Turner ever since."

He loosed his hands and retrieved a handkerchief from his pocket. With great effort, he wiped a bit of spittle from the corner of his mouth. "One day my feet got tangled up, and I fell against my metal cot, cutting a gash over my eye." He turned his face so Copper could see the zigzag scar that bisected his left eyebrow. "They took me to the third floor, up to surgery. I sat on a table under the skylight while Doctor Corbett stitched my wound. He talked to me like I was any other person, and when he finished he said, 'Tommy Turner, you don't belong here.'"

"Dr. Corbett signed me out that very day and secured a room for me at a boardinghouse. Then he made sure I was gainfully employed." Tommy straightened his shoulders proudly. "I clean offices and Mr. Upchurch's bank and make more than enough tomeet my needs. I have my room, my books, and most of all my freedom, and I owe it all to the good Lord for sending Dr. Corbett my way."

Copper patted Tommy's shoulder. "I learn more of my husband's goodness every day."

Dark clouds tumbled across the sun, and a quick, hot wind whipped up her skirts as she collected the tea service. "I'd better get home before the rain," she told Tommy. "Come for supper soon?"

"Dr. Corbett and I usually play chess on Tuesdays. I'll come a little early one evening."

⚜

Copper tossed and turned most of the night. She worried about Mr. Clough and wished Simon would come home. Near dawn, a pounding on the front door startled her awake.

"Hey," Andy Tolliver yelled, "anybody awake in there?"

"Land's sake, child," Copper heard Searcy say. "Stop caterwauling and come on in here. Eat some breakfast while Searcy wakes Miz Corbett."

"I'm up, Searcy," Copper called, pulling the sash of her robe tight and hurrying down the stairs. "Andy, how is Mr. Clough?"

"Can I eat while we talk? My belly's so empty it's sticking to my backbone."

Copper sat with Andy at the kitchen table, a cup of tea in her hand. He dug into his sausage and eggs. She didn't stop him talking with his mouth full.

"Mr. Clough's hurting right smart. I got to take some kind of medicine back." He patted his shirt pocket. "I got it wrote down. Doc said the next twenty-four hours will tell the tale."

Searcy poured cold milk in a tall glass and dished two biscuits onto his plate.

Andy sopped up gravy and stuffed half a biscuit into his mouth. "Reuben come home so's he can milk the cows and all, but I'm going back soon's I see about my ma and the girls. Doc's letting me ride Pard. Don't that beat all?" He stood up and handed Copper a script in Simon's fine hand. "Miz Corbett, you'll need to go to the office to get this here medicine."

Dressed and ready for the day, Copper hurried to the office and carefully followed Simon's written directions. She measured drams and grains and drops, dissolved morphine with alcohol, rubbed camphor gum and chloral hydrate together, added oil of cloves and cinnamon, then poured the solution into a four-ounce bottle.

She had to stop more than once, taking deep breaths to calm her shaking fingers, fearful of making a mistake. Simon said you could kill a patient with the wrong dose of medication. The first week she worked with him he'd had her practice over and over the names of all of the medicines and preparations in the pharmacy cabinet as well as different measurements. Grains and drams, millimeters and centimeters—she was glad for the Latin Mam had insisted she learn. But more than that, she was glad she could do something to help Mr. Clough.

Finished with her task, she wrapped the bottle of medicine in newspaper and secured it in a poke for Andy to take back to the farm. She wished she could accompany him, but somebody needed to open the office.

About ten o'clock, patients of Simon's began to come by the office. Mrs. Schulz had a sty on her eyelid, which Copper treated with hot compresses.

Tony Brock was inebriated once again and only wanted attention. Copper showed him to the hammock on the back porch and encouraged him to sleep it off.

The only serious problem was Mrs. Ashcraft's two-year-old son, Zack, a handsome boy with dark hair, big brown eyes, and chipmunk cheeks, who presented with a mild fever, a runny nose, and loud breathing. His mother reported that he'd woken after midnight with a loud, barking cough.

Copper's intuition told her Zack had the croup. Should she tell the young mother how she tended to her own brothers when Willy or Daniel would wake in the night with the same symptoms? But what if little Zack had whooping cough? Then a teapot of hot, steamy water and half a teaspoon of turpentine would be of no help. Instead she instructed the weary mother to take him down the street to Dr. Thornsberry.

She stood in the doorway and watched Mrs. Ashcraft struggle down the sidewalk, Zack bouncing on her hip, her pregnant belly causing an ungainly waddle to her walk. Where did the confidence come from to diagnose illness? What if she told someone the wrong thing and they got worse or even died because of what she did or didn't do? The very thought made Copper shudder.

She pulled the door closed and turned the key in the lock. Seemed funny to lock the door, but they kept those drugs in the little pharmacy. Simon said you shouldn't tempt folks; you shouldn't be their stumbling block. Thinking of Birdie, she understood.

Copper went around to the back porch to check on Mr. Brock. He was out cold. One arm hung over the side of the hammock. An empty whiskey bottle lay beside his outstretched hand. His breathing was unlabored, regular and deep.

There was nothing to keep her from calling on Alice, though she dreaded the visit. Alice had sent word to the office yesterday that she wasn't feeling well, but Copper had forgotten all about her during the excitement of the day. *No help for it now,* she thought as she started down the walk. *Might as well get on with it.*

A maid escorted Copper to the bedchamber where Simon's sister reclined on a fainting couch. Alice wore an elegant gray covert-cloth dressing gown edged with pink piping. Its flared collar framed her face in ashen shadow. She dabbed a fine sheen of perspiration from her upper lip with a dainty hanky. Not a hair was out of place.

"How kind of you to fit me into your busy schedule, Laura Grace." Alice's dark eyes stabbed at Copper. "My, you look like a common shopgirl."

"Goodness, I'm sorry, Alice. I forgot to leave my apron at the office. You look ill. Is there something I can do for you?"

"What has become of my brother?"

Without being asked, Copper perched on the edge of a green silk lady's chair. "He spent the night caring for Mr. Clough. You must have heard about the accident."

Alice looked like she had that day in the garden when Paw-paw stuck his nose up the cat's tail. "I should think you would want more for your husband than nights spent in some run-down farmhouse caring for people who have no intention of paying him." When she dabbed at her lip again, her collar fell open. A violet stain marred her swanlike neck.

Copper stared hard. "Alice?"

Alice pulled her gown tight and held it there, turning her face away. "Simon could treat the best of society if he didn't have an office full of paupers. He can't expect people of affluence to sit in that waiting room and catch head lice."

Copper felt heat rush to her cheeks. "We'd be glad to have the rich folks bring their nits in the back door if that would make them feel better. The last thing we want in the office is mixed nits," she fired, then bit her tongue. Better leave before she said something she couldn't take back. "Can I get you anything before I go?"

"I think not." Alice's handbell rang with a dismissive toll. "Joseph will show you out."

Copper hurried down the elegant, curved stairway without stopping to admire any of the oil paintings or even the crys-tal chandelier. She was so angry she thought she might have a stroke. Stopping on the manicured lawn, she fanned herself with her offensive apron. Thoughts of mayhem raced through her mind. She pushed Alice down the curved staircase; she stabbed her with a rat-tail comb; she held her hostage among the riffraff in Simon's waiting room; little Zack Ashcraft wiped his runny nose on Alice's skirt.

Copper marched down the sidewalk, giving no thought to her sister-in-law's distress. Righteous indignation clung to her like a shadow cast at high noon and trailed her all the way home.

⁘

Simon was home in time for supper. Mr. Clough had stabilized enough to be transported to the hospital, but he could not move his legs.

Simon praised Copper for the mixture of pain-relieving morphine. "Between you and Andy," he said, "I couldn't have had better assistance."

She had so much to tell him, so much to ask, but he fell asleep at the table with his fork in his hand. She drew a bath and laid his nightclothes on the bed. When at last he lay down, she rubbed his shoulders with liniment until he slept. Kneading the knots from his neck, she whispered, "Lord, please be with Mr. Clough tonight and with Mrs. Clough. It must be so hard for her. And, Lord, keep me away from rat-tail combs."

Before she climbed into bed, she retrieved the letter that had come for her that morning. Finally, Mam's reply. Disappointment, nothing but disappointment. Giddy with pleasure when she'd found the light blue envelope in the post, Copper had rushed to the stable to saddle Rose. She had to be away from the house and all its restraints before she delved into the secrets of her past.

Reuben intercepted her, finishing the task although she hadn't asked for help. "Careful, missus."

"Oh, Reuben, I'll be safe, and I won't be gone long. It's just that . . ." She felt in her pocket for the folded envelope before she saw the wary look in his round brown eyes. Mounting the horse, she choked back her words. She needed to be careful not to overstep her bounds.

It had felt so good to be alone—alone and free—just her and Rose and nobody watching. It was nearly like home, where some days she'd wander the woods for hours all by her lonesome. She hadn't realized how much she missed that. But, oh, she had Mam's letter. The letter that would help her figure out why Alice didn't like her. With understanding, surely friendship would follow. She'd looped the horse's reins over a low tree branch and hurried down the bank to Willow Springs, her and Simon's special place.

Now she stood in her nightgown and pulled the heavy drapes against the night sky. Taking the pins from her hair, she shook it free and stood pondering the navy blue ink of her stepmother's words. There was no help there, but news of the boys and Daddy had been welcome. *Funny*, she thought, *even on paper Mam's words can sting*. The lavatory door closed softly behind her. She crossed the floor, lifted the lid of the indoor toilet, and pulled the handle. Tiny scraps of blue paper swirled away, down and out, leaving only the trace of unanswered questions behind.

❧

Life returned to its normal pace soon after Mr. Clough's accident. Copper was careful to treat Alice with respect whenever she came to call. She'd even begun to accompany her sister-in-law on some of her societal duties, rolling bandages at the hospital auxiliary and attending missionary meetings. She was determined to worm a place into Alice's cold heart because she knew that would please her husband.

Simon was continually busy, spending much of his time on house calls. Sometimes he took the buggy, but most often it was just him and Pard and a saddlebag full of supplies.

Copper kept the office humming; she learned quickly and started caring for minor problems—superficial cuts and colds and such—on her own. Her days were pleasantly full with her work, her charitable duties, and now a Bible class every Wednesday morning for Searcy. But still she missed her mountain home. She had a mantra: *Someday*.

Once a week she wrote to her family, but she'd stopped asking hard questions. Correspondence from home was always from Mam, with an occasional note tacked on from Daddy. He always said the same thing: *We are fine. The weather is good. Take care of yourself.* It seemed strange, all those words from Mam and so few from Daddy, when it was she and her father who talked when she lived at home. Every night rocking in side-by-side chairs on the porch or in front of the fireplace, Daddy with his pipe and his Bible, Copper with a cup of tea and a piece of embroidery. Words on paper made some folks shy, she knew, but she'd give a pretty penny to know how her father really was.

Mam told her lots of things—that the boys were growing like weeds, that the family had postponed their move for a time. It seemed Daddy was dragging his feet, but his health had improved somewhat. Copper was thankful. She couldn't imagine her family living anywhere but on Troublesome Creek no matter how much Mam hoped to be elsewhere.

⁂

Tommy Turner had a standing invitation to supper and chess with Simon every Tuesday night. One evening after their game, Copper and Simon stood in the doorway and watched him leave. When he reached the corner, he turned and gave a jerking salute.

"Simon?" Copper asked. "I've been wondering why you don't pay Tommy to clean your office. It doesn't seem right somehow."

Simon removed his spectacles and polished the lenses with a square of soft linen he always kept in his breast pocket. "When Tommy left the asylum, he had lived off the welfare of others his whole life. I arranged a loan to give him a start. Now he's paying me back a little at a time. It's a matter of pride. His."

She turned to kiss his cheek. "You're just about the best man I ever knew."

"Just about?" He held her arms. "Come clean, Mrs. Corbett. What other man has impressed you as much as I?"

She tapped her cheek with her index finger. "Hmm, let me think. Henry Thomas comes to mind. He's quite an impressive chicken thief."

"Ah, the wily Henry. But I'm the one who bought your pie."

She fluttered her eyelashes against his face. Butterfly kisses. "But would you dare steal for me, Dr. Corbett?"

Pulling her close, his voice was husky in her ear. "I would filch the chickens, the rooster, and the fox himself if you asked me to. I guess you'd have me be a common thief in order to prove myself."

"That could be interesting, Simon." She pulled away and started up the stairs. He followed. Stopping on the landing, she turned to face him, teasing. Enjoying, for a moment, her power over him. "A common thief married to a common shopgirl. We could start a whole new life."

"A shopgirl?" He looked up at her, perplexed.

She hooked her hands in his suspenders and pulled him close. "Dear husband, I wonder how you'd look in stripes."

CHAPTER 12

It was an August day so hot you could fry an egg on the side-walk. Midmorning, Copper opened all the office windows and propped the doors in order to catch the slightest breeze.

Simon had gone out into the country that morning to treat a young woman burned when her dress sleeve hooked a frying pan of smoldering grease. Her family had buttered her up, then sent for the doctor.

The bank teller came in for his usual script, and Mrs. Johnson brought her brood: three husky, stair-step sons and baby Matilda, who was wailing and pulling on her ear.

"Matilda is so delicate," Mrs. Johnson said as she hefted her pudgy daughter onto the exam table. "My boys never gave me a minute's worry, but this one . . . I'm up every night with something or other."

It was difficult to discern any delicacy in the roly-poly baby so chubby that her eyes disappeared in folds of flesh when she cried. She was such a charming infant. It was all Copper could do to stop herself from kissing her dimpled knees.

Matilda's brothers stood guard as Copper examined the infant, until a raucous noise drew them to the open window. *Whoosh*, suddenly the three little boys charged out the door.

The ladies followed to the porch. Matilda snuggled against Copper's neck; a few drops of warmed sweet oil held in place by a plug of cotton batting soothed the baby's earache.

The city was astir. People spilled onto the sidewalk from every office and business up and down the street. Mrs. Johnson's sons joined a pack of boys tagging after an oddly dressed stranger who was nailing playbills on the lamp poles. The man was dressed in a baggy orange suit, and his face was painted white. A ruby red smile stretched from ear to ear. The top of his tall black hat hung askew like the lid of a partially opened tin can, and a tiny wizened monkey peeked out. A yapping dog nipped at the heels of the stranger's silly floppy shoes. From the pocket of his billowing pants, the clown extracted a child-size trombone and with great gusto blew a long rusty note. The dog turned tail and ran under the office porch.

The excitement in the air was as thick as caramel icing. The circus was coming to town!

Several days later, Copper sat on the porch swing and waited for Hester. Simon was escorting them to the circus parade. Copper and Searcy had filled a basket with fried chicken, potato salad, cabbage slaw, corn-bread muffins, and lemonade. For dessert, Reuben had a big watermelon cooling in the washtub.

After the parade, there would be a picnic for everyone in the town park. Copper had thought Searcy and Reuben would share with them, but Searcy told her they'd spread their quilts in the place set aside for them. It was hard to keep it straight, this everybody being different. She'd never get used to it.

Copper adjusted her straw hat in the reflection of the parlor window. Its rolled brim was adorned with a blue grosgrain ribbon, which complimented her blue-and-white-striped silk taffeta resort dress. The overskirt of her dress was trimmed with white silk fringe, and she had a blue parasol to protect her from the sun. Copper laughed to think of that. Why, this time last year she would have been hoeing weeds from the cabbages in the garden with no thought to her face or hands. She stretched out her legs and admired her new white kid high-button shoes. These were surely not for hoeing weeds.

Just as Simon stepped out the door, smartly dressed in a blue-and-white pin-striped cotton shirt, a red tie tucked in at the fourth button, tan knickerbockers with long stockings, and boot-cut shoes, Hester bounced onto the porch and plopped herself beside Copper in the swing.

"Oh my, I may wilt in this heat," Hester complained. Picking up a church fan, she waved it mightily at her ruddy face and helped herself to a glass of lemonade and one of the sugar cookies Copper had put out on a tray. A bit of her drink spilled onto the bosom of her white poplin dress. "Fiddlesticks. I'm always spilling something. Simon," she bossed, "fetch me a cloth."

He handed her his clean handkerchief.

"Simon always minds me. He's used to bossy women." Hester's jolly face broke into a huge grin at Simon's discomfiture, and she poked Copper in the ribs with her elbow. "Don't take offense. My mother says I was born without a filter." She ate another cookie and drank her lemonade. "We may not be kin, Simon and I, but we're as close as kissing cousins."

Leaping up, Hester planted a noisy kiss on Simon's red cheek before opening her white dotted swiss umbrella. "Shouldn't we be going? All the good viewing spots will be taken if we sit here and gab all day."

They found a spot among the crowd of people on Main Street, directly across from Benton's bank. A scrawny locust tree provided sketchy shade. Copper could scarcely contain herself as she took in the sights. Children dashed back and forth, jockeying for the best position, while adults stepped back to let the smallest ones stand in front.

Vendors hawked their wares. "Popcorn! Get your fresh-roasted peanuts! Ice treats!"

Simon bought red and purple ices. Copper's tasted of grape and made her mouth numb. She and Hester exchanged glances, then burst out laughing to see their colored lips.

A man dressed like President Lincoln, top hat and all, sold toy monkeys on sticks. Copper bought two to send to her brothers. When she squeezed the sticks together, the monkeys did flips. She wished Willy and Daniel were here. What fun they would have.

Music thrummed their way; you could hear it with your ears and feel it through your feet. Shading her eyes against the glare, she looked down the street. Here came the parade! First the band, all members dressed in uniform, marched past, music blaring; then acrobats flipped past them just like the monkeys on sticks. A man juggled colored balls higher and higher and never missed a beat. A dark-haired woman dressed in a skimpy jeweled costume stood on the back of a white horse led down the street by a midget. They stopped right in front of Copper. The woman looked at her and smiled, then raised one leg over her head and held it there as the horse high-stepped away.

Hester grinned and nudged Copper in the side.

Copper averted her eyes; perhaps they should take offense. But then the clowns came bursting along! They were everywhere at once, pulling nickels from children's ears, chasing dogs, stealing men's hats, and making a funny loud racket.

Copper leaned into Simon and laughed until her sides ached. And all the while the band played on.

Copper had never had so much fun. She glanced about the crowded street and was surprised that she knew so many people. There was Tommy Turner leaning against a lamppost across the way. Waving at the Johnson family, she laughed when Mrs. Johnson waved baby Matilda's hand back at her. She caught a glimpse of Tony Brock weaving in and out of the crowd, nearly falling off the curb. Hopefully he'd find an alleyway and sleep it off. If she saw him at the picnic she'd get him to eat something. And was that Mrs. Archesson with her carpetbag? Just a flit of her behind Mrs. Johnson? Copper hoped the bird lady was enjoying herself and that she'd stay on her side of the street.

One frowning face in the midst of all the smiles caught her attention. On the balcony above the bank's closed doors, Alice stood glaring at her. Whatever would warrant such a look? Copper was using her parasol, and her gloves were the proper length. Uh-oh. Paw-paw had wagged his way to her side and stood drooling happily at her knee. It was impossible to keep him in the backyard, and she refused to keep him tied all the time. Copper dropped one hand and placed it on Paw-paw's nose. With just a little pressure he was soon secreted behind her. Maybe Alice would forget she'd seen him.

The Lincoln clown, now on stilts, strutted past the crowd as he hoisted a large American flag. Everyone quieted as he went by. A wagon followed, hauling a load of veterans, some minus an arm or a leg. The men removed their hats, and some folks saluted.

And then—oh my—elephants! As if they were in Africa or India, a string of large gray beasts strolled up Main Street, tail to trunk to tail to trunk, and the last one was a baby! Copper clapped to see such a thing.

Lastly, to signal the end of the parade, a sturdy pony pulled a cage on wheels past the crowd. Inside lay the king of the beasts. His magnificent head rested on huge crossed paws.

Copper turned her face away; the lion's golden eyes made her sad somehow. She fancied he mourned for his freedom as she often grieved the loss of her own.

Following the parade, Copper, Simon, and Hester joined the rest of the revelers at the park, where picnic tables groaned under baskets of food and bright quilts beckoned under every shade tree. Simon was commandeered for a round of lawn tennis, so Copper and Hester settled themselves in wooden folding chairs to watch.

"I hope this doesn't take long," Hester fussed. "I can't wait to get to that fried chicken. Aren't you hungry?"

"Not really," Copper replied, sipping on the lemon ice Simon had bought her. "I ate so much at the parade, I might never eat again."

"Perish the thought!" Hester said as she shifted her weight, the chair beneath her popping and squeaking in protest. "Life wouldn't be worth much without breakfast, dinner, and supper. I'll be right back, Copper. I'm just going to get a nibble of my mother's deviled eggs before they're gone. Can I bring you anything? A tablespoonful of air perhaps?"

"I'll save your seat," Copper said. "Oh, look! Simon made a great serve."

Hester soon returned with a napkin full of goodies. "What's going on over there?" She indicated a commotion on the other side of the tennis game. "Mrs. Johnson seems to have lost something."

Indeed, Mrs. Johnson did seem distressed as she shook out the linens from the basket where her baby, Matilda, had been sleeping. Copper could hear her calling as she searched frantically.

"I'm going to see what has happened," Copper said. "Stay here and enjoy your eggs. I'll be right back."

"What's wrong, Mrs. Johnson?" Copper asked as she reached the distraught mother.

"Oh, Mrs. Corbett, I seem to have misplaced Matilda." Mrs. Johnson shook her head in disbelief. "She was sleeping right here in her basket while I helped my youngest son to the outhouse. I took him myself because his brothers were rolling hoops with some other boys, and my husband's gone to fetch our picnic basket."

"Are you sure you didn't hand her off to one of the other ladies?" Copper asked as other women started to join them. "She didn't just disappear."

"No. I left her right here! Right here sleeping in her basket!" Mrs. Johnson's voice rose in panic. "She must have crawled out of the basket and come looking for me."

Copper took the frightened mother's hands in her own. "I'm going to get Dr. Corbett and your husband. We'll find her. Don't worry."

Soon everyone had gathered around the Johnson family. Their oldest boy was sent to find a police officer, which caused Mrs. Johnson to cry out and collapse to the ground. Several women waved at her with pasteboard fans, and one mopped her face with a rag dipped in ice water.

While waiting for the police to arrive, Simon instructed the men to fan out, each covering a portion of the park that stretched for many tree-covered acres and was bisected by Town Branch, a swiftly flowing creek whose waters could be treacherous.

The search continued, but evening came much too quickly,

bringing darkening skies and the threat of a summer thunderstorm. Mothers collected baskets, quilts, and children, holding their own close to their sides. Fathers placed intact families in buggies and wagons to be carried home to their safe houses. Fireworks were disassembled and packed carefully in wooden packing crates to be used at another time.

Mrs. Johnson wailed piteously, her cries a stark reminder to everyone of how quickly disaster could strike, how quickly joy could turn to grief. Her husband walked her to their carriage, he on one side, Copper on the other, both murmuring words of encouragement that fell on deaf ears. Matilda's brothers tagged behind, perplexed as to what had happened, the oldest carrying the basket that had been the baby's bed.

Copper overheard the police captain mention dragging the creek in the morning as soon as it was light. The men, Simon included, assembled before him, nodding in agreement. The creek seemed the likely place to find baby Matilda.

Copper listened but doubted. It seemed someone would have noticed. What were they thinking? That someone had drowned Matilda? Who would do such a thing?

Simon had opened his office to get some calming powders for Mrs. Johnson. Mr. Johnson said they would go to the home of her sister for the night. The police captain assured the baby's parents that they would continue their search despite the lightning that danced across the sky.

Simon and Copper walked home hand in hand, sharing thoughts, each wondering where baby Matilda was. Simon had delivered the little girl after an uneventful pregnancy and an easy labor. He was attached to her, as a doctor is to every child he brings into the world. Copper had seen Matilda only twice in the office, but that was enough to forge a bond, and she grieved for the chubby baby and for her mother. She worried that the baby was alone and frightened of the coming storm.

"Do you think Matilda is in the creek, Simon?" she asked.

"We looked everywhere, behind every tree, beneath every bush. It's the only place we haven't searched. It doesn't make sense, but where else could she be?"

"Simon, someone had to take her. A little baby doesn't just fall in the creek by herself."

"Who would take her? We were picnicking there, close to the banks of the water. Perhaps she just toddled in."

"Oh, that can't be. Besides, she wasn't walking yet. She'd barely learned to crawl." Copper stopped under a gaslight, shaking her head. "A baby can't be here one moment and gone the next. This makes me too sad. Isn't there something else we can do?"

"We must pray, Copper. Pray that the police find the baby before it is too late."

Copper and Simon were surprised to find Andy Tolliver waiting at their house with Simon's medical bag in hand and Pard saddled up.

"Hey, Doc," Andy said. "I figured you'd be home shortly. Doc Thornsberry sent me to fetch you. Thought I might as well get things ready while I waited."

"What has happened?"

"Doc T. said there's a big bust-up this side of Paris. Said a train overturned and scattered bodies all along the track. Said they needed every doctor they could get." Andy stroked Pard's long nose and looked at Simon hopefully. "Can I go with you?"

"Sorry, Andy, but I don't know how long I'll be gone. You'd better stay here." Simon reached out and patted the boy's shoulder. "You did a good job, son. I'm proud of you."

"You should change your clothes, Simon," Copper said. "While you do that, I'll fix a poke of food and some coffee for you to take along."

Copper hurried to the kitchen, Andy right on her heels. She measured the coffee, glad she had ground the beans that morning, and added cold water to the coffeepot. While it perked she made thick ham sandwiches, and she twisted boiled eggs sprinkled with salt into waxed paper to put in Pard's saddlebag. Simon would need a repast considering he had not eaten at the picnic supper. Everyone had been too busy searching for the baby to eat.

A gulp of coffee, a quick kiss, and an admonishment to stay in out of the weather, and Simon was gone. Off to another crisis, leaving Copper to fret to Andy about how he could keep up the pace, how he could handle so much misery all the time.

"Well, Miz Corbett," Andy explained in all seriousness, as if Copper expected him to come up with an answer to her hypothetical question, "Doc can handle it because he's got something to do about it. It's us that has to wait that has the hardest time. Yep, waiting's the hardest part, I expect."

CHAPTER 13

Copper shivered and hugged herself, though the air was close and warm. Heat lightning shimmered across the sky as she and Andy sat in the porch swing and watched.

He fiddled in his overalls pocket and came up with the egg she'd given him when she made Simon's. Untwisting the waxed paper, he gobbled up the egg.

Copper marveled at how much Andy could eat. It seemed he was always half starved. Did his mother ever feed him? She was glad he was here. Very glad for his companionship this unsettling night.

Carefully, he straightened out the little piece of waxed paper, folded it, and stuck it back in his pocket. "Say, Miz Corbett, how 'bout that baby that got lost? Did anybody find it?" He pushed his foot against the porch floor and set the swing moving. "I had to watch my sisters all day, and I took them home when the baby went missing."

"Why, Andy, I wish you had introduced your little sisters to me."

"Marydell and Dodie was pulling me ever' which way. I was too busy for introductions." Dragging his foot, he stopped the swing before turning to face her. "Did they? Did they find the baby?"

Copper shook her head. "Everyone looked and looked until finally the police chief asked us to go home. I can't imagine what happened to her. The police questioned everybody to see if anyone had noticed anything out of the ordinary or a stranger lurking about."

"Hmm." Andy turned thoughtful. He propped his elbow on his knee and said, "Only thing I saw that was maybe a little strange was that old, skinny woman. You know, the one that hangs around wanting tonic all the time. A couple of days ago she came to Doc's for a refill. She acts half crazy."

"I'll have to agree with your assessment of Mrs. Archesson, Andy. But what did she do that seemed different to you?"

"Well, for one, she had that big old bag of hers slung over her arm. She was sort of wearing it across her chest instead of dragging it like she usually does. It was plumb full of something when she walked past the girls and me. And she was talking to it. That's strange even for her, don't you think?"

"I don't know. She was talking to herself the day I had a run-in with her in Dr. Corbett's office. She's an odd duck."

The sky had turned an ominous green-black before full night descended. Thunder rolled, and the air was charged with energy.

Copper stood. "You'd better stay here until the weather clears up some. I should have sent you home earlier. Your mother will be worried."

"Nah," Andy answered, holding the screen door open for her. "She likes me gone at nights when her friend comes over. Hey, Miz Corbett, you got any more of them oatmeal cookies?"

Copper readied herself for bed and braided her hair. She would have left it down if Simon had been home because her hair was his delight.

Just that morning, as he had every Saturday morning since their interlude in the creek, he had washed her hair with Cashmere Bouquet soap as she bent over the claw-foot bathtub. He refused to let her use diluted vinegar for a rinse, for he didn't like the smell, but insisted on a little fresh lemon juice mixed in warm water. She loved the attention, but her hair was hard to manage nowadays. Seemed no matter what she did her curls refused to be tamed.

Plumping up the pillows at her back, she took her Bible from the bedside table, searching for a word of comfort. She'd prayed and prayed for the baby, but the threatening weather outside her bedroom window offered no surcease from her worry. A hard spatter of wind-driven rain tapped out a question against the windowpane: *Where is Matilda?*

Copper wished she could fly on the wings of a turtledove back to Troublesome Creek and on up the highest mountain to where her friend Remy lived. Remy was as canny as a fox; she'd know just where to look for the baby. Settling back against the bolster and smiling in spite of her worry, Copper remembered her friend and how once Remy had also been lost to her.

It had been an out-of-sorts time in Copper's life when she'd first met Remy Riddle. Trying to find a place to run away to, a place to get away from her stepmother's threats to send her to boarding school, Copper had discovered the fey girl living in a cave by herself.

They had become fast friends, and Copper sorrowed when she had to leave Remy behind. That was almost as hard as leaving her home, the place as dear as life to her. With one finger Copper tapped her chest directly over her heart—Remy's reminder that people always came before place . . . even her beloved mountains.

Try as she might to sleep, a nagging disquiet kept her awake. Finally she gave up and made her way downstairs. What was it Andy had said about Mrs. Archesson and her carpetbag before he bedded down in the foyer? He'd made a pallet with blankets and pillows right in front of the door after refusing to either go home or sleep comfortably in the spare bedroom.

"What if Doc comes home and finds me sleeping instead of keeping watch?" he'd asked. "Be just like that story he told me of Jesus in the garden and His buddies sawing logs while He was doing all the praying. Nope, I'll just stay right here where Doc can find me if he comes home and needs me."

Poor little lad, Copper thought as she leaned down and brushed his unruly hair from his eyes. *Why is no one looking out for Andy? Someday I'm going to have a visit with his mother.*

"Andy? Andy, wake up." Sorry to have to wake him, she shook him gently. "I need to talk to you."

He sat up abruptly, rubbing his eyes with balled fists. "Has Doc come back? Do I need to give Pard a rubdown?"

Copper gathered her robe around her and took a seat on the bottom step. Lamplight spilled down in a yellow puddle around them. "It's something you said earlier about Mrs. Archesson. I can't get it off my mind."

"Huh? What'd I say?"

"Something about her talking to her bag. It's nagging at my mind."

"Ah, she's nuts, Miz Corbett."

"I don't know. She's sane enough to get just what she needs." Copper shrugged her braid back from her shoulder. "I remember something. . . . The day Mr. Clough was hurt she was in the office, and she held little Matilda. She seemed so calm while she cradled the baby, and she told me she lost a child years ago. You don't suppose . . . ? Andy, I think Mrs. Archesson has Matilda!"

"I wouldn't be a bit surprised," Andy replied. "It makes perfect sense as far as crazy people go."

Jumping up, Copper knit her brow. "We should find a policeman and have him go search Mrs. Archesson's house."

"Why don't we go ourselves? A policeman would just scare her. They'd have to bust her door down; then she'd hightail it out the back with the stolen goods."

Copper peered out the foyer window. "How would we ever find her house? It's pitch-black outside."

"Oh, I deliver groceries for Mr. Cook. I pert near know where everybody lives." Andy folded his blanket and shoved his feet into too-small shoes. Someone—his mother?—had cut half the tops off so his toes stuck out like a litter of wiggling puppies. "Most times Mrs. Archesson makes me leave hers out back on the cellar door. She don't never let me past the kitchen. Her and her aunt—a real old, old lady I ain't seen for weeks—live there all by their lonesome." He stuffed his shirt in his trousers and pulled up on his belt. Every bit the man of the house. "Them two never cut the grass or carry off any trash. They're both tetched, I reckon."

Copper wasn't sure. It was one thing to have suspicions, one thing to malign Mrs. Archesson to Andy, but to actually go to her house and accuse her? Best to get the law and do this correctly.

Andy looked at her expectantly. "Let's do it, Miz Corbett. Let's go see if that old bat took baby Matilda."

"I think we've disparaged Mrs. Archesson enough without calling her names, but, yes, let's go see if that old bat took baby Matilda." She took his bedclothes and started for the stairs. "I'll just need to get dressed. Why don't you get a lantern? And grab some matches from the kitchen. I'll meet you on the front porch in a couple of minutes."

After pulling on a pair of Simon's old trousers, a dark sweater, and her work boots, Copper coiled her braid and tucked it beneath her black sunbonnet. There, now she was ready to go hunting for Matilda.

The night had turned wilder still; tree limbs thrashed about, and heat lightning crackled across the sky, leaving the air tainted with the smell of sulfur.

"Feels like whirlwind weather to me," Andy said while looking critically at her. "I hope we don't run into nobody. They'd call the law for sure, seeing as how that getup makes you look like a burglar."

"I can't go creeping around looking for kidnapped babies in a dress and petticoats. Men's clothes are so much better for working in." She reached out for him, whispering, "Hush now, and take my hand. How far is it to Mrs. Archesson's house?"

"We don't need to be so quiet yet," he replied. "Nobody will hear us over this storm. It ain't too far."

The small hand that clutched Copper's was sturdy and strong. She might have been back home walking with Willy. His hand was just like Andy's, while Daniel's would feel as soft and fragile as a baby's. A lump of longing formed in her throat, but Andy dashed it with his chatter.

It seemed strange to be out in the night like this, just she and Andy, passing dark houses full of sleeping people. They'd walked about a mile when Andy started chattering again. "The old ladies live in a big, run-down house that was probably real nice at one time. The oldest one—Aunt Annie, she's called—has whiskers and a mustache. Ain't that funny?"

Lightning flashed and revealed a sagging two-story house with closed shutters and a crumbling wraparound porch.

"Here it is," Andy said, his voice gleeful. "Oh, boy, this is spooky."

The dwelling had a brooding air as they approached. Andy tightened his grip on Copper's hand when she tripped on the root of a tree in the overgrown yard and nearly fell to her knees.

"We'd better go round back," Andy cautioned. "She'll know

for sure if we try to get in the front door. Anyways, it'll be locked up tight."

Slowly, hugging the walls, ducking under the windows, they sneaked around to the back.

"Here's the cellar door," Andy whispered. "Take this lantern, and let me see if I can get it open." He grasped the handle of the door and tugged mightily.

The door swung outward on its rusted hinges, creaking as loud as a gunshot in the stormy night.

"There's stairs here," Andy said. "Just a few."

The air in the cellar under Mrs. Archesson's house was so murky and thick that you could have cut it into ribbons with a pocketknife and so menacingly silent that Copper could feel the stillness like little pinpricks all over her body. Sweat trickled down her back, and her underarms itched something fierce. "It's so dark," she murmured. "How will we ever find the stairs?"

Andy fished in his back pocket. "Let me get a match. . . . There, that's better."

A flickering gleam from the lantern illuminated the crowded space. Gargantuan shadows danced on the damp rock walls.

"See, what'd I tell you?" He prodded an overturned baby carriage, and its wheel spun slowly, trailing long strands of cobwebs.

Copper sneezed loudly, biting her tongue in the process and tasting her own salty blood. She stifled another sneeze and scrubbed her nose with her shirtsleeve.

Andy led the way through the maze. "Bunch of junk," he said under his breath. "There's the stairwell. Best I remember, it opens into the kitchen."

"How do you know all this?" Copper couldn't resist asking as she followed him. Andy was full of surprises.

"I once stole in here on a dare from Todd Bowman. That Todd's always doing something crazy. He dared me to see if Mrs. Archesson's aunt was a witch like people says. But, nope, she's just kinda scrunched up, like a dried-up apple. She can't even hear no more. Ain't that sad, Miz Corbett?"

Andy paused with his hand on the door latch. "Anyways, I was all over this here house. The bedrooms is upstairs. Betcha that's where we'll find Matilda."

The kitchen door bumped open, and they crept in, Copper behind Andy, the lantern dark once again. She held on to Andy's shoulder as he led her to the front of the dank, dark house . . . to the rickety stairway.

They paused for Andy to get his bearings. Copper strained to hear any hint that told her there was a baby in this decrepit house. But it seemed they were trapped in a dark void where nothing stirred, no light shone faintly from candle or lamp, and no one slumbered peacefully in the night. Fear snaked up her backbone and lodged in her brain. Something terrible lay waiting. The faint, almost hazy perfume of death assaulted her. Perhaps if there had been any sight or sound to distract, she would not have noticed, so vague was the scent that mingled with the other slightly fermented odor produced by an old house occupied by old people.

What had she led this young boy into? Steeling herself, she clutched Andy's dry hand with her own clammy one. "Careful," she cautioned, taking control. "Follow me."

They mounted the steps and inched along the wall of a lengthy hallway, pausing before each door.

They had passed three such doorways when Copper motioned for Andy to enter with her. The stench was stronger here, strong enough to make her hold her breath. "Something's very wrong. Light the lantern."

That was not necessary, however, for before Andy found his pocket a dramatic bolt of lightning illuminated the many-windowed bedchamber in which they stood. The momentary, brilliant flash revealed a stiff body with mouth agape on the four-poster canopied bed square in the middle of the room.

Horrendous screams assaulted their ears. Panic struck as Copper and Andy fled in tandem to the open doorway. Stars exploded before Copper's eyes when she struck her right hip on the doorjamb, while Andy, lantern clanging, ran full force into the other side. He was flung backward onto the floor of the very room they were so desperate to escape. Copper pulled him to his feet and clung to him tightly. With a ragged laugh, she caught her breath. The screams she heard had been theirs.

"Hand me a match," she said, then with a trembling hand lit the wick. "Is this Aunt Annie?"

"Well," Andy answered, his face as white as milk toast, his freckles as dark as raisins, "I reckon it was."

"Are you all right, Andy?"

He swaggered toward the bed, his voice full of shaky bravado. "This don't scare me none. I've seen dead people before, you know. I help at the undertaker's sometimes."

"There's not much you haven't done, is there?" Copper

asked, wanting to reassure him, feeling guilty for his witnessing such a dreadful thing. She held the lantern high. "Oh my, look."

What they saw was Mrs. Archesson's aunt in a silk dressing gown, propped up by pillows and surrounded by empty tonic bottles.

Andy upended one bottle, and a clear drip of medicine wet the bedcover. "Well, I don't expect she took baby Matilda. Let's go poke around some more."

Pulling the spread over Aunt Annie, making a lumpy ghost of the body, Copper answered, "We might as well, since we're here. But if all our screaming didn't bring Mrs. Archesson running, she must not be home."

Slowly, slowly, they tread down the stairs, into the hall, and back toward the kitchen, careful to step in the little circles of light the lantern cast before them.

What now? Copper pondered. *I've broken into a house I have no business to be in and frightened Andy half to death just to find a body we weren't even looking for.*

Suddenly a snoring bray filled the hall. Up it soared, groaning and bumping around them until with a halting hum it stopped, and the house was quiet once again.

Andy looked quizzically at Copper.

"Someone's in there." Copper pointed to a room directly off the hallway to their right.

"Sounds like Mrs. Archesson's sleeping off her tonic," Andy answered, tugging Copper's arm. "Come on. Time's a-wasting."

They found Birdie slumped in an overstuffed chair in her sitting room. Stacks of old newspapers, books, clothing, and general trash impeded their progress.

"Careful with that lantern. We don't want to start a fire," Copper said. "What in the world?" She sank to her knees. "Oh no. Oh no. Lord, please, not this." She moaned a prayer as she pulled the limp, blue form of a baby from the carpetbag at Birdie's feet.

"Oh no, the little thing's smothered," Andy cried. "She couldn't get no air in that old purse."

What to do, what to do? The horror of the situation clanged about in Copper's head. Surely it was not too late for Matilda. "Help me," she prayed again, knowing God wouldn't want her to accept this baby's death. "Andy! Where could we get cold water?"

"Run her out back, Miz Corbett. The cistern's out there by the cellar door."

Dodging the piles of clutter, Copper held baby Matilda tightly in her arms and followed the trailing light as Andy ran for the kitchen door.

Once in the yard, he seized the handle of the cistern pump. Water trickled out in little spits, then began to flow. Copper held the baby under its stream, bathing her face and rubbing her chest until she heard a little gurgle, a thin gasp for air. Then the Matilda she remembered wailed away like the siren of the new fire engine they had heard at the parade just hours before.

"Oh, boy, we did it. We did it!" Andy whooped and hollered and pounded Copper on the back. Finally he settled down long enough to ask, "You ain't gonna make me drag Mrs. Archesson out here and sober her up under that pump, are you?"

Copper knelt with the baby snuggled to her chest. Matilda had stopped crying and now nuzzled Copper's neck. "We just need one more thing. If you'll fetch a blanket or a dry rag to wrap Miss Matilda in, we'll take her home. We'll let the law deal with this house and its contents."

CHAPTER 14

Very early that morning, Copper, Simon, and Andy witnessed a sweet reunion when the police chief brought Matilda's family to fetch her. The pudgy baby girl, no worse for her ordeal, gurgled and smiled as her brothers made funny noises and silly faces just for the pleasure of seeing her reaction.

Mr. Johnson clasped Copper's hand in his own. "Mrs. Corbett, how can we ever repay you for saving our baby?" His face contorted, and he choked back a sob. "You were so brave to go into that crazy woman's house. I shudder to think what would have happened if you hadn't found little Matilda when you did."

"Thank you, Mr. Johnson," Copper replied, "but Andy is the one who deserves the plaudit. He remembered that Mrs. Archesson was acting strangely, and it was Andy who found the way to Matilda. Praise the Lord, and thank Andy that we made it in time."

A small crowd had gathered on the porch, and people lined the street beyond. Everyone wanted to get a glimpse of the now-famous baby and her rescuers. Even the mayor was there, his walrus mustache bobbing as he laughed. He shook hands and generally worked the impromptu gathering. Election Day was just a few months away, and it seemed he never missed an opportunity to grab a vote.

Standing on the top porch step, the mayor held up his hand to silence the crowd. His rich voice boomed, "I hereby declare this Matilda Johnson Day. Seeing as how we missed the fire-works last night, I invite each and every one of you to the park this evening. We'll have our celebration, and there'll be water-melon for all! There will also be a special ceremony of commen-dation for this young fellow, Andrew Tolliver."

Andy pulled on Copper's sleeve and stretched up to whisper urgently in her ear, "What's a commendation? I ain't in trouble, am I?"

Copper whispered back, "No, Andy. It's a reward, like getting a medal for being so brave."

"Andrew—" the mayor motioned for Andy to come his way— "say something to the folks."

Andy stepped up beside him. "Shucks, Mr. Mayor. I don't need nothing for helping Miz Corbett here save baby Matilda." He rubbed one toeless shoe against the heel of the other. "It's the good Lord sent us to that old bat's—sorry, Mrs. Archesson's house, I reckon."

The crowd broke out in applause as a gang of boys led by Andy's friend Todd Bowman, his broken arm still plastered, hoisted Andy to their shoulders and paraded him down the sidewalk.

Finally the crowd faded away. The Johnson family gathered their children and, with one last hug for Copper and calls of "We'll see you tonight" and "Thanks again," were slowly driven away in the police chief's carriage.

Copper leaned against Simon as she waved the buggy away. "I'm so glad you're home. I thought you'd be gone all day."

Catching her in a tight embrace, he rested his chin on the top of her head. "I could sleep standing up." He stifled a yawn. "Let's go in and catch a nap."

The screen door squeaked open, and Searcy poked her head out. "You all come in now," she said and frowned at Copper. "Ain't enough you try to get yourself killed traipsing around all hours of the night, going places you got no business going; now you be trying to starve yourself." The door swung wide on its hinges. "Come on in here and eat your biscuits and gravy."

Copper's stomach growled in appreciation when Searcy set her filled plate on the table. Bacon, fried eggs, sawmill gravy, hash browns, and a slice of ripe red tomato vied for the first bite. "What would we do without you, Searcy?"

With her hands planted firmly on her hips, Searcy surveyed the young couple, then walked to the stove and seized the handle of the coffeepot with a yellow pot holder. "Be pitiful thing to find out," she muttered before she came back to the table. Fresh black coffee trickled into first Simon's cup and then Copper's.

"Taking care of you two be Searcy's pleasure. Now eat up." Seemingly satisfied, Searcy headed out the door.

Lingering over the meal, Copper turned to Simon. "I forgot all about the train wreck. Was anyone hurt?"

"We were as fortunate as baby Matilda," he replied, pausing between bites. "When Dr. Thornsberry and I got there, we found many passengers with cuts and bruises but thankfully no deaths. The conductor suffered a fractured leg. His was the most serious injury."

"Seems the Lord blessed us all last night," Copper said.

Simon looked at her over his coffee cup. "What am I to do with you? Seems I can't trust you out of my sight."

"Simon . . ."

He loosened his tie and leaned back in his chair. "I'm serious, sweetheart. You could have gotten yourself killed last night. I've a good mind to lock you in *our* cellar."

"What would you have had me do?"

His eyes held the same blend of alarm and pride her father's had shown the time Copper killed a wildcat outside the chicken coop. She'd clocked the marauding varmint dead as a doorknob with only a pebble fired from a slingshot, just like David slew Goliath.

"You should have sent Andy to the police station with your suspicions instead of going off by yourselves the way you did," Simon fussed.

"I just had the strongest feeling I was barking up the right tree. You have to listen when God gives you insight. Besides, if we had waited for help, I think Matilda would have been dead when we found her." Copper stood and scraped the remnants of their breakfast into the slop bucket Searcy kept for the hog. Through the window over the sink, she could see the house-keeper in the garden, gathering vegetables into her bunched-up apron, already preparing for the noon meal. "What's going to happen to Birdie?"

"Birdie?"

"Mrs. Archesson, I mean. She's such a flighty little thing that I nicknamed her Birdie."

Simon laughed, holding out his mug for a refill. "That's perfect. She does get her feathers ruffled quite easily. When the police chief intercepted me on my way home from Paris, I went to the Archesson house with him to sign commitment papers. The undertaker was there with the mortuary wagon to get Annie Archesson's body, but *Birdie* took no notice."

"Why did you have to sign papers? Didn't they take her to jail?"

"She's not a criminal, just a confused and sick woman. I commended her to the lunatic asylum. She'll be safe there. They'll protect her from herself."

"But, Simon, she could have killed Matilda. She should be tarred and feathered."

"Judge not lest ye be judged. You don't know why she felt compelled to take the baby."

His soft rebuke shamed her, but he hadn't seen that precious little girl stuffed like so much garbage in a dirty old bag, her very breath stolen away, while drunk Birdie slept the night away. And of course, she'd never told him about Birdie nearly strangling her that day in his office. Still, her temper flared. Simon could suffer fools if he wanted, but she would not.

Anger cut her tiredness as slick as a hot knife through butter. Simon started for the stairs to rest a bit, but Copper decided to find Andy. "May I take him to the dry-goods store and select something appropriate for him to wear to the celebration tonight?" she asked.

"You may go if Reuben has time to take you. Just have your purchases added to my account." He paused for a kiss before continuing his instructions. "And be careful. Andy doesn't live in the best part of town."

"Thank you, dearest," she said, tying her bonnet under her chin and drawing on her gloves, her ill feelings all but forgotten.

"Indeed, Dr. Corbett was right as usual. This is not the best part of town," Copper said to Reuben as she bounced on the buggy seat beside him. Reuben had brought the Sunday carriage around for their trip, but when he opened the door for her, Pawpaw jumped in instead, so she sat beside Reuben on the driver's bench. You could see much better that way.

"Yes'm," Reuben answered.

No matter how Copper tried she couldn't get more than a word from the taciturn man. She guessed he wasn't used to a woman who had as many opinions as she did.

Bump, bump, bump . . . They made their teeth-rattling way down a crooked alley lined on both sides with meager shotgun houses. The dwellings sat cheek by jowl as if leaning on each other for support. In the ditch that lined the road, stagnant brown water released a noxious odor.

The noise of children shrieking as they ran through a large mud puddle mingled with that of a red-faced housewife who loudly harangued someone as she leaned out a second-story window. "Just get out!" Copper heard her shout. "If you can't bring any of your pay home to feed these brats, then what do I need you for?"

As they passed by, Copper could see a man dressed in an undershirt, idling on the porch, drinking from a long-necked brown bottle. He seemed unperturbed by the woman's harsh words or by the dishpan of dirty water she flung from the window.

Copper swiveled around trying to take it all in. The dress she wore slicked across the leather seat. "Whoops!" she cried in alarm as she jammed her feet against the floorboards. Reuben put his hand out before she righted herself and sat back. "Sorry," she said.

"Yes'm," he answered, his eyes straight ahead.

Taking in every detail of the passing scene, she was appalled but not surprised. She had seen much poorer sights up the hollows of the mountains, but these seemed sadder somehow. Where she came from, no matter how bad off you might be, it was not so open for everyone to see. It didn't seem so squalid to live in a shanty when there was space around you and the beautiful mountains to look at. But here the yards were so small you couldn't tell your chickens from your neighbors'. And there were chickens of every sort pecking and scratching at the bare ground.

She wished for a handful of cracked corn to fling at the pitiful things.

Nearly every door stood wide open. "Goodness gracious," she remarked, "you could throw a cat through the front door, and it would sail clean through the house." She caught herself gawking; she'd never seen so many people's lives laid bare. "I suppose they leave the doors open to catch some air. I'll bet the flies are thick, for I don't see any screens."

Amazingly, Reuben found his voice. "Probably so, but these folks be wearied by more than flies."

Chagrined, Copper cast a sideways look and studied his face. She hoped she hadn't offended him. Her mind flitted to her mountain home and how they would drag out the screens first thing every summer. Who could forget scrubbing those windows with vinegar water and polishing them with newsprint before propping them open with the fly screens? Mam always said it didn't take wealth to be clean.

Reuben's face betrayed no emotion as they approached the end of the narrow street. "Here now. I think this be where young Andy lives."

The house sat nearly level with the road. The tiny front yard looked tidy compared to that of its neighbor, which was strewn with all manner of odds and ends, the most curious of which was a wooden rowboat, oars still attached.

They're ready for the flood, Copper thought but kept it to herself. She figured she'd already said enough.

Holding her skirts aloft, she stepped across the drainage ditch and into the yard. Paw-paw yipped and whined to come with her, but she left him in the carriage. The gray, lightweight-wool calling suit she wore with its short, fitted jacket trimmed with crystal-beaded swirls of purple ribbon seemed woefully inappropriate, and she wished she'd worn anything but the jaunty hat of gold and purple feathers. The emperor in his new clothes couldn't have seemed more out of place.

Unlike most of the other houses, the door to Andy's was closed. Flakes of white paint floated to the rough stone stoop when Copper rapped loudly. "Andy," she called when she got no response, "are you in there?"

The door opened a crack, revealing a dirty little face framed by tangles of hair the color of rich cream. "What do you want, miss?" the little girl whispered.

"Hi there. I'm Andy's friend. Is he home?"

"He ain't here." The door opened wider, and the girl stared up at Copper with round blue eyes. Wash her face and this child would be beautiful. "I wish he'd hurry back. Me and Dodie are hungry."

"Could I speak to your mother?" Copper asked.

The child made no move. "My ma's asleep."

"Well . . . ," Copper started, unsure what to do. She couldn't just barge into a house uninvited. Could she?

A dull *thunk . . . thunk . . . thunk* emanated from somewhere in the room.

The girl looked over her shoulder. "That's the baby. She's mad 'cause there ain't no milk." Her voice sounded resigned and old beyond her years.

"Should I come in and see about her?" Copper asked.

"Andy says don't let nobody in without permission. You wait right here." The door closed behind her.

Half a minute passed before it swung back open. "Dodie says come on in," the girl said.

The room Copper entered surprised her. Expecting few and humble furnishings, she saw instead a camel-backed sofa of elegant brown brocade and two plush chairs of the same material, one with a brightly colored fringed shawl draped over the arm. In one corner sat a curio cabinet, lavishly dressed dolls covering its mirrored shelves. Just steps beyond the sitting room was the kitchen, where an odd-looking baby banged her head against the back of a wobbly wooden high chair.

"I'm Marydell," the girl said, sliding her hand between the chair back and the baby's head. "And this is my sister, Dodie."

In stark contrast to the parlor the kitchen was nearly bare. Strings of brightly colored beads hung from a doorframe separating it from the room beyond. Through the beaded curtain, Copper could faintly make out the form of a woman lying on a bed.

The toddling-age baby continued her head banging, smashing against Marydell's hand.

"I'm six," Marydell continued without even a grimace of pain. "Can I wear your hat?"

"It's nice to meet you, Marydell." Copper fumbled with her hatpin and handed her hat to Marydell. Leaning down, she unfastened the tray and slid the baby out. "Does Dodie mind if I look in the cupboard?"

Marydell put her ear to her sister's mouth. "Dodie says, 'Help yourself,' but I already looked and it's empty as my belly."

Copper drew aside a panel of printed cotton that hung from a length of twine strung between two nails. Indeed, the kitchen cupboard was empty. The shelves held only a bottle of clotted milk and a withered potato sporting a long white sprout.

"Muk," the baby said and reached toward the bottle.

"Reckon she could eat it off a spoon?" Marydell asked. "It won't pour. I already tried."

"We need to wake your mother." Copper peeked between two strands of beads.

The woman slept with one slender arm thrown across her eyes. Stirring, she propped herself on one elbow. Clouds of hair the color of clover honey spilled around her heart-shaped face. "Marydell," she whined like a petulant child, "you know I need my sleep. Can't I ask the least little thing from you?"

"I'm sorry, Ma." Marydell laid Copper's feathered hat on the table before she slipped into the room. "Let me fix the blanket." The child drew the coverlet across her mother's chest and patted it into place. The woman's droopy eyes closed before Marydell finished.

"Here, lady," Marydell said, grabbing Copper's free hand. "Let's take Dodie outside."

The scent of ammonia stung Copper's nose. "Do you have a clean diaper?" she asked as they stepped out.

Reuben had turned the carriage around and waited up the road a bit in a shady spot. Copper could see Paw-paw's head hanging out the window.

"That Dodie's always needing something. Come round back

with me." Marydell edged through the narrow space between her house and her neighbors'. "I hung this nappy out this morning. It should be dry by now."

Taking Dodie from Copper, she laid the baby on her back on a patch of grass. Deftly she exchanged the wet rag for a dry one. "There now, is that better, baby?" she asked as she hung the used diaper over the same rusty wire from which she had taken the dry one. "When they're smelly I have to rinse them out in that bucket. Andy keeps water in it all the time."

Copper knelt and took the baby in her arms. Dodie leaned back as far as she could and grinned. A string of drool wet the front of her stained gown. She was a wiry baby, long and thin without a trace of fat. Her perfectly round, slick head sat on her shoulders like the stopper in a bottle, and her ears stuck out like the handles on a jug.

Copper fought her inclination to rouse the children's mother. How could she lie abed when her little ones were hungry? Instead she followed Marydell to the front stoop, where they sat to wait for Andy. A fine anger settled in her chest like a smoldering ember. Righteous wrath.

Before long, Andy came strutting down the street—a resplendent Andy all dressed up. "Hey, girls. Hey, Miz Corbett. I sure didn't expect to find you here."

"I came to see if I could take you to get something special to wear to the ceremony tonight, but I see someone's beaten me to it."

Marydell ran to her brother's side and stroked the arm of his brown-and-gold glen plaid jacket. He had knickerbockers to match and long black stockings tucked into shiny brown boots. "Andy, you look beautiful," she said.

"Yes, Andy, you are quite handsome," Copper agreed.

Andy smiled. "I expect I feel right handsome." He set a box of groceries on the stoop and doffed his new brown-and-white-striped billed cap. "Would you believe the mayor took me to the dry-goods store to get me a suit of clothes, and Mr. Massey wouldn't let him pay? Said it was on the house. Don't that beat all? Just for helping you get Matilda back."

The baby held her arms up, and Andy settled her on his hip. "Glad you're dry for a change, girl." Dodie squealed and pulled at his tie. "These here shoes are a mite big, but they'll do." He squared his shoulders. "Mr. Massey said a growing boy needs a big shoe."

"You deserve every bit of it," Copper said. "Did the mayor buy these groceries?"

"No, ma'am," he replied, his chest puffed out. "I bought these with my earnings."

"Muk!" Dodie cried. "Muk."

"Yes, girly-girl, milk." He opened the door but did not invite Copper in. "I'd best fix Dodie a bottle. See you tonight, Miz Corbett."

CHAPTER 15

Standing on tiptoe, Copper searched the crowd in vain for Andy's mother and his two little sisters. "Surely they'll be here. I can't believe his mother would miss the award ceremony."

Simon slipped his hand under her elbow. "Did you meet Annalise when you went to her house today?"

"Is that Andy's mother's name? How pretty. No, she was still abed." It was near dusk, so she furled her parasol as they walked along. "I met his sisters, Marydell and Dodie. That baby tickles my mind. There's something familiar about her, but I can't put my finger on it."

"Don't you think babies look pretty much the same?" Simon asked. "Like Humpty Dumpty, all head and no necks?"

Copper laughed. "Dodie's not the prettiest little girl I ever saw, but I don't think she looks like an egg. Marydell's a different story. She reminds me of a wildflower with all that yellow hair around her little dirty face." She stopped to face Simon. "I don't think their mother takes very good care of them."

"Annalise is an inattentive mother, but she's not mean, and they've got Andy." He escorted Copper to a front-row seat in front of the grandstand. "Look, there're the Johnsons with baby Matilda."

The crowd clapped enthusiastically as the mayor escorted Andy to the podium, where Mr. Johnson shook his hand and Mrs. Johnson hugged him tightly.

As if he spent every day in front of a crowd, Andy started right in. "Alls I can say is I couldn't have saved baby Matilda here without Miz Corbett's help, and her praying didn't hurt none. And I ain't never going in anybody's cellar after dark again."

"You're awfully quiet," Simon said as he and Copper strolled home following the ceremony and the fireworks display. "Did you enjoy the evening?"

"Oh yes. I couldn't imagine anything more beautiful than the fireworks. It was like watching the brightest star burst in the heavens. I wish I could have shared it with Willy and Daniel. They would have been so excited. I should write Mam in the morning and tell her all about it."

Their Bible reading that night was about Jesus and a woman nearly stoned.

"Simon," Copper said when he had finished reading, "do you ever get angry at your patients?"

"Anyone in particular you have in mind?" he asked as they kneeled for prayer.

She turned to face him. "Well, Andy's mother for one. It makes me mad that she was sleeping when her children were hungry. And Birdie, too, for heaven's sake. You act like it doesn't bother you that she nearly killed Matilda."

"Sweetheart, one thing you have to learn when you practice medicine is not to rush to judgment. It's easy to think we would do better than people like Annalise, but how do we really know, never having lived their lives?"

Bowing her head over folded hands, Copper tried to concentrate as her husband led their prayers. His words about judgment stung, though she knew he hadn't meant them as a rebuke. The anger she'd welcomed toward Andy's mother that morning churned in her stomach like a lump of soured dough.

That night Copper dreamed she lived in Bible times. She walked along a winding road, her sandaled feet kicking up little puffs of dust. A clay water jug rested on her shoulder. Shading her eyes against the fine sand stirred up by a quick, hot wind, she saw a crowd gathering on the steps of the Temple. In her haste to see what was happening she twisted her ankle on a rock that lay in her path.

"It's the Lord of the Jews," she heard one man tell another, his voice thick with sarcasm. "He's talking to that harlot."

People milled around, picking up stones; angry words called out for violence. The wind, laden with the feel of an approaching storm, swirled faster until the crowd faded away and left Copper staring into the dark-pooled, beseeching eyes of a woman drawing water from the well.

Past midnight she woke with a start, her hand aching from the stone she'd clenched so tightly. Slipping from bed, she fell to her knees and asked Jesus to grant her eyes like her husband's, eyes that could see past people's ways and into their hearts.

Glumly, Copper stared at her breakfast plate. For once she didn't have an appetite. After her late-night prayers, she'd stolen downstairs and out to the porch. Wrapped in a quilt, nestled in the porch swing, she spent long hours wrestling with her conscience. Birdie's pinched face kept intruding into her thoughts. *"I had a baby once. Had a baby once,"* Copper could hear her say. What did it mean? What would drive Birdie to steal another woman's baby?

"Cat got your tongue?" Simon asked.

Pushing a bit of biscuit into a puddle of gravy, Copper said, "I'm worried about Mrs. Archesson. I want to go to the hospital to see her."

Simon's face clouded. Somehow she'd known it would. "She's not really in a hospital," he said. "The asylum is not a fit place for you to visit."

"But . . ."

He looked over his spectacles at her like Mam used to do, as if to say, "Obey me."

"Simon, I won't feel at peace until I see her. How bad could it be?"

Sighing, he gave in. "It's a depressing place, but if you must go, I'll get Tommy Turner to escort you. He knows his way around."

Suddenly hungry, she dug into her food. "Thank you. I feel better already. It can't be as depressing for me as it is for Birdie."

⁂

Copper was pleasantly surprised when she and Tommy Turner approached the administration building. The asylum was nothing like the prisonlike structure she had pictured it to be. The complex sat back from the road on manicured lawns, albeit fenced ones, and was remarkable for the profusion of flowers of every kind. Fruit and shade trees bordered curving paths where nurses walked their charges, who looked remarkably alike in shapeless robes washed to the same dull gray.

Copper drew her skirts aside to allow the passage of an elderly woman who plucked imaginary objects from the air. "Let's go find Birdie."

They entered the three-storied central pavilion through an arched fanlighted doorway. The reception hall was clean and airy. Sunshine streamed through huge many-paned windows on either side, and the polished, dark-marble floor echoed with their footsteps, announcing their presence.

"We are here to see Mrs. Archesson," Copper informed the man who sat behind the first desk they saw. "We have permission from her admitting physician, Dr. Corbett."

"Yes, ma'am." He chewed on the stub of a lead pencil and barely looked up. "Let me see. . . . She's a new admit, so she's in A. I'll send for Nellie; she can escort you. The gentleman will have to wait here. No men callers but family allowed in that part of the institute."

"I'll wait for you outside," Tommy said, heading for the door.

Copper wondered what painful memories of this place were hidden behind his pleasant demeanor.

A few minutes later Nellie arrived and led Copper down a long, wood-paneled hallway to a heavy door, which she opened with a jangling set of keys, then locked behind them. Bright light gave way to shadow as gas lamps hissed and spit out stingy rays barely illuminating stone steps descending to Women's Ward A.

The open, airy feel of the asylum's grounds seemed a thousand miles away from this dismal stairwell that smelled of lime from the damp, thickly mortared rock walls.

"This is where the real crazies are kept," Nellie informed Copper in a clipped accent Copper couldn't place. "Them as what hurts somebody."

The narrow hall opened into a wide corridor, revealing a row of barred floor-to-ceiling doors through which Copper glimpsed what seemed to be the same poor woman over and over again. Each small cell held an iron bedstead tethered to the wall with a heavy chain and not much else, save the hapless creatures living within. The smells of unwashed bodies and stale urine mixed with moans and screams of despair.

"A moment, please," Copper said, placing one gloved hand on Nellie's arm, ashamed of her reaction. What made her think she could be of any help in such a place? She should have listened to her husband.

"Here, miss," the nurse said with concern. Her round, pink-cheeked face and robust figure made Copper think Nellie should be milking cows, not living like a mole. "Let's sit a bit. The kitchen's just up ahead. We'll have a spot of tea before you see your friend."

Nellie steered Copper to the kitchen and pulled out a straight-backed chair before she poured dark steeped tea into two gray granite mugs. "I'd sweeten that some." She handed Copper a lidded bowl. "You're looking a mite peaked."

"Thank you for being so kind," Copper replied, stirring sugar into her tea. "I'm sorry to cause trouble."

"No trouble, miss. I was more than ready to sit a spell." Nellie took a long, loud sip and looked over the rim of her cup. "Who might you be to the lady who tried to kill that wee baby?"

"I'm just an acquaintance, really." With trembling fingers, Copper carefully took a sip of tea, then set her cup on the matching saucer. "I met Mrs. Archesson in Dr. Corbett's office, and I came to visit with her for a bit, just to see if she's all right. I don't mean to stay but a minute."

"This is not how we usually does things," Nellie said, rising. "We don't get many visitors on Ward A."

"Surely they don't stay here forever," Copper said.

"Most will get better—quieter anyway—move upstairs, and have privileges. Some work on the farm. They go home when they can if they have someone to watch over them. Mrs. Archesson's not so bad. Her brain's just clouded from all that tonic she drank."

"May I visit with her now?" Copper asked, feeling stronger from the sweet tea.

JAN WATSON

"Surely, miss, just let me get her hooked up."

Copper followed Nellie to the cell door and watched as the young woman clamped a metal shackle around Birdie's left ankle before tethering it to the foot of the bed.

"Really," Copper began, "I don't think that will be necessary. . . ."

"That's the rules, miss, else you can't visit with her."

"I understand. Thank you, Nellie." Copper entered the room where Mrs. Archesson lay, stiff as a corpse, upon a lumpy mattress.

"If you need anything, I'm just next door, taking care of Mrs. Porter," Nellie said, her voice as sunny as if she were tending flowers in a garden. "Talk about society. Her Highness thinks she's Mary Todd Lincoln. Everything has to have a gold rim, else she won't touch it."

Copper had never felt at such a loss, not even on that dreadful night with Andy in Mrs. Archesson's house. What was she to do now? What solace could she give to this poor woman? *Help me, Lord*, she prayed. *Show me what to do.*

"Mrs. Archesson? Birdie?" she said softly, slipping into the nickname she had given for need of a bit of comfort. "Birdie?" she repeated, easing herself onto the uncomfortable bed and stroking Mrs. Archesson's shoulder.

Hooded eyes blinked once, twice. Birdie looked at Copper without a trace of recognition. "Are you an angel? Here to help me find my baby?"

"Don't you remember me, Mrs. Archesson?"

Birdie struggled with the shackle, her face creased in frustration.

166

"I'm Copper Corbett. Dr. Corbett's wife. I met you at the office when you came for a visit."

"I feel so fuzzy-headed." Mrs. Archesson took a big breath and shook her head. "I can't remember where I put the baby."

Marshaling her thoughts, Copper opened her mouth to explain about finding baby Matilda.

But Birdie spoke first, staring over Copper's shoulder with faraway eyes. "He must be hungry by now. He's a big baby, Robert Jr.–the apple of his father's eye."

The chain holding the shackle clanged as loud as a church bell, and Copper jumped up and stood looking down at Birdie.

"Can you get me loose from this thing?" Birdie cried, writhing on her bed. Dry corn shucks rustled in protest. "Aunt Annie will be mad if I don't get supper started."

Alarmed, Copper nearly called for Nellie.

But just as suddenly as she had started, Birdie seemed to give up and slumped back against the wall, whispering, "She never liked me, you know. Never liked me. We wouldn't be living with her, Robert and I, if he hadn't been hurt in the war."

Copper stood beside the bed holding Birdie's brown-speckled hand. *Birdie must be over fifty*, she thought, *but she's thinking she has a baby and that her husband, not to mention Aunt Annie, is still alive.*

Birdie managed to pull herself to a sitting position at the end of her comfortless bed. She rocked there, back and forth, bony arms around bony knees. "I didn't mean it, Robert. Don't you know I'd never hurt our baby?" Falling back, she pounded the mattress with her fists. A fine dust made Copper sneeze. "Oh, why does she hate me so? What did I ever do to her?" Her eyes begged Copper. "Make Aunt Annie give me my boy."

"Shh," Copper said, reaching under her own full skirts and removing the muslin half petticoat she wore over her knee-length drawers. She ripped a small hole in the seam of Birdie's mattress and removed some of its mildewed contents. Reaching down her bodice, she extracted a length of the blue ribbon from the lace and openwork top of her camisole, hooked it with her teeth, and tore it in two pieces.

"Shh," she cautioned yet again, lest Birdie's racket summon attention. Quickly Copper began to stuff the petticoat with shucks. This done, she tied a length of blue ribbon around each end of the petticoat. If she'd had her watercolors, she would have painted a little face.

"Look, Birdie." She rocked the pillow in her arms. "Here's your baby. Here's Robert Jr."

"Oh, my baby. My baby," Mrs. Archesson crooned, taking the "baby" from Copper. "Mama won't lose you again, never lose you again. Here, precious, are you hungry?" Gathering her corn-shuck baby to her flat chest, she looked up at Copper with the bright, clear gaze of a young woman. "Excuse me. I need to feed my baby now. Perhaps you can visit another time?"

"Certainly, Mrs. Archesson. Thank you for letting me visit." Copper's knees wobbled like jelly as she went to the door and called for Nellie.

"What do you have there?" Nellie questioned as she observed her patient. "She's not allowed any contraband."

"That's not contraband." Copper squared her shoulders,

standing as tall as her five-foot-three-inch frame would allow. "The doll is a therapeutic remedy approved by her doctor. It is to remain at the bedside." The shame of her lie colored her cheeks. But Simon would approve, wouldn't he?

"Good-bye, Mrs. Archesson," she said with a merry lilt to her voice as if she were leaving a tea party. "Nellie, will you show me out?" While *Please, Lord, get me out of here* was what she prayed.

CHAPTER 16

Copper dressed carefully for her fifth visit to the lunatic asylum. The morning was hot and sticky, with not a breeze to cool the day, and so she selected a light poplin frock in a somber shade of brown. Choosing a plain straw bonnet, she tucked the last stray strand of hair under its brim.

"There," she said to her reflection in the mirror. "Tommy is sure to approve." He was to be her chaperone again, and he had cautioned her to dress simply. Some of the inmates at the hospital were so starved for color, Tommy related, that they might rip a fancy hat right off her head.

They sat quietly as Copper guided the buggy down Fourth Street and reined the horse to a stop under the branches of a maple tree.

"Tommy, does it bother you to come here?" she asked as he gave her his gyrating hand and helped her to step down. "There must be some unpleasant memories."

Tommy held himself as still as he could. He had a way of locking his hands behind his hips, which seemed to still the worst of his jerks. "The strangest sensation overtakes me. I'm afraid I'll be sucked right back into my old ward. I know my bed is still there, just waiting for me. It's not that I had such a bad life. People were good to me, and I had plenty to eat, but now I've had a taste of freedom. I don't ever want to go back."

"Why, Tommy, that won't happen. You do perfectly well on your own."

When they reached the administration building, Tommy stood back. "I wish I could go along. You'll be careful, won't you?"

"Sure, I will. But really, I'm not afraid of Mrs. Archesson. I don't think she meant to hurt anyone. She just got confused."

The stone stairway seemed familiar to Copper this time as Nellie led her down the dank corridor. In no time they were at Mrs. Archesson's cell, and the shackle was applied as on previous visits.

The frail-looking woman lay on her side, cradling her corn-shuck baby.

"She's been more content since you left her that doll," Nellie said. "She even ate some breakfast, but now she's wanting her dead husband." She rolled her brown eyes and grinned. "Suppose you can make a *man* out of a shift and corn shucks? If so, there's a few of us nurses wants to place an order." She guffawed at her own joke before the cell door clanged shut behind her. "Call out if you need me."

"Thank you, Nellie," Copper replied, her confidence waning as she watched Birdie mother the pillow.

"Please sit beside us," Birdie said, pulling herself into a semi-reclining position, resting her head against the bed frame. Her hair hung in greasy gray strings around her sallow face. "It's so good to have a friend. When will you be taking me and Robert Jr. home?" She put the little bundle over her shoulder and patted it firmly. "And where is my husband? It's not like him to be away this long. I'll just bet it's that awful aunt of his, that Annie. Really, Mrs. Corbett, she's a dreadful person. A dreadful person."

What do I do now? Copper thought. *It doesn't seem right to continue this charade. How did I get myself into such a mess?* She'd visit for just a minute, then leave the tending of Birdie and her baby to Nellie.

A commotion in the next cell over pulled her from her thoughts. A great clinking and clanging nearly obscured the sound of a woman screaming, "Call me by my title or don't address me at all!" More crashing continued before they heard, "My husband is the president of the United States, and I am the First Lady. Must I tell you servant girls the same thing every day? I want my own china. I want flowers on my tray. My family, the Todds, will have you all fired!"

Nellie ran past Birdie's room, her apron stained with what appeared to be tomato soup. "Mrs. Lincoln, indeed," she muttered. "Even Honest Abe, God rest his soul, couldn't put up with the high-and-mighty Abigail Porter turned Mary Todd Lincoln."

"Just imagine," Birdie remarked, her eyes sparkling, "what folks at church will say when I tell them Mrs. Lincoln and I had our lyings-in at the very same time . . . my baby born in the same hospital as President Lincoln's son."

Copper's head was fairly spinning. Spying a chair by the door, she dragged it over and sat down. My goodness, she was beginning to understand why folks called this place the loony bin.

"Mrs. Archesson, Nellie has left your meal tray. Will you take a bite of this tomato soup? And look, here is a lovely piece of milk toast. Um, looks delicious." Copper spooned soup into Birdie's open mouth. "You need to eat to regain your strength."

"I will eat every morsel if you will promise to take me home," Birdie said before a great tremor shook her body and her eyes clouded once again. Her head dropped to her chest, and she wiped tears with the sleeve of her gown. "I don't have a baby anymore, do I? Something has gone terribly wrong with my life, and I don't know quite what it is."

Copper spoke carefully, weighing each word, hopeful to make a connection that would last. "Mrs. Archesson, may I call you by your Christian name?"

"My given name is Mary Martha, like the ladies in the Bible, but you may call me Birdie. No one besides you ever liked me enough to give me a nickname, except for Robert, of course, and he called me darling. Robert called me darling."

Pushing the tray table aside, Copper scooted closer. "Tell me about yourself, Birdie. Tell me about your life."

Birdie's face crumpled. "I've always been an afterthought,

never important to anyone besides my husband. I was my mother's change-of-life baby, and I grew up taking care of my parents."

Copper fished in her pocket and handed Birdie a delicate, embroidered handkerchief.

"I don't think they ever really loved each other. Not like my Robert and I did anyway." The doll fell to the floor, but she didn't move to pick it up. "What we had was so special. We married when I was eighteen. Our house had a red-tin roof. I remember like it was yesterday—the sound of rain on that red roof."

Strange, Copper thought as she tried to figure Mrs. Archesson out. *She seems to flit between stages of her life. If we could trap her mind in the present time, maybe we could help her.*

"So, anyway, that's how we came to be there in that awful house."

Copper's ears perked up.

"But I don't blame Robert," Birdie continued. "He was hurt fighting for what he believed in."

"Pardon me, Birdie, but I missed something. Are you talking about the house with the red roof? I thought you loved that house."

"We had to leave our house because Robert couldn't work after his leg was amputated—an old war wound—and his army pension was a pittance. I helped as much as I could. I made the prettiest hats, you know, but then I got in the family way and couldn't work anymore." One thin hand twisted the mattress cover. "That's when Robert went to his aunt Annie for help. Oh, I wish we'd just stayed in our place and starved to death. It wouldn't have been much worse."

"What was so bad about Aunt Annie?" Copper asked, leaning forward, sharing Birdie's space.

"She hated me," Birdie said, her voice flat. "I should have run the first time I laid eyes on that evil old woman, but Robert wouldn't hear a bad word about her. She raised him after his parents died of the smallpox. So I was stuck. Stuck to do her bidding while Robert faded away before my very eyes. He never got over the awful things he saw in the war. He would wake screaming, saying his leg was hurting. He would beg me to rub it, and I would stroke thin air."

A little smile creased Birdie's lips. "The only thing that cheered him was thoughts of the baby. He said once it was born we would move to Tennessee. I yearned for that day when we would be far away from Aunt Annie."

"Wasn't Aunt Annie excited to have a baby in the house?"

"She acted that way for Robert, but she let me know what a bother I was. She kept a log of every bite I took and counted every egg I ate. I lived for the birth of my baby so we could escape from her influence, but she was only biding her time. She was not going to let us go."

Copper barely noticed when Nellie came for the meal tray. "What happened next? What happened when your baby was born?"

"This is the hard part," Birdie cried. "This is why I needed tonic for my nerves. It helped me to forget." She tugged Copper's hand and drew her to the bed. "Oh, sit close to me. I feel as if I might come apart."

"Should I send for the doctor?" Nellie asked from behind

Copper. She hadn't left with the tray. Copper understood. Birdie's story was enthralling.

"Maybe you shouldn't talk about it now, Birdie," Copper said. "Maybe we should wait until your doctor is here."

Lifting her shoulders, then letting them fall, Birdie said, "I need to tell it now while my mind is good. I need to sort out what happened to me. Just stay close to me until my story is finished."

Nellie slipped around to the end of the bed and released the shackle. Catching Copper's eye, she nodded. "We'll both be right here," she said as she rubbed a red mark on her patient's ankle. "Take all the time you need, dearie."

"The morning my baby was born it was raining sleet," Birdie continued. "Ice covered every tree and bush. When the sun shone, it sparkled like jewels. The doctor took a long time getting there—the roads were so treacherous—but I didn't really need him." A blush crept up Birdie's neck. "The doctor said I could birth a dozen.

"Robert Jr. was an easy baby. He just slept and ate, slept and ate. I would put him beside me in the bed, and he would eat until the milk ran out the corner of his little mouth. I loved that baby so. One night I tucked him in his cradle. It sat right beside me, next to my side of the bed. I slept the night through, and when I woke I was afraid because the baby was so still. 'Robert,' I screamed. 'Something is wrong. Something is wrong with Robert Jr.' My husband climbed right over me and grabbed his son. 'He's dead, Mary Martha!' Robert cried out. 'Oh, Lord, help us.'"

Copper couldn't help but cry. Silent tears slid down her

cheeks, and Nellie's broken sobs provided tender music to Birdie's story.

"Aunt Annie said I poisoned my baby. That my milk was tainted. She said healthy babies don't just die of their own accord lying right next to their mother. She carried his little body out of the house and buried him under that twisted apple tree that sits beside the summer kitchen, said there was no need to spend money on a funeral.

"I begged Robert to stop her, to get a minister to bury him, but as always, he let her have her way. She always got her way. Robert was never himself again after that. It was almost a relief when I found him hanging from a rafter in the barn. Then I knew I had paid the price for killing my own baby. God took my husband, the only person who ever loved me. I never tried to leave Aunt Annie after that. It was my penance, caring for her."

Finished, Birdie sat up and put her feet on the floor. As she took Copper in, her gaze begged for understanding. "At first I just took the tonic to help me sleep, but before long I had to have it to stand being awake; then I had to have it all the time. I took mine and Aunt Annie took hers, and then I wound up here thinking a corn-shuck baby was my own."

"Oh, Birdie," Copper said as tears dripped from her chin. "I am sorry you had to suffer so much. What can I do to help?"

"You help me by just being here," Birdie replied. There were no tears in her eyes. Copper supposed she'd used them all up. "No one ever listened to my story before." Her fist thumped her own chest. "No one saw *me*. They only saw a foolish woman in a fancy hat. Do you think I can make it, Mrs. Corbett? Do you think I could live like normal people?"

Folding Birdie into her arms, Copper answered, "If ever anyone deserved a normal life, it is you. Let me talk to Dr. Corbett and find out what we need to do. And, Birdie, listen to me. God has not been punishing you. He doesn't work that way."

Kneeling on the stone floor beside the hospital bed, Copper asked if Birdie and Nellie would pray with her. "Heavenly Father, surround Your daughter Mary Martha with the light of Your truth. Give her strength, dear Lord, and peace. These things we ask in Jesus' name. Amen."

"I believe," Birdie whispered, sinking onto the bed, resting her head on the pillow Copper tucked under her head. "I believe God forgives me."

A summer storm must have broken the sweltering heat, because Copper could feel the rumble of thunder through the soles of her shoes as it shook the very foundation of the asylum. It seemed she'd been underground for a very long time. Tommy would be worried.

Drawing a coverlet around Birdie's shoulders, she signaled to Nellie her desire to leave. "I'll be back soon," she promised. "And I'll send the reverend to pray with you."

Birdie didn't answer, just lay with her eyes closed, but it seemed to Copper that her face held hope.

Why would such a thing happen? she mused as she followed Nellie up the stairs. *How can a person get so far away from God?*

Nellie paused on the last step and turned toward Copper. "Miss, could you come back sometime and pray for me?"

Copper patted Nellie's plump arm. "I would be glad to, but did you know you can talk to God whenever you want? You don't need me."

"You've got to be good to talk to Him, miss. And I've not always done them things I should."

"Neither have I, Nellie. But God is ever forgiving if we have a repentant heart. You have but to ask."

The wind and rain swept Copper through the door and into the foyer, where she stood for a moment furling her umbrella. As she put it in the tin-lined tray of the hall tree, she could hear Simon's low voice mixed with Alice's querulous one. She wished for a moment to catch her breath, to digest Birdie's story, but instead she stepped into the parlor.

"Well, finally you see fit to come home." Alice's greeting hurt. "I suppose it slipped your mind that I was coming by to take you to our missionary meeting."

My own Aunt Annie, Copper thought as she kissed Simon's cheek. "Forgive me, Alice. Have you had lunch?"

"Simon and I were forced to dine without you."

"We were fine, sweetheart," Simon interjected, "just a little concerned about you."

"Truly, I didn't mean to be away so long, but Mrs. Archesson needed me, and then the weather . . . Alice, perhaps the ladies in the missionary society would like to help her. She is all alone."

"That would hardly be appropriate," Alice replied. "The missionary society was formed to help convert savages in uncivilized nations, those who have not had a chance to hear the Word of God. Mrs. Archesson is an old sot, hardly deserving of our time." She pulled the rarely used bell cord, summoning Searcy into the room. "Fetch my umbrella," she demanded before pulling on her gloves and trailing the housekeeper to the foyer.

Simon and Copper stepped onto the porch with Alice. The rain had nearly stopped, but Simon opened Alice's umbrella.

"I will apologize for your absence," Alice said to Copper, "but you must learn to take your obligations seriously."

"I'm sorry. I'll be ready next time."

"It amazes me, Simon, that you do not have better control of your wife," Copper heard her say as brother and sister walked head to head toward the waiting carriage. "Benton would have a fit if I set one foot on the grounds of that madhouse."

Copper strained so hard to hear Simon's reply that she nearly fell off the porch.

"And that, my dear, is between you and your husband as this is between my wife and myself."

"Well!" Alice shot back. "Pardon me for trying to save her from humiliating herself."

Simon came back to the porch and slipped an arm around Copper's waist as they watched Alice settle herself in the carriage.

Waving good-bye, he said, "Off to save the heathen in far-away lands. Heaven save us from the ladies of the missionary society."

"Alice has her way and I have mine. That doesn't make her wrong," Copper responded, surprising herself.

"No, just misguided," he said. "Now tell me what has made

you so late to lunch. Must you let your husband starve?" He nuzzled her neck. "Do I have to be a heathen to get your attention?"

"Simon," she said, pulling away, "the neighbors."

"Sometimes I wish I'd stayed with you on Troublesome Creek; then I could kiss you anywhere I pleased. There'd be no one to see but bears and raccoons."

"Don't tease me. I could pack my trunk in nothing flat."

"Maybe someday. One never knows what God plans for the future."

Copper couldn't help herself. Simon's words had opened a little window of hope. Might she someday have her heart's desire? Might they return to her beloved Troublesome Creek? She turned the thought over in her mind, then tucked it away in her heart for safekeeping.

CHAPTER 17

Birdie's house sure looked sad in the daytime. Weeds and brambles snatched at Copper's clothing as she made her uninvited way across the overgrown yard. Birdie wouldn't mind that she was here; they were friends now. But Simon would be angry if he discovered she'd sneaked away without someone to accompany her. Sneaked off! She, a grown, married woman, had had to steal away in order to take a walk alone. A walk that just happened to lead to the outskirts of town and Mary Martha Archesson's uninhabited house.

When she and Andy had been here before, she hadn't realized how big the place was nor how decrepit. The round support pillars of the wraparound porch were rotting, and the roof sagged dangerously. Simon had told her that he and the undertaker had to take Aunt Annie's body out the back door for fear they'd fall through the floorboards if they tried to carry her across the porch.

The house must have been grand at one time, sitting back from the road as it did on an expansive lawn. Despite the peeling paint, you could tell it had once been pristine white. Large gaslights flanked the double doors, and faded black shutters hung askew at the long, many-paned windows. It was probably the site of lots of parties with its two-storied grandeur.

Copper followed a trail marked by flattened weeds to the back. There was the cellar door and there the cistern where Andy had pumped water to wake baby Matilda. Wandering, lost in thought, she passed a small stone building set a short distance behind the house. Farther along, an ancient apple tree sported knotty green fruit. *Is this where Birdie's baby is buried?* There was no marker of any sort. Tears came to her eyes, and she sat on the steps of the stone building to rest a minute. Sad though she was, she felt a comforting presence, as if an angel sheltered her with his wings.

Somewhere in the distance, a clock struck noon. She'd have to hurry to beat Simon home. With a last look around, she returned to the front and set off toward Willow Street. Someday she'd have to ask Simon for her own carriage. What a blessing it would be to come and go as she pleased, though Alice wouldn't approve. Copper wished she didn't care so much what her sister-in-law thought.

Simon was pacing the porch when Copper made her way up the walk. The heat of the day had forced her to remove her hat and gloves, and now she had no time to make herself proper before he saw her.

The chain of his watch sparkled in the sun as he stared down the steps. With an exaggerated sigh, he tucked the watch back in his pocket. "Laura Grace, where have you been?"

Ah, the dreaded *Laura Grace*. It took her right back to her childhood and her stern stepmother. Stubbornly, she didn't answer, just made her way to him and bussed his cheek. "It's good to see you too, Dr. Corbett."

"I don't come home from the office to eat my noontime meal alone," he reprimanded.

She didn't wait for him to open the screen door but barged through and let it slam behind her, then slapped her hat and gloves down on the hall table before going to the dining room.

Simon followed, sitting silently at the head of the table, cutting each bite of his food as precisely as if he were in surgery before forking it into his mouth.

Copper's anger dissipated as quickly as it had formed, and she felt ashamed. She wiped her mouth with the edge of her napkin, then cleared her throat. "I'm sorry, Simon."

His eyes met hers. "You worry me. And Searcy . . . she had no idea where you were."

"I didn't set out to go so far, but I walked all the way to Mary Martha Archesson's house." Pausing while buttering a yeast roll, she pointed her knife in his direction. "Something will have to be done before she comes home. The house is falling down, and the lawn is a mess."

"If you will promise to stay away, I will send someone around to see about Mrs. Archesson's house."

"That would be wonderful," she replied, jumping up to kiss his cheek. "You're the best husband in the world."

"What am I to do with you? Don't you understand you're not expected to fix everyone's problems?"

"Well, of course not, Husband." She tickled his mustache. "Just those I know about." Seating herself again, she pushed green beans around with her fork. She hadn't had much of an appetite for days—must be the heat. "When will Birdie get to come home?"

"Thank you," Simon said after Searcy stepped in from the kitchen and poured more ice water. "It's not as simple as it may seem. She has to be declared competent before she is released, and she has to have somewhere to go."

"Could she come here for a while until her house is repaired?"

"That is out of the question," Simon said. "She's safe where she is for now."

"You be eating them beans, Miz Corbett," Searcy interjected. "Searcy didn't cook all morning just to slop the hogs."

Copper took a big bite. "Delicious."

"Don't worry about Mary Martha Archesson," Simon said as he stood and patted her shoulder. "She stands to inherit all of Annie's property. She'll be able to take care of herself."

Copper followed him to the foyer where he retrieved his hat.

"Keep out of trouble this afternoon," he admonished. "I expect to find you here when I return."

"I'll be right there in the porch swing. I'm going to an auxiliary meeting with Alice, but after that I have a new ladies magazine to read."

✧

An hour before supper, Copper sat in the porch swing, *Woman's
Home Companion* open on her lap, languidly stirring the air with
a church fan and sipping iced lemonade. The title of an article
caught her eye: "What Man Does Not Love Beauty? Mrs.
Pinkham Counsels Young Wives to Keep Their Attractiveness."
She glanced about, embarrassed by the racy title but captivated
all the same.

> *Seven-eighths of men marry a woman because she is beautiful
> in their eyes. What a disappointment, then, to see the fair young
> wife's beauty fading away before a year passes over her head!
> Strengthen yourself so you will not break down under the new
> strain on your powers.*

The church fan whipped the humid air, faster and faster.

> *Keep your beauty; it is a precious possession. Your husband loves
> your beauty, and he is proud to be seen in public with you. Try to
> keep it for his sake and your own.*
>   *The pale cheeks, the dark shadows under the eyes, the general
> drooping of the young wife's form—what do they mean?*

Copper read on, pushing the swing slowly with one foot.

*They mean that her nerves are failing, that her strength is going,
and that something must be done to help her through the coming
trials of maternity.*

A jolt like lightning surged through Copper. Maternity! That
meant the family way . . . being with child. . . . *Oh, my goodness,
I'm going to have a baby.* The open magazine plopped to the floor
when she jumped up and hurried into the house.

The mirror hanging in the foyer was in shadow, so she
leaned forward, nose to nose with her reflection, and stared hard.
Were there just the faintest of shadows beneath her eyes? And,
yes, her shoulders were definitely drooping. Her nerves didn't
seem to be failing, however, so what did that mean? Did you
have to have all the signs or would two do? Perhaps she should
read more of Mrs. Pinkham's counsel.

Settling back in the swing, one leg tucked under, she found
her place in the magazine.

*Build yourself up at once by a course of tonic with specific
powers, such as Lydia E. Pinkham's Vegetable Compound.*

A letter of commendation followed.

*To my suffering sisters,
Let me write this for your benefit, telling you what Lydia
E. Pinkham's Vegetable Compound has done for me. I am but
nineteen and suffered monthly with painful cramping, dizziness,
burning sensations at the back of my ears and on top of my head,*

nervousness, soreness of muscles, bearing-down pains, could not sleep well, tingling in my feet and legs, and, oh, how I longed to be well! One day I wrote to Mrs. Pinkham telling her all, knowing I could do so in perfect confidence. She replied with a lovely letter telling me exactly what to do.

Paw-paw circled a spot of sunshine, an unwelcome distraction. "Lay down!" Copper said more sharply than she'd meant. His old brown eyes looked up sadly. "I'm sorry–" she fished a sliver of ice from her lemonade and let him slurp it from her hand–"but I need to finish this before Simon gets home." Satisfied, Paw-paw plopped down on the top step. "Let's see, where was I? Oh yes, the letter."

After taking nine bottles of compound, one box of liver pills, and using one half package of sanative wash, I can rightly say I am cured. I am so happy, and I owe my happiness to none other than Mrs. Pinkham. Why will women suffer when help is near? Let me, as one who has had some experience, urge all suffering women, especially young wives, to seek Mrs. Pinkham's Compound. You can avail yourself of it at any druggist.

Standing, Copper retrieved letters from home stuck deep in her apron pocket. Her foot tingled painfully. Was that another sign? She'd have to ask Simon. For now, she couldn't wait to reread the letters from this morning's post, one from Mam and one from Brother Issac.

It seemed a lifetime, not mere months, since she'd waved

good-bye to them in June, the day of her wedding. Brother Isaac had married her and Simon in the little church in the shadow of the mountains. He had been her minister for years, and she missed him dearly. Her heart beat fast at what his letter told her. He was coming for a visit! How wonderful it would be to see someone from home.

Mam's letter was not so cheerful. Daddy had been sick again. Nothing serious, Mam wrote. Nothing that couldn't be helped by mustard plasters. Laura Grace was not to worry; they'd be leaving for Philadelphia in two weeks.

Lost in thought, Copper tapped her chin with the envelope from Mam's missive. Mam and Daddy and Willy and Daniel had been preparing to leave for Philadelphia since Copper left Troublesome Creek with Simon. Mam wanted to take the boys to a place where they could get an education, and Daddy had agreed. They should have been there and settled by now. Copper felt uneasy. Was Mam telling her everything?

But Isaac was coming. He might be here any day now, and he would tell her all the news from home.

Over supper, Simon shared news of his own. Mary Martha Archesson was to be released from the asylum. She was considered to be of sound mind. Graciously, baby Matilda's parents did not press charges against her. As soon as the men Simon had hired finished repairing her house, Birdie could come home.

Copper clapped with joy. "I am so excited for Birdie. I just hope she doesn't get too lonely living in that big house by herself."

"The passing of time brings change for everyone. If Mary Martha is unable to reconcile herself to her new life, then she will have to return to the asylum."

"Oh, that mustn't happen," Copper replied, standing and scraping their plates before taking them to the sink. "We must pray that God will send a way to keep Birdie busy. . . . 'Idle hands are the devil's workshop,' you know. Mam must have said that a thousand times while I was growing up." She filled the sink with water and took a bar of lye soap from the ledge. "Go on now, Searcy." She shooed the housekeeper away. "You'll be late to your Bible study."

Searcy wrapped her Bible in a starched and ironed tea towel before tucking it in her basket. "Searcy don't feel right leaving you with these dishes," she said as she tied the strings of her bright blue bonnet under her chin.

"A little dishwater won't kill me. Now, go on. Go show the girls what you've learned this week."

"You be leaving them skillets, Miz Corbett," Searcy said as she stepped out the door. "Searcy be doing them in the morning."

Copper washed and Simon dried.

"What's this about Bible study?" he asked. "I've never known Searcy to leave before her work was done." Turning a plate, he studied a chip in its rim. "We'll need to replace this one."

Copper took the plate to the pantry and put it in the basket they kept for donations to the poor. She'd never get used to the waste in this house. She came out of the narrow room talking. "You know I've been teaching Searcy to read the Bible. Well, she's already learned half the alphabet, and she can write her name. She's so pleased with herself that she is teaching the other housekeepers and maids on the street. They meet once a week at Searcy's house."

Simon took a platter from Copper. "How did you get the ladies to let their maids have an evening off?"

"That took some finagling and arm-twisting." She laughed and smiled at him. "I found they couldn't turn me down when we're rolling bandages together at the hospital auxiliary meetings."

Copper scrubbed the cast-iron skillets and dried them in the still-warm oven before she sized them with a dollop of lard. Then she untied her apron strings. Was it her imagination, or did the waist of the apron feel a little too snug? Best share her news with Simon.

"Come sit on the porch with me," she said, reaching for his hand. "There's something I want you to see."

It was a pleasant evening. A cool breeze had swept away the lingering mosquitoes, and a harried hummingbird darted in and out of the trailing red trumpet vine that inched its way to the roof. Copper and Simon sat together on the swing, and she shyly handed him her *Woman's Home Companion*, now dog-eared at Mrs. Pinkham's column.

"What is this, my dear?" Simon smiled at her indulgently and seated his spectacles on the bridge of his nose. "What in this bit of folderol could possibly be of interest to me?"

"Just read it." A blush rose from her collarbone and washed across her cheeks. She busied herself smoothing the front of her dress.

He read aloud, "'What Man Does Not Love Beauty?'" then read silently for a while.

Copper could not meet his eyes when he stopped and peered at her from over the top of the magazine. She had not felt such a remove from him as she did at this moment. To her, since their time at the creek, he had seemed as much a part of her as her heart or her right arm, but now she was aware of their dissimilarity. . . . Her body was a vessel, and she could carry life. It seemed to set her apart somehow.

Laying the magazine aside, Simon reached for her wrist and placed his fingers at her pulse. She could feel the throb of her heart at the base of her throat . . . the very same beat that he discerned with his fingertips.

"Are you ill?" he said with some alarm.

At his tone, Paw-paw roused from his sleep and came across the porch to lay his head in Copper's lap. She rubbed his head and scratched behind his ears. "Not ill, but surely you've noticed a difference in me."

"I've a good mind to make a bonfire with this tripe!" He flung the magazine across the porch. "If you think for one moment that you are any less beautiful to me than the day I first met you on Troublesome Creek . . ."

"You're missing the point." With a little shove, Copper diverted the dog to his spot of sunshine before facing her husband. "Look at me. Really look. Don't you see it?"

"I'm sorry, but I'm at a loss."

"The shadows under my eyes? The drooping of my shoulders? My apron strings too tight? Forevermore, Simon, you're a doctor."

"Copper," he said, as serious as a judge, "you don't need a tonic. Maybe a nap in the afternoon?"

"Good grief, Dr. Corbett, I don't want Mrs. Pinkham's tonic or her little liver pills!" Copper ran her hands through her hair and shook her head. "I'm trying to tell you we're going to have a baby."

If she'd balled her hand into a fist and socked him in the belly, he would not have gone any whiter. "Are you sure?" he asked.

Surprise and disappointment overtook her. His reaction was not what she'd expected. Maybe it was the shock. The swing rocked when she hopped up to fetch the errant magazine and push it in his face. "Ouch, my leg is tingling again. It's one of the signs."

His hand covered his mouth, but she could see him smile. "Sweetheart . . . ," he managed before he threw back his head, nearly choking with laughter.

"What, pray tell, is the matter with you, Simon Corbett?" She rushed to the steps, her leg on fire, and sank down to bury her face against Paw-paw's furry head. "I don't find this one bit funny!"

Simon leaned down behind her, cupped her elbows in his hands, and lifted her to her feet. "Let's go inside. This conversation begs a moment's privacy."

Simon led Copper into his study and settled her in his favorite reading chair. Pulling the hassock close, he took a seat. "I'm sorry I laughed at you," he said, leaning toward her. "That was unkind and I did not mean to be, but, dearest, you cannot learn about female complaints from a silly magazine."

"It seems I cannot learn them anywhere," Copper replied, feeling humiliated and near tears. "Married people have babies, so how do you know we're not having one? Tell me that."

In a gesture all too familiar to her, Simon took off his spectacles, cleaned them, and set them back on his nose. He was giving
himself time to think.

He pushed back the hassock, stood, and cleared his throat.
Taking a few steps away, he looked at her sternly. "I have a few
questions to ask. Some might make you uncomfortable, but they
are necessary if I am to determine the state of your health."

"Simon Corbett, I am not your patient, and you will not treat
me so. Either you sit with me and ask your questions as my husband or I will make an appointment with Dr. Thornsberry."

He sat and took Copper's hands in his. His knees touched
hers as he gently guided her through a maze of embarrassing
symptoms, none of which she had.

"I'm sorry," Simon said at last. "I hope you are not disappointed."

"I am a little," Copper answered, "but I still don't understand
why I'm not having a baby. Is it because we haven't been married
long enough?"

He stroked her face. "You are the dearest thing in the world
to me. I want so badly to protect your innocence, but in my need
I have denied your own."

Standing, Simon turned a key in the one bookcase he still
kept locked against her and retrieved a leather-bound tome.
"When you have finished reading chapter 9, come to me and we
will talk more."

Stroking the burgundy cover, she took in the book's inky
scent. Seemed to her even roses didn't smell as good as books.
Her shoulders squared, she sat up straight as the pages fell open

to chapter 9: "Nursing and Midwifery." Simon was trusting her with this knowledge, and she felt humbled. They'd come so far, she and Simon.

Lost in the book, she'd read well past the chapter he'd bidden her to when he came back in and lit the lamp. Outside the open windows, twilight turned to night. A persistent cricket struck up his band of brothers in a raucous serenade, but she paid no attention, caught up as she was in Simon's book. He didn't laugh again but answered her every question and told her stories of some of his patients, of deliveries gone well and deliveries gone bad.

Fascinated, she couldn't get enough. To think of God's design. Her soul stirred with a knowing sent straight from her heavenly Father. She must be a part of this somehow. She must. "Could I be a doctor? Might I bring babies into the world?"

Simon's honest face clouded, and he strode about the room as he studied the issue. She knew he didn't want to disappoint her. "I think not," he said finally. "It just wouldn't be proper."

Copper was determined not to beg, so she sat quietly, watching as he closed the windows and tidied up the room. If her desire was meant to be, God would work out the details. It gave her pleasure when she saw that Simon didn't lock the bookcase against her after he put the heavy book back in its proper place.

He studied the room as if he hoped for more chores to do before he knelt at her feet and took her hand in his. "Sometimes I fear it is my destiny to lose you in one way or another."

"What do you mean?" she asked, frightened by the thought. "Don't you know I love you? Don't you know I'd never leave you?"

He leaned forward and kissed her with a kiss so full of longing she thought she might swoon. "I want to keep you as I found you," he said. "I want to be enough for you."

"Simon . . . ," she started but stopped and giggled. "Remember the night you first saw me? My dress was torn. My feet were bare. I had blood on my face from sucking copperhead's venom from my little brother's wound, and I smelled from the clabber Mam splashed all over me when Willy came screaming from the woods. Are you sure that's what you want?"

He pulled her up, then took the chair and reached out for her. "Ah," he sighed as he began to tease the pins and combs from her hair, "that night."

It seemed his sigh transported them both back to Troublesome Creek, back to the fateful night they first met. They sat in silence for a moment, each remembering what had transpired the night he, a stranger, had stepped onto the porch of the house where Copper's little brother Daniel lay still as death. Simon would admit he was smitten, love at first sight. And Copper would concede that Simon mesmerized her, though it had taken some time for her to truly love him. If she searched her heart, she would have to admit there were still days when she wished she'd never left that little cabin on the creek.

Simon's arms tightened around her, claiming her, as if he knew her thoughts.

She turned in his arms and asked, "You don't want a baby, do you?"

"Someday, sweetheart. Someday. Let me keep you to myself for just a little longer."

CHAPTER 18

Searcy stood in the kitchen, waiting for the coffee to perk. The heat of the warming pot felt good to her hands, for the late September morning held a chill that warned of the winter to come. It was the day of Copper's dinner party for her friend Isaac, and Searcy was thinking of the ham soaking in a lard bucket beside the stove. She needed to pour the water off and replace it with fresh yet again so it wouldn't be too salty when she baked it. *Soon enough, right after breakfast,* she thought as she opened the back door. *Then them beaten biscuits needs starting.*

She discovered a pasteboard box as she reached for the broom to sweep the porch. What was a dirty old box doing on her clean porch? *Full of cats,* she figured, hearing the mewling sound coming from inside the box with its crisscrossed flaps.

Wonder if Mr. Doctor wants to pick one for the barn before Reuben gunnysacks the rest. Best take care of them before Miz Corbett sees. Else we be having cats living in the kitchen, sleeping on the beds, they long tails twining round Searcy's legs.

She swept around the box, clearing the fallen leaves that had collected on the porch overnight. "Don't know why folks can't take care of they own discards."

⚜

A shimmer of leaves fell outside the window as Copper sat at the table eating her breakfast. Pale gold, bright red, and jeweled orange offerings so beautiful she knew she had to have a bouquet for the dining room, a centerpiece for the supper she was having for Isaac.

"I'll be right back," she told Simon and Searcy. "I have to have some of those leaves."

"But your breakfast be getting cold," Searcy said, moving in front of the door. "What if Searcy gets them leaves for you?"

"Oh no, thank you, but I can't wait to get my hands on them. They are so beautiful." Copper pushed open the door and laughed as leaves flew into the room.

As she stepped out to greet the shower, she heard Searcy say apologetically, "Forgot all about that box of cats, Mr. Doctor. We in trouble now."

An unassuming box sat there like an unopened gift, a little sound of distress leaking out its seams. Leaves and bits of debris swirled around it from the wind. "Cats?" Copper heard Simon say as she knelt before the box. She wouldn't mind a kitten or two. Tugging, she popped open the top flaps. "Oh, my word, Simon! Come quick!"

"What is it?" he asked as he hurried out to the porch and leaned over her shoulder. "Run and get my bag!"

In a flash she was back to meet him at the kitchen door as he came inside with the bundle of bloody rags. "Get me the suction bulb and a towel," he said.

The baby was slick with what looked like lard, and it gurgled instead of crying. Simon turned it upside down and smacked its tiny fanny. He wrapped it in the towel and dried it with vigorous strokes. "My goodness. Where did you come from?"

Soon Simon had the baby dried and wrapped in clean towels. He laid the little thing in a dishpan and set it on the open oven door to keep warm. "Searcy, we'll need a wet nurse."

"Reuben will go," she answered. "Janie Mark will be glad to come. She got milk enough for hers and twenty more."

"Tell Janie she'll get paid," Simon replied.

"Probably won't take nothing. She been praising you for weeks, Mr. Doctor. Ever since you delivered her upside-down baby."

"Janie's baby was breech. A stubborn little thing," Simon told Copper. "Go on then, Searcy, and tell Reuben. We'll need Janie soon."

"Didn't I tell you we were going to have a baby?" Copper gushed as soon as she and Simon were alone in the room with a dishpan full of newborn.

"Copper," Simon said so sternly that she knew he meant business, "I will say this only once. This is not our baby nor will it be. We will care for it and see to a proper placement, but we will not keep it."

"But, Simon—"

"This is not open to discussion."

Peeling back the towels covering the tiny body, Copper asked, "But who will take him? Who will take a baby with just one arm?"

<hr/>

At noon, when Simon returned from the office, his kitchen was restored to order. He smelled country ham baking and saw Copper at the kitchen table rolling biscuit dough. A smidgen of flour dotted her cheek. Searcy basted the ham. Janie Mark sat in a rocker near the stove, and her face broke into a wide grin when he walked into the room.

"Good afternoon, ladies," he said. "Janie, it's good to see you."

Janie didn't say a word, just kept rocking and smiling, two babies—her own and the foundling—tucked in her ample arms.

"Copper?" He opened the dining room door, and she followed him from the steamy kitchen.

With one thumb, he wiped the flour from her face, and then he pulled her into the circle of his arms. "Are you all right? Finding the baby was quite a shock for you this morning."

"I'm not an egg. I won't break." She leaned back and looked up at him. "Once Janie got here, everything fell into place. But we've been as busy as bees."

He took his place at the table, where a full plate sat waiting for him. Copper poured cold water into his glass. "Aren't you eating?" he asked, picking up his fork.

"I've been nibbling all morning. Hester came over to help out and brought two lemon meringue pies Mallie made."

"Are you sure it's a good idea to have Hester and her mother here on Isaac's first night?" Simon asked. "He'll not be able to get a word in edgewise."

"I thought Hester could keep an eye on Alice. Someone will need to keep your sister from drowning."

Simon sat there, dumbfounded. "Drowning?"

"You know, like turkeys in the rain. They throw their heads back so far they'll drown in a downpour. Alice is kind of like that, don't you think? With her nose always so far in the air?"

Simon just shook his head as she rambled on.

"Anyway, I'm not hungry because I couldn't wait to try Mallie's pie. We each had a slice, even Searcy, though she fussed the whole time she ate. It was such fun—a kitchen full of women and babies. It reminded me of John Pelfrey's house when I was growing up." She sighed. "His mother was constantly cooking or baking, and it seemed like there was always a new baby."

"I wonder if he's forgiven me," Simon said softly.

Copper took a chair beside him, leaning forward on her elbows. "What do you mean?"

"John Pelfrey. I wonder if he's forgiven me for stealing you away."

Her thumb rubbed the back of his hand. "John could never bear a grudge. All he cared about was my happiness."

"Are you, sweetheart? Are you happy?"

"Most times I am," she replied. "And always when I'm with

you. . . . Now eat. I need to set this table for supper. I want everything to look nice for Isaac."

⁂

Dressed in a dark rose alpaca shirtwaist and skirt, Copper
stood fretting at the front door. She fiddled with the sheer
frill of lace that adorned her collar and turned to the mirrored
hall tree to check her hair for the umpteenth time. Smoothing
an errant curl, she tucked it into the French braid Hester had
plaited for her. They'd had such fun dressing each other's hair
that afternoon while Searcy finished cooking and Janie fed the
babies.

Copper was beside herself with anticipation. Isaac should be
here any moment. She hadn't seen any of her family since June.
Isaac was as close as kin. He knew all her folks; she knew all his.

"Oh my, here he is," she called toward Searcy in the kitchen.
"He's handing off his horse to Reuben. I can't wait any longer."

She flew out the door, screen slamming behind her, jumped
down the steps, and flung herself into Isaac's waiting arms.
"Isaac! Oh, Isaac! Stand still and let me smell the mountain air
that clings to you."

He grabbed her in a bear hug and swung her around and
around the yard. "Let me look at you, girl." He held her at arm's
length. "Pretty as a picture." He kissed her on each cheek, then
swept her around again.

Overcome, she began to cry. "I've missed you all so much."
She fished an embroidered hanky from her sleeve and patted her
cheeks dry. Words tumbled out with sobs. "Tell me everything.

Is Daddy really better like Mam says? How big are Daniel and Willy? And John Pelfrey—does anyone hear from John?"

"Hold up, Copper." Isaac put a finger to her lips and laughed his great booming laugh. "Let me dust this red clay dirt off my pants and scrape my boots so I don't dirty up your rugs. My, little girl—" he paused—"appears you've done right well for yourself."

She watched him take in the two-storied house with its many windows and large front porch, the soft blue wooden siding set off by pristine white gingerbread trim, and the formal front garden with its meandering brick path and splashing fountain. "Isaac, I'd trade this quick as a cat—" she made a sweeping motion toward the house and gardens—"for the roughest cabin up any holler on Troublesome."

"Enough talking on the sidewalk." He slapped dust from his gray felt hat. "Where's the well house? I need to wash up some, and I sure could do with a long, cool drink of water."

"You come on in the house. Searcy and I have your room all ready. There's sweet tea with ice waiting for you. Hurry and clean up, though. I want to visit with you before Hester and our guests get here for supper."

"Hester? What have you gone and done?" Isaac stroked his bushy black beard.

"Don't fret. We're just having a little party to celebrate your coming. Now let me show you to your room."

The day had turned warm, and Copper waited on the porch for Isaac.

Finally Isaac, freshly washed, dressed in a faded but clean black suit, his worn boots polished to a sheen, joined her in the swing. "Girl," he began, putting one arm around her and pulling her close, "I'm happy as a coon in a holler log to be here with you. It's amazing. One day you're setting on the porch on Troublesome Creek, and next thing you know you're in Lexington. Thank the good Lord for fast horses." He squeezed her shoulder. "Before we catch up on home folks, tell me about your own sweet self."

They spent a good hour exchanging information. Isaac heard of Copper's escapades. Copper learned that Daniel had fully recovered from the snake bite that nearly crippled him over a year ago. Willy was taller; Mam was the same; Daddy's cough was no worse. They had been packing for their move when Isaac left. Hard to picture Will Brown in the big city of Philadelphia. And, yes, Mrs. Pelfrey had received several postcards from John.

"You know, Copper," Isaac said, "you just about broke John's heart when you left. He will pine over you as long as he lives."

"Please don't say that." Copper dropped her head and wove her handkerchief through her fingers. "He was probably glad to see me go. John had plans of his own."

"Did he ever. Who would have thought he'd leave the mountains? Now he's off somewhere on a merchant ship, last I heard."

They sat for a moment in companionable silence, watching the activity up and down the street. A carriage pulled into the drive next door, and a small boy with a stick chased a hoop down the middle of the road while a fat-bellied puppy tried to keep up.

"It's busy here, isn't it?" Isaac's question answered itself.

"Too busy. Too noisy," Copper replied. "I miss the peace and quiet of the mountains."

"But you're happy, aren't you? You wouldn't really go back, would you?"

Swirling pieces of chipped ice around in her glass, Copper pondered that for a moment. Would she? Could she give up all the comforts of her city life? "In a heartbeat, Isaac. I'd fly back on eagles' wings if Simon would go with me."

"That puts me in mind of that verse from Exodus. You know the one I mean?"

"'I bare you on eagles' wings, and brought you unto myself,'" she quoted, then dared to tell her preacher friend of her deepest wish. "Sometimes I pray that God will bear me on swift wings back to Troublesome Creek." She raised her face to look into his brown eyes. "Is it selfish to be that way?"

"You can't help your feelings, little girl." Isaac took a long draw from his glass. "Man, that's good," he said and then turned his thoughtful gaze on her. "Just mind that old saw 'Be careful what you ask for lest you get it' . . . or something like that."

"That sounds like something Daddy would say. But tell me, did you come all this way just for a visit with Simon and me?"

Isaac stood and spread his arms. "I've been convicted, Copper. The Lord God has called me to gather souls for the harvest. I'm here to assemble supplies for my journey. I'm on my way to Africa." The swing creaked when he sat back down.

"Oh my. Weren't there enough heathens on Troublesome Creek? Why, the Jaspers alone must have ten heathens in their family, and what about Digger Pennington? Did you give up on him?"

Isaac shrugged. "I'm afraid there's not much hope for old Digger. He's convicted of his unconviction. But you'd be surprised by the Jaspers. Once I got Papa Carl under the water, near every one of them has been baptized."

Copper's face broke into a grin. "I sure would have liked to see that. There must have been a lot of hallelujahs the day Carl Jasper was saved."

"It was a sight. You know, Carl must weigh three hundred pounds. His belly's as big as a nail keg, his shoulders near broad as a corncrib door. I had to take him to the river to find a pool deep enough, and when he went under, I did too! I thought the Lord was calling me home for sure." Isaac fished a red bandanna from his pocket and mopped his face. "Both of us come up gasping and praising God." He paused and chuckled. "Believe it or not, Carl's been called to preach. He's taking over the pulpit at Troublesome Creek."

"Well, I never." Copper shook her head at the thought. The errant curl she'd so carefully tucked away popped back out. "I can see why God has called you to the harvest field. But why Africa? You could do a world of good right here in Lexington, where the pews are filled with lukewarm Christians."

"The people here have heard the Word. Africa is ripe with possibility. Praise the Lord." He raised his hand to the sky. "I want to do my Father's bidding."

Copper ran her hands up and down her arms. "You're giving me goose bumps. Simon and I want to help you with your mission. What can we do?"

"Actually, Simon talked with me in June when you were wed. He offered to support me when I went to the missionary field. You married a man of God."

"God blessed me. Look, here he comes now with Hester. You'll have time to get acquainted before everyone else arrives. You need to see our new baby, too."

The blood drained from Isaac's face.

"No. No. Not that," Copper stammered. "A foundling was left on our doorstep. He needs your prayers."

CHAPTER 19

Copper took out a sheet of lavender-scented stationery that bore her title, Mrs. Simon Corbett, embossed across the top and began to write.

> *Dear Mam,*
> *It is cold and snowing here this late November day. Simon is away, teaching a seminar in Cincinnati, so we will not open the office today. Searcy has lit a fire in the parlor, and I sit here with a cup of tea and my pen and think of you.*
> *You will be as shocked as I to learn of the happenings here in Lexington over the last couple of months. Isaac and Hester are to wed! Simon and I just shake our heads to think of what one little dinner party has wrought. Hester is wonderfully happy and thanks me daily.*

We have been to the dressmaker's a number of times. Mam, Hester's wedding gown is lovely. It is made of white satin with lace trim. The sleeves are capped with a pinaforelike lace flounce, and the hem is finished with ermine. A coronet of crystal-beaded flowers will secure her floor-length veil. She will carry a bouquet of white roses and orange blossoms. Simon is to give her away (Hester's father died in the war), and I shall be her attendant. I will wear an orchid silk ensemble with a dear little hat of orchid-colored violets and feathers. It ties with ribbon under my chin.

We have had no easy time convincing Isaac that he must allow Simon to have his tailor dress him. He laughed at the white tie and tails and thus far has refused to trim his beard, but, as you well know, we women will have our way. I suspect he will be well groomed come the wedding day. The bride and groom will leave soon after the wedding and board a ship bound for Africa.

I shall miss Hester—we have become fast friends—but I am so happy she has found someone dear to her heart. Hester was afraid she would wither on the vine, never finding a husband.

You asked about the foundling baby when last you wrote. We never found his mother, but I am relieved to answer that he is doing well. I took him to meet Mrs. Archesson—Birdie. Just as I thought, she took to him like a brown thrush to corn. They are a comfort to each other, and, Mam, Tommy Turner is helping with the baby. To keep from being lonely, Birdie takes in boarders, and Tommy is one of several living there. He will set a good example for Bobby. Birdie named the baby for her own dead son.

Janie (remember me telling you about the wet nurse, Janie Mark?), along with her children, now lives in the little stone

house behind Birdie's and helps with Bobby and the lodgers.
Isn't it wonderful, Mam, how God brings just the right people
together?

Please reply soon and tell me of yourself and Daddy, Willy
and Daniel. Does it snow much there in Pennsylvania? I pine for
all of you.

Sealing the envelope with mucilage, Copper hurried outside, where the wind whipped the snow into white showers, to hand her letter to the postman. She wished the office were open even in Simon's absence, but he insisted she stay in when the weather was inclement.

On Troublesome Creek, she would have spent a day like today shoveling a path to the stable in order to milk the cow and care for the other animals. She wondered if she would ever adjust to forced idleness.

Back in the house, she shook snow from her shawl and hung it by the kitchen stove to dry. "Move, Paw-paw," she said, giving the hound a gentle shove with her boot. He gave up his spot in front of the stove and curled up on his bed in the corner.

"That old dog sure sucks up heat," Searcy said.

Copper smiled. It had taken some persuasion to get Searcy to accept an animal in the house. But now, she noticed, Searcy kept the choicest table scraps for him and never made him move when she swept the floor. Simon didn't forbid it as long as Paw-paw stayed in the kitchen. Copper guessed Simon had learned when to give up.

"This would be a good day to clean," Copper said. "I can't

laze around a minute longer. What about the pantry? I've been meaning to sort through the canned goods for ages."

"Searcy ain't so sure about spring cleaning in November. Seems like you be mixing ever'thing up. What be next? Planting onion sets?"

"Let's," Copper teased as they headed to the pantry. "We'll get Reuben to plow the garden."

The pantry was a long, narrow room. Open shelves above marble countertops lined the left wall. A row of small windows near the ceiling let in what light was available on such a gloomy morning. Crocks of sauerkraut and bread-and-butter pickles lined the back of the counter, while the shelves held green beans, tomatoes, corn, blackberries, peaches, apples, and other foodstuffs. A cured ham, ready for baking, hung from an exposed pipe. Flour, sugar, cornmeal, and oats were stored in pull-out tin bins in the cabinets below the marble counters. Bags of dried beans leaned against the wall. Potatoes, onions, and apples, layered in straw, sat in boxes on the floor.

An old pie safe stood against the far wall and held seldom-used cooking utensils. On the right, cabinets with windowed doors held all manner of plates, bowls, cups, and saucers. Deep drawers protected linens from dust. Searcy kept her flatirons, as well as the wooden ironing board, behind the pantry door.

"Doesn't this make you feel blessed?" Copper asked.

"Blessed with hot work and a sore back," Searcy replied, wiping the jar lids free of dust as Copper handed each one to her. "But Searcy surely do like looking at all them jars lined up in rows like that. Looks like summertime."

"Let's put some of these in that bushel basket," Copper said, a jar of beans and one of tomatoes in her arms. "I want to check on Andy's mother and the girls as soon as this snow lets up. Annalise is so fragile; I'm afraid she'll forget to get groceries in for the children."

"Fragile!" Searcy huffed, her hands on her hips. "Lazy be more likely. Laying around like a plucked chicken, too ornery to fix any victuals for her young'uns."

"The Bible says, 'It is more blessed to give than to receive.'"

"Ain't be talking about no receiving. Be talking about working. God don't give rewards to them that don't."

"There's truth in that for sure. But we have plenty here—" Copper opened her arms to the full pantry and tapped a trapdoor with her foot—"and more below in the cellar. Besides, if I take a basket, it will give me an excuse to visit. You don't really mind, do you?"

"Don't be casting pearls before swine, the Good Book say."

⚬⚬⚬⚬

Searcy fussed, but she filled a poke with potatoes and onions. Before Miz Corbett came, Searcy had slipped food to Andy nearly every week to keep the little Tollivers fed. Miz Alice would have pitched a fit if Searcy had been caught.

"You might as well take some of them fried-apple pies when you go. That Andy, he loves Searcy's fried-apple pies. . . . And take a round of corn bread."

It surely was right to feed those raggedy children. From the things Miz Corbett had told her, Searcy had her own opinion of

Annalise Tolliver. No other woman she knew stayed in bed while her hungry little children were left to fend for themselves, that boy Andy working like a man.

But there was no use saying anything ugly. Miz Corbett never saw bad in anyone save maybe Miz Alice. And she couldn't rightly help that. A body would have to have her eyes poked out to be around Miz Alice and not see something bad. Miz Corbett was like sunshine . . . chasing shadows from dark corners.

⚜

Jouncing along on the seat beside Reuben, Copper was in her element. It made her feet itch to spend too much time indoors. She couldn't get enough of the cold, crisp air. And snow . . . snow blanketed yards and roads, decorated trees like coconut icing, and muffled the sound of the horse's hooves and the creak of the buggy.

They had just got started when Copper spied trouble up ahead. Clip-clopping down the street came Alice's horse pulling Alice's fancy carriage driven by Alice's groom, and oh no, Alice's stern face poked out the open window before one gloved hand shot forth, palm out.

Without a word, Reuben pulled their buggy to the side of the road and sat, passively waiting.

Alice's liveried chauffeur hopped down, procured a broom, and proceeded to sweep a path from carriage to buggy before he opened the door and escorted his mistress across the slippery road.

Alice looked up at Copper. "One does not sit beside one's driver, Laura Grace," she chastised in a voice as cold as the wintry day. With a toss of her head she turned her wrath on Reuben. "I would have thought that you had more sense than to seat her this way."

"Yes'm," Reuben said, staring straight ahead.

"I will be reporting this to Dr. Corbett."

"Yes'm," Reuben repeated.

Copper allowed Alice's groom to assist her down and into the buggy, where she perched on the edge of the seat. Leaning out the door, Copper choked out, "I'm sorry, Alice. I just wanted to enjoy the fresh air and feel the snow on my face. It makes me think of home."

"*This* is your home, Laura Grace. You are a doctor's wife and a Corbett. Please conduct yourself accordingly."

Copper sat, mortified, and watched as the ice queen slid across the street. Unable to bring herself to answer Alice's dismissive wave, she hung her head. Anger percolated through her heart like strong black coffee. Try as she might, despite her prayers, she couldn't make herself like Simon's sister.

With a jerk the buggy moved forward. Shoving her hands deep inside her Persian lamb muff, Copper settled back. The basketful of canned goods on the seat bounced every time they hit a bump. Through the window she noticed the snow was not as sparkly as when she'd first come out, and the air she drew into her lungs was damp and oppressive. *Alice is only trying to teach me city ways,* she thought, contrite. *She's only trying to help. I've got to make my peace with her somehow.*

Then a mean little vision stole into her mind. A snowball flung with lethal accuracy slammed against a regal head. Copper laughed.

The small house on James Street was stifling. Reuben set the bucket of coal Copper had brought beside another scuttle filled to its brim before he returned to the buggy.

Following Marydell, Copper carried the basket to the kitchen. Dodie sat in her rickety high chair, gnawing on a drumstick. When she saw Copper, she waved the meaty bone in the air and kicked her bare feet. The remains of a meal sat congealing on the kitchen table.

"Looks like you have plenty to eat, Marydell," Copper said.

"Ma's friend brought lots of things." Marydell twisted a strand of hair around her finger. "Dodie got a new dress, and Ma got a new doll." Grabbing Copper's hand, she pulled her toward the front room. "See? Ma put it in the cabinet so's me and Dodie won't get her dirty. Do you want me to take her out?"

"No, thank you, Marydell. Your mother will show it to me if she wants to. Is she sleeping?"

"Yeah. She said for me to keep Dodie quiet, but she wouldn't mind if I showed you the doll. She likes you, Miz Corbett."

Copper drew a handkerchief from her pocket. "Take this and wipe Dodie's face and hands, please, while I see about your mother."

Copper drew back the beaded curtain separating the bedroom from the kitchen. "Annalise? I've brought some things for the children."

One hand emerged from the mound of covers on the bed and pushed golden hair from startling blue eyes. "Copper—" she slurred the slightest bit—"you're just too good, but we don't need anything. You shouldn't bother." Annalise made a wan attempt to sit up before falling back against velvet-covered pillows. An empty bottle clattered to the floor and rolled beneath the bed. "Oh my, what time is it? I was up all night with Dodie. She had another of her earaches." Annalise smiled, revealing perfect teeth.

Marydell walked in with the squirming Dodie and dumped her on her mother's bed. "She's been a good baby today, Ma. And she slept straight through last night." Marydell bent over and blew a wet kiss on the baby's skinny belly.

Annalise seemed to take no notice that Copper had caught her in a lie.

Dodie made a game of sliding off the far side of the bed, causing Marydell to run around to catch her. Dodie crowed with delight, then climbed into her mother's arms and began to suck her thumb.

"Ma, can I show Miz Corbett the new doll? I'll be very careful."

"Don't whine, Marydell," Annalise answered, her eyes drooping. "Don't you be getting her dirty."

"I won't." Marydell's eyes shone with excitement. "Come on, Miz Corbett. This one's ever so pretty. She kinda looks like you." Wiping her hands on her skirt, the little girl opened the door of the curio cabinet and took a doll from the middle shelf.

"My, she is lovely," Copper said. "Why, I've never seen such a beautiful dress."

The doll was wearing a replica of a woman's formal calling suit made of dark green taffeta with a short, fitted jacket. Her stand-up collar, jabot, and wrist flounces were of lace. Marydell pulled up the skirt, revealing silk underclothes, hose, and black patent leather pumps. Fastened to her wig was a tiny hat trimmed with feathers, and she carried a rose-colored parasol that could be opened and closed.

"See why she looks like you?" Marydell reached out and reverently stroked the doll's head. "See her pretty red hair? Look, we can take her hat off and her hair will come loose and you can comb it. If I could just find a comb . . . Ma won't let me use hers."

Copper put the doll back in the cabinet and closed the door. "Why, Marydell, the doll on the top shelf has the same color hair as yours. Pretty as sunshine. I think I like her the very best."

Marydell leaned against Copper. "When I grow up, I'm gonna be just like you. I'm gonna have me a fine horse and buggy, and I'm gonna have a hired man to drive me and Dodie around."

Copper cupped Marydell's face. "I hope when you are a young lady, you will be allowed to drive the buggy for yourself."

A knocking at the back door caught their attention.

"Who could that be?" Marydell ran ahead of Copper and cracked the door.

A child somewhat older than Marydell stood shivering on the back stoop.

"It's Lizzie." Marydell opened the door wide.

The child ignored Copper's urging to come inside. Instead she clutched at Copper's dress. "Please, ma'am, come with me. Mrs. Reardon saw your buggy, and she said come fetch you. Mama's bleeding real bad, and the baby won't come. She said you'd know what to do."

"But I'm just the doctor's wife," Copper stammered, alarm coursing through her. "I can't deliver a baby. You'll have to get someone else."

"There ain't time for nobody else, lady. You got to help my mama." Lizzie nearly dragged Copper off the stoop.

"Just a minute . . . let me think. Marydell, go out front and tell Reuben to fetch Dr. Thornsberry. Tell him it's an emergency and to come right away. Tell him to come to . . . where do you live?"

"Just there." Lizzie pointed to a two-story house on the street behind. "We live in the back there."

"All right," Copper replied. "I'll see what I can do. Marydell, you show Reuben where I will be."

The apartment was just two cramped rooms. A curtain fashioned from a brown brocade dress that had seen better days covered the one window in the bedroom. The bodice hung, drooping, over the long skirt. Piles of dirty laundry occupied each corner, and on a bed kitty-corner to the room, a youngish woman looped her hands through knotted bedsheets that had been secured to the bedposts.

"Thank goodness, you've come to answer my prayer," the woman called to Copper. "I can't take this much longer."

Another woman, with a body as round as a bushel basket, turned and introduced herself to Copper. "I'm Mrs. Reardon, Sally's landlady. I live upstairs." The sweet-faced woman shook her head. "I tried to help Sally, but something is bad wrong. I seen the doctor's buggy pull up to the Tollivers' and seen you go in. Folks say you know about medicine."

"Oh, it's starting again. Please do something," Sally screamed. "Somebody do something."

"I've got the water boiling in the kitchen there," Mrs. Reardon said.

The kitchen was not in any better shape than the bed-sitting-room, but there was indeed a kettle of water roiling away on top of a stove. A white kitchen table swayed under a stack of dirty dishes, and a pot of oatmeal, thick as glue, rested on the seat of a straight-backed chair. Two little boys stood barefoot by the chair. They seemed not to notice either Copper or the frigid air that seeped in around the window and whistled through a crack in the wall, so intent were they with their spoons and the oatmeal.

Taking a deep breath, Copper prayed, *Heavenly Father, if I'm the answer to this woman's prayer, she's in a heap of trouble. I know I said I wanted to learn about birthing babies, but don't You reckon this is a bad idea? Help that woman, Lord, and please send Dr. Thornsberry quick.*

Copper's fervent prayer was interrupted by an unearthly yell. She hurried back to Sally, who writhed in pain. All Copper saw was red. Red seeping across the bed and dripping to the floor, each drop so heavy Copper could hear it plop. A smell like rusted iron filled the room. Sally's very life was leaking out. Copper saw stars and felt light-headed. She wished she had some smelling salts.

Sally grunted and began to drum her heels on the bed. "Help me, Joe! Help me!"

"Joe's her husband," Mrs. Reardon explained. "He lit out like the hound dog he is as soon as I got here."

Lizzie started crying, and the little boys rushed into the room.

Copper straightened her spine and took charge. "Children, your mother's going to be just fine. Mrs. Reardon, please take them upstairs and bring me back some clean linens."

In the kitchen, Copper dipped water from the steaming kettle into a granite pan. On the windowsill over the sink, she spied a bar of lye soap on a cracked saucer, and, incongruously, a potted red geranium. The flower made her want to cry for Sally. Instead she rolled up her sleeves and scrubbed her hands and arms until they stung.

Back at the bedside, she touched Sally's shoulder. "Is it all right if I examine you now?"

Groaning, Sally complied.

Expecting to see the top of a baby's head, as she'd seen in Simon's book on obstetrics, Copper was shocked to find a tiny foot thrusting its way into the world instead. "I think the head is supposed to come out first."

"I don't care what comes first!" Sally pounded her fists against the bed. "Just get it out of me before I split right in two. Oh, I got to push."

With a great heaving and straining, Sally grabbed her knees and bore down until Copper could see one little leg to the knee.

"Okay, I think we're getting somewhere."

Sally fell back against the bed. The little leg disappeared before Copper's startled eyes. Copper fought a swell of panic; then Sally pushed mightily, and Copper could see the leg again.

Lord, help us. Show me what to do, Copper pleaded. She

touched the little foot, and perfect toes flared against her palm. Timidly she ran one finger up the baby's leg until she could feel the knee but not the lower leg on the other limb. *It's going to be like the foundling baby. It's missing some of its parts.* Just then her touch made out the other leg, bent upward on itself. Carefully, ever so gently, she continued her probing up the baby's backbone until she could feel the shoulders. *Lord, help us!* she prayed again, for the baby's head seemed caught in a tight vise of its mother's making.

Sally screamed like a banshee and pushed with all her strength.

"Wait, Sally! Take easy breaths and don't push again until I tell you." The vise relaxed, and gingerly Copper pressed against the back of the little skull and tilted the head forward. "Push now. Push! Push! Push!"

The slick baby girl slipped into Copper's waiting hands.

Mrs. Reardon, a stack of linens in her arms, looked over Copper's shoulder. "You got to cut the navel string with them scissors boiling in the pot." She fished in her pocket and handed Copper two pieces of string. "You tie it off, and I'll fetch them." Soon she was back, leaning over Copper again. "You tied it in two places. That's good. Now just cut between the ties. Careful, it'll splash blood on you."

Just as Copper began to cut her way through the thick, jelly-filled cord, she heard a welcome voice. Dr. Thornsberry had come. Copper nearly cried with relief to see the jolly, white-bearded doctor. She sat back on her heels, too shaky to stand.

"Let's see what we have here," the good doctor said. His

voice always had a laugh about it. He picked up the baby and gave her a quick once-over, then looked at Copper over the rim of his half-moon glasses. "Mrs. Corbett, you've done a wonderful job."

Copper took in the bloody mess of the room, the exhausted mother, and her own ruined dress. Things didn't seem too wonderful to her. "I just did what I could. Simon is away, you see."

"Yes, Cincinnati, isn't it?"

Copper nodded and placed both hands on the bed to steady herself as she rose. "I'm so glad to see you, Dr. Thornsberry," she said as if they were meeting at a dinner party.

Copper watched the doctor carefully after he took over the mother's care. It seemed the afterbirth was delivered with little effort, and Sally's bleeding slowed to a trickle. The doctor soon had order restored, and Copper stepped into the kitchen with him. With a courteous gesture he indicated for Copper to use the washbasin first. Mrs. Reardon had thoughtfully placed clean towels for their use.

She scrubbed and scrubbed, then emptied the waste into a slop bucket and fixed fresh hot water for Dr. Thornsberry.

He leaned his considerable girth against the sink as he dried his hands carefully, one finger at a time. "You did yourself proud, my dear. You must have delivered dozens of babies up there in the mountains to become such an expert."

He must be teasing, Copper thought. He was a big bear of a man, and she had always found him easy to be around. "Dr. Thornsberry, my mam would hardly let me out of the yard much less go about delivering babies. I nearly died of fright in there."

"You really don't know what you've done?"

"Poor Sally did all the work. I just prayed."

He slipped his arm around her and gave her shoulder a squeeze. "The infant would have more than likely died without your assistance, Mrs. Corbett. A foot presentation is fraught with danger."

"I knew it!" Copper exclaimed. "I knew the head should be first."

Dr. Thornsberry laughed so hard his belly shook. "How did you know what to do?"

"I did what seemed natural. I was scared, but it seemed like God was by my side."

"I'd say the good Lord has blessed you with a rare talent. Now let's go check on your patient."

Remarkably, Mrs. Reardon had already stripped the bed, and Sally was wearing a clean gown.

Dr. Thornsberry took the baby from her mother's arms and laid her on the foot of the bed. "See, the flattened head and these petechiae bear witness to her distress."

"Petechiae?"

"These purple hemorrhagic spots indicate trauma, but she'll recover nicely."

"They look like pinpricks," Copper mused. "Will her head always be like this?"

"She'll shape up nicely in a few days. Babies are remarkably resilient." Rewrapping the infant, Dr. Thornsberry handed her back to her mother, then turned to Copper. "Now home with you. Mrs. Reardon and I will finish up here."

CHAPTER 20

Dear Mam, Copper penned while the wind moaned down the chimney and swirled sparks from the fire onto the carpet. "Forevermore!" She jumped up, spilling ink across the page, and smacked a live ember with her carpet slipper. "Simon, won't this dreadful weather ever let up?"

"Hmm?" He barely looked up from the open book on his lap. "What's that, dearest?"

"Oh, never mind." She parted the heavy drapes Searcy had pulled against drafts. "I'm sick of being cooped up."

"Uh-huh," he said, paying her no mind. Copper knew he could be happy for days with nothing more than a stack of books for entertainment.

Leaning against the window frame, she peered out at the

piles of drifted snow. Her mind wandered. This would be a
perfect day for checking trotlines. Back home, John Pelfrey had
sometimes let her tag along when he went to check his traps.
Pest, he always called her. She smiled to think of the good times
they'd had growing up together, exploring and hunting. John
was her best friend. Well, he used to be until love got in the way.
Until John decided he wanted more than friendship.

Shivering, she drew her shawl around her shoulders and
pressed her forehead against the cold windowpane. That was
a terrible time, she remembered. A time of loss and pain when
Simon had come into her life and turned it upside down. A time
when she'd hurt John. Now here she was with her face pressed
against the window, wishing for escape, and John was out there
somewhere at sea. She wondered if he ever thought of her.

The clock ticked. . . . Simon thumbed a page. . . .

Copper turned from the window. She settled herself with
her lap tray, her pen and ink, her lavender stationery and started
writing again.

Dear Mam,

*You would be proud to know how much I am learning. Simon
allows me access to his library, and I am studying the parts of the
body.*

*Did you know the heart is a pump? It has four rooms called
chambers that pulse and push blood here and there. The blood
it pushes has many parts called cells. They're like little buggies
carrying around the air we breathe, oxygenating everything, even
our fingers and toes.*

Alice is mad at me again. I think she does not get enough oxygen. Her little buggies are frozen like her heart. She says I am not a proper wife. She said I was shirking my duties when she found me researching instead of finishing the needlepoint cushions for the dining room chairs. I'm afraid you might agree with her.

You must understand, Mam. I felt more alive and more in tune to God's purpose for my life when I was helping Sally deliver her little flat-headed baby than I ever have before. I just can't live out my days doing nothing more than keeping house and taking tea with the ladies of the missionary society. Assisting Simon on the days the office is open helps, but it is not enough. I can't tell Simon. He thinks I don't love him unless my every moment is light and happy. There must be something wrong with me. Why can't I be like other women? Why can't I be satisfied?

Crumpling the paper, Copper tossed it into the fireplace. A little tongue of flame licked out, erasing her words. Mam would not approve. Instead she wrote of Hester's wedding, of the beautiful bride and the handsome, clean-shaven groom.

Would you believe that Isaac shaved his beard! That was such a surprise. We've all been in a dither helping them get ready to leave. They will board a train as soon as the weather clears. Then it's off to the mission field.

Hester and I have been culling her things. They can take only what they can transport easily on their own. Hester had four trunks of clothes alone, and it was with many tears that she put aside her beautiful things in order to pack cooking utensils, soap

*powders, and first-aid supplies as well as sturdy shirtwaists and
heavy boots. We fashioned a muslin underskirt with many pockets
and filled them with toilet water, face soap, hair ribbons, and the
like. She looked lumpy when she tried it on under her traveling
frock, but as she said, at least she will have the necessities.*

*What will happen when she uses up all her necessities? I am
afraid love has clouded her reason, as it does for all women, I
suppose. I promised to mail packages, but I wonder if they have a
post office where Isaac is taking her. We must keep them covered
with prayer.*

Copper laid her pen aside. Finally a letter she could send.
The smell of the woodsmoke comforted her.

A little mucilage and a two-cent stamp bearing George
Washington's likeness and it was ready for the post. The mailman would retrieve it when he brought the afternoon's mail. So
convenient. So unlike home, where waiting for the mail meant
listening for Mr. Bramble and his mule, Sweetie. Mr. Bramble
brought the mail once a week if Sweetie had a mind to.

Copper stepped out onto the only patch of porch not covered by snow. The street was quiet, with houses hunched and
brooding under the overcast sky, as if it, too, were weary of the
long winter.

Simon filled the space behind her. His hands rested on her
shoulders. "Why are you out here in this weather? Why are you
standing here alone?"

"I was remembering the mailman from home, Mr. Bramble,
and his mule, Sweetie," Copper replied. "I wonder how they are."

"I wish you would get over this melancholy. It's not good for you to think so much of the past."

She leaned against him, and he wrapped his sweater around her. A fierce wind howled round the corner of the house, showering them with snow and billowing up her skirts. "Do you want to hear a story?" she asked. "A funny story about Mr. Bramble and Sweetie?"

He drew her back inside. "Searcy made tea. Come sit by the fire and tell me your story."

They opened all the curtains, turned out the gas lamps, and pulled the settee close to the fire. Safe and warm, snuggled up under Simon's arm, Copper began her story, a tale she had heard her daddy tell many times.

"Mr. Bramble was a proud man, as quiet men often are. It was his considerable duty to carry the post to all the families scattered up and down the hollers of Troublesome Creek. Most days his mule, Sweetie, was happy to oblige and carried her saddlebags willingly. But sometimes, as mules are wont to do, Sweetie took a contrary turn and forced Mr. Bramble to follow her home, the mail half delivered.

"Besides having the most stubborn mule in the county, Mr. Bramble had the unfortunate fate to be wed to a self-willed woman with eight obstinate daughters. Some thought Mr. Bramble was beat down by circumstance, but he would tell you that knowing women made him an expert on mule behavior. He didn't have a lot to brag on, but he was proud of the way he had with Sweetie.

"One hot summer's day, Mr. Bramble's wife and her eight

cantankerous daughters set their minds upon a fancy mahogany bedstead and wardrobe they found at Mrs. Oriander Wilson's moving sale. Mr. Bramble said nary a word; he just went to fetch Sweetie and a wagon.

"Several men attending the sale helped him wrestle the bedstead and wardrobe onto the bed of the wagon. Then Mr. Bramble's self-willed wife spied a washstand and a set of dishes that soon found themselves nestled in among the furniture. Mr. Bramble wiped his face on his red bandanna, moved his ever-present pipe from one side of his mouth to the other, and proceeded to lead Sweetie toward home.

"Well, as stubborn mules will sometimes do for no discernible reason, Sweetie took offense. After only a turn and a half of the wagon's wheels, Sweetie stopped, standing as rigid as a fence post in her tracks. Poor Mr. Bramble. If the men hadn't been watching, if his wife and her eight daughters hadn't been standing with their hands on their hips, if he hadn't had a queen's ransom on the bed of his wagon, he would have let Sweetie have her way and come back for the wagon another day.

"To his considerable credit, Mr. Bramble tried every trick anyone could think of: covering Sweetie's eyes with cloth, a flick of a whip to her flanks, pushing on her rump . . . nothing worked. Sweetie stood there, her long face complacent, occasionally flipping a fly off her back with her tail.

"Then Mr. Bramble tried the sure cure for Sweetie's stubbornness. Fishing a green apple from his overalls pocket, he held it in front of her wrinkling nose. The mule leaned forward, her lips drawn back, her big yellow teeth open for a bite. The crowd held

its collective breath as Mr. Bramble moved just out of reach. But Sweetie held her ground.

"Mr. Bramble flung the apple aside. His manhood was at stake. For once, Sweetie had to do his bidding. He gathered a few pieces of wood and stacked them under Sweetie's ponderous belly. Knocking the ash from his pipe onto the kindling, Mr. Bramble looked up from under the mule, his mouth stretched in a wide possum grin.

"'You'll move or else,' he said and stood back as a spark took hold and licks of flame curled upward. 'Now we'll see just who is boss,' Mr. Bramble's grin seemed to say as Sweetie strained forward. The wagon creaked as the wheels went round and round and . . . stopped . . . the wagonload of furniture positioned just so over the fire.

"Mr. Bramble flung his hat to the ground, but his face took on a look of resignation. He unhitched the mule and helped the men, with a great heaving and groaning, move the heavy wagon past the fire. Sweetie rolled her dark brown eyes and snorted until Mr. Bramble came and, with a great sigh, took the bit from her mouth. Ever so delicately, the stubborn mule nibbled the green apple treat he held in his hand.

"'Just goes to show, fellows,' Mr. Bramble told his laughing friends. "'Ain't no man alive can make a mule or a woman do what she don't want to do . . . for she will always make you pay.'"

"Isn't that the truth," Simon teased between bursts of laughter.

Tickled, Copper flung a pillow at his head. He tossed it back and picked up another. She whooped and ran toward the door. A nice fat snowball would answer his assault.

She drew up short as the doorbell trilled. The day had turned to night, and the wind still raged outside. Who would be out in such weather?

Having caught up with her, Simon opened the door.

A man swept off his hat. "Beg your pardon for coming to the front, but the snow is deep, and Mr. Collins say for me to hurry fast."

"Come in, Clarence," Simon invited. "Come in out of the cold."

"Nah, sir, but thank ye. Just came to tell you Mr. Collins say come soon as you can. He say it's Mrs. Collins's time." Snow caught on the man's thick black hair and in his beard. "You want I should wait with my buggy, Dr. Corbett?"

"Yes, thank you. We shan't be long."

"We?" Copper asked as Simon closed the door. "Am I to go along then?"

"You can't learn about birthing babies sitting here alone, little wife."

"Oh, Simon." Throwing her arms around him, she kissed him soundly. "I promise you won't be sorry."

"The only sorrow I have right now," he said as he helped her into her Persian wool coat, then bent to receive the muffler she wound around his neck, "is that I won't be here to claim more of those kisses."

CHAPTER 21

The house in which Nora Collins labored was imposing even in the stark light of the cold winter evening. Huge oaks lined the macadam driveway and clung with stick fingers to the dead leaves of autumn that rustled in the whining wind.

Copper drew her coat tight and leaned into Simon as the carriage followed the horseshoe-shaped driveway. He pointed out gargoyles, illuminated by gas lamps, perched atop the roofline before they parked under an ornate porte cochere.

"They're so ugly," she said. "They make me think of demons. Why would anyone want them on their house?"

"The Collins family is like the Upchurches . . . old money," Simon replied, as if that explained the sinister statues. "Phillip Collins's grandfather Dexter Collins clerked in a law office, taught himself what he needed to know, and became an important man in political circles. He invested every dime he ever made in newspapers and left it all to Phillip's father and thus to Phillip himself."

"Don't you like Phillip Collins?" Copper asked as they climbed the stairs leading to the front door.

"I don't know him well enough for like or dislike. Let's just say I wouldn't spend the evening in his presence were it not for Nora."

A tall, thin man threw open the double doors. An overcoat was draped across his shoulders. He paused to shake Simon's hand. "Jolly good to see you, old bean," he said, then tipped his hat to Copper. "Beastly evening. Say what? Sorry I can't stay, but duty calls, you know." With that he danced down the walk, words flying back over his shoulder. "Nora couldn't be in better hands . . . her mother here as well . . . dining with Benton . . . home late . . ." He fairly flung himself into the carriage Simon and Copper had just vacated. "I'll send Clarence back here," he called before his groom closed the door, "in case you need him."

"Don't put yourself out," Simon said barely under his breath as he escorted Copper through the door. "And that, my dear, was Phillip Collins."

"Why does he talk so funny?" Copper shook the snow from her wrap before handing it to the waiting butler.

"He and Benton attended school together in Europe," Simon answered when the butler disappeared into the cloakroom. "He glommed on to the language, thinks it makes him aristocratic. Thankfully Benton was not so affected."

Following the butler up a curving marble staircase, they

paused before a heavy closed door. Two sharp raps from the butler's gloved hand and the door cracked open.

"It's the doctor," a young maid said over her shoulder.

"Oh, thank goodness," an older woman replied. "Not a moment too soon. Bring him in, Girt."

"Now, sweetheart," Simon comforted, his hand at the small of Copper's back, "don't be alarmed at what you see tonight. This should be an easy delivery, physically anyway. Nora has had the best of care, and she is well built for childbirth."

Nora Collins lay on a four-poster, ensconced by layers of red toile curtains, propped up against piles of lace-covered pillows. "Phillip," she said in the tiniest squeaky voice. "Phillip, I need you. I suffer so."

"Oh, Dr. Corbett!" the elderly lady exclaimed. "I'm so relieved to see you. Nora is in great distress."

Simon bowed. "Good evening, ladies," he said and made introductions all around. "Let's see how our mother is progressing." He strode to a waiting washbasin and began to scrub.

Copper followed suit, nervousness churning her stomach.

Simon rested one hand on top of the bedclothes and took out his pocket watch. "Just here." He motioned for Copper to place her palm below his.

Concentrating so hard she was nearly cross-eyed, she watched the second hand tick.

"You will feel a tightening and then a release. That is one contraction. Time it from beginning to end and the space between each one. That's one way to predict how far along she is."

Nora's forehead was slick with perspiration. She squinted with each tightening of her belly.

Simon snapped his watch shut. "Nora, do you remember what we discussed on my last visit? I told you about an internal exam, and now it is time. Mrs. Corbett will be assisting me, and your mother should stay, of course."

"Mama." Nora clutched at her mother.

"Nora, you must let the good doctor take care of you. Here, I shall hold your hand." Nora's mother settled herself in an armless chair at the bedside, her back to Simon and Copper.

Girt tented the blankets, dissecting the bed. Everything was clean and in order, so different from Sally's delivery. Copper stood at the lower side of the bed and, under Simon's instruction, blindly examined her patient. At least with Sally she could see what she was doing.

"A fingertip," she answered Simon's unspoken question. "She's only a fingertip dilated."

"As I thought," Simon replied. "We were summoned much too soon."

The maid brushed Nora's fine brown hair away from her face as Simon continued, "Nora, you are in early labor. I suggest you try to sleep and you also, Mrs. Bellwether."

Mrs. Bellwether pried Nora's fingers loose, then slowly stood. "I shall have Girt make my bed in the adjoining nursery, Dr. Corbett. You must promise to call me when she is imminent."

"Mama," Nora pleaded, "I cannot bear this pain alone."

Leaning heavily on her ivory-handled cane, Mrs. Bellwether paused in her slow trek across the room. She turned back toward the bed. "Darling daughter." One liver-spotted hand caressed Nora's flushed cheek. "Suffering in childbirth is a woman's curse and her delight. Why, the doctor despaired for my life on the night you were born after thirty-six hours of travail. It was quite the worst experience I have ever had."

Nora turned away, moaning. "I shan't be able to stand it."

"Of course you shall. The good doctor and his wife will help you."

Simon drew Copper and the maid to the door. "Put the windows up, Girt, and place a screen near the bed to protect Mrs. Collins from drafts. And do remove the bed curtains. We need a clean, unencumbered room."

"Yes, Doctor." Girt curtsied, her maid's cap bobbing on top of her frizzy, ginger-colored hair. "Should I begin the preparations?"

"Wait until we return. Mrs. Corbett will assist you."

In the expansive hallway, Copper leaned against the wall under the wavering light of a candle sconce. This was a big responsibility. It seemed so matter-of-fact in Simon's books but so scary when there was an actual person before her. She had a million questions. "Why would Nora's mother scare her so? And why do men disappear just when they are so badly wanted?" she asked, remembering Sally's husband.

One finger to his mustached lip, Simon steered her to the staircase. "Let's find the kitchen and have a cup of coffee. It's going to be a long night."

The kitchen was just as pretentious as the rest of the house. "Searcy would call this uppity," Copper said as a maid poured coffee into china cups. Simon took his black, but Copper doctored hers with cream and sugar. She didn't like coffee, but if that's what would help get her through the coming delivery, then she'd drink it.

"Usually I'm not called this soon," Simon said quietly once the maid had left them alone. "It's a waste of a doctor's time to attend to the necessities of childbirth easily handled by the women in the house. But Nora is . . . shall we say . . . delicate." He reached across the table and took Copper's hand. "It will be an excellent experience for you."

"What do you mean by delicate? I thought you said she should have an easy delivery."

His thumb stroked the back of her hand. "I said physically easy, but Nora is a little fey. Occasionally she has spells . . . perhaps absence seizures. I wanted her to go to Cincinnati to be seen by an expert in diseases of the brain, but Mrs. Bellwether would have none of it. If Nora's illness progresses, I fear she'll wind up at the asylum."

"There's a woman near home, up the holler at Crook Neck, who has fits," Copper said. "When she gets to acting strange, her family ties her to a tree."

"A tree! That's barbaric."

"It keeps her from falling off a cliff, and it keeps her home. Mountain folks take care of their own."

"There's truth in that," he replied. "Now finish your coffee. You need to get back to your patient."

Copper poured more cream. Her spoon clanked against the china cup as loud as a ringing bell in the quiet kitchen. "I feel so ignorant, Simon. Girt is only a little older than me, yet she seems so experienced."

"A lady's maid learns these things. Girt has been present each time I called on Nora. I feel comfortable she will be a good teacher for you."

"But where will you be?"

"Stretched out on the nearest bed. You won't need me for hours yet."

Copper sipped her cooling drink; the coffee was not helping her jittery stomach. "Why would Nora's mother say those things about having babies? Why scare her daughter more than she already is?"

"Women like to share horror stories. You'll learn it's best to get your patient's mother out of the room as soon as possible, before she turns into a shrew."

Copper set her cup aside. "That's unkind."

Simon smiled at her over the top of his cup. "Perhaps, but true nonetheless."

Copper stood and stretched. "I'm so proud that you are trusting me to do this."

Simon chuckled and pushed their chairs up to the table. "You'll find midwifery a humbling profession, my dear." He tucked an errant strand of hair behind her ear. "Administering Nora's enema will take care of your pride."

Hours passed. Simon slept in a room just down the hall. Girt rested in a straight chair pulled up to Nora's bed. Copper had learned from Girt how to prepare an occupied bed, and now her patient dozed fitfully, the drawsheet underneath her drawn tight.

JAN WATSON

A fire roared in the fireplace to offset the chill from the half-open windows, and a standing screen protected the bed from drafts. Three basins—one for washing, one for rinsing, and one for antiseptic solutions—sat waiting on the washstand. A rolling tea cart draped with boiled linens held instruments previously sterilized.

Too overwhelmed to take advantage of her patient's nap, Copper stood at the window, thankful for the cold wind that swirled in. It was imperative, Simon had told her, to keep stale, unclean air from the room. Her mind slipped back and forth between Sally's outrageous, fearsome delivery and this sterile, controlled labor. It seemed unfair to her that wealth made such a difference in a woman's life.

Near 4 a.m. Nora moaned, "My back. My back."

Instantly Girt was on her feet.

Copper rinsed her hands in the antiseptic solution and pulled back the covers at the foot of the bed. Just then a great gush of water soaked the patient's diaper pad and the drawsheet.

"Now we're getting somewhere," Girt said, her milk white complexion flushed with excitement. "The doctor will want to know."

Copper went to fetch him. "Simon." One whisper of his name and he sat up. "Girt says it's time."

A commotion in the stairwell caught their attention. Copper saw Phillip Collins stumbling up the steps. Approaching the landing, he rocked back on his heels. Simon reached out a hand to steady him.

"Shellabrating," Phillip slurred as if they'd asked. "Shella-

brating the birth of a son wish Benton the banker!" His laughter ended in a hiccup. "That wush funny. Benton the banker!"

"You've begun your celebration a little early," Simon said.

"It wush a boy, right? My fair Nora didn't let me down?"

"Phillip?" A plaintive cry. "Phillip, I need you."

"Would shumbody shut her up?" Phillip said as Simon
steered him down the hall toward the room he had just vacated.
"I've got a dreadful headache."

Moments later, Simon was back.

"He should be horsewhipped!" Copper fumed. "Make him
come be with Nora."

"Best let sleeping dogs lie," Simon replied. "Now let's check
on our patient."

The room whirled with activity: Nora groaning, knees to
chest; her mother pacing in front of the fireplace; instruments
clanking; Girt calling, "Push! Push! Push!" Copper kneeling,
hands ready to receive a miracle. A baby born.

"Oh." A collective sigh.

Copper grinned from ear to ear. "She's beautiful. Just beautiful."

"She is that," Simon added. "Nora, God has blessed you with
a lovely daughter."

Supported by Girt, Nora leaned toward the newborn Copper
held for her to see. Suddenly Nora's focus shifted. She turned
away but not before Copper saw a shadow cross her face.

"Let me see my granddaughter," Mrs. Bellwether said, taking
the flannel-wrapped infant. "My, but she's a pretty thing."

Simon touched Copper's arm. "There's more to be done.
More for you to learn."

Awed, Copper assisted Simon. When the afterbirth was delivered and Nora's bleeding had slowed, Copper took a moment for herself and stood at the now-closed windows. Sometime during the long night the snow and wind had stopped. Dawn was breaking. Soft rays of morning's first light streamed down from heaven and blessed each snow-covered bush, each icicle-tipped tree branch. Then the light surrounded her, touched her soul, and filled her with contentment.

CHAPTER 22

On the morning of Nora's tenth day of confinement, Copper mounted the now-familiar staircase to her patient's bedchamber. Her leather doctor's bag, a gift from Simon, slapped against her leg with each step.

Nora lay in bed, as prescribed, the back of one hand against her forehead, and with the other she fingered the length of ribbon decorating her gown. The baby lay across her chest, supported by pillows. Nora sighed and gave Copper a wan look before she motioned for Girt to take the baby. Furious crying at the interruption followed.

"Now, Nora," Copper said, "you must finish nursing or you'll get engorged. Besides, Phillipa is still hungry."

"I have had enough of her for the moment," Nora replied. "It's obvious I don't have enough milk to satisfy her."

"Of course you have enough milk. Phillipa gains weight daily." Copper took the baby and patted her back. "Girt, please fetch the scales so we can show Nora how well she is doing."

Girt left for the nursery and returned with the baby scales on a rolling cart. Mrs. Bellwether followed.

Deftly, Copper undressed the baby, except for the bellyband, and laid her on the scale. "Look, Phillipa weighs seven-ten. Two ounces more than her birth weight." After fluffing the bolster at Nora's back, Copper repositioned Phillipa to finish nursing.

Nora stared blankly. Her stiff arms barely supported her baby.

Mrs. Bellwether slipped her hand into the crook of Copper's elbow and nudged her toward the nursery. Gently, she closed the door. "I know you mean well, Mrs. Corbett, but you mustn't upset Nora. I fear nursing is too much of a strain on her delicate disposition." She tapped her cane insistently against the floor. "I want you to get a wet nurse."

"We must consider the baby's health also," Copper said. "There have been three infant deaths from diarrhea in the community in the last two weeks, and two of those babies were wet-nursed. I don't think we dare take that risk with Phillipa."

"Many children are raised on boiled cow's milk with no ill effect," Mrs. Bellwether countered. "Why, Nora herself was a bottle baby."

Copper covered the old woman's hand with her own. The cane stopped tapping. "It seems a shame to stop what is working so well."

"Then what can we do?" Mrs. Bellwether asked. Fatigue etched her face with a spiderweb of worry.

"This is beyond my ability to decide. I'll ask Dr. Corbett to call." Copper turned down the coverlet on the nursery cot. "Meanwhile, I prescribe rest for you, Mrs. Bellwether."

"If I must." Mrs. Bellwether handed her cane to Copper and sank onto the bed.

"Can I get you anything?" Copper smoothed the cover over the frail woman's shoulders.

"No, dear." A tear trickled sideways from her faded blue eyes. "I'm just so worried."

"You don't need to fret, Mrs. Bellwether. Really, we'll work this out."

Copper found Girt in the kitchen taking her morning tea. She jumped up and poured a cup for Copper.

"Thanks, dear," Copper said. She'd grown close to Girt and enjoyed their chats during her twice-daily rounds on Nora. "Have you seen Nora in seizure before, Girt?"

"Yes, many times," Girt answered around a bite of sugar cookie. "Poor thing looks blank as a new sheet of paper and can't do the least thing for herself."

"When does it usually happen?"

Girt looked thoughtful. Finishing one cookie, she dunked another in her tea. "Her nervous disposition can't handle anything like loud noises or taxing situations." She glanced around the kitchen and lowered her voice. "It's especially bad when the master is about."

"Is Mr. Collins mean to Nora?"

Girt cleaned the tablecloth with a brush, sweeping bits of

cookie into the crumb receiver. "No, not that I've ever seen."
She whispered in Copper's ear, "It's quite the other way round,
I think."

"Hmm. Don't you think it's odd that Nora didn't have one
seizure while she was in labor?"

"I guess I never noticed," Girt responded. "We were that
busy."

"We certainly were." Copper stood and folded her napkin.
"Have some more tea. I'll tend to Mrs. Collins for a while."

Copper leaned over the cradle, listening for the sweet sounds of
a baby in slumber. With a little grunt, Phillipa raised her head a
fraction of an inch.

"Hey, little turtle." Copper stroked the baby's head. "You're
so strong, aren't you? Yes, you're so strong." Laughing, Copper
looked at Nora. "Wonder why we repeat everything we say to
babies. Do you find yourself doing that?"

"Hardly," Nora replied. "Why would one bother talking to an
infant?" A hint of frost wilted each word.

Nora seems so flat, Copper thought. *So flat in every way.* She
was thin and bony with a narrow face, brown hair, and protrud-
ing brown eyes that seemed to reflect no light. Girt and Copper
had done everything for her for ten days.

Even when they changed her huckaback toweling binder and
pinned it with two-inch straight pins, Nora made no effort to
help. It was quite a task to wrap her from her upper abdomen to
her thighs when she wobbled around in the bed as though somebody had stolen her backbone. "Doing her binder's like stuffing

a sausage," Girt had commented one day in the kitchen, making Copper laugh.

"Let's get you up today." Copper pulled the chair close to the bed. "You must be tired from lying in bed so long."

"I can't," Nora whined. "I'm much too weak."

Copper's patience snapped. *She'll get up if I have to drag her out of that bed.* "You'll do fine," Copper said, determined. "We'll have you on your feet in no time. Now just ease over this way."

In minutes that seemed like hours, Nora groaned her tortuous way to the side of the bed. Sliding her arm behind Nora's back, Copper sat her up, then swung her legs over the side. "Now, doesn't that feel good?"

A long, drawn-out moan was Nora's only answer.

Her fingers at the pulse of Nora's wrist, Copper observed her patient carefully. Her heartbeat was steady. Her face was pink, and her reflexes were good. It should be fine to stand her up long enough to pivot her to the chair. Copper was good at pivoting. She'd practiced on Searcy until Searcy had refused to be her guinea pig any longer. Taking a deep breath, Copper eased Nora until they were standing face-to-face.

Nora was on her feet! Copper was smiling ever so proudly when suddenly Nora stiffened and fell. Off-balance, Copper clutched her patient to her chest as they crashed backward to the floor.

Copper prayed a fervent, silent prayer: *Lord, please don't let anyone come through that door until I figure out how to get this woman off my chest.*

Reaching for her chatelaine, Copper withdrew the vial of

ammonia she always carried. She snapped the glass ampoule
with her thumb and waved it right in front of Nora's nose, getting a stinging whiff of it herself. Soon both nurse and patient
were gagging and gasping for breath.

Then Nora was back in bed, propped in a sitting position by
as many pillows as Copper could stuff behind her back. Nora's
face went blank, and her hands twitched.

*What have I done? Why didn't I listen when Nora said she was
too weak to stand?* Once again her fingers found Nora's pulse—full
and steady, and her face still held good color. What had made
her faint? *She must be flooding! I've caused her to hemorrhage! Please,
Lord, help us!* she prayed as she threw back Nora's bedcovers.
Thankfully there was only a stain on the diaper pad, no bigger
than it should have been.

Pacing, Copper studied on what to do. Ammonia stung her
eyes like fire, but she hardly noticed, so worried was she about
her patient. It was time to send for Simon. Pausing, she leaned
in close to Nora's dressing table and dabbed at her eyes with a
clean hanky from her pocket. There reflected in the mirror was
her seriously ill patient. A smug smile turned up the corners of
Nora's pencil-thin lips. As Copper watched unobserved, Nora
lifted a steady hand to smooth her hair.

Baby Phillipa began to cry, and Copper saw Nora slacken her
face . . . saw the calculated tremor in her hands commence . . .
saw the turning away from her daughter's need.

Copper didn't need the smarting fumes of ammonia to see
red. She'd had just about enough of the deceitful Nora Collins!
She had to get away . . . had to spend some time with a mother

who loved her baby. Against her burning desire to slap Nora into common sense, Copper instead loosed her unresponsive patient's gown and helped the hungry baby eat. But as soon as Girt came back, Copper was out the door.

CHAPTER 23

Sure of her welcome, Copper ignored the brass knocker and cracked the door to the big white house. "Hello? Anybody home?"

"Come in. Come in," she heard Birdie call. The smell of something warm and spicy enticed her toward the kitchen.

The room bustled with activity. Birdie leaned over the open oven door, a pan of cake in her hand, a big smile on her face. "Sit down. Sit down," she chirped.

Tommy Turner attempted to rise from his chair before Copper put a hand on his shoulder, easing him back down. "Copper! Have dessert with us."

"Mrs. Corbett," one of Birdie's boarders greeted, "how's that fine husband of yours?"

"He's well. Thank you for asking," Copper said.

"Hey, Miz Corbett," Andy Tolliver chimed in from his place at the table, "you'll love Miz Mary Martha's cake."

"Hello, Andy," Copper replied. "I haven't seen you all week."

"This boy can smell my gingerbread from the other side of town," Birdie said as she slid the first piece onto Andy's plate. "Grab a cup, Copper. I'll just get the whipped cream . . . whipped cream."

"Not until I get a piece of this." Copper scooped baby Robert from his high chair and bussed his little round cheeks.

The baby chortled and waved the stump of his arm.

"Watch this," Andy said as he folded a quilt in fours, then put it on the floor. He took Robert from her and put the baby on the pallet.

Robert raised his head much like she had watched Phillipa do earlier that morning. But Robert was older and much stronger, and he stuck out his neck like a turtle.

"Watch," Andy said again and lay on the floor beside the quilt. "Roll over, Robert. Roll over."

The baby rocked with all his might and with a grunt flipped onto his back.

"Yea!" Everyone clapped. "Yea, Robert."

"I'm having my cake right here," Copper said, sitting on the quilt with the baby. She took in the room: Tommy Turner at home at the table; one of Birdie's boarders, a widow of many years, her gray hair well dressed, Copper knew, by Birdie; Andy Tolliver obviously welcome in this house, licking whipped cream from his plate; the crippled baby fat and happy; and Birdie . . .

who would have thought? Birdie was sober and holding court in her own kitchen.

A memory tugged Copper home to Troublesome and across the creek to John Pelfrey's house. John's mother's kitchen was just like this, so nurturing . . . so inviting. It wasn't gingerbread she remembered but wheels of yellow corn bread. It seemed there was always one freshly baked, sitting in the warming oven ready for the little crock of sweet-cream butter kept in the middle of the table. And Copper knew from long-ago observations that Emilee Pelfrey's thirteenth baby was just as precious to her as Robert was to Birdie. She would give a pretty penny to be in that kitchen once again.

"I got to go," Andy interrupted her daydream. "Did you need any more chores done, Miz Mary Martha?"

"No, not today, Andy. Thank you," Birdie said. "Don't forget that extra pan of gingerbread to take home."

"I won't. I'm on my way to Doc's office, Miz Corbett. I'll tell him I seen you."

When Andy opened the door, a blast of cold air tried but couldn't dilute the warmth of the room, heated as it was by contented souls.

Copper's eyes misted over. *Thank You, Lord. I praise Your name for answered prayer.*

Soon it was just Birdie with baby Robert sleeping in her arms and Copper at the round kitchen table.

Birdie's sharp black eyes found Copper's. "What's troubling you? What's the trouble?"

"Birdie, I've had a puzzling day. Perhaps you can help me understand how it is that a mother falls in love with her baby."

"Well. Well," Birdie said as she shifted Robert to her shoulder. "I haven't had much experience, what with losing my Robert as I did. And I've had this one for such a short time."

"But you love him, don't you?"

Tears shimmered but did not fall from Birdie's eyes. "I didn't love him at first. Not at first."

"But you were so excited when we brought him here that night. You took right to him."

Birdie took her time to answer. "I didn't say I didn't want him. I wanted him in the worst way, and I was so thankful to Dr. Corbett for letting me have him. But it was very hard. Very hard." Robert stirred and cried out. Birdie tightened her hold and began to gently rock in the age-old way a mother soothes her baby. "You see, I wanted him for myself. I wanted him to be the baby I lost, but he wasn't." A single tear slipped down her face.

"What made you come to love him?"

"It was simple, really; he needed me. No matter who was here, it was me his eyes searched for. I was the only one who could soothe him. There's power in a baby's need."

Copper saw the look of adoration on Birdie's face before she bent her head to kiss the top of baby Robert's head. She'd found the missing piece to Nora's puzzle.

❧

The next morning was cold and sunny. Copper wasn't in the best of spirits as her buggy made its way to Nora's house. She had backslid once again. Seemed every time she thought she'd conquered her judgmental attitude, someone like Nora Collins came along. "Judge not lest ye be judged," she could almost hear Mam preaching. She'd prayed about it last night on her knees and again this morning, but her heart still didn't feel right.

A cardinal flew past the buggy window and landed on a wooden fence post. Dried sunflowers drooped over the fence, catching the bird's attention. Determined, he hung upside down and tugged seeds from the frozen pods. Copper set her mind on the task ahead. She'd have to be just as determined as the cardinal on the sunflower in order to carry out her plans for the day.

Mrs. Bellwether, wrapped head to toe in fur, was just leaving the house as Copper entered. Off to a club meeting, she informed Copper.

Good, Copper thought, *now you won't get in my way.*

Nora was sitting in a chair in front of the fireplace. Sparks hotter than the ones that sailed up the flue shot at Copper from her eyes.

"Good morning," Copper said as if she didn't notice. "It's good to see you up, Nora."

Girt smoothed a top sheet in place. The room was toasty warm and smelled of recently ironed linen—a homey, comforting fragrance. "Dr. Corbett called on us last evening," Girt said as she reached for a pillowcase. "He left orders."

Copper suppressed a grin. Simon had been more than a little put out with Mrs. Collins when he heard Copper's story over noon dinner yesterday. "You're not to go back to be treated that way," he'd said angrily before she pleaded her case. She had to see that baby Phillipa got what she needed. Finally he'd given in to her, but only after he had called upon Mrs. Collins himself.

As Girt gathered up the bedclothes, Copper emptied the baby hamper. "Why don't you do the baby's things this morning, Girt? I'll see to Phillipa's bath."

Today would be the baby's first dipping bath. Phillipa cooed and wiggled all over when Copper put her in the water. "Oh, you're a good baby. Such a good baby," Copper said as she lathered the delicate skin with fine castile soap. "Look, Nora. I believe she could swim if I turned her loose." And indeed Phillipa paddled with her hands and feet, splashing water in all directions.

Nora didn't say a word, just moved away from the spray.

"Oh," Copper said, "I forgot to get clean clothes for the baby. Could you fetch something, Nora?"

You'd have thought I'd asked her to plow the north forty, Copper thought, listening to Nora's huffs and puffs as she pawed through dresser drawers.

"This? Or maybe this?" Nora asked as she held up little gowns and tiny wrappers as if she needed Copper's approval.

Then it dawned on Copper. *Why, she's afraid. Nora is afraid of her own baby.* "Choose the clothing you like best. Anything will be fine."

Nora flung a pale yellow knit dress with matching cap and booties on the baby's dressing table.

Copper finished with the bath, then oiled Phillipa and showed Nora how to powder her own hand before gently patting the baby with it. "That will keep her from sneezing," Copper said as she folded and pinned a clean nappy.

"I could never do that," Nora fretted. "I'm afraid I would hurt her."

"Just tuck your hand between Phillipa's skin and the pin." Copper demonstrated. "Be careful not to stick yourself." She rolled the baby's dark hair around one finger. "I believe she's got natural curls. Do you want a ribbon?"

"Yellow," Nora said. "Yellow to match her dress."

"I'm just going to tuck her in the cradle now," Copper said. "I'll be back in a few minutes."

"But Mother's gone and Girt's downstairs. You can't leave me alone with her."

"She's asleep, and I'll only be a moment. You'll be fine." Closing the door, she leaned against the wall. It seemed Nora was softening just a bit. If Mrs. Bellwether didn't come home early, her plan just might work.

Copper massaged a crick in her neck. She'd been bent to the keyhole for nearly half an hour. Nora made no move toward the cradle, just sat in a chair, a length of yellow ribbon in her lap.

Soon Girt was leaning over Copper's shoulder watching with her. "What are we doing standing out here?"

"We're waiting for Phillipa to need her mother," Copper whispered.

Just when Copper thought her back would break, just when the crick had become a steady pain, Phillipa began to stir with little mews at first, testing the waters in her baby way, seeing who would come to her rescue. Through the keyhole, Copper could see Nora begin to pace. She strode about the room, casting anxious glances toward the cradle, the ribbon twisting in her hands. Phillipa began to cry in earnest.

Girt reached for the doorknob, but Copper stopped her.

"But the baby," the maid said, her voice drowned out by the angry wail coming from the bedroom.

Copper had opened her mouth to answer when suddenly the hall was quiet. She and Girt vied for the keyhole. Copper won, and there was her reward.

Nora rocked her daughter, baby Phillipa nursing greedily, a yellow ribbon in her pretty dark hair. Unbelievably, Nora began to croon, "Rock-a-bye, baby, in the treetop . . ."

Girt nudged Copper aside and had her own look-see. A big grin split her face before she grabbed Copper and danced her down the hall. "You're a gem. There's hope for Nora and Phillipa now."

Copper's prayers were easier that night. She had done the right thing for Nora. But still she prayed for tolerance. She reckoned with people like Nora Collins and Alice Upchurch in the world, she'd need a heaping portion of that.

CHAPTER 24

Christmas surprised Copper with its quick appearance that winter. She had been so busy with Nora and Phillipa that suddenly it was two weeks before the big day. Outside, wreaths hung on the windows, their red bows merrily wishing joy to each passerby. Inside, a stately pine with candle-tipped boughs ushered in the holiday season as if it had sprung fully decorated from the foyer floor. All accomplished by Simon and Searcy.

"Why," Copper mused to Searcy before supper one evening, "I haven't cracked the first black walnut for jam cakes. Mam would be ashamed of me."

Searcy flung open the pantry door. "Did you think Searcy be sitting on her hands while you birthing babies?"

"My word—" Copper cupped her nose with her hand—"it smells like somebody smashed a still in here."

Searcy ladled more whiskey over a dozen cakes wrapped in cheesecloth and placed in round tins. "Ain't no sense making fruitcake if they ain't soaked in spirits. They be dry as dirt. Taste like dirt too."

"I should have been helping you," Copper replied. "I did get my presents mailed. All but one, anyway. I'd best get it wrapped and in the post."

Standing at the dining room table, she was busy with scissors and twine when Simon came home, his cheeks red from the cold. He watched as she tucked a pair of leather gloves into a small box. "I thought you mailed your parcels to Philadelphia last week."

"Oh, I did." She stopped to kiss his cheek. "These are not for Daddy. They're for John."

"John Pelfrey?"

"Uh-huh. I'm mailing them to his mother in hopes that she will send them to him. I sure wish I knew where he is."

"Why?"

"So we could keep in touch." The festive red paper she had chosen for wrap crinkled as she worked. She smoothed it flat and tried again. "I miss John so much," she said, then felt Simon's questioning gaze.

"Copper," he said, "why would you be thinking of John Pelfrey? Much less sending him gifts?"

"Why," she said around a lump in her throat, "John and I grew up together. He's always been my best friend."

"More than friend, I would say." Simon's voice was tight, his words clipped. "As I remember it, he wanted to marry you."

Copper took a shuddery breath. The present smoldered like

sin in her hands. "Have I done something wrong?" She could barely see through the tears threatening to spill over.

Suddenly he crushed her to his chest. The box tumbled to the floor. He held her so close she could hardly breathe, and his heart beat against her cheek. "I'm sorry," he whispered gruffly. "Dearest, I'm so sorry."

Tears quickly gave way to sobs. Copper cried and cried as Simon led her to the parlor, where a fire chased away the chill of the day. Settling into the wing chair, he held her. It seemed she would never stop crying even though he begged his apology.

Finally spent, she rested her head on his broad shoulder and listened to his endearments. "What did I do to upset you?"

"It's just when I saw you with those gloves and you mentioned his name . . . well, I . . . something came over me. I can't bear to think of anyone else touching you."

"He hardly *touched* me. We were only friends, Simon. You know that."

"Did you let him kiss you?"

"Yes," she answered truthfully, and her answer took her back home to the Indian summer day under the hickory nut tree, not much more than a year ago when John had asked, "Could I kiss you, Pest?" She had made John cry then just like Simon made her cry now. How could love hurt so much?

Simon's hands captured her face. "Show me. Show me how he kissed you."

Resigned, her lips brushed his tenderly for a moment of promise before she drew away. "Satisfied? Should I demand if you've kissed before?"

"Forgive me." He hung his head. "But I'm so afraid of losing you."

"Simon," she snapped, "do you think John might sail up the creek on his merchant ship back from the Orient or some such place? Maybe tempt me with exotic spices and bolts of silk from China? And do you think I'd hop aboard like a ship-sick sailor and leave you without a backward glance?" She tried to get up, but his arms held her fast. "If I was going to leave—" she struggled against him as words she'd never meant to say slipped out—"I'd have gone when you and Searcy put up that sham of a Christmas tree while I was seeing to Nora Collins."

He quieted her with a long, hard kiss that took her breath away. John's kiss had promised, but Simon's claimed her as if he owned a bit of her soul. It wasn't likely she'd walk away from that. She settled into his strong embrace and kissed him back.

Later that night she was glad when supper was over, the fire banked, and the clock wound. Glad for the cold winter night and the warmth of their love.

The next morning as Copper followed Simon down for breakfast, she saw him pause at the bottom of the staircase.

"What's wrong with this Christmas tree?" he asked.

Copper could reach out and touch the graceful angel ornament that had belonged to his mother. The tree was beautiful. Each evergreen branch bowed with heaps of ornaments collected by his family through the years. Silvery icicles reflected the light in the foyer, and mounds of cotton batting looked like real snow at its base. Why couldn't he have forgotten her hateful words from the day before?

"It's just not a *real* Christmas tree," she replied.

"How can it not be real?" he asked with a sweep of his hand. "It's Christmas, and this is definitely a tree."

"Oh, Simon." She tucked her skirts to the side with one quick motion and plopped down on the landing. "For one thing it's a pine tree, and for another it's too straight and its branches are much too even. Why, it doesn't look like anything's ever lived in it."

He shook his head. "Sweetheart, I looked all over the tree lot to find the perfect specimen for you."

"That's just it. A perfect tree tells no story." A wave of longing washed over her. At home she'd have scoured the mountain behind the cabin until she found just the right bushy cedar, one with an abandoned bird's nest tucked up in its center. Daddy would take a hatchet to the trunk, and they'd haul it home on the sled, Willy and Daniel riding atop, catching snowflakes on their tongues.

Once in the house, they'd have to turn the tree a dozen times to find the best side, what with its bare spots and crooked branches that told of summer's drought and winter's storm. You could tell the tree had suffered just by looking at it, but she'd make it proud with blue jay and cardinal feathers and paper chains the twins had made.

Christmas Eve, Mam would hold her long-handled corn popper over the fire in the fireplace until the corn pop-pop-popped; then they'd gather round the tree while Daddy read the Christmas story from Papa Brown's Bible. . . . Anytime she woke that long winter's night, the clean scent of cedar reminded her that it was Jesus' birthday. A body should be home for Christmas.

"I favor the smell of cedar . . . ," Copper started, then saw his fallen face. "But this is fine." She hurried down the steps and slipped her hand into the crook of his elbow. "Just fine. Why, really, it's quite beautiful." She ushered him along to the kitchen. "Do you want my help at the office today?"

"Don't you have a luncheon with Alice?"

Alice! How could she forget? Her stomach flipped as homesickness made way for indigestion. But she bit her tongue. She'd said enough for one day.

⚜

Copper was determined to be pleasant on the long ride to the ladies-aid luncheon at the home of Mrs. Inglebrook. "Are you ready for Christmas, Alice?" she asked, her words desperately chipping at the frosty silence between them in the carriage.

"What does one do to be *ready*, Laura Grace? Do you mean, is my house in order? Certainly it is. I put my household first, unlike some who flit about town meddling in the affairs of others."

Copper measured her reply. "My work is important and a great help to Simon. My midwifery frees him to see other patients. Besides—"

"Oh, for heaven's sake, don't clatter on so." Alice shrugged and arranged her red-fox wrap. The matching muff lay in her lap. "Babies made their way into the world long before you came to Lexington."

Suddenly the buggy jounced, springs groaning, into a deep

hole. "Steady! Steady!" the driver instructed the horse as Copper flew across the seat, her teeth rattling from the jar, and landed smack up against Alice, whose arm shot up to steady them. The leg-of-mutton sleeve of her purple velvet coat rode up, revealing paper white skin.

Copper reached out to help. Her fingers brushed a lump as purple as an eggplant and just as foreign on the inside of Alice's thin limb. "What is this?"

Alice jerked the sleeve to meet the top button of her short, dove gray glove. "It's nothing." She turned away. "I had a fall at home."

How could you hurt the inside of your arm by falling? Copper wondered. "Did you show this to Simon?"

"Please don't fuss so!" Alice exclaimed, her chin trembling, her face stretched in a horrid grimace. "It's of no consequence. And I'll thank you not to mention this to my brother."

"I'm sorry," Copper said, frightened, though she couldn't say why. "We're here," she sang out gaily, falsely. "Goodness gracious, look at the wreath on Mrs. Inglebrook's door! Don't you just love Christmas?"

⚜

In truth, Copper easily forgot her sister-in-law's distress, for when she returned home that afternoon full of stories about Mrs Inglebrook's lovely Christmas decorations, full of delicious cookies and cocoa she had shared with the other ladies, a surprise awaited her. The beautifully decorated pine that had stood so formally in the foyer was no more. An unkempt, lopsided tree had taken its place. The fulsome green scent of cedar thickened the air. And Simon stood waiting on the stairs.

Dropping her coat to the floor, Copper rushed forward, arms flung wide as if to embrace the tree. "Oh," she cried, "there was never a lowly cedar so honored as this one." His mother's fragile glass ornaments trembled on the cedar's drooping boughs, and the Christmas angel swayed dangerously atop a spindly branch.

Simon's arms encircled her from behind as he parted the evergreen's girth to reveal a nest of twigs and mud snuggled up against the trunk. Silky milkweed seed still lined the little refuge, and a bit of red ribbon was boldly knit into its rim. "A tree that tells a story," he whispered in her ear.

She leaned against his warmth. "A tree to hold a nest for a bird who longs for beauty."

"As do I." His whisper turned urgent and caught against her heart. "I long for beauty also."

Worldly cares fell away as Copper turned to her husband . . . turned to the man who made her feel truly loved and as beautiful as a cedar tree.

CHAPTER 25

The next morning found Copper on the way across town with a basket of goodies for Andy and his sisters.

As usual, Marydell met her at the door. Dodie clung as tight as a monkey on her skinny hip.

"Where's your mother this morning?" Copper asked, taking the baby.

"She ain't here," Marydell said matter-of-factly, as if that was no surprise. "Andy said he had to go rustle up some coal somewheres before we all turn into icicles. Is that true, Miz Corbett? Would we turn into icicles if the fire goes out?" She went to the window and pulled aside the tattered, dirty curtain. Long, skinny icicles with pointed tips hung halfway down the window. "They're pretty, ain't they?"

"What happened to the coal pile, Marydell? There should have been plenty."

"Oh, probably somebody stole it. Andy says some folks would steal the pennies off a dead man's eyes. If you're dead, why do you need pennies?"

Copper started to the kitchen. Marydell was too young for some answers. "Is there anything to eat in the pantry?" She rummaged around in the now-familiar cupboard, finding cheese, bread, and a full bottle of whiskey. She had half a mind to toss it out the door.

"That there belongs to Ma's friend," Marydell said as if she could read Copper's mind.

Copper hitched Dodie a little higher on her hip. "Friend?"

"I ain't never seen him, but I know when he's coming 'cause Ma makes me and Dodie go to bed." Marydell shook her finger in mockery. "'And don't you dare come out!' Ma says." The girl twisted a long strand of butter-colored hair around one finger. "Dodie always sleeps, but sometimes I just pretend like this." She scrunched her eyes tight.

Copper's stomach dropped. "What about Andy?"

"He leaves. Want to know a secret?" she whispered.

Dodie wriggled in Copper's arms and patted Copper's face with one grimy little hand. "Sure, I'd love to know a secret."

"Ma's friend's buying her a present today!" Marydell thrust a baby bottle toward Dodie. "Don't tell nobody."

Parting the beaded curtain to the bedroom, Copper laid Dodie on the bed. "I have an idea. Why don't you both come home with me? We'll bake Christmas cookies."

Marydell's brow furrowed. "What if Ma comes back and needs me?"

"We'll leave a note, and you can make some cookies for your mother and for Andy."

"Well, okay, as long as we get home before dark. Ma's scared of the dark." Marydell dropped to her knees and looked under the bed. "There's Dodie's shoes. I can't reach them."

Copper fetched a yardstick from the kitchen. Kneeling, she swept dust balls, a silk stocking, a hairbrush, and a piece of gold jewelry from under the bed. Holding the cuff link up to the light, she noticed fancy swirled initials. It looked expensive. She'd best tuck it in her pocket and give it to Annalise when she brought the girls back.

After a time of struggle, she had the baby shod. "My, Dodie—" she couldn't help but smile—"you certainly look fetching."

Dodie looked up with a lopsided grin. While Copper was busy with her feet, the baby had pulled the errant stocking down over her ears. Laughing from deep in her belly, she tugged it off.

"Here, Dodie," Marydell said. "You can wear my toboggan. I don't never get cold anyway."

After easing out her hatpin, Copper plopped her beaver cloche on Marydell's head. "Now," she said, carrying Dodie to the door, "are we ready?"

Marydell caressed the deep brown fur of her borrowed hat, then set the decorative ostrich plume to trembling when she opened the door. "We're ready; ain't we, Dodie?"

The kitchen smelled of cinnamon, nutmeg, and ginger. Puffs of flour dotted Marydell's pinafore and Dodie's bald head. Curls of raw dough stuck to the countertop. Mixing bowls and spoons and cookie cutters of every sort littered the table.

"What's this?" Simon exclaimed, coming in for his noon meal. "Fairies and elves have taken over my kitchen. Where did you find such beautiful creatures, Copper?"

"Doc Corbett!" Marydell squealed at his appearance. "Don't you rec'nize us? Don't you remember putting drops in Dodie's ear?"

"Hmm, your voice does sound familiar." Chin in hand, he took a closer look. "Why, it's Marydell Tolliver under that apron. But who is this beauty?" Swooping Dodie up, he swung her over his head.

Marydell laughed as loud as the baby. "It's Dodie. Dodie Tolliver."

Copper was amazed. Had she ever heard Marydell laugh before?

"Are you baking these for me?" Simon teased and swiped a cookie. "I've never eaten a tree before."

"If you'd wait just a little minute," Marydell huffed, "I'd put some of this green icing on it." She held up one already decorated with icing and silver sprinkles. "See? They're supposed to be like Miss Copper's Christmas tree, not just any old tree in the forest."

"Uh-oh, I can't resist. . . . Delicious! The trunk didn't need icing anyway, did it?"

Marydell rolled her eyes. "Doc Corbett, you and Dodie are eating up all my presents. Now I won't have one to put your name on with this red icing." She stuck her finger in and tasted the sweet confection. "See? I already done Andy's—'course, Miss Copper helped."

"I'm sorry. Take this back and decorate it for me. I won't care if the trunk is gone."

Seeing Simon's questioning look, Copper steered him over to the stove. She cracked the oven door and peeked at another pan of browning cookies. "Annalise left them alone, and Andy's out scrounging up coal so they won't freeze to death. What was I to do?"

"Annalise does the best she can," he started, as if Copper had been criticizing.

"I can't believe you're taking her side!" Copper countered, waving her pot holder.

Marydell looked their way, a cookie clutched close to her chest, one protective arm around Dodie.

Chagrined, Copper lowered her voice. "What if the house had caught fire?"

"These children are well-off compared to most I see in that neighborhood." Simon removed his spectacles and pinched the bridge of his nose. "Little boys crippled from rickets and little girls nearly blind from eye infections. Annalise is not a bad person, just childlike herself, and the children do love her." His eyes reflected the burden of other people's sorrows.

Copper felt ashamed and wished she could hold him, maybe take some of his weariness into herself, but the children watched and Searcy puttered around the kitchen, and so she patted his arm. "You're right, but it makes me sad when I remember the Christmases I had growing up."

Simon relieved her of the pot holder and slid the tray of cookies from the oven. "Would that we could wish happy memories for every child."

She slipped an apron over his neck. "Maybe we can't do that, but we can make happy memories for these two. Get ready, girls. We've more decorating to do."

Everyone settled at the table—Simon teasing, Searcy wiping flour from Dodie's head with the corner of her apron, Marydell laughing, Dodie licking icing from a spoon—all full of Christmas cheer.

"Sure smells like Christmas," Searcy said. "This house ain't smelled like this since Miz Lilly passed."

Copper paused and took it all in. Seemed like Simon's weariness just fell away, and there was Searcy smiling while two little ragamuffin girls messed up her kitchen. And the girls laughed and played as children should. What was it about Christmas? How did it happen that a baby born in a manger so very long ago still had the power to turn an ordinary day into Christmas? She left to fetch her Bible. This was a good time for everyone to hear the story of that night in Bethlehem.

Simon carried Dodie to the dining room and plopped her down atop a stack of books before pulling her chair close to the table set for supper.

"Here," Searcy fretted, "that child be tumbling off lessen

you . . ." As quick as a wink she slid a linen towel around Dodie's middle and tied her to the chair.

"I'll just have cookies for dinner," Simon said. "No roast beef for me."

Marydell flounced to the table. "I told you, Doc Corbett, you can't eat all them cookies now, else me and Dodie won't have any ornaments to put on our tree. Did you know Miss Copper's getting us a tree?"

"Might it be that beautiful pine I just threw out?"

"The very same," Copper replied. "Reuben trimmed it some so it will fit in Annalise's front room. And Santa left presents to put under the tree."

"Presents for Ma?" Marydell asked from her chair beside Dodie.

"No, Santa leaves gifts for good boys and girls. He said these are for Andy, Dodie, and Marydell. Now quiet, everyone, and listen to the story," Copper said.

"'And it came to pass in those days, that there went out a decree from Caesar Augustus that all the world should be taxed,'" she read.

"Tacked?" Marydell said with alarm. "You mean like carpet tacks?"

A finger to Simon's lips quieted the girl as Copper continued, "'And all went to be taxed'—that means paying money, Marydell—'every one into his own city. And Joseph also went up from Galilee, out of the city of Nazareth, into Judaea, unto the city of David, which is called Bethlehem; (because he was of the house and lineage of David:) to be taxed with Mary his espoused wife, being great with child. And so it was, that, while they were there, the days were accomplished that she should be delivered. And she brought forth her firstborn son, and wrapped him in swaddling clothes, and laid him in a manger; because there was no room for them in the inn.'"

"Oh, I know. I know." Marydell waved her arm. "Can I tell the rest of it?"

Copper's eyes met Simon's twinkling ones. Whatever would Marydell say?

"Then," Marydell stood and pronounced, "the shepherds came with their sheep, and the smartest men rode on camels and followed the brightest star. They brought presents for baby Jesus. I reckon Santa gave them to the smart men to put under the baby's tree."

Surprised, Copper said, "That is beautiful, Marydell. Who told you the story of baby Jesus?"

"Sometimes Andy takes me to Sunday school. Andy says girls who don't go to Sunday school grow up to be heathens. I don't want to be no heathen."

Lord, Copper prayed, *protect these precious children*. Close to tears, she busied herself tucking a clean dishrag under Dodie's chin as Searcy put serving bowls on the table.

"You've got lots of utensils," Marydell said from where she sat primly on the edge of her chair. "We use spoons."

"You're right." Copper picked up Simon's and her forks and knives and placed them in the silver cabinet. "No one needs all this extra stuff. Now, bow your head for grace."

"God, our Father," Simon began, "bless this food as You bless

Your servants gathered here. Help us do Thy will in all things and in all ways. In Jesus' blessed name, amen."

Dinner was satisfying after all the sweet treats. Copper and Simon exchanged smiles as they chased roast beef and potatoes around their plates with spoons while Dodie gummed peas and Marydell ate daintily from her fork.

Children are good for a home, Copper surmised as she readied herself for bed that night. Marydell with her funny ways brought back memories of her brothers, especially Willy.

A letter had arrived yesterday with Mam's Christmas box. The twins were excited about the holiday. Daniel was growing and nearly as tall as his brother. Willy liked school, and Daddy was working in a dry-goods store. His cough was nearly gone now that he no longer went down in the mines. Mam wrote nothing of herself; she never did. Would she forever remain a puzzle, like Alice, with a piece always missing?

After removing her hairpins and combs, Copper pulled the navy blue dress she'd worn all day over her head and put it on a wooden hanger. She'd never liked navy—made her think of funerals. Oh, dear, she'd lost a button. A foreign weight in the pocket caused the dress to sag when she shoved it in the back of the closet with the other clothes needing repair. She'd get around to them eventually; it was just that she hated to sew. Maybe she should take them to the dressmaker. Would that be lazy? Mam would say so.

Leaving her hair free, as Simon liked it, she settled at her dressing table and rubbed Pompeian Massage Cream on her elbows. The cream had cost a fortune–one dollar for the squat blue bottle. It seemed wrong somehow to waste money on such a frill, but it sure smelled better than the concoction of mutton tallow, gum camphor, and turpentine she and Mam had used at home.

Something nagged her. She slathered more cream on her hands and searched her mind. It must be the button. Such a silly thing to worry about.

CHAPTER 26

The long winter had come and gone, and the first warm day was welcome. Puffs of white smoke drifted heavenward from fires under numerous washtubs, and laundry flapped on lines as far as the eye could see. It seemed all the maids on the street vied to get their wash out first, but Searcy's rival, Mallie, nearly always won. Searcy swore Mallie got out her washboard at the stroke of midnight on Sunday just to be first to the clothesline on Monday morning.

Copper held the screen door half open, enjoying the April air. A pot of soup beans simmered on the stove. A round of corn bread waited in the warming oven. Beans and the chicken left over from Sunday dinner and maybe some green onions from the garden would make for an easy meal on such a busy day. It was a wonder they had any chicken left since Benton and Alice had visited with them after church. Benton was a hearty eater. *Greedy*, Copper thought. *Benton is greedy about everything.*

The screen door slapped softly behind her as she stepped out onto the still-wet grass and made her way to the lines. *The sheets won't be dry yet*, she thought. Still, she reached out and pulled damp linen to her face, inhaling the fresh, clean smell.

Could it really be almost a year since she came to Lexington? Seemed like ages since first she'd seen Searcy at the washtub scrubbing clothes. It bothered her a little that Troublesome Creek was fading in her memory, blurred round the edges like a distant tree at twilight.

Other folks seemed more real than her own family now: Alice replacing Mam, Andy and his sisters stealing Willy and Daniel's place. And what of Daddy? She had to think hard to see his face, couldn't imagine him living in the city, but he seemed to prosper in Philadelphia. Mam wrote that they had found a church where Daddy was a deacon, and he liked helping people in the store. And, she surmised, Mam was happy. She had what she'd always wanted—a place away from the mountains she despised.

With absent mind, Copper resettled the clothespins on the sheets, smoothed the pillowcases, and shook wrinkles from a cotton towel as she took stock of all the changes in her life. She assisted with most of Simon's deliveries now and did much of the follow-up care. Simon teased that soon there'd be no need for him. She had a way, he said, a natural way with women in labor.

Simon had left this morning to go to Cincinnati for another

medical meeting. She missed him already. Their partings were getting harder and harder. The taste of his last kiss lingered on her lips.

She sidestepped Old Tom, who pounced right in front of her, just missing the mouse that scurried down a chipmunk's hole. The sun raised itself a notch in the cloudless blue sky. The warmth of its searching rays was welcome among the wet laundry. Contentment settled in her heart as she surveyed her day dresses hanging next to Simon's shirts, shirts so white that sunlight bounced off them. All was right in her little world—for a moment anyway.

Copper raised her hand, a shield against the sudden glare, and noticed Searcy, a clutch of clothespins in her fist, standing at the fence listening to Mallie. Odd that either of them would take even a moment's rest on wash day. Mallie's hands flapped, and she cut her gaze in Copper's direction. The wooden pins scattered on the ground at Searcy's feet.

"What is it?" Copper asked. "Is Mallie's daughter having her baby?"

"It be Miz Alice," Searcy replied, her eyes rounded in fear. "Mandy told Mallie that Beulah said Jenny told her that Joseph say Miz Alice been in the closet all last night and this morning and won't come out. Joseph, he don't rightly know what to do, and Mr. Benton be gone since yesterday late. Mallie say Mandy say Beulah say Jenny say Joseph wants you to come."

This is better than the telegraph, Copper thought as her scalp prickled with alarm. "I'll go right now. It won't take me but a few minutes to walk over there."

"You'd best let Reuben fetch Dr. Thornsberry," Searcy said.

"Alice won't like it if we make a fuss. I'll send Joseph for the doctor if need be." Copper looked down the long row of connecting yards. "Meanwhile, Searcy, do what you can to put out these smoke signals."

A gloom as thick as clotted cream settled around Copper as she ascended the spiral staircase; even the sparkling chandelier seemed to cast only a feeble light. A clock somewhere in the vast spaces of Alice's house chimed the hour like a portent of doom.

Taking a deep breath to steady herself, Copper turned the heavy glass knob and cracked the door. "Alice?" she asked, unsure of her welcome and more than a little afraid. Alice would have her head on a platter for invading her private place.

"Lord, what should I do?" she asked in reverence. Clearing her throat, she pushed the door farther and stepped in. "Alice," she squeaked.

Something was amiss. The curtains were still drawn and the room lay in shadow, but Copper could easily see the disarray. The covers were pulled back, the bedspread neatly folded on the bench at the foot of the bed, but Alice's gray robe lay in a heap on the floor along with several pieces of writing paper and a book of poetry. Wordsworth, Copper noted, stepping closer. A gash in the wall marked the landing place of a wooden jewelry casket that now lay at the baseboard, its trays slid out, disgorging all manner of gold, diamonds, and pearls upon the floor. *What in the world?*

A keening whimper pricked her ears. Joseph had said Alice was in the closet, and it sounded like she was. But why? Once again Copper found herself in a place she didn't need to be. She'd go back downstairs and send for help. This was clearly none of her business.

At the staircase, she clasped the rail, her hand shaking like a palsied old woman's and her knees threatening to give way. She collapsed on the top stair and covered her ears against the whimpering sound that followed her out the door. As soon as she could trust her legs, she'd go find Joseph.

***

Searcy was in a dither. Seemed like she couldn't pull herself together enough to finish the laundry. But she had to, didn't she? Had to stop the prying eyes and gossiping voices that came at her over the fence. Miz Alice wouldn't like other folks knowing her business.

Sliding wooden pins into her apron pocket, Searcy made her way down the line. The day was fast heating up. She had to hurry so the ironing pieces wouldn't overdry. Searcy fretted as she worked. Poor Miz Alice. Was she sick? Had Mr. Benton hurt her feelings again? She thought about the first time Miz Alice had come home after she married that mean man. She'd flung herself on the floor at her mother's feet and sobbed about mistakes.

Searcy remembered Miz Lilly's words to her only daughter as if it had happened yesterday. "When you dance you have to pay the fiddler." Like that made any sense to anybody. Like that took any of Miz Alice's pain away.

Searcy tightened the kerchief on her head and wiped a bead of perspiration from her face. Worrying herself didn't do any good, but it seemed like Miz Alice was not meant to find happiness. As a girl she was forever trying to please her mother with flowers plucked from the garden or some such thing, hoping to garner a little praise from a woman who had none to give. She was a pretty little thing, Miz Alice was. But pretty didn't make happy.

Searcy thought she'd try a prayer like Miz Corbett had taught her. Now how'd it go? Bend your head and close your eyes and talk to the Lord. Let's see. *Father, it be Searcy asking You to lift up Miz Alice's sorrow. It be all right if You settle it back down on these here shoulders. Amen.*

There, that felt better. Made a body walk a little taller. Funny—as much as Searcy had seen white folks pray around the dining room table over food she herself had cooked, she'd never known that God would listen to her, too.

If she hurried with the wash, maybe she'd have time to figure out a little of the Scripture in her Bible. Last evening she'd puzzled out a piece from Luke: "Mine eyes have seen thy salvation." That was a pretty word: *salvation.*

Searcy raised her eyes to see a second pair of hands as brown as her own neatly folding dried laundry into a willow basket. Mallie was doing Searcy's work while her own clothes were still hanging on the line.

CHAPTER 27

Light-headed, Copper held fast to the railing as she took the steps down ever so carefully. She'd been sick after breakfast, and her stomach still felt funny. But she was also more than a little afraid. Something was terribly wrong in that closet upstairs. She'd reached the curve in the open, S-shaped stairway before she could see Joseph standing below, looking up at her.

"Miz Alice?" he asked and started up.

Copper could see concern on his face. Her backbone stiffened with resolve. She was being a ninny. "I was just coming for you, Joseph. Would you mind to wait in the hall while I see about Mrs. Upchurch? I might need you to go for Dr. Thornsberry."

"Yes'm." He positioned himself like a sentry outside the bedroom door.

Copper's rap at the closet sounded tentative even to her own ears, so using the heel of her hand, she pounded with authority. "Alice! It's Copper. Open the door."

With her ear pressed tight to the door, she thought she could hear a body shifting about, but the door did not open. "I'm coming in." Easing the door, she stopped when it caught on something. "Alice, if you don't let me in, I'm having Joseph take this door off the hinges! You know I will."

Hot air smelling of stale cedar met her when the door swung open. The closet was a good size, as big as Copper's dressing room. Men's suits and shirts hung neatly on wooden rods. Well, some did; most were piled on the floor, where Alice nested like a deranged bird. A pair of scissors glinted wickedly in her hand. "I fell asleep," she said, "or I would have finished."

"Finished?"

"Buttons, Laura Grace." The scissors snip, snip, snipped, and several buttons lost their purchase. "Can't you see I'm busy?"

Copper saw she had indeed been busy. There must have been a hundred buttons, not to mention a few dozen shirtsleeves and collarless jackets, in Alice's nest. Copper sank to her knees and reached for the scissors. "Are you hurt?"

Alice released her weapon and turned away from Copper. "It's nothing," she said, but the keening cry started again.

Has a night in the closet unhinged Alice? Best get her out of here. "Come, Alice, let me help you up."

Alice acquiesced, leaning unsteadily on Copper as they made their way to the bed.

Copper nearly gasped when she saw Alice's black eye, her

puffy lip, and the dried blood from her nose. With gentle fingers she probed the damage until Alice slapped her hand away. "I'm going to send for a doctor."

Alice drew herself up in bed. "You'll do nothing of the sort."

"Forevermore, Alice. I just want to help you. You could have a broken nose for all I know."

"Hand me a mirror."

Copper handed her a silver-backed hand mirror, then poured water from a pitcher into the washbowl. Holding a dampened towel, she watched as Alice surveyed her damaged face.

"Oh," she yelped as the mirror fell to her lap. "Benton never did this before. He never hit me where it would show."

Copper dabbed at the crusted blood. "Why did Benton do this?"

Alice crumpled against the headboard like a rag doll leaking stuffing. "It was all my fault." Tears fell from her swollen eyes. "He never would have done this if I hadn't made him mad."

"Nothing you could have done warrants this." Copper's voice rose in anger.

Somewhere in the house a door slammed.

Alice nearly jumped from the bed, her eyes wide with fright, and Copper's heart beat wildly. Rushing to the closet, Copper grabbed a valise from the high shelf. "Oops!" she cried when an errant button caused her to slip and slide across the hardwood floor. Her ankle turned dangerously, and she nearly fell. Tucking her hair behind her ears, she limped back to the bedside.

Copper opened the case and put Alice's slim volume of Wordsworth into its yawning mouth. "You're going home with me." She emptied the contents of a dresser drawer atop the book. "Nobody has to live like this."

"Who asked for your opinion? Or your presence, for that matter?" Alice flung the mirror across the bed. "Life is so simple for you, Laura Grace. Like a game you always win."

Copper's face stung with the slap of Alice's words. Upending the valise, she dumped cotton undergarments back into the dresser drawer and plopped the volume of poetry to the floor where she'd found it. Were it not for her aching ankle, she'd have kicked the valise across the room. Instead she snapped it shut and stretched to set it on the closet shelf. She was finished with Alice Upchurch. See if she ever darkened this door again.

"You need to put a beefsteak on your eye, Alice," she said as she headed for the door. "That will cut the swelling."

She nearly made it. Nearly severed the tenuous tie that bound her to a woman who would never be her sister. She grasped the doorknob between duty and freedom. But something she'd never thought to hear called her back.

"I'm sorry," Alice croaked, as if the words had been stuck in her craw for a very long time.

"Pardon me?" Copper replied, her back to Alice, though she'd heard well enough.

"I said I'm sorry, Laura Grace." Alice's voice broke on a sob. "I'm so sorry."

Copper wiped the smile from her face before she turned around. "Thank you."

Alice whipped her head back and forth on the bolster pillow. "Nobody could ever love me. I'm a wretched, ugly woman."

Willow Springs

Copper's triumph was short-lived as she witnessed Alice's humiliation. *Lord,* she petitioned, *will You ever let me bear a grudge? You know I have a right. Why, Alice is as mean as a striped snake. If she bit her tongue she'd poison herself. Must I always turn the other cheek? How many times must I forgive her?*

Her knowledge of Scripture pierced her angry satisfaction. "Seventy times seven," Jesus had told Peter when he asked the same question as they tarried in Capernaum. Seventy times seven and beyond.

Copper pinched her lower lip between thumb and forefinger and paused in front of Alice's dresser to study the situation. Was she any better than Alice, really? How many times had Mam cautioned her to mind her tongue? Once she'd had to print Psalm 140 verse 3 until her slate was full only to have her stepmother erase it with one swipe and make her write it yet again.

The mirror over the dressing table caught her eye, but she turned away. She didn't want to see a hypocrite. "I'll be right back, Alice. I'm going to need a few things."

Joseph waited patiently right outside the door.

"Joseph, go with me to the kitchen. I need a tea tray and a beefsteak."

"Yes, ma'am," he said, standing back.

"You'll need to go first." She rested her hand on his broad shoulder for support and hobbled down the steps, testing her ankle. *No harm done,* she thought when she reached the landing and headed to the kitchen.

As soon as the water in the teakettle rose to a boil, she

assembled an invalid tray with tea, toast, and orange marmalade as well as a mound of chipped ice tied up in a soft cotton towel.

Joseph fetched a small beefsteak and carried the whole lot up the stairs to Alice's room.

"Thank you," Copper said after he placed the tray on a serving table.

"Will you be needing anything else?" he asked, his face impassive, as if he didn't see the carnage in the room.

"I'll use the bell if need be, Joseph. You can go on about your day."

Alice lay with closed eyes upon the bolster pillow. The sight of her hands, her beautiful hands, lying defenseless upon the counterpane nearly caused Copper's undoing. Obviously she hadn't fought back. One good whack with the heavy gold candlestick from the mantel would have cleaned Benton's clock. Poor Alice; she needed a backbone.

"Alice? See if you can eat a little something. You need to get your strength back."

"Perhaps a little tea." Alice winced as she sat up , allowing Copper to place the tray on her lap and pour her tea. "There is no spoon for the honey. I can see I need to teach you to prepare a proper serving tray."

"Forevermore." Copper stirred honey into the teacup with the handle of a knife. "Hot butter's not the only way to choke a hound dog. Make do, Alice. Make do."

"Ouch!" Alice exclaimed as a hint of a smile stretched her split lip. "Laura Grace, you say the most ridiculous things."

"I talk like my daddy talks and his daddy before him. It marks where I'm from." She shook out a starched napkin and tucked it under Alice's chin. "Did you ever study Paul's letters? Mam had me memorize this verse in Colossians: 'Let your speech be always with grace.' But then it also says 'seasoned with salt.' Well, my folks like to use a little salt in our speech for flavor. I don't think God judges us for that, do you?"

One trembling hand covered Alice's eyes. "If God is judging anyone in this room, it's me. If there's any fault, it's mine. Benton says I'm no better than a dried-up old maid, and he's right."

"Alice, you're making me mad. How can you dismiss what he's done to you so easily?"

Alice choked down a tiny piece of dry toast and a sip of tea. "He's not always like this."

Copper began to tidy the room, righting an overturned chair and laying Alice's dressing gown across the foot of the bed. "I don't see how you can blame yourself. I'd feel ever so much better if you'd let me send for help."

"No, I told you!" Alice's voice rose in alarm. "I couldn't bear for anyone to see me this way. Please, leave me a little pride."

Pulling the backless stool from the dressing table to the bedside, Copper sat and took Alice's hand. "Tell me what happened."

"I angered Benton. He was looking for . . . he couldn't find . . . I-I can't talk about this. I'm so ashamed. You must promise to keep this to yourself." The eye that was not covered with beefsteak beseeched Copper.

"Benton has hurt you before, hasn't he?"

"A pinch maybe or a twist of my arm when I upset him." One finger traced the bruise on her face. "Never like this." Her voice became quiet, dreamy, as if she were relating a small piece of fancy, not something real, not a bit of her own life.

Copper tucked her hands under her hips to keep from reaching out, breaking the spell, putting herself in the way of Alice's story.

"Benton chose me. Of all the girls he could have had, I am the one he wanted." Her laugh strangled from her throat. "He said my beauty cast a spell over him."

Mesmerized, Copper watched Alice stir her tea with the knife handle. Round and round she stirred though she never took a drink.

"My father was just like Simon, forever putting everyone else in front of his family. I can't count the number of times he let some drifter, some tramp, sit at our dinner table like an honored guest. I could never entertain in that house, never be who I was meant to be. And then Benton and I wed." A sweep of her hand took in the room. "I was so proud to have all this."

Carefully, she set the knife on the edge of her saucer and pressed the monogrammed napkin to the corner of her mouth. "It's no small thing being Mrs. Benton Upchurch."

Shame for Alice burned Copper's face. How could she revel in Benton's wealth while he disrespected her so? What was that Scripture Brother Isaac had preached a dozen times? "Lay not up for yourselves treasures upon earth, where moth and rust doth corrupt, and where thieves break through and steal."

Copper kept her silence though Alice's violated face shouted corruption, and the broken jewelry box spilling riches across the floor stank of rust and the dry, powdery dust of moths.

"Did you know Benton is the fourth Upchurch to own the bank?" Alice asked as if it mattered. "Tradition is important to him." She set the tea tray aside and leaned back against the pillow. Her white hands pleated and smoothed the ribbon edge of the bedcover. "I tried, you know. It wasn't for the lack of trying, but I couldn't seem to hold a baby in my womb."

The air in the room grew dense, close, as if a summer storm threatened. Copper wished she had opened the curtains, wished she had propped the window, wished she were home folding the sun-sweetened laundry. Quietly, she waited for the rest of the story.

"It was after the fifth pregnancy—or was it the sixth? Oh, I don't even know anymore—that he moved across the hall." Her head whipped back and forth again.

Copper reached out and caught the beefsteak and laid it on the invalid tray beside the melting ice pack.

Alice's words clotted together as if she were trying to stop the bleeding out of her painful memory. "I loved him. I loved him. I loved him." Her fists beat against her thighs as she choked, "I only had to do this one thing for him, and he would have loved me back." She raised her shoulders as she took in a deep breath, then let them fall with a long sigh of resignation. "I'm barren. Benton deserves better than me."

Copper was at a loss. There were no clever words to ease Alice's suffering. "Alice," she started, then stopped. "I don't know what to say."

"I couldn't stand the sight of you when Simon brought you here. Did you know that? Your very presence offended me. Now, somehow, your presence gives me comfort. Can I trust you with my secrets?"

Against her better judgment, Copper gave all she had to give. "You can trust me. I won't tell Simon, but I hope you will. He needs to know."

"I want to sleep now, Laura Grace. You can send the maid up to sit with me."

"What will happen when Benton comes back?"

"Nothing will happen as long as I don't interfere, as long as I leave him alone."

"Let me put this right before I go." Stooping, Copper picked up the ornate jewelry chest. Ropes of pearls and loops of beaded jet slithered through her fingers. A diamond ring glinted in the shadow under a table, and beside it a little lump of gold beckoned. Down on her knees, Copper captured the pretty pieces. The ring fit perfectly in a section of one of the trays, but the other piece caused her brain to pucker. Why did it feel so familiar to her hand?

CHAPTER 28

High overhead, the sun said it was only a little past noon. It seemed to Copper as if she'd been in Alice's bedchamber all day. It was good to be outside, away from that room swirling with secrets. Her head pounded with all the words she'd had to digest, but at least she felt she understood Alice a tad better. Maybe she shouldn't have refused the carriage ride home; her ankle still ached a little, but she just had to be alone for a while, alone with a secret of her own.

Lord forgive her, but the piece of jewelry she'd found under the table now burned a hole in her pocket. Like a game of old maid, she couldn't wait to get home to see if she held the winning pair. Did that other bit of gold, also tucked away in a dress pocket, match this one?

Standing still, she shaded her eyes. Was that Andy across the street? "Andy?" she called.

He waved but did not stop. Strange–that wasn't like him. Had the whole world gone mad? Alice was talking and Andy was not.

Copper dropped her hand and walked on. She was in a bit of a hurry herself.

Copper paused to select just the right hat to go with her blue-and-white pin-striped blouse and conservative gray skirt and jacket. Stepping in front of the cheval glass, she adjusted the broad-brimmed gray felt hat with its mass of ribbon bows. Her stomach fluttered with apprehension, but she ignored it. She was taking the carriage to the bank and that was that.

"Afternoon, ma'am." The doorman tipped his hat and swung open the heavy glass door proclaiming People's Bank and Trust; Est. 1854; Benton Upchurch, Esq., President. "May I take your parasol?"

"No, thank you," Copper answered. "I might need this pointy end."

"Pardon?"

"Never mind. I'm here to see my brother-in-law, Mr. Upchurch."

At that moment Benton stepped into the lobby. He struggled to button the jacket of his brown serge suit over his ponderous belly. "Laura Grace, what a pleasant surprise," he boomed as he escorted her, his hand resting familiarly on the small of her back, into his inner office.

After closing the frosted glass door, he pulled out the chair fronting his enormous desk for her. "My, you look fetching this afternoon. Do you mind?" Not waiting for a reply, he clipped the end of a hand-rolled Havana and, after a brief flare from a match, puffed noxious fumes into the air. His piggish, bloodshot eyes never strayed from Copper.

She remained standing as he rolled back in his armed chair and placed one booted foot upon the polished surface of the desk.

"I've just left Alice," she began.

His eyes narrowed. "Did she ask you to talk to me?"

Copper paused, taking in the room. She saw his heritage in portraits of his father and grandfathers, like the ones in Alice's dining room—imposing oils of men with the same round face and prominent ears as himself. "No, she doesn't know I'm here."

"So what brings you here?"

"You hurt her badly." Copper leaned on her hands and met his cold stare across the desk. "And I'm here to tell you that won't happen again."

Benton took a long draw on his cigar and released smoke in her face. "Your regard is strangely placed, my dear. Alice despises you, you know."

"She doesn't have to love me for me to love her. You sit in church every Sunday. Isn't that what Jesus teaches? Love for one another. Even you, Benton, though that might take some praying, considering what I saw this morning."

"What I do in my house with my wife is no business of yours."

"You are right, of course," she said, leaning farther toward him, "until you harm her and I find out; then it becomes my business."

His foot dropped to the floor, and he met her eye to eye. "What are you going to do? Shoot me?"

"That's an idea," she said, "but I'd thought more along the lines of going to the elders in the church."

"Ha!" He laughed and held out his beefy paw, palm up. "They sit right here. You've got nothing on me."

Copper rolled a set of cuff links across the desk like a pair of dice. "One of these was in your jewelry case. Guess where I found the other one?"

He grabbed the studs before they skittered off the edge. A pulse throbbed at his temple, and he dabbed sweat from his forehead with a monogrammed handkerchief. The same mono-gram—*BU*—Copper noted, as the one on the cuff links. She might have shot him, he lost hot air so quickly and dropped back into his chair with a thud.

"What do you want?" he asked, suddenly not able to meet her eyes.

"Benton, where you choose to spend your time is indeed none of my affair. All I ask is your word of honor that you will never touch Alice in anger again."

The cigar smoldered in a cut-glass ashtray, smoke curling up like a question mark. Copper thought she'd never felt so sick, but she stood her ground.

Benton juggled the studs in his hands, back and forth, back and forth. "I care for her, but a man has needs. I lost my temper when she threw her jewelry casket at me." He stared at the floor. "I never meant to go so far."

"Do I have your word?"

"On my honor, Laura Grace, you have my word." Benton rose from the chair and pulled a watch fob from his vest pocket. Flipping the watchcase open, he gazed at it as if time was of sudden import. "That's settled then." He stuck the cigar in the corner of his mouth and spoke around it. "Ladies first."

"Thank you, but no," Copper replied. "I'll see myself out."

CHAPTER 29

I shouldn't have eaten that second pancake, Copper reckoned. *It's made me queasy this morning.* Chickens clucked and the rooster preened as she leaned against the henhouse door with a bucket of water in one hand and a poke of shelled corn and oats in the other. "Here, biddies. Biddy, biddy, biddy."

Chickens and doodles circled round her feet, scratching and pecking at the feed as she scattered it about, completing her favorite chore, one she'd had to wrest from Searcy. She scooped up a tiny ball of downy fluff and held it close to her face.

The chick peeped its high-pitched call. Copper set it in front of the watering tray.

"Here, little doodle, have a drink. No, I didn't say drown yourself, silly." Laughing, she pulled the piece of fluff from the watering tray. "Like this." She tipped the chick's beak in the water, then tilted its head so water could trickle down its throat. "That's not so hard, is it?"

Copper watched the baby chicks closely as they ate and drank, occasionally pecking on the floor with her fingernail, mimicking a mother hen. The doodles weren't blessed with brains, but she loved them nonetheless. And once it figured out how, a chicken would eat anything, some of which she'd rather not think about.

Black specks swam before her eyes when she bent over the last water container. She pried off the circular tray and poured water into the small tank before tapping the tray back on and upending the whole thing. "Now we're in business. Scat, Old Tom." With one foot she scooted the curious cat out the hen-house door. "No chicken for your breakfast. How about some warm milk? Let's see if Reuben has saved any for you."

She savored the feel of dew-soaked grass as she walked barefoot to the stable with her full egg basket.

The tomcat butted his head against her ankle.

"Hey, what are you doing? Your bowl is full." Giving in, she scratched the insistent cat behind the ears.

"Miz Corbett? You all right?" Reuben stepped from a stall with a brimming bucket. "You looking white as this here milk."

Copper steadied herself with one hand against the barn door. "I've been rushing around too much. I'm just so glad to be outdoors."

"You want I should walk you to the house?"

"Thank you, Reuben, but really, I'm fine." At her feet, Old

Tom lapped at the sweet morning milk. "But could you drive me to the Tollivers' this afternoon? It's such a pretty day. I'd like to take Marydell and Dodie out for a while."

"Andy ain't been by all week. Usually stops for milk in the evenings."

Copper pinched her lower lip. "That seems strange. I haven't seen him either. Maybe I'd better go check on them this morning instead of waiting."

"I'll get the carriage whenever you be ready," Reuben said. "You let me know."

On her way back to the house, Copper stopped to admire the garden plot. Reuben had already plowed the ground, and now the rich, dark soil lay waiting to be planted.

The garden gate stood open, so she stepped inside and bent to scoop up a handful of soil. She could almost smell green onions and ripe red tomatoes as she held the dirt to her nose. And cucumbers—soon they'd plant cucumbers, and before you knew it she and Searcy could make pickles. Just the thought of crunchy bread-and-butter pickles made her mouth water and cleared up her queasy stomach. She wondered if there were any left from last year.

Back in the kitchen, Copper put the eggs in the pantry and then washed up. Her mind wandered as she leaned against the sink, gazing out the window. It was nice talking with Reuben, she thought, but sad to think of the loss that had opened their friendship.

Paw-paw had been dead since midwinter, a season so severe that the creeks froze solid and birds huddled in masses, too cold to fly. She'd found her pet after she went searching in the snow when he'd missed breakfast and then dinner. Copper found him out behind the barn, sheltered by an ancient lilac bush.

Reuben had come across her sitting there, the dead dog cradled to her chest like a baby, tears leaving frozen tracks down her cheeks. "He was trying to get home, Reuben," she cried. "I shouldn't have let him out of the house."

Reuben knelt in the snow, stroked Paw-paw's head, and ran his hands down Paw-paw's back. "He was a good old dog."

"I didn't take very good care of him," Copper confessed between sobs. "Once I left him in a cave for days, and now I've let him die scared and alone."

"Looks to me like Paw-paw died being a dog, Miz Corbett. Looks to me like this old hound died doing what he wanted."

Copper shifted a little under the dog's weight. The cold seeped from the ground into her very bones. "What do you mean?"

Gently, Reuben pulled a tuft of white fur from Paw-paw's mouth and held it out. "He almost had hisself a rabbit. Caught its cotton tail anyway."

"But if I'd kept him in the house, he wouldn't have been hunting in this awful weather."

"Miz Corbett, would you druther die cooped up in the house or running free?"

"That gives me comfort." She captured Reuben's hand between her mittens. He didn't pull away, just put his other hand over hers and patted.

Copper bent her head and kissed the matted fur of her loyal companion. She couldn't imagine a day without Paw-paw. "Life is hard, Reuben."

"It be's that way sometimes." He lifted the dog from her arms. "It sure be's that way sometimes."

✳

Copper settled back inside the carriage on her way to the Tollivers'. She held a basket of foodstuffs on her lap, and a can of milk rested at her feet.

She leaned forward when they passed Alice's house. Three weeks had passed since the incident in the closet, and Copper had visited nearly every day. Alice turned everyone else away. Gossip was Alice had the vapors. Nobody bothered a woman with the vapors. Even Simon didn't question it. Men could be dense sometimes. Alice was venturing out today, however. The hospital auxiliary was electing officers, and everyone expected Alice to be president.

Copper had sent her regrets. She had other things on her mind. When had she last seen Andy? In her concern over Alice had she neglected Marydell and Dodie?

The crooked, unpaved streets and narrow alleyways of Lexington's other side were as familiar now as her own neighborhood. This was where, nine times out of ten, their patients lived. Seemed it was always deep in the night when the knock on the door came for Simon. Something about the dark frightened laboring women. They could walk off pain all day or deliver twins with only the help of a neighbor, but when night settled in, fear intensified pain, and panic crowded out faith in their own ability. Simon trusted Copper to do the follow-up care for his new mothers, and she loved doing it.

Andy's house was closed up tight. Not a window was cracked even in this heat. Reuben helped Copper down and carried the tin of milk to the stoop.

Carefully, Copper set the eggs down before she knocked. Expecting something sinister, she was pleasantly surprised when Andy opened the door. He looked just fine. She was getting jaded, always expecting the worst.

"Hey, Miz Corbett," he said.

"Hi, Andy. I thought I might take Marydell and Dodie to the park if it's all right with your mother. Would you like to go with us?"

Dodie ran to the door smiling, her arms in the air.

Swinging her up, Copper kissed her surprisingly clean cheek. Annalise must have turned over a new leaf. The little girl smelled of sun-dried diapers and talcum powder. Her ever-present baby bottle sparkled. Where did Andy get milk if he wasn't coming by the house? Something smelled, and it wasn't Dodie's diaper. "Where's Marydell?"

Andy cut his gaze away from Copper's stare. "She's gone with Ma."

"Reuben says you haven't been by for milk all week."

He stared at his shoes. "I been coming by late and taking some from the springhouse. I didn't think you'd mind. Miz Reardon watches Dodie if I ain't gone too long."

"I don't understand why you're here alone with Dodie."

"Miz Corbett—" he squared his shoulders and met her eyes— "there's things I cain't tell you."

"I'm your friend. I'd like to help if something's wrong."

His shoulders slumped. Fat tears spilled down his cheeks and washed away his boyish pride. "She left us. Ma just up and left, and she took Marydell with her."

"But how—why?" Shocked, Copper stumbled into the small kitchen. She sat in a straight-backed chair and held Dodie in her lap. "How long has she been gone?"

"Two weeks, I figure. At first I didn't count 'cause it didn't seem right somehow—counting the days your ma'd been gone."

Copper searched her mind. She'd have to choose her words with care. "Looks like you've been doing a good job here. Why, Dodie's cheeks are as fat as a chipmunk's."

Dodie popped the bottle nipple from her mouth, then laughed from deep in her belly and popped it again.

Andy's shoulders rose a notch. "I been cleaning and putting things away."

"I can see that you have, but don't you need some help with the baby?"

"Dodie's my responsibility now."

Copper saw that the boy was desperate to keep his little family together. He needed a man's advice. She'd take him home to Simon. "Who's doing your work while you're keeping Dodie? Who is delivering groceries for Mr. Cook? And who's doing errands for the undertaker? You must be missed all over town."

"I expect you're right." He took Dodie from Copper and sat her on his hip. "But Dodie comes first."

"What if you and Dodie stay at my house for a while? Just until we get this all straightened out. Besides, there're a million things Dr. Corbett needs your help with."

"I'll think on it. I sure thank you for coming by."

Copper made her way to the door. "I'll stop by again tomorrow. Maybe you'd let me sit with Dodie for a while."

It was the hardest thing she'd ever done, turning her back on Andy and Dodie. Simon was out in the country, she knew, doing patient rounds. It would be evening before he got home–a long time to wait. All the way back to Willow Street she prayed for God's protection over the children and for guidance.

CHAPTER 30

Simon was as perplexed as Copper when she told him the story of Annalise. "That doesn't make any sense," he said, dropping his shoes to the floor. "Why would she leave Andy and Dodie? Why would she take Marydell?"

"I don't know," Copper responded, following him to the lavatory, where he soaped and rinsed his face. "Why would she?"

Ever the surgeon, he leaned toward the mirror, precisely trimming his mustache. She got no answer, just a raising of his eyebrows.

Her nightgown billowed around her as she sat on the edge of the claw-foot tub watching the tidy movement of his hands. It seemed he never wasted a motion. Always meticulous, he caught each dark hair in a towel as it fell. Unbidden, her finger traced her upper lip, where his mustache tickled each time he kissed her.

"Dearest?" Simon asked as his eyes met hers in the reflection of the looking glass.

Copper dropped her gaze. "We need to talk about Annalise and the children."

"Can't that wait until morning?"

Standing, she walked through the open door into their bedroom. "I reckon it can," she answered as he followed close behind. "I reckon it can."

The front door stood open when Copper and Simon came downstairs at half past six the next morning. The seesaw squeak of the porch swing accompanied a pair of little brown shoes that sailed in and out of vision through the screen door.

"You got company," Searcy said with a nod toward the door.

"Indeed we do," Simon replied as they stepped out to the porch. "Good morning, Andy."

"Dodie here wanted to visit," Andy said.

Dodie sat curled against her brother, her thumb in her mouth, her eyes shut tight in sleep.

Simon scooped her up. "How'd you get here, Andy?"

"Walked," he answered. "We started early."

"Looks like we need a couple of extra eggs this fine morning, Searcy."

"They already cracked, Mr. Doctor." Searcy held the screen door open. "Bring them children on inside."

As they sat at the table, Dodie shoved biscuits and gravy into her mouth with both hands. Delighted to wake in their company, she worked the room with her brown eyes, fluttering her eyelashes at Simon and tracking Searcy's every move.

She might not be the prettiest little girl, Copper thought, *but she's got a spark. How could Annalise leave this sweet baby?*

Andy ate very little, sitting ill at ease in the kitchen where he'd always seemed like a happy-go-lucky boy. A boy full of answers to the problems life had dealt him. Copper's heart ached. What were they to do?

Following breakfast, Simon took his coffee mug and headed for the backyard. "Let's check out the garden, Andy. Reuben might need your help out there."

Andy stopped at Dodie's chair as if to take her with him.

"Searcy and I would like to visit with Dodie for a while, if that's okay with you," Copper said.

There was no mistaking the relief that crossed Andy's face. "I expect Dodie would like that. And I'm way behind in my chores." He straightened, hitched up his britches, and swaggered after Simon. "I expect Reuben will need help with the planting."

Copper and Searcy were mixing pickling spices, and Dodie was down for a nap before Simon and Andy came back in. Simon's hand rested on Andy's shoulder. Out the window, Copper could see Reuben bringing up the horses.

"Andy and I will be gone for a few days." Simon's eyes looked determined and hard, but they softened when he met Copper's gaze. "We've got a man's job to do."

❧❧❧

It was fun having Dodie to play with while Simon and Andy were gone. Early one morning Copper left Dodie in Searcy's care while she went to Massey's Mercantile and bought every dress of Dodie's size in the store. Her heels clicked importantly on the well-oiled wooden floor as Mr. Massey trailed her up and down the wide aisles. Pausing now and then before glass-fronted cabinets, Copper also selected several sets of children's soft knit chemisette tops and full-cut muslin drawers, white and dark hosiery, various hair ribbons, and even a wee buttoned corset waist of cotton twill with garters to hold Dodie's stockings up.

"Did you see these?" Mr. Massey asked, holding up the tiniest pair of white leather pumps with ankle straps.

Copper fished in her shopping bag for the pasteboard cutout she'd made of Dodie's foot. "Do you have this size?"

Mr. Massey set several small boxes on the counter. Holding the cutout, he matched it to the bottom of one shoe. "This is perfect, but you better take one size up. Children's feet grow faster than weeds."

Soon Mr. Massey had the whole lot wrapped in brown paper packages tied with string. "Good day, Mrs. Corbett. I'll have these sent round this afternoon."

"I'll take one with me," Copper replied. She couldn't wait to see Dodie all dressed up.

❧❧❧

The baby was in the bath when Copper got home. Searcy had a dishpan on the kitchen table and was scrubbing away.

Plopping down in a chair, Copper laughed along with Dodie as Searcy got soaking wet.

"This here little girl needs some training, Miz Corbett," Searcy said.

"What do you mean?"

"Well, she's near two years old, and she still be acting like a baby. Time to pitch her diapers and that bottle."

Copper frowned. "You're right. I guess it was easier for Annalise to treat her like a baby than to take the time to train her. Where should we start?"

"I taken the liberty of borrowing this little chair." Searcy indicated a child-sized wooden commode chair sitting in the corner. "Dodie visited it once already. She a smart little thing, given half a chance."

Copper took the towel and wrapped Dodie in her arms. "You're a marvel, Searcy."

"Suppose her mama's coming back?"

Resting her chin on top of Dodie's sweet-smelling head, Copper answered, "I've had a sinking feeling ever since they left. I wish Simon hadn't gone off after her. I wish he'd sent the law instead."

"Don't you expect Mr. Doctor think he had to take Andy? Reckon he thought the boy needed to see the truth of the matter."

"I know you're right," Copper replied, fiddling with Dodie's wispy brown hair. "But I'm worried all the same." Retrieving a purple ribbon from her package, she tried mightily to get a bow to cling to Dodie's locks, but as soon as she tied a knot it slipped right out. "This is not going to work, Miss Priss," she said as Dodie wiggled out of her arms. "But we can still dress you up."

After Searcy had Dodie visit the pot again, Copper slipped on her little undergarments and wrestled her feet into the new white pumps. Surprisingly, Dodie held up her arms for the floral organdy frock with chemisette yoke Copper had selected. "She has to see herself, Searcy. Let's take her upstairs."

Dodie marched right up to the cheval glass and pointed at her reflection. "Pretty baby," she said.

And pretty she was. The blue dress with white lace trim was perfect for her. Copper couldn't help but laugh when the little girl held up first one foot and then the other as if showing her new shoes to the child in the mirror.

"I can't stand it," Copper said. "I have to show her off. I'm going to try that ribbon one more time; then we're going to visit Alice." That Copper even thought of visiting her sister-in-law spoke volumes about the turn their relationship had taken. For the first time since her arrival in Lexington, Copper felt welcome in Alice's home. She just made sure to visit when Benton was unlikely to be there.

Now she'd have to be doubly careful. Taking Dodie was a risk, but if she and Andy were going to be living with Copper and Simon, her sister-in-law would have to see them. There was no way around it. Besides, Alice didn't have to know about Annalise. She and Simon would keep the secret, and Benton would never tell. It would be best, Copper convinced herself, to just show up with Dodie.

Dodie did her best to show off for Alice. She twirled around to make her dress stand out and tapped across the floor in her new shoes. Finally, exhausted, she accepted the pallet Copper had made for her on the floor of the dining room and drifted off to sleep while Alice poured tea.

"She is a charming little girl," Alice said, slicing a piece of lemon pound cake for Copper. "Tell me more about her circumstance."

The story of Annalise and the children tumbled out. Of course, Alice knew Andy. Everyone knew Andy. Copper thought she saw a glint of recognition when she mentioned Annalise Tolliver, but obviously Alice had no notion of the girls. Why would she? Annalise was not the type of woman Alice would want to know very well.

"I have a suspicion," Alice started. She stopped herself and asked instead, "When do you expect Simon home?"

"Soon, I hope." Copper put down her fork. The cake tasted strangely metallic. "Oh, Alice, I'm worried that something bad will happen."

"It's not like you to worry over nothing, Laura Grace. I'm sure Simon can take care of himself and the boy."

"I know. It's just . . ." Copper felt tears well up. "I don't know why I'm feeling like this."

"It's the strain," Alice replied. "You've been left in an untenable position. Hopefully these children's mother will do the right thing by them."

"That's just it." Copper pushed her cake aside. "I don't know what the right thing is. I've prayed and prayed about it. I know God will reveal His perfect plan for them. I sure hope I get to be part of it."

"I'm sure it's wise to leave it in His hands. It would be best if they go to their mother in Ohio or wherever it is that Simon finds her." Alice folded her napkin and stood. "Please excuse me for a moment."

The sound of Alice's swishing skirt mingled with the baby's soft snores as Copper stared at her teacup. Even tea tasted funny. Whatever was the matter with her?

A man's voice startled her from her reverie and wakened the little girl from her nest in the corner. Dodie stretched and began her trek across the room.

Benton Upchurch burst in. "Where's Alice?"

Dodie smiled and made her way toward him. "Hiben," she crowed. "Hiben." The toe of her new shoe snagged on a wrinkle in the plush Turkish rug, and Dodie nearly fell.

Benton had no choice but to catch her. He swung her up in his arms as if he held a baby every day.

Dodie rewarded him with a crooked smile and the purple ribbon she clutched in her fist. "Pretty baby," she sang. "Pretty baby." The ribbon she stuck on Benton's bald pate sat there reproachfully, as out of place as a teacup on safari.

"'Hi Ben' indeed," Alice said as she entered the room, her face white.

"Alice," he said, "what's going on here?"

"Perhaps you should tell me." Her voice was tight as her hands found a resting place on her hips.

"I would say it's your little sister-in-law here making trouble again," Benton said.

"Wait a minute," Copper interjected, but they paid her no mind.

Benton swung away from Alice, Dodie still in his arms.

"Trouble!" Alice hissed. "You think Laura Grace is causing trouble! Look on the wall, Benton. Your very ancestors reveal your secrets."

The room spun as Copper watched the scene play out. Benton held a baby whose round, nearly bald head and jug ears exactly matched those of a series of distinguished bankers captured in oils.

"Alice—" he started toward her—"believe me; I didn't know."

"Huh," Alice snorted. "How could you look at her and not know? I knew before I even saw you holding her."

Copper felt sick. Her suspicion was true. She had been so wrong to bring Dodie here, to think Alice wouldn't know.

"Things have been so much better between us these last few weeks," Benton pleaded. "Surely you can forgive this indiscretion, this mere dalliance."

"A mere dalliance doesn't produce a child. Did you think I was unaware of your goings-on?" Alice's cheeks flushed. She stalked toward Benton as if she carried a loaded a gun.

Suddenly Copper remembered the jewelry casket splayed against the wall. What would happen next?

Dodie held out her arms, and Alice took the little girl, snuggling her tight. As if aware her future hung in the balance, Dodie laid her head in the crook of Alice's neck, and one little hand reached up to pat Alice's cheek.

"I want this baby," Alice said simply.

"Have you lost your mind?" Benton's face turned red. He

flung his arms about and shouted, "People will talk. Think of my reputation."

"I've lived your reputation for fifteen years." Alice's voice ran cold as springwater. She paced the room, rocking the child in her arms. "For what? The only person who cared for me in my time of need was Laura Grace, the woman I despised for fear she'd ruin that *reputation*."

Benton met her at the window. From where Copper sat, they looked like a family already. When he reached out, Alice didn't flinch; she merely let her body rest against his. His arm circled her. "I want her, Benton." Copper saw his face soften as Alice's voice turned raw with need. "You know how much I've wanted a child."

Copper dropped her eyes. Some moments shouldn't have a witness.

"People will think we're doing it out of charity," Alice begged. "No one would dare question you."

⁕

When Copper arrived home, she didn't have the energy to go inside. Giving Dodie over to Searcy, she collapsed on the porch swing and pondered what had happened at Alice and Benton's.

In a way, it was like the transformation she had witnessed in the relationship of her father and stepmother back home on Troublesome Creek. All of her growing-up years had been marked by the tension between her parents. And then, right before she left the mountains, they had become like sweethearts. How sad to waste your time that way.

A warm zephyr gusted round her, the scent of petunias and roses riding its wake. She bowed her head and prayed, *Father, is this the answer You've sent for Dodie? Is she to be Alice's daughter? What about Marydell and Andy? And why do I carry this dread in the pit of my stomach?*

She laughed at herself then and pushed the swing with one foot. *I'm sorry, Lord. That wasn't much of a prayer. The children are Yours. I accept Your will. Please bring Simon home safely. Amen.*

It felt good . . . safe . . . to sit here as the afternoon wore away, but her arms felt strangely empty. Silly, but Copper had begun to picture Dodie as her baby and Marydell and Andy as hers also. Now Marydell was missing, Andy was despondent, and Alice claimed Dodie.

Oh, she missed her husband. He'd make everything right again. Besides, she had something to tell him. Something she'd been keeping secret until she was positively sure. She only hoped he would be as happy as she was.

CHAPTER 31

Simon and Andy were gone for two weeks. Copper thought she'd die of loneliness before she spied their horses coming down the street at a fast clip. It was all she could do to stay on the porch and wait, as a patient wife should. "Searcy," she called through the screen, "bring Dodie out."

Simon met her with arms outstretched. Had a kiss ever been so sweet? She pulled back as befit their audience.

"Later," Simon whispered in her ear as she clung to his arm.

Dodie shouted, "Andy! Andy!" before her brother had her seated on his hip. His boyish face had hardened, and Copper saw a hint of the handsome man he would become. "Mardee?" Dodie questioned. "Andy, where Mardee?"

It was much later before Copper heard the full story of Annalise
Tolliver. First there was supper and getting the children settled.
Reuben had fetched Dodie's crib days earlier, so she went right
off to sleep, but Andy was a different story. Simon had to take a
firm stand with the boy or else he would have lit out for the little
house on the other side of town. Finally he agreed to sleep on
the porch and now lay bedded down in the swing.

"You won't believe this story, Copper," Simon said from
upside down as she washed the road dust from his hair.

She massaged his favorite Larkin's Tar Soap into his scalp
before finishing with a rinse of cold water.

"We caught up with them in Three Mile, Ohio. Annalise and
Marydell were staying with a woman on the outskirts of town.
Rosemary Hitchfield, her name is—Billy Hitchfield's mother. Billy
is Marydell's father. Annalise says Billy's the only man she's ever
loved."

"What does a woman who abandons her children know
about love?" Copper asked.

"Not much." Simon towel-dried his hair as he talked.
"Annalise was thrown out of her house when she was four-
teen and pregnant with Andy. She said his father was the
mayor's son, but he wanted nothing to do with her or with
Andy. Imagine it—just a girl herself and turned out in her
time of need."

Remembering her own father's love, Copper replied, "I can't
imagine. How terrible for Annalise and for Andy."

"That's the thing; she kept her baby. She really tried. Then
she met Billy, the love of her life. She winds up pregnant with

Marydell, and he gets thrown into jail for killing a man over a game of cards. Seems Billy Hitchfield is quite the gambler. Story goes that the other man drew first, hence Billy's relatively short time in prison." He sprinkled his toothbrush with dentifrice and talked around a mouthful of foam. "Annalise came to Lexington because she had a sister here. She was waiting out Billy's term."

"My goodness," Copper said, "how terrible."

"It gets worse," he said and rinsed his mouth. "Annalise's sister was no better off than Annalise was. She trailed off after some man not a year after Annalise arrived here. So what was she to do? She had Andy and Marydell and no means of support."

Copper sprinkled cleanser on a cloth and cleaned the sink as he talked. She bit her tongue to keep from jumping ahead of the story, while her mind screamed, *Where is Marydell now? What has happened to Marydell?*

"Thankfully Billy's mother tracked her down, by Billy's request, and rented the little house you found them in. Mrs. Hitchfield doesn't have much herself, but she's tried to do right by Annalise. So Andy has one father, Marydell has another, and who knows who Dodie belongs to."

Copper raised her hand as if she were in school asking for permission to speak. "I know."

Simon slipped the nightshirt she'd put across the end of the bed over his head. "Whatever do you mean?"

"She's Benton's, Simon. Dodie is Benton's daughter."

He sank onto the bed, his face a mask of disbelief. "What did you say?"

As she told him her story, the downstairs clock chimed midnight, surprising them both. "That's all of it. Except that Alice wants Dodie."

"What would convince my upright sister to raise her philandering husband's daughter?"

Stifling a yawn, Copper took down her hair and sat on the bench in front of her dressing table. "There's so much more to tell. I guess it had best wait until morning. But please tell me; where is Marydell?"

Standing behind her, Simon wielded the silver-backed brush and began to work the tangles from her hair. "Don't be upset, but we had to leave Marydell behind."

"Why?" Copper could see her own tears in the shadowy mirror. "I don't understand how you could think of doing such a thing."

"I had no jurisdiction over the girl. I couldn't force her to leave with Andy and me." He ran his hands through Copper's thick mane. "Annalise gave Marydell the choice, and she chose her mother."

"Didn't that just make you sick, Simon? Leaving her there?"

"I was more worried about Andy than Marydell. I like Mrs. Hitchfield. She assured me she'd keep track of her granddaughter, but Annalise didn't even ask Andy what he wanted nor was she concerned for Dodie. She just assumed we'd take them both in."

Finishing, Simon laid the brush aside and took Copper in his arms. "I guess I assumed the same thing. I certainly never entertained Alice wanting Dodie. Let's get some sleep now. We'll unscramble all this in the morning."

⚜

It took more than one morning's talk to put everything together, but within a week things had fallen into place. Dodie was living with Alice and Benton, and Andy had his own room at Birdie's boardinghouse. Benton had had a charitable moment, and Andy's room and board were secured. Copper was sorely disappointed to give up Andy. But she understood his explanation.

"Miz Corbett, you don't need me except for this and that. Now Dodie don't need me either—" he dashed at tears with his knuckles—"but Miz Birdie does. She's got all them boarders and her little crippled boy to think about. Besides, Tommy Turner's going to teach me to play chess." He allowed an embrace then.

"I'm so sorry," Copper said. "I wish things had turned out differently."

His hug was brief but fierce. "It's for the best. Ma was happy, and that other lady will see to Marydell."

"I love you. You must promise to come to me if you need anything. Anything at all."

"I will," he said. "Doc said I was like a son to him. Ain't that something, Miz Corbett?"

"Yes, it is," Copper answered, her arm still around the boy. "That's really something."

⚜

In the wee hours of the morning on the night after Andy left to live at Birdie's, Simon awoke with a start. Copper's side of the bed was empty.

Lighting an oil lamp, he searched the house for her. "Sweet-heart?" he asked when he came upon her sitting on the floor of the pantry. "Whatever is the matter?"

"Oh, Simon," she said matter-of-factly, as if he found her eating pickled cucumbers in the dark every night. "I woke up hungry." Juice trickled down her chin, flashing silver in the lamplight. "Want one?"

"Not right now." He saw the weighted wooden disk cast aside, watched as she speared another pickle. She was going to have such a bellyache.

"I dreamed I was back home," she said around a crunch, "going to the cellar to fetch some of Mam's bread-and-butters. I woke with such a yearning; I couldn't wait another minute."

"Why didn't you wake me?"

Laying her fork aside, she reached into the crock with both hands. "I didn't think you'd be hungry."

Catching hold of her, he entreated, "Stop now. You're going to make yourself sick."

Standing, she swayed a little. Her gown was wet and clung to the little swell of her belly. He could have smacked himself on the head. Though he guessed she was not more than six weeks along, how could he have missed this?

"Oh, dear," she said. "I think you're right."

Soon Simon had the mess cleaned up and Copper in a clean gown. After tucking her into bed, he leaned over her, smoothed the hair from around her face, and placed his palm on her forehead.

"I feel fine now, Simon. Do you think there's any sauerkraut left from supper?"

He shook his head. "Dearest," he started but stopped when her eyes drooped and closed. Settling the light quilt over her shoulders, he whispered, "You can have sauerkraut with your eggs in the morning."

Simon pulled a chair close, then turned up the oil lamp and opened his Bible to a favorite Scripture: "Thus saith the Lord, thy redeemer, and he that formed thee from the womb, I am the Lord that maketh all things; that stretcheth forth the heavens alone; that spreadeth abroad the earth by myself."

Simon set the Bible on the nightstand. He extinguished the wick and knelt beside the bed, where his wife lay sleeping. This was a night to give thanks.

CHAPTER 32

The porch swing squeaked a protest as Copper settled down, resting her feet on a small stool, stationer and pen in hand. Her dressmaker had paid a visit this morning to let out the darts in her blouses and move the buttons on her skirts. Soon she'd need new clothes—dresses with no waistbands and billowy wrappers. And no corsets; that was very good.

It was July, and she was five months along according to Dr. Thornsberry's calculations. She smiled to remember the kindly man pulling on his white beard as he counted the months backward, then added days until he came up with the probable time of her confinement, give or take two weeks. The baby would come, Copper reckoned, when it was ready.

The only hard part of being with child was staying in. The

doctor would allow her only short trips in the buggy. And, of course, once she started showing it was indecent to be out in society anyway. She missed church the most, but Simon told her everything the minister said and served her Communion himself.

Shuffling pen, paper, and ink against her expanding belly, she sighed and gave up. Her lap had disappeared. She'd have to go inside and sit at the table to answer a letter from Hester and Isaac, but first she'd enjoy the bright summer day from her porch swing and try to contain her growing excitement.

After supper last night, she and Simon had taken a stroll around the yard and stopped to admire the roses and the hollyhocks, the marigolds and the lilies. "We're going to have some company," he said, plucking a pink rosebud and holding it for her to smell.

She caught the gleam in his eyes, and she knew. She just knew. "Is it Daddy and Mam?" she asked, clapping.

He put his hands on her shoulders as if she needed holding in place. "Now don't get too wound up; you must think of the baby."

"Simon!"

"Yes," he said, "they're coming by train the first week of August, and Willy and Daniel also."

Now the swing swayed when she waved at a neighbor lady who passed by on the sidewalk. "My family is coming for a visit," she called out, unable to contain her happiness.

Pausing on the sidewalk, the lady shaded her eyes against the sun and called back, "That's wonderful news."

"Yes, it is," Copper replied. "It is the most wonderful news."

It seemed as if Copper's world had shrunk to nothing more than waiting—waiting for Simon to come home from the office each evening, waiting for her family's visit, waiting for the baby to come. Finally she marked August 5 off the calendar hanging on the pantry door. Her mother and father and eight-year-old twin brothers were on their way.

Simon wouldn't let her accompany him to the train station to pick them up—too much hustle and bustle there—and so she waited some more. Trailing through the house, she dusted already-spotless furniture and rearranged knickknacks until Searcy gave her a mess of green beans to break.

It was Willy's voice she heard first—his voice and his pounding footsteps across the porch floor. "Sissy! Sissy!" he hollered.

Then they were all in the foyer, hugging and laughing while Simon stood beaming in the open door.

How had the boys grown so tall in such a short time? Willy reached her shoulder, and Daniel was not far behind. Daniel held Copper's hand, smiling a little shyly.

Willy told her all about the train in his nonstop way, his eyes dancing with mischief. "We flew down the tracks fast as greased lightning, a thousand miles an hour or more."

"The average speed was thirty-five miles an hour, Sissy," Daniel interjected in his studious way. "The brakeman told me."

"Me and Daniel got to go to the coal car and watch the fireman sling coal in the furnace."

"And we went to the observation deck," Daniel said, tugging on her hand. "My hat blew off."

"Felt like we were going a thousand miles an hour when you lost your hat, didn't it, Daniel?" Willy teased.

"Daniel, Willy," Mam said, "go help with the luggage."

Mam, her hair a faded replica of Copper's own, was dressed in a fawn linen suit with a white handkerchief-linen blouse. She looked . . . how did she look? Surer maybe, steady, with a light from within. Copper realized her stepmother looked like she was supposed to look, like she would look if she'd never left the city to live on Troublesome Creek. Copper's heart softened; maybe she'd finally be able to understand why Mam had taken Daddy away from their mountain home.

There were tears in Mam's eyes as they embraced. "I'm so happy for you, Laura Grace, so happy."

And then Copper was in her father's arms. He might have seemed a little thinner, but his hug was as strong as ever, and she saw that his face had good color. When he stood back to look her over, his smile stretched from ear to ear. "A grandbaby," he said. "I'm right proud of you, girl."

A flurry of activity interrupted them as Simon and Reuben brought in the humpback trunks and hefted them up the stairs, followed by Willy and Daniel carrying valises and hatboxes. Searcy called lunch, and Andy came by to take the twins off exploring.

"You must eat first," Copper said. "You too, Andy. Searcy's been cooking all morning."

A veritable feast awaited them: chicken and dumplings, can-

died carrots, green beans, creamed corn, yeast rolls, and chocolate meringue pie.

Simon's blessing was heartfelt if short. "Lord, we thank You
for safe journeys, welcome family, and good food."

Copper was nearly too full of gratitude to eat. All her most
loved people were gathered around one table. Even though
Searcy didn't sit, still she was here.

Willy was the first to push back from the table. "May I be
excused? And may Daniel and Andy too?" He wiped his face and
tucked his napkin neatly by his plate. "I can't wait to get outside."

Mam's eyebrows rose in an expression Copper remembered
well. "Once the table is cleared and the dishes washed, you boys
may do as you please for the rest of the afternoon."

A great clinking and clanking arose from the kitchen. Copper
knew Searcy would be in a dither with three boys in her kitchen,
but it was good of Mam to offer their help. She was raising them
as she had raised Copper—to be of service to others.

⚜

The two weeks of their visit sped by. On weekday afternoons
Copper and Mam and Alice received lady guests. Everyone
wanted to meet Copper's mother. Some were Mam's friends from
long ago. While they were entertaining, Simon would see patients,
the boys would tear around town with Andy, and Daddy would
go off to the barn, where he was working on a surprise. Copper
was forbidden to go anywhere near his workshop.

In Copper's eyes, the best part of the visit was late evenings
after supper. As if by design, she and Daddy had the porch to

themselves, just like all those nights on Troublesome Creek. The only difference was the view—the house across the street instead of the mountains shooting up around them.

"Are you happy, Daddy?" she asked one evening as she watched him chew on the stem of his pipe. "I mean, really happy?"

He took the pipe out of his mouth and chuckled. "I'd be happier if your mam would let me have some tobacco for this pipe."

She took the pipe from him and turned it over and over in her hands. "Don't tease me. I want to know."

"I don't think on that very often, Daughter." He stroked his short-clipped white beard. "I reckon I'm as happy as a man has any right to be. I feel better since the move, and I like working in the store. Gives me a chance to meet all sorts of folks. And Grace, well, she's like a different person. It pleases me right smart to see her happy."

The lights came on in the house across the street. A mosquito buzzed near Copper's ear. She pulled a light shawl around her shoulders. "We'd better go in, Daddy. The mosquitoes will eat us up."

He reached to take her hand. "How about you, Copper Brown. Are you happy?"

"Oh, Daddy, I love Simon so much, and now this." She laid his hand upon her belly. "But I miss the mountains. If I could do it over, I'd make Simon come there and set up his practice. I miss how life used to be. We could have been happy on Troublesome Creek."

Her father stuck the stem of his empty pipe back in his

mouth. She knew he was thinking on the best answer. Daddy never spoke until he was sure of his words. "Don't let yesterday take up too much of today, Daughter."

Copper strained to see his wise face in the waning light. "What do you mean?"

"When life takes you by surprise, when it takes you places you never thought to be, remember Paul. I reckon one of my favorite Scriptures is in Philippians where he says, 'For I have learned, in whatsoever state I am, therewith to be content.'"

Copper stood on tiptoe to buss her father's cheek. "I'll try, Daddy. I'll try to be more like Paul."

He opened the screen door and held it as she stepped into the welcoming light of the entry hall. "I reckon if Paul could stand shipwrecks and prison, you and I can handle this soft city life, girl."

Much too soon it was the last night of Copper's family's visit. They'd enjoyed a big supper with Benton, Alice, and Dodie. Andy had come as well, and Birdie brought little Robert. Tommy Turner couldn't make dinner, but he came by for dessert. Nobody would willingly miss out on Searcy's banana pudding.

After supper everyone gathered in the parlor so Daddy could present his surprise. Willy stood behind Copper's chair and covered her eyes while Daniel and Andy helped carry it in.

"Look!" Willy said, moving his hands.

Tears shimmered in Copper's eyes as she knelt before the cradle her daddy had made. "I think I could fit two babies in here," she said, setting it to rocking with the lightest touch.

"Perish the thought," Simon said, causing everyone to laugh.

"I have a little surprise myself," Mam said, fishing for a beautifully wrapped box hidden behind the sofa.

Copper sat right where she was on the floor and took Mam's gift, running her hands over the lavender-colored paper and sliding the orchid silk ribbon through her fingers. "It's too pretty to open."

Willy plopped down beside her. Retrieving a small knife from his pocket, he opened one of its shiny blades and neatly slit the orchid ribbon. "Look, Doc Simon." He held the knife up for all to see. "Daddy finally let me have the pocketknife you gave me for Christmas that time."

Everyone laughed again as Copper peeled off the paper and opened the box. "Oh!" she exclaimed, pulling out a crocheted cradle canopy and a matching coverlet. "Mam, this is beautiful." Awkwardly, she struggled to stand. Simon rushed to her side, helping her up. "I can get down, but I can't get up," she said, blushing, going to her stepmother and then to Daddy with hugs and thanks.

The men and boys gathered round the cradle to assemble the thin pieces of wood that would hold the ecru lace canopy in place, while the women oohed and aahed over Mam's fine stitches. Copper's baby would have a bed fit for a king or a queen.

It felt like Christmas morning later that night when Copper stole down the stairs while everyone else lay sleeping. She just had to see the cradle again. Funny—the front door was ajar. Surely Simon hadn't forgotten to latch it.

"Daddy," she said, not really surprised to find him on the porch, "can't you sleep either?"

"Just counting the stars, Daughter. I get the same number no matter where I'm counting from." He circled her shoulders with his arm and pulled her close. "What's got you out of bed?"

"I want to see the cradle again. I want to picture my baby in it."

Quietly, they went in together. The cradle sat under a window in a wash of golden moonlight.

"Thank you, Daddy."

"I made it of burled walnut," he said. "I like to see the knots in a piece of furniture. Shows the tree has lived awhile and weathered some storms."

"It's perfect. I love it."

"Just like life, it's as pretty as you make it. Sand the hard times smooth and slap some varnish on and nobody will know the difference."

Copper had to cover her mouth to stifle a giggle. "Oh, Daddy, I miss you already."

CHAPTER 33

The summer had been long and sweet, lasting through October. Copper had hoped it would never end. What was it about the change in seasons that made her so despondent? Perhaps it was the rustling of the dying leaves or the grass turning brown beneath her feet as she trod upon shed flower heads and the discarded seeds of once-fertile plants.

Casting a look around, Copper retrieved the rake that leaned against the garden fence and began to comb her flower bed. She'd keep the marigold, zinnia, and hollyhock seeds in used envelopes she'd saved all summer. A smile played on her lips as she thought of the one she'd added to the stack just yesterday–Mam's first letter since their visit. Oh, to bring back that time just past when Mam and Daddy and the boys came all the way from Philadelphia.

Lost in reverie, Copper scratched about with the rake. She picked up a sunflower stalk and hung it over the fence. The heavy seedpod drooped sadly, like the lid of the trunk that Mam had packed for her family's homeward journey. Copper had fretted after them until she made herself sick, until Simon came up with a solution to her misery. "The train runs two ways," he'd declared. Next year, after the baby was born, after she was strong again, they'd hop aboard and return the visit. The very thought made her shiver with anticipation and lifted some of her melancholy.

A sudden shower of jeweled leaves descended on her just-raked ground. Stubbornly she swept them up, determined to make some progress before someone caught her at the task and took the rake away.

The screen door screeched, announcing Searcy's presence. "Miz Corbett," she called, as Copper had known she would, "what you be doing with that rake? You be careful you don't strangle that baby."

"Forevermore, Searcy. I can't just sit in the house all the time. Why, my great-grandmother killed a bear and helped build a log cabin while she carried my daddy's daddy, and she never strangled him. Anyway, I don't believe all those old wives' tales."

"Well, you ain't be building no cabins nor killing no bears on Searcy's watch. Besides, who you think be telling all them tales? Old wives, that's who. Old wives that had their share of babies."

"I'll be careful," Copper promised. "See, I'm just doing a little scratching around."

"What be going on down at the barn?"

"The farrier is here. Both horses are being shod today."

They could see men watching and hear the tap-tap-clang, tap-tap-clang, as the smith's hammer shaped iron against the anvil.

A messenger approached from the side yard. Tipping his hat, he asked for Dr. Corbett.

"He's there—" Copper pointed toward the barn—"with the horses."

She saw Simon take a note, saw him confer with Reuben, watched as he handed over Pard's reins and then strode across the yard toward her.

"Mrs. Wilson's family sent for me," he said. "She's in a bad way."

"Send someone else," Copper said. "You don't have a horse."

He led her to the arbor and kissed her there under the faded morning-glory vine. For once she didn't care who could see as she threw her arms around him. "I don't want you to go, Simon."

"Keep this up and I shan't," he murmured. He tipped her chin and kissed her again. "What's wrong, dearest?"

"Nothing," she replied, feeling silly. "Of course you must go. Poor Mrs. Wilson."

"It's her time. She's had a long and fruitful life, but I want to be there when she crosses over."

She hugged him as hard as she ever had, as hard as the swelling of her belly would allow.

"You hold me longest this time," he whispered, teasing, for it was she who always broke their embrace.

After he left for the livery station, Copper stayed for a while under the arbor, holding on to their sweet moment until Searcy came worrying about her.

The day was warm, and a pleasant breeze blew from the west. There'd not be many more days like this. Restless after lunch, Copper found her wide-brimmed straw hat and went back out to the garden. It was fruitless to try to keep ahead of the fallen leaves. The trees were nearly spent; they'd produced a bumper crop this year.

She laughed at her ungainly self, belly as big as a summer pumpkin. She was thirty-four weeks, according to Dr. Thornsberry. The baby would soon be here. Her hands cupped her gift, her son or daughter. Simon was convinced she carried a girl, although he had yet to come up with a name. But she knew it was a boy, and they'd name him William Alexander. William for her daddy and Alexander, which was Simon's middle name. They'd call him Alec. The name rolled off her tongue, and already she could see him, all dark hair and round dark eyes. How did women stand the wait? Her arms yearned for the weight of her baby. She was so blessed.

⚜

Way out in the country, an old blacksnake uncurled on a sun-warmed boulder. He was hungry; last week's field mouse was long gone. His eye slits widened and took in the flash of a chipmunk in the weeds across the road. Tasting the air with his forked tongue, he silently slithered toward his prey.

It was late October, but the air was still soft and warm across Simon's shoulders. His mind was not on the road he traveled. He usually enjoyed being out in the country, especially in such fine weather, but today he'd rather be home. He hated to leave

Copper. Her time was growing close, and though he wouldn't actually be attending her, he wanted to be there.

His thoughts were of Copper and the baby she carried. Secretly he wanted a daughter, a little copy of his wife. She had charged him to come up with a name, and he was thinking on it. Maybe Grace for Copper's stepmother . . . or Alice? No, better not name her Alice. Though things were decidedly better between his wife and his sister, he'd better not push it. Lilly came to his mind; that would be a pretty name. Yes, Lilly to honor his mother.

The horse he'd rented from the livery was skittish. He should have kept his attention on the ride, but he let the reins go slack just before he saw a snake from the corner of his eye. Suddenly the horse reared, shrieking, hooves pawing the air, and flung Simon from the saddle.

Simon fell hard against a rock ledge that jutted from the hillside, then slid as slowly as the serpent had crossed his path to crumple into a heap upon the ground. A thin trail of blood marked his fall, and a sticky red pool spread beneath him. His shattered spectacles lay just beyond his reach; the horse's hooves crushed his new felt hat.

With a final fearsome scream, the horse wheeled and sped back toward town, leaving the trampled snake and the battered man to their fate.

⚜

Copper shaded her eyes to watch as a flock of blackbirds took flight from a nearby field of dry cornstalks. As if driven by a fierce wind, they blew east then west, forming a big swooping S in the nearly cloudless sky, the sound of their echoing caws as lonesome as a train whistle. Mesmerized, she watched the dance until they flew off en masse, probably to rob someone else's cornfield, leaving the day strangely quiet.

A chill shook her and she wrapped her arms around herself. "A goose has walked over my grave," she told Old Tom.

The cat purred and wound around her ankles.

"Laura Grace?" Alice called from the back porch. "What are you doing out here all alone?"

Inordinately glad to see her sister-in-law, Copper hurried to the house.

Alice held the screen door. "Dodie and I have come for tea," she said, then whispered, "We're practicing our manners."

Copper nearly laughed before she saw that Alice was quite serious, for at the dining table, Searcy had laid three places, and Dodie was sipping milk from a china cup.

"Mardee," she cried, her little face lit up with pleasure. "Mardee!"

"Oh, dear," Alice said. "She thinks you have Marydell. I hoped she had forgotten."

"I suspect it would take a long time to forget a sister." Copper stooped to cover Dodie with kisses before she took her seat. "How are things at home?"

"A minor miracle has occurred. Benton took supper with us last night." She broke a piece of sugar cookie and put it on the baby's plate. "He can't get enough of this child." Her eyes met Copper's across the table. "Laura Grace, I can never thank you enough."

"God is blessing you and blessing Dodie through you."

Alice placed a small parcel in front of Copper. "I've brought something for us to do. Open it."

Tiny drawstring gowns, half a dozen bibs, and embroidery floss of every color spilled out in Copper's lap.

"We need to get busy on a layette for Dodie's little cousin," Alice said. "I thought we could start this afternoon."

Dodie snared a loop of bright gold. "Me help," she said, dunking the yarn in her milk and drawing a circle of white on the tablecloth. "Me help."

Copper was glad for the distraction as scissors and needle whiled away the afternoon. Soon a row of ducks paddled their way across a flannel sleeper, and a green frog hopped on a fancy bib.

"Frog," Dodie said and hopped across the floor. "Dodie be a frog."

"My, how time has flown," Alice said while securing her sewing supplies in a small woven basket. "We'd better get this table cleared before Simon comes in expecting supper."

"He'll be late," Copper replied. "He's gone out in the country to Mrs. Wilson's. It's her time."

"Why don't you come and eat with us? Joseph can bring you home afterward."

"Thank you, Alice, but not tonight." Copper stood, her hands gathered at her lower back. "I'm suddenly tired. It will be an early bedtime for me."

Early to bed but not early to sleep. No matter what Copper tried, rest would not come. She would have gone down for warm milk,

but she didn't want to wake Searcy and Reuben. They'd taken
to staying over on the nights that Simon was gone, sleeping in a
small room off the kitchen. Simon would not hear of her staying
alone. And, she must admit, knowing they were close by was a
great comfort.

The small of her back ached, and her shoulders seemed
tied in knots. That's what she got for wielding the rake today.
Turning on her side, she buried her face in Simon's pillow. His
scent—just-ironed linen with a hint of lavender—comforted her.
Searcy had taught her to make the lavender water she sprinkled
his starched shirts with before ironing.

As if it were yesterday, Copper remembered the first time she
had noticed that scent . . . when she was back on Troublesome
Creek. Her brother Daniel had managed to get himself bitten
while playing at snake handling with a copperhead. He wanted to
be like the dancing preacher he'd witnessed at a revival meeting.

As an answer to her family's fervent prayer, up rode a
stranger to save her brother's life. Copper had been lost from the
first moment she saw Dr. Simon Corbett, although she'd struggled mightily against her fate. Now she couldn't imagine that
she'd ever thought she could live without him.

She rolled out of bed and opened the curtains. The big, silver moon shone as bright as day. He'd find his way back easy
enough with that light to guide him. Simon would be home
soon.

It seemed Copper had just fallen into a deep and dreamless slumber when a commotion downstairs awakened her. In truth she'd

slept for several hours, for it was four o'clock in the morning. Sitting up in bed, she pushed her hair from her face and tried to make sense of the noise. Someone was crying.

"I'll go for Alice and Benton," a man's voice said.

"Keep it down," came another.

"Searcy, get hold of yourself and go wake Mrs. Corbett, but gently." That sounded like Dr. Thornsberry.

She must be dreaming. Why would he be in the foyer? Then the worst sound came—a long, low moan of pain.

"I'm here," Copper called, wrapping herself in a robe and flying to the stairs. "What has happened?" Searcy met her midway, and the look on her face made Copper's stomach lurch. She sat down right there, her vision blocked by Searcy. Very, very slowly, she turned, as if to crawl back up the steps. If she didn't see, then nothing bad had happened. She'd just go back to bed and make it go away.

"Miz Corbett—" Searcy touched her shoulder, let her touch linger—"it be Mr. Doctor. He done got hisself hurt."

"Is it bad, Searcy?" Copper asked.

"Dr. Thornsberry's here. He goin' look Mr. Doctor over soon as we get him settled."

Copper bent over her knees. Through the stair rails she could see her husband lying in a stretcher of arms. "Bring him up," she said, standing, tightening her sash. "He'll want to be in his own bed."

CHAPTER 34

It was Simon's stillness that bothered Copper. Truly, he looked the same. Every morning Reuben bathed him and dressed him in a starched white shirt and brown suit pants as if he would wake at any moment and go to his office. Every morning Copper would stand in the doorway and watch as Searcy and Reuben rolled him like a timbered log from one side to the other to make the bed with fresh linen. Every morning Mallie from next door appeared on the back porch for the bundle of laundry. She insisted, and Searcy gave in. Every day but Sunday, Simon's wash dried on Mallie's line. And every day he lingered, still as death, without speaking.

Five long days had passed in this manner since he was found on the side of the road. Poor Mrs. Wilson had passed on without his witness. It was the swelling, Dr. Thornsberry assured Copper. Simon's brain had sustained quite a blow. He'd wake up as soon as the swelling subsided, the doctor insisted, though Copper noticed each time he said so his voice held less conviction.

"When?" she demanded this morning when the doctor held his stethoscope to Simon's chest.

"Now, little mother," he answered, his kindness shattering her patience as he patted her arm, "we must let nature take its course."

They'd put a chair and a little table to hold a Bible and a lamp right outside his door. A steady stream of folks came to keep watch with the family, and most tarried there, searching the Scriptures and praying. Alice practically moved in, and Benton came every evening. Food piled up in the kitchen until Copper couldn't stand the sight of it. Then Reuben would pack everything up and take it to the poorhouse.

Copper stayed next to Simon's bed, knitting little sweaters and hats. She really didn't mind her vigil. It was pleasant sitting beside her silent husband, and as long as she sat there he was alive. The warm days lingered with gentle breezes through the open window. But she could tell that cold was coming; frost was creeping their way.

Then a miracle happened. On the morning of the sixth day, as Copper embroidered yet another infant's gown, Simon woke up. "Sweetheart," he rasped weakly, "water."

He sipped a small amount through the invalid's straw before his head fell back against the pillow. "What happened?"

She told him what she knew as his eyes tracked her face, loving her still.

It seemed for the next day or two that Copper would get to keep Simon. Even Alice took heart and went home to care for Dodie. Dr. Thornsberry was pleased when Simon ate a little broth and some milk toast. Once he even sat up on the side of the bed, his thin legs dangling.

Copper had just picked up her sewing when Dr. Thornsberry made his final call. "He's sleeping," she said when she spied the burly doctor filling the doorframe. "He's just taking a rest."

He made his doctor motions again—lungs, heart, pulse, skin turgor; she knew the drill by heart—before he fixed her with a pitying look. "I'll be back soon," he said as he stepped into the hall, where Searcy stood waiting. "Fetch Alice and Benton," Copper heard him say. "It won't be long."

Ever so carefully, she folded the little gown on which she worked and put it squarely in the middle of the nightstand. Taking a moment, she rearranged flowers on the dresser brought by friends yesterday. Flowers so bright and gay in a yellow vase.

"I'm so cold," Simon said from far, far away. "Take down your hair and warm me."

Pins and combs fell to the floor as her hair tumbled free. Just one more task before she went to him. There, just at the top of the doorframe, was the key they never used. She took it down and turned the lock. He'd be hers alone for a while.

Somehow Simon had managed to turn to his side, and he held out his arms to Copper. Gently she lay down. It seemed so long since he'd held her. She could feel his shallow breath as he laid his head on her shoulder. Slowly, so slowly, he traced the mound of their baby, her hand resting on his.

Quick as a darting minnow came the response.

"Our daughter moved," he said.

"Alec, our son," she teased, desperate to keep him there. "You've picked no name for a girl."

He raised himself on one elbow as if his strength were restored. "Lilly. Name her Lilly . . . Gray . . . Gray . . . everything's fading . . . but look! Do you see?" His hand lifted and pointed. "Angels in the corner!" His arms slackened around her. He fell back, still against the pillow.

Copper leaped up, screaming, "Go away! You can't have him." She grabbed the yellow vase of flowers she'd just arranged. It shattered against the far corner, followed by the cut-glass vase full of mums.

Voices shouted, "Open the door." Fists pounded. "Let us in."

"Go away!" she screamed again, throwing one item after another until her dressing table was clear and every little bottle and pot of perfume and elixir was broken. Nothing was left but a pair of scissors from her sewing basket. "Go away," she cried to the people pounding at the door and to the angels in the corner. "Go away."

The doorframe splintered, and strong arms circled her from behind. She kicked and struggled as Dr. Thornsberry wrested the scissors from her hand. A hypodermic flashed and then a needle's prick. Faces swam in and out of her vision—Searcy's and Alice's, Benton's and Tommy Turner's, and even Simon's, growing cold. The crunch of broken glass and horrible screaming bounced off the walls and echoed down long hallways filled with rushing water and many doors. None of which opened for her.

A thick film held Copper under. She swam in dark green water; the prick of the hypodermic needle became as welcome as a warm drink on a cold day, taking her pain away. Words, muffled as if spoken through yards of cotton batting, came at her, but rarely could she make them out. When she did she heard, "contractions . . . labor . . . too soon . . ." She couldn't concentrate enough to make sense of them.

⚜

Three days after the funeral Copper didn't get to attend, her tiny daughter was born in a night of blinding pain. Little Lilly Gray, born of sorrow, swaddled and whisked away while her mother swam in the dark green pool.

⚜

"Laura Grace," Mam said, "what have you done to yourself?"

Copper fought to sleep. She didn't want clear words, didn't want the light that streamed in from open curtains to penetrate her gauzy mind. Where had Mam come from? Was she back on Troublesome Creek? Had this nightmare been just that—an awful dream?

Discomfort woke her. Her chest hurt. Cramps tightened her belly. A binder wrapped her tightly from just under her shoulder blades to her hips. "Lord, help me," her parched lips mouthed, though the prayer didn't make it past her throat. "Bring back my husband. Bring back my baby."

A glass straw was held to her lips—was that the same one she'd offered to Simon? She wanted to knock it away, but she couldn't lift her hands, so she drank. It wouldn't do to disobey her mother.

"A bath." Mam leaned over her and straightened the pillows that lumped behind her head. "That's what you need. A bath, and then we'll see what we can do about this hair."

Mam and Searcy washed her with quiet efficiency. Soon a clean wrap replaced the soiled one, though if she could have, she'd have ripped it off and thrown it out the window. "It's worse than a corset," she squeaked, her voice sounding weak and child-like. The bed linen and even her clean gown smelled of roses, not lavender. For that she was thankful. "Can I get up?"

"I think so," Mam said. "Searcy, please bring that chair. It will do her good to be out of bed for a short time."

Strong hands lifted her. Her wobbly legs wouldn't hold her. Where had her strength gone?

"How about Searcy fetch some of that chicken soup off the stove?"

"Yes," Mam replied. "That would go down well. I believe she's ready to eat more than the little bits of broth she's had these last few days."

Why was everyone talking over her head? Did they think she'd lost her mind as well as her strength? Had she? Copper slumped back against the chair, too weak, too weary to care.

Mam made a little exclamation of despair. "What shall I do with your hair?"

A comb caught on Copper's hair, the pain welcome to her.

Pain was the only thing that felt real in this room of grief–the pull of the comb, the tightness across her chest, and the sharp cramp of her belly. Simon was gone, and Mam was here instead, teasing the tangles from her hair. *Lord, help me,* she prayed again. A litany against despair. *Lord, help me.*

Dr. Thornsberry approved of Mam's ministration when he came to call. He was glad to see Copper up. Glad to see her eating. "A little walk around the room," he encouraged, he on one side, Mam on the other. "A little walk and then back to bed."

Settled against the pillows, Copper caught his hand before he had a chance to leave. "What happened to my husband? Please tell me. Why did Simon die?"

"Now, my dear," the good doctor started, patting her hand, "you'll only upset yourself."

"I have to know." Her voice was a haunting need. "I have to set it right."

"Why, what do you mean?" he asked.

"There must have been something we could have done. Some way to save him."

The doctor let go of her hand and scrubbed his face as if weary beyond words. "I thought we had. When he started eating, I felt he'd turned the corner, but it seems he'd lost more blood than we knew, much of it pooled inside him, secretly sapping his strength. I'm so sorry."

With those sincere words, the dam was broken. Copper's wailing could have been heard from the street corner.

They let her cry for many minutes. Finally, just when she

thought she might drown in her own tears, Dr. Thornsberry said, "For heaven's sake, somebody fetch her baby."

Copper's mind went still. Her baby? Had she heard right? Could it be that her baby was alive?

Lilly Gray was a tiny bundle and the meanest baby Dr. Thornsberry said he'd ever seen. Copper laughed through tears when he said that, when he explained what he meant. He'd never thought she would live, he told Copper, weeks early and delivered to a mother in shock. But as soon as she was released from the womb, she started kicking and squirming. They could barely keep her swaddled she wiggled so in her pasteboard box in the warming oven. They couldn't get her to take milk from the wet nurse, so Alice and Searcy and Birdie had set up a command post in the kitchen and fed her around the clock from an eyedropper.

When Copper held her baby, her binder flooded with milk. "Why did you wrap me in this thing?"

"I thought it best," Dr. Thornsberry said, "to dry up the milk."

Copper held her daughter, her baby never expected to live. Dark hair as fluffy as dandelions gone to seed, eyes shut tight, little limbs swimming, using up needed energy trying to find her mother.

"Loose this thing," she said, not caring who saw. "Let me nurse my baby."

Such relief. Copper felt as though an elephant had stepped off her chest. Blessedly, the room was empty except for Mam, who sat at the foot of the bed, her head turned away. And, of course, Lilly Gray, who made no motion to suck. Copper stuck her finger in the baby's mouth; she made a mewling sound. She'd never get nourishment this way.

"Help me, Mam. Tickle her feet."

Mam leaned over and stroked the baby's foot. Lilly tried to jerk away, but Mam continued. With her knuckle, Copper pulled down on the baby's chin, opening the little bird's mouth. There— just a tiny suck, but it was followed by another then another. "Hand me that cup, please. I'll just catch this extra."

The day was spent in this fashion. Lilly Gray eating in minute bursts of sucks, none lasting long enough; Copper using the eye-dropper between, even while the baby slept, then massaging the small throat to make her swallow. Her own pain was forgotten in the wonderment of her daughter—the physical pain, anyway; nothing could assuage her broken heart.

Over the next few weeks it was a blessing to have her mother here, although secretly Copper wished for her father. But Will was with the boys, who were quarantined with a light case of the measles. Their whole neighborhood was locked up tight. Mam had had to slip out even though she posed no threat of spreading the dread disease.

They had time those quiet days. Time to make amends for a lifetime of misunderstanding. And time for Copper to get the answers to questions long locked away in Mam's vault of repres-sion. It was her way of protecting herself, Copper came to under-stand, and the only way she knew to protect the niece she had raised as her daughter.

"Times were different then, Laura Grace," she said one day in answer to Copper's prodding. "It seemed best to keep family secrets just that. And how was I to know you'd ever find out that people here gossiped that your grandfather Taylor took his own life?"

Mam's cheeks colored as if just talking about it brought back the shame she must have felt. "He was a broken man after my mother's death. He couldn't adjust to losing her. You can't imagine what I went through just to get him buried next to my mother."

Mam's hands worried each other, twisting about in her lap. "It's against the law, you know—against man's law and God's. The caretakers of the cemetery had rules against laying suicides to rest with *proper* folk." She stood from her perch on the side of Copper's bed and walked to the window. "It was as if his very body was unclean."

Copper tried to bite back her question, but it pushed past the wall Mam had built so many years before, crossed over the barrier Copper had never been brave enough to breach. "Did he? Did Grandfather Taylor kill himself?"

Mam's sigh lifted her shoulders, and she let them drop. Her eyes looked a hundred years old. "He tried to go on. He suffered Mother's death for many years and then . . ."

Copper laid the baby on the bed and went to her mother. Embracing her from behind, she murmured, "I'm so sorry, Mam. What a terrible time for you."

Rarely had Copper felt her mother's embrace, but now Mam turned to her. "I made so many mistakes in raising you, Laura Grace, kept so much of myself hidden away. For that I'm sorry."

"You owe me no apologies," Copper replied, tears seeping through her closed eyelids, Mam's long-suffering sorrow mixing with her own.

※

"Come home with me," Mam pleaded before she left. "You don't have to stay here alone."

Copper turned it over in her mind. Being with Mam and Daddy and the boys was tempting. But she wasn't ready to leave Simon. She hadn't even visited the grave. She might never go there. *He's not really dead if I never see a grave.* Voice was never given to this thought. People would think she was crazy, and maybe she was. But one moment he had been naming their daughter and the next he was pointing to angels. How could that happen? How could life end so quickly in a strong and vital man? Maybe if she had attended his funeral instead of swimming in Dr. Thornsberry's drug-induced sleep, she would believe. But then she wouldn't have her daughter. The doctor had bought Lilly needed womb time, and Copper couldn't fault him for that.

"Laura Grace?" Mam's voice pulled her back to the present. "Would you consider it at least? You could have your own place close to us. We'd all like that."

"I dream of going home," she answered wistfully, "home to the mountains. The farm is there. I know I could make a go of it."

Mam's face grew stern. "Your daughter's needs come first. It would be best if you put Troublesome Creek out of your mind."

Copper sighed. "I know you're right, Mam. But dreaming doesn't hurt, does it?"

CHAPTER 35

It was a long, cold winter. Copper never left the house, glad for the excuse of Lilly Gray. How easy it was to turn invitations away. "Lilly Gray is colicky," she could say, or "I think Lilly Gray may be coming down with a cold." It was out of the question that she would leave her in the care of Searcy or the young downstairs maid Alice had hired to help with all the added work a baby brings into a home. Most days she never left her room but stayed cocooned in covers and quilts with baby Lilly Gray.

What a darling girl her baby was. She demanded nothing and was content to lie in her mother's arms for hours at a time. Alice said she was spoiled, and Copper knew Searcy agreed, for Lilly Gray never cried. There was no need. *Funny to see Alice and*

Searcy in collusion, Copper thought. Finally united in effort to *save* Copper from herself.

"Who wants saving?" Copper said to the baby, whose legs had dimpled with fat over the course of the winter, who now had a double chin and eyes as round as saucers. She would talk to her daughter in such a fashion, as though there were answers to be found in the knowing eyes that held her fast. Sometimes she felt as if she could get lost in the depths of those gray eyes. "We can live right here in this room. We don't ever have to leave, do we? You won't leave me, will you, Lilly Gray? You won't ever leave your mama." Tears started again. Oh, she hated the weeping, the never-ending sorrow that held her in such a hard grip.

What had happened to her life? It seemed Copper no longer knew who she was. For one thing, she didn't recognize herself. The mirror reflected a sickly woman whose bones jutted out like a plucked chicken's, all elbows and knees.

She twirled her hair into a bun and secured it to the back of her head. Who cared what it looked like anymore? But Alice was coming by, and she had to make some effort to be presentable. She pinched her cheeks for a little color, then turned away from the mirror. Fatigue filled her with its heavy fog, and she crawled back into bed. She'd rest while she waited for her sister-in-law to come calling.

She had to admit that she enjoyed Alice's visits. Her sharp tongue and bossy ways seemed right somehow. Everyone else tiptoed around Copper, keeping distance as if her grief were contagious, but Alice was not afraid.

Spring was coming. Copper could see the changes outside

her bedroom window. Buds were forming on the trees, and a robin had started a nest. Lilly Gray had nodded off to sleep, a thin drool of milk on her chin, when Alice came for her daily call.

"Where's Dodie?" Copper asked.

"I left her at home," Alice responded. "I'm taking Lilly for a while."

"What do you mean?" Copper answered, her nerves jangling.

"Let me hold my niece." Alice took Lilly Gray and snuggled her tight. "Good morning, precious. Guess what Auntie Alice has brought for you?"

"Where are you taking her?" Copper asked as Alice dressed the baby in a sweater.

"I've brought a perambulator, so Lilly Gray and I are taking a stroll," Alice stated, as if Copper had no say. She put a frilly white bonnet on Lilly and tied the ribbon under her chin. "Is this not the sweetest thing you've ever seen?"

Lilly Gray looked over Alice's shoulder. The bonnet revealed startled eyes and round cheeks, her little mouth puckered like a rosebud.

"I'm not ready, Alice. I'm just not ready to go out."

Alice turned, her eyes weary, her mouth set in a straight line. "Laura Grace, you can stay here and waste away if you choose, but this is not what Simon would want for his daughter. She needs fresh air, and frankly I'm tired of coddling you."

As quick as that, the room was empty. Copper's blood boiled. Angrier than she'd ever been, she threw back the covers and ran to the window. Craning her neck, she could just see Alice turning the corner with a hooded wicker stroller that held her daughter. *Her* daughter! How dare Alice make decisions concerning Lilly Gray. Wait until she told Simon!

The enormity of her loss came as swift as roiling floodwater. Falling to her knees, she prayed hard and fast. Her words tumbled together. *Lord, please, give me some peace. If You won't send him back, then show me how and why to live without him.*

Spent, she lay on the floor, her face pressed into the rug. What would happen if she never got up? Could she lie here forever, not feeling, not caring? It would be so easy. The thought of her baby got her to her knees, then to her feet. She was so tired of being tired.

Four black crepe dresses hung from the rod in her dressing room. Delivered to the house by her dressmaker, they waited to announce her widowhood. Though her hands shook, she pinned the piece of hair jewelry Alice had made for her to the front of one and slipped it on before finding her shoes.

It seemed she could hear her bones clanking as she descended the stairs. "Them bones, them bones, them dry bones," she said and laughed at her foolish self.

The new maid—Aimee, was it?—jumped a foot when Copper joined her at the kitchen sink. She looked as if she'd seen a ghost. "You scared me silly, Mrs. Corbett. Weren't expecting to see you up."

"I'm sorry. I didn't mean to startle you." Copper accepted the chair the maid pulled out for her and sipped gratefully at a cup of tea sweetened with honey. "Where is Searcy?"

"Trailing after Mrs. Upchurch and the baby. They'll be back

soon. It's the baby's first outing." Aimee colored. "Begging your pardon, Mrs. Corbett. Of course you already know that."

"It's all right. It's just—I've been ill."

"Oh, right, ma'am, I know," Aimee said while drying her hands on a corner of her apron. "Somebody's here nearly all the time praying for you. We keep the coffeepot full and the teakettle on simmer."

Touched, the dreaded tears welling again, Copper asked, "Who comes?"

"Everybody. It's like they're taking turns. I know most everyone from making my shopping rounds. Everyone except those ladies who come after dark."

"Why would they come after dark?"

"I don't know, ma'am, but half a dozen or so just show up every so often." She nodded toward the back porch. "Searcy passes mugs of coffee out the door."

Copper surmised they were Simon's patients, the poor and the prostitutes, who came to the back door when they needed help, now coming to the back door in support of her.

She'd just petitioned the Lord to show her how and why, and clearly here was her answer. While she lay abed upstairs, sickened with grief, folks from every walk of life gathered below and lifted her up. She felt buoyant, as if her soul floated near the ceiling. "Will you pray with me?"

Aimee knelt as Copper prayed, "Thank You, Father, for the witness of the many who have prayed for me. Thank You for answered prayer. Forgive my selfishness. In Jesus' name, amen."

Copper moved to stand, but a tug on her skirt kept her

sitting as Aimee added a prayer of her own. "Dear Lord, I just come today asking for Thy continued hand of healing on Mrs. Corbett. Hold her in the palm of Thy hand. Hide her suffering in the shadow of Thy wings."

"Thank you, Aimee. I think that's the most beautiful prayer I've ever heard."

Aimee picked up Copper's cup and saucer. Her fair skin bloomed. "I've learned powerful verses from Searcy. She shares one every morning; then I mark them in the Bible she gave me."

Standing, still shaky, Copper said, "I guess I'll go and find my daughter."

"I've a better idea, ma'am," Aimee answered. "Let me fetch a wrap, and you can wait for Mrs. Upchurch in the porch swing."

CHAPTER 36

Copper stood at the kitchen window staring out, taking stock. A cup of strong tea kept her company as a cold March wind rattled the window. It was her birthday, and the cake Searcy insisted on baking cooled on the sink, its rich chocolate smell tempting her.

Could it be she was twenty years old? Where had the time gone? Since Simon's death, long days turned into months of sleepless nights and now a year and four months of melancholy.

The first year hadn't been so bad—once Alice got Copper out of bed. Simon's presence was still so strong, and on each day that passed she would remember a matching day from the year before. "On this day I told him I was expecting. On this we walked to Willow Springs and had a picnic. Oh, and here he kissed me by the morning-glory trellis." Truly, the first year wasn't so bad.

But now . . . the first anniversary of each moment with him was over, and Copper had to do the seconds. Touching her forehead to the cold windowpane, she gave in to a moment of despair. Life stretched out in front of her like an unending highway of loss. She still remembered Simon's face and the rich sound of his voice, but memory wouldn't put his arms around her nor keep her warm on a cold March night.

The sound of wooden blocks tumbling and of Lilly's surprised laughter made her turn around. Copper leaned against the sink as she sipped her tea and watched Dodie build a little tower again, then let Lilly knock it down. Lilly laughed from deep in her belly as if she hadn't just done the very same thing only minutes before. Dodie was a big girl now, mothering Lilly Gray like Marydell once mothered her.

Not for the first time, Copper wondered if her decision to leave Lexington was the right one. Lilly would miss Dodie, and she would miss Alice and Searcy and Reuben. Not to mention Birdie, little Robert, Tommy Turner, and Andy. Although Andy flourished under Tommy's tutelage, she felt he needed her mothering. He had been the hardest to tell. Even though Alice had been angry for weeks and accused her of being foolish and Searcy cried, it was Andy who broke Copper's heart.

"It will be all right, Miz Corbett. Me and Tommy will come and visit you. Wouldn't that be something, me coming to see you in the mountains?" Andy's eyes flashed as he teased. "I never liked wearing shoes nohow."

She had no doubt he would show up for a visit on Troublesome Creek one day.

Thinking back, Copper realized Andy had been on her side since she'd first come to Lexington nearly three years ago. Everyone else asked why she wanted to leave. Why would she do such a thing? But Andy never questioned.

The girls were tired of building blocks, so Copper brought out the rag dolls and the small cardboard suitcase of doll clothes Lilly had gotten from Santa last Christmas. Dodie loved playing dolls, and Lilly loved whatever Dodie was doing. It was time for Lilly's nap, but it could wait. Alice would be back from her meeting soon.

The kitchen was cozy and warm. Lilly's eyes were drooping, and Dodie's followed suit. Copper let them nap where they lay on the braided rug in front of the cookstove, blocks, dolls, and tiny clothes scattered all around. It was a pretty contrast to the blustery gray day Copper could see outside the window. Her tea had grown cold, but she sat at the table and drank it anyway. She didn't want to disturb the girls by reaching for the kettle.

Copper thought back to late summer, when she'd realized her skills as a midwife were becoming de rigueur. Much like the newly fashionable polonaise walking suit or nannies imported from Europe, she was in demand. It seemed anybody who was anybody or—at the very least—married to somebody wanted that nice Mrs. Corbett to deliver her baby. At least that's what Dr. Thornsberry had told Copper when she questioned all the please-call notes delivered to her house. He was proud of her, he said, and, of course, Alice was delighted.

But Copper wasn't so sure. She quickly grew tired of all the demanding postdebutantes with their overdone houses and overwrought ways. On the other hand, she never tired of delivering the babies that her society mothers soon handed over to nannies and maids.

Mrs. Lemuel Cain was a case in point. She was expecting her third baby in as many years, and she was delighted when Copper agreed to attend her. Toward the end of Mrs. Cain's confinement, Copper's visits became more frequent. She liked to keep a close eye on her patients.

The Cains' home was in Alice and Benton's neighborhood and was even more pretentious. A pillared portico protected visitors from the elements while they waited to be admitted.

Mrs. Cain usually received Copper in the drawing room, a space so full of heavy, dark wood furniture; billowing drapes; and needlepoint pillows that it made Copper feel smothered. Even the piano, sitting kitty-corner to the fireplace, was dressed with an artfully draped shawl.

Helen Cain was very nice to Copper, even insisting that Copper bring Lilly when she came to call. Lilly loved to visit the nursery and play with the children, a two-year-old girl and a one-year-old boy. Helen was fortunate to have the same nursemaid who had cared for Helen herself as a child. Everyone called the maid MeMe. Copper thought it strange that she never saw the children with their mother. Wasn't she worried MeMe would take her place in their hearts?

It was well after midnight when Helen Cain delivered her third baby, another beautiful, healthy daughter. Copper wondered why babies so often liked to make their presentation in the middle of the night. But she didn't mind as long as their deliveries went as well as this one. Mr. and Mrs. Cain were delighted

with their little bundle from heaven and expressed their appreciation to Copper.

Toward the end of Copper's six-week follow-up visits with
Mrs. Cain, she found her patient weeping into a lace handkerchief. "It's MeMe," Helen said when Copper questioned, afraid
her patient was unwell.

"MeMe," Copper said, sounding like a parrot.

Helen touched the hankie to her nose. "It's not as if I'm dismissing her, Mrs. Corbett. My husband said she is welcome to
stay on in the kitchen."

"I'm afraid I've missed something," Copper said. "Is MeMe
unable to care for the children? Perhaps you could get someone
to assist her until the baby is older."

Helen sighed and tucked her handkerchief up the cuff of her
sleeve. "I simply can't have MeMe if everyone else has European
nannies. How would it look when they go to the park?"

"Your children seem to thrive under MeMe's care," Copper
said, thinking of the elderly but spry maid and how quickly Lilly
had taken to her.

Two perfect tears trembled at the corners of Helen's blue
eyes. "Yes, I know. This is very difficult for me." The hankie
was retrieved from its hiding place. "You just don't know, Mrs.
Corbett–" she paused to dab her cheeks–"how stressful it is,
keeping up with fashion."

Less than a week later, Copper was on the front porch
knocking at a mud daubers' nest with the end of the broom
handle. The daubers loved tucking the meticulously fashioned,
pipelike nests up under the gingerbread trim. And Copper loved

to knock them down. Mud and debris showered onto the floor as she pounded. Spiders, with the daubers' wormlike larvae attached, disentangled and crawled from the splattered mud tubes.

Copper's skin crawled as she swept the mess away. "Go somewhere else," she said. Thinking of the poor spiders, stuffed into the prison of the daubers' cells, waiting to be eaten when the larvae grew into grubs, gave Copper the willies.

"Forevermore," she said, noticing someone at the end of the walk. Laying the broom aside, she started that way. An elderly black woman was sitting on a brown valise. "Do you need help?" Copper asked.

"No, ma'am," she said, "Thank you anyway. I'm just resting a bit."

"MeMe!" Copper said, recognizing her. "Where in the world are you going?"

"Well, first I'm taking myself to the train station, and then I'm taking myself to Atlanta, Georgia." Her warm brown eyes looked up at Copper. "Do you know of Atlanta, Miz Corbett?"

Before Copper could answer, MeMe continued. "It's the prettiest place, flowers everywhere."

Copper could hear the woman's knees creaking when she helped her up off the valise.

"Whew," McMe said, "it's a long way to the train station."

"Surely Mrs. Cain would have seen you to the station," Copper said.

"I didn't give her the chance. I walked until I got tuckered out, and then I remembered this is where Searcy works, and I thought I'd sit and rest a spell. I could tell from when you came calling on Miz Helen that you have a good heart."

MeMe removed the hatpin from her hair and held her bonnet trimmed in silk violets out for Copper to see. "Miz Helen gave me this and some walking money. Did you know I took care of her since she was a baby? After twenty years, this old hat and thirty dollars is all I'm worth to her." The woman's shoulders sagged. "I spent all those years thinking she needed me. Looks like she could have given me a new hat at least."

"I'm sorry, MeMe," Copper said, although it didn't seem sufficient. "What can I do to help?"

"I've got a sister in Atlanta and more nieces and nephews than you can count. That's home. Don't you worry about me; I'll be fine once I get there."

Copper slipped her arm around MeMe's waist. Lifting the cracked leather valise with her other hand, she guided her toward the kitchen door. "I have a train schedule in the kitchen. Let's get you a glass of cold sweet tea, and then we'll figure out when we need to get you to the station."

MeMe paused to settle the hat back on her head, expertly slipping the hatpin in place. She squared her shoulders, ready for the journey. "I expect old ladies ain't out of fashion in Atlanta."

After Copper saw MeMe safely to her train, she sat on a park bench in the depot and watched the foot traffic. Men, women, and children all scurrying to get somewhere else. "All aboard!" She heard the conductor's loud call. "All aboard!"

She had turned MeMe's words over in her mind. MeMe wasn't afraid to face the future. She wasn't put off by the thought of change. It didn't take an old-fashioned hat and thirty dollars for Copper to make a decision. She was going home. MeMe had shown her the way. She reckoned she'd still be welcome on Troublesome Creek.

Copper's thoughts swirled like the tea leaves at the bottom of her cup that cold March day as she remembered making the decision that would send her in a new direction. She'd been packing and sorting all winter. One wagon full of furniture and tools had already been sent ahead to be unpacked on Troublesome Creek. She and Lilly Gray would leave early in June. Isaac and Hester would be home then to await the birth of their baby, due in late summer. Isaac would accompany her to the mountains and stay for a short visit while Hester stayed in Lexington with her family.

There was one more thing Copper had to do. One she'd put off far too long. As soon as the weather warmed a little, she had to go to the cemetery. She had to visit Simon's grave.

CHAPTER 37

The Corbett family plot was down a winding cemetery road banked by flowering trees of every sort and sectioned off from the other graves by a wrought iron fence with fleur-de-lis edging. Copper had brought a willow sapling from Willow Springs, the creek she and Simon loved so much, and Reuben planted it where she asked so that when it grew tall the drooping branches would weep upon Simon's resting place.

Inclined to throw herself upon his grave, she stood instead and traced the inscription on the smooth granite.

Simon Alexander Corbett
Beloved Physician, Husband, Father, and Brother
1856–1884
The Lord Giveth His Beloved Sleep.

Inside the fence, a statuary figure towered with wings outstretched, keeping watch. Michael, Copper decided, the archangel, leader of the righteous angels. It was only right that Simon should be in Michael's care.

Her heart was a cold, gray lump leaking ashes. A simple mantra kept her from screaming and tearing her hair: "He is not here. He is not here."

Finally she allowed herself to kneel and smooth her hand over the grassy mound. "Simon, please understand I'm not leaving you." Her fist tapped her chest. How did her heart survive when his did not? She guessed hers now beat for both of them. "I'll carry you with me always."

She had no idea how long she knelt there, only that the sky darkened before Reuben moved from among the shadows to touch her shoulder. "We'd best be going, Miz Corbett. They be closing the gate soon."

He had to help her up, hold her steady, this wonderful friend. The man who'd been afraid to touch her for so long now allowed her to lean against his sturdy frame as he led her away. "He is not here," she whispered, tasting the salt of her tears. "Praise God; he is not here."

It was a long way back to Troublesome Creek. Thankfully Copper had Brother Isaac as an escort. He was a good companion, entertaining both Copper and Lilly Gray with his stories from the Dark Continent of mischievous monkeys and regal lions but quiet when Lilly napped—Copper's thinking time.

There was so much to store away. So many good people

she'd had to tell good-bye. Alice and Dodie, who cried for Lilly Gray before they'd even stepped off the porch. Andy Tolliver— how could she leave Andy? Tommy Turner and Birdie and little Robert. Birdie insisted on making Copper's going-away hat. Surprisingly simple, it was fashioned with removable flowers so Copper could wear it to church or while working in the garden.

And then there were the townspeople, people from church, her patients, and her good friend Dr. Thornsberry. How could so many people steal so much of Copper's heart in three short years?

Hardest, of course, had been saying good-bye to Searcy and Reuben. Copper had thought to leave the house to them, but Benton convinced her, rightly so, that such a move would hurt them more than help them. Lexington was progressive, but it was still not ready for mixing. So Copper sold the house. There was enough money in the bank to keep Searcy from scrubbing any floor but her own for the rest of her life. Reuben added land to their place to house all the chickens, horses, pigs, and cows, including Molly. He still wore his old straw hat, and he'd always have work-worn hands, but now he called himself a gentleman farmer. It made Copper smile to think on it.

Of all the animals, only Old Tom made the trip with Copper. Caught up in a wicker basket, he was too old to give much protest.

After much thought as to what she should take, the wagon was ready. A lilac slip from over Paw-paw's grave and a sapling from Willow Springs wrapped together in wet burlap were last to be loaded. Everything else, after Alice took family heirlooms to save for Dodie and Lilly Gray, from furniture to pots and pans and bedding, was parceled to Searcy and to Birdie for her burgeoning boardinghouse. Some special items of Simon's were given to Tommy Turner, who would in turn leave them to Andy.

Copper wasn't a foolish woman. She'd listened to Benton's advice carefully. She would have a small income of her own and money for Lilly Gray's education when the time came. There was no virtue in hunger as far as she could tell. Alice had promised to see to Andy and to Marydell, if need be, and so Copper was set free, in a sense—free to seek solace for her aching heart, a balm from Gilead.

Now as the buggy covered the miles, Copper said to Isaac, "I wonder what the home place will look like."

"Way different, I expect. Once Daniel and Emilee Pelfrey moved away, there probably wasn't anybody checking on it. Do you ever hear from John?"

"Not for a long time," she mused. "He could be anywhere in the world by now. Where was it his ma and pa went?"

"Emilee's father died and left them a good-size farm in Virginia. Can you imagine moving all their young'uns?"

Copper laughed. "They had twelve, outside of John, who had already left. Makes my move seem easy, doesn't it?"

Lilly Gray slumped against her, napping, and Copper nearly drifted off herself, the sway of the carriage lulling her. What would she find when she got home? She feared raccoons would have taken over the cabin. There wasn't a window or door that could keep them and their nasty destructive ways out of an abandoned house. If nothing else, they'd come down the chim-

ney. And she lamented the garden, probably run over with jim-
sonweed. It would take months to get it ready for planting, too
late for a crop this year. Fortunately, she had plenty of Searcy's
canned goods plus enough dried beans, flour, sugar, and lard to
stock a good-size grocery store.

"A penny for your thoughts," Isaac said to Copper.

"I was just thinking of all the work that lies ahead. Do you
think I'm foolish to try to make a go of Daddy's farm by myself?"

He turned his soft brown eyes on her. "It won't be easy, but
I could see you were losing yourself in the city. Once Simon was
gone it wasn't home to you anymore."

"It never really was," she said. "The only time I was in my
own skin was when Simon was next to me or when I was helping women in their time of need. That's why I'm coming back.
To find myself and to birth some babies." She stretched her arms
up over her head. Lilly Gray stirred beside her. Smiling, she
looked at Isaac. "I should find some babies to birth somewhere
up these hollers; don't you think?"

He had to stop the horses he laughed so hard. Jumping
down from the buggy seat, he slapped his hat against his thigh.
"We might as well stretch our legs," he said between whoops.
"Girl, you haven't changed a whit."

She loved Isaac for his bushy beard and his laugh so loud it
scared the birds from the trees. He was like having her daddy
near. And he believed in her, she knew, just like her daddy always
did. Surely she hadn't forgotten how to scrub a house with lye
soap, and as for her garden, there was always next year.

CHAPTER 38

There is no place akin to the mountains in the springtime. Redbuds and dogwoods dotted the landscape like cones of cotton candy, and every time a soft breeze blew, petals showered the buggy with fragrant rain. Copper's stomach knotted with anticipation as the miles passed.

Finally, the place dearer to her than any other began to make itself known. "There's the big rock!" she shouted to Isaac as if he didn't know. "There's the swimming hole!"

Soon—soon—just around the bend and down the narrow lane. She could barely keep herself in the buggy, and Lilly Gray protested when she hugged her too hard. Her heart beat fast, her breath quickened, and there it was! *Oh, Lord, thank You*, she prayed. *Thank You for keeping this place for me.*

Somehow the overgrown farmland she'd expected was not what greeted them. Instead the fencerows were clean, and the cabin looked much like she had left it. As they passed by the garden, she could see little hills of potatoes and green shoots of corn.

"I don't understand," she said, turning to Isaac. "It looks like someone is living here."

"It had to be Brother Jasper," Isaac replied. "I let him know you were coming home. He must have sent some of his congregation over to clean things up."

Copper clasped her hands to her chest. "This is wonderful. What a beautiful homecoming. Take Lilly Gray, please. I can't wait to get inside."

For the first time since Simon died, Copper slept the night through. The crowing of somebody's rooster woke her at sunrise.

A fire was laid in the woodstove, and she lit it to brew coffee. When it was ready, she poured a cup and stepped barefoot onto the split-log porch. Everything was the same right down to the granite bucket and dipper on the shelf and the rocking chairs under the windows. The burble of Troublesome Creek called to her in the distance. She went back in to check on Lilly and pull the blanket up over her shoulders.

Lilly burrowed under, her lovey close beside. She'd sleep another hour or two.

Fog hung in the air and swirled like long gray ribbons when Copper walked into its midst. With every breath, she savored the taste and the scent of the mountains: coal smoke and clay

dirt and shale rock. Her chilled feet found the familiar path.
Troublesome Creek was as beautiful as she remembered—clear as
window glass with a music that soothed her soul. Stooping, she
cupped the water and drank until it spilled down her chin. Cold
as it was, she could have bathed in it.

Her soul spilled over. "'The Lord is my shepherd,'" she said
from memory, "'I shall not want. He maketh me to lie down in
green pastures: he leadeth me beside the still waters.'"

Just as she had found her way through the fog to the creek,
she would find her way in life. Later she and Lilly Gray would
decide where along the creek to plant Simon's willow.

Copper had been gone just minutes, and the coffee was still hot.
Thankful for Lilly's sleeping, she settled in a rocker with her cup.
Perhaps she'd sit here on the porch all day taking it in. Home.
The sun warmed a notch, burning off the fog. A familiar shape
materialized. A cow? Forevermore, a cow lost in the fog? Setting
the cup on the floor, she leaned forward as if her eyes were playing tricks.

"Thought you might be needing this." A deep voice startled
her. She wasn't dressed for company.

"I beg your pardon," she said.

"I heard you was coming home, Pest. I knew you'd be wanting a cow."

"John?" Could it be her dear friend? "John Pelfrey?" She
couldn't believe her eyes. "I thought you were long gone."

"I been back a spell, farming the home place and chunking
coal." He stood at the edge of the porch, the rope that tethered

the cow in his hand. "I was right sorry to hear about your husband. He was a good man."

"I know," she replied. "Thank you." The least little bit of sympathy and tears started again. She'd hoped to leave them behind. "Do you want a cup of coffee?"

"Is it as good as your mam used to make?"

"Probably not, but it's hot."

"All right then. I'll get this one to the stable first." He turned and started off, then paused to look back over his shoulder, taking her measure with the green eyes she remembered. "You'll like her. She's a good milker."

From somewhere the rooster crowed again, refusing to give up the dawn. Sunlight streamed across the yard and each tree; each blade of grass was bathed in its golden light. Lilly Gray called from her crib. The cow's hips swayed as John led her across the lot to the barn.

Copper Brown Corbett was home, and she was thankful.

ABOUT THE AUTHOR

A retired registered nurse of twenty-five years, Jan Watson specialized in the care of newborns and their mothers. She is a charter member of Southern Acres Christian Church and lives in Lexington, Kentucky. Jan has three grown sons and a daughter-in-law.

Willow Springs is the sequel to Jan's award-winning first novel, *Troublesome Creek*. Her awards include the 2004 Christian Writers Guild Operation First Novel and second place in the 2006 Inspirational Readers Choice Contest sponsored by the Faith, Hope, and Love Chapter of the Romance Writers of America. *Troublesome Creek* was also a nominee for the Kentucky Literary Awards in 2006.

Jan's hobbies are reading, antiquing, and taking long walks with her Jack Russell terrier, Maggie. Currently she is writing the third book in her Copper Brown series, *Torrent Falls*.

Jan invites you to visit her Web site at www.janwatson.net. You can contact her through e-mail at author@janwatson.net.

CROSSINGS®
THE BOOK CLUB FOR TODAY'S CHRISTIAN FAMILY

A Letter to Our Readers

Dear Reader:

In order that we might better contribute to your reading enjoyment, we would appreciate your taking a few minutes to respond to the following questions. When completed, please return to the following:

Andrea Doering, Editor-in-Chief
Crossings Book Club
401 Franklin Avenue, Garden City, NY 11530

You can post your review online! Go to www.crossings.com and rate this book.

Title _____ Author _____

1 Did you enjoy reading this book?

❏ Very much. I would like to see more books by this author!

❏ I really liked_____

❏ Moderately. I would have enjoyed it more if_____

2 What influenced your decision to purchase this book? Check all that apply.

    ❏ Cover
    ❏ Title
    ❏ Publicity
    ❏ Catalog description
    ❏ Friends
    ❏ Enjoyed other books by this author
    ❏ Other _____

3 Please check your age range:

    ❏ Under 18   ❏ 18-24
    ❏ 25-34   ❏ 35-45
    ❏ 46-55   ❏ Over 55

4 How many hours per week do you read? _____

5 How would you rate this book, on a scale from 1 (poor) to 5 (superior)?

Name_____

Occupation_____

Address_____

City_____ State_____ Zip_____